The Forbidden Fling

EMILY WRIGHT

THE FORBIDDEN FLING
Copyright © 2026 by Emily Wright.

Warnings: This book contains sexually explicit material which is only suitable for mature readers. Please view the full list of trigger warnings on the websites below.

For information contact:
Emily Wright
www.emilywrightwriter.co.uk
Purple Clouds Press
www.purplecloudspress.co.uk

Book and cover design by Diana L
Published by Purple Clouds Press
ISBN: 978-1-0676148-1-2

First Edition: April 2026

Subscribe to my newsletter to stay in touch and also receive a free sapphic novella!

www.emilywrightwriter.co.uk/contact

'Hope is the thing with feathers
That perches in the soul,
And sings the tune without the words,
And never stops at all'

— Emily Dickinson

ONE

Faye

When Faye imagined jet-setting to the warm shores of Portugal, she pictured clear blue skies and sunshine warming her face as soon as the crew opened the aeroplane doors. Instead, they circled the airport for an hour, waiting to land, and Storm Reneé met them on the tarmac like a smack in the face. Rain pelted Faye's bare arms, the metal steps trembling underneath her feet. A man's cap flew at her like a missile, and she screamed as it clipped the back of her head, smashing her brand-new sunglasses onto the tarmac.

Great. Just…great.

The wind howled as she hurried towards passport

control, her dark hair whipping across her vision and into her mouth. Babies wailed as the wind tried to outroar the aeroplane engines. Pieces of paper flew loose from passengers' magazines.

Once inside the building, Faye parted her hair like heavy curtains, the tangles wet between her fingers. She sighed, shifting her heavy rucksack from one shoulder to the other as the line slowly inched forward. To ease her worries that her luggage might accidentally end up in Asia instead of Europe, she'd packed most of her ostomy essentials in her carry-on. Her muscles ached from lugging around the extra weight, but it was worth the sacrifice.

Tell that to your back in the morning.

Even travelling under perfect circumstances would give Faye a migraine. The combination of being six months post-op and travelling on her own for the first time resulted in her imagining every fictional scenario, from the plane in flames to her being sucked down the cabin toilet.

Logically, she knew she'd be fine. She could last up to six hours before she needed to empty her bag— depending on what she ate—and it was a short flight. But the what-ifs always circulated in the back of her mind—a quality that made her the most organised twenty-six-year-old she knew but also frequently left her with a throbbing headache. Her brain didn't know how to rest.

Hence, the enrolment on the Sandy Springs "Reset Your Life" course. A wellness retreat on a remote

Portuguese island that—her dads were convinced—would give her the kick up the arse she needed.

David's "You need to relax" meeting Lukas's "Get out there and start living" had meant Faye couldn't get a word in edgeways. She assumed it was the same with anyone's parents, regardless of gender, but their end sentiment was the same: Faye had become a hermit who treated other humans like foreign lifeforms. And that needed to change.

Finally, the grumpy, stout man at passport control waved her forward. She'd been practising her Portuguese on a loop ever since taking her aisle seat on the plane. All those months spent hiding away from everyone weren't totally unproductive.

You can do this. Be confident. Be clear.

Faye flashed a smile she didn't feel and greeted the man with a "Boa tarde", digging her nails into her palms. He glanced at her and muttered something incoherent—either Faye's Portuguese wasn't quite up to scratch, or he was a chronic mumbler. When she didn't reply, he raised a fuzzy eyebrow.

Shit. Did he ask something?

Just as she imagined being dragged away in handcuffs for disobeying orders, he stamped her passport and called the next person forward. Hiding the warmth coating her cheeks, she thanked him anyway and headed towards the luggage carousel.

She fired off a quick Landed safe and sound text to her dads, then scanned the board, her fingers twitching under the strap of her rucksack. Her flight wasn't listed. She blinked, the words jumbling together on the screen. They were delayed, but surely their luggage should have arrived by now?

Someone bumped into her, knocking her off balance. More bodies closed in, scurrying like rats. Her mouth opened, but she couldn't say anything. What if her suitcase never turned up? *Oh god.* She was going to end up stranded in the airport forever because she had the physical aggression of a comatose manatee.

Pain throbbed in her shoulders. The speakers overhead crackled, stumbling over a muffled message. Maybe they'd just announced her luggage had been diverted to Reykjavík. Faye didn't know. She was going to die in this airport, the stale AC her last lingering memory of existence.

Then a flash of magenta caught her eye. She hurried to the adjacent belt, her trainers squeaking against the shiny floor as she weaved through the crowd. Suitcases piled up on the carousel like Jenga blocks. The knot in her chest loosened a smidge.

Hers was impossible to miss. She could hear David's voice in her head. "Excellent job, Miss Pankhurst." Her history-teacher dad loved the suffragettes and often compared Faye's organisational skills to the founders of the movement. Faye wasn't going to complain about that compliment.

Prepare for the worst and never be disappointed.

Strong women inspired her. Rosa Parks's bravery,

Ada Lovelace's creativity, Amelia Earhart's ambition. Faye believed there was a special essence in every person that surged when they faced adversity. Something she'd lovingly called the "enigma". She just needed to find her own.

She inhaled a shaky breath.

It starts today, she reminded herself. *Get a grip*.

She tugged her suitcase free and started towards arrivals, sidestepping an enormous family of tantrumming children with snotty noses. Her head spun as her gaze combed the many placards. *Get me out of here.*

She spotted a sixty-something woman holding up "Faye Donovan" in sharp black marker, and her lungs let out another sigh of relief.

She wasn't going to die in the airport. *Hooray.*

She noted the woman's name badge: Carla.

"*Olá*. You're finally here! Welcome." A big grin spread across her weathered but kind face. A long, loose ponytail of dark hair dangled down her back, a silver septum piercing drawing attention to her button nose. She grabbed Faye's suitcase and wheeled it away. "We must be quick. The weather is getting worse."

Carla wasted no time speeding out of the cluster of taxis, pulling red, oversized sunglasses from the dashboard even though the sun was nowhere to be seen. Remembering the broken ones in her bag, Faye sighed. She should've brought spares.

A quiet settled, the radio a low murmur of chattering voices as the wind raged outside, rocking the car. Carla tapped her painted fingernails on the steering wheel, tutting as the stream of traffic refused to let her merge onto the *autoestrada*.

Faye chewed her lip. If she wanted to make friends on this trip and prove she could be a functioning human, she needed to practise her conversational skills. But… words. It was so painfully English to discuss the weather, but it was a classic dialogue opener.

"Windy today, isn't it?" Faye cringed hearing the words leave her lips. Interacting with people shouldn't be so difficult.

Carla nodded, keeping her eyes on the road. "Yes, the storm is getting worse."

Faye had read about the storm early this morning when she couldn't sleep. The worst of it wasn't supposed to arrive until tomorrow, when she'd already settled safely on the island. But Faye's luck wasn't worth betting on. She'd never imagined living with a stoma, becoming a recluse under thirty, and running away to a volcanic island. But here she was.

"Ah, poor bugger," Carla commented as a woman's umbrella turned inside out, dragging her down the street. Leaves swirled around her, the rain pelting her face.

Faye couldn't help the questioning glance at the use of the colloquial English, and Carla laughed. "I like English phrases," she explained, eyes locked on the scene outside the window. The woman tried and failed to bend the broken metal ribs back into place, hitting herself in the nose. "Cheap as chips. Piece of cake. The boss always teaches me." Carla turned to Faye. "Do you know any more?"

"Hmm." Put on the spot, every word in the English language left Faye's brain. Then her dad, Lukas, popped into her mind. His Italian background meant he loved English phrases too, and he had a favourite. "Do you know 'the dog's bollocks'?" she asked.

Maybe not the best example to teach a stranger, Faye.

But before she could scramble to say something else, Carla chuckled. "What?" She grinned as she inched the van forward through traffic. "What does it mean?" The worsening weather drew dark clouds over them, and the wind rocked the van with a whistle.

"It means really good. Like..." Faye pulled a half-eaten bar of chocolate from her rucksack and held it up. "This chocolate is the dog's bollocks. It's the best."

"Not made of dog, right?" Carla eyed her, waiting for Faye to confirm.

Faye laughed, relaxing a little. "No. No dogs were harmed. Don't worry."

"Can I try?"

She had promised her dads to say yes to more things, but sharing her chocolate was sharing her heart. Like the mimic octopus camouflages itself into a jellyfish or a venomous sea-snake, Faye had to fit in, she supposed, so she begrudgingly let Carla snap off the top chunk.

"Mmm." Carla nodded her approval. "The dog's bollocks."

Faye popped a square into her mouth too, pleased at her progress. Even if she had to sacrifice her chocolate.

"I like you." Carla pointed at her. "What more can you teach me?"

***

Two hours later, Carla pulled the minibus up to the port, only to find it closed. They'd been on a wild goose chase—Carla liked that saying too—due to falling trees blocking the roads. Faye had hoped to leave the worst of the weather behind them, but judging by the roll of thunder and the violent waves splashing the dock, it was just getting started.

She hadn't prepared for this. She laid a hand over her abdomen, subtly gauging her bag's fullness. The last thing she wanted was to leak all over Carla's car. Then shit would hit the fan. Literally.

Carla tsked, eyeing the orange tape blocking the entrance with distaste. "Looks like we're not getting to the island tonight."

Oh no. Another clap of thunder ricocheted across the sky. With it, Faye imagined an explosion coming from her stomach, coating the inside of Carla's car and killing them both.

Her breathing quickened, pressure building in her chest. What was she thinking, coming here? She was hundreds of miles away from home, from her dads. She couldn't handle this by herself. She couldn't handle anything. A dizzying wave passed over her as her lungs squeezed. Tightened.

Suddenly, she was back between the thin sheets of her hospital bed. She groaned, confused by the monotonous beeps. The sharp bite of needles under her skin. Feeding tubes growing off her arms like roots. A new pain throbbed in her abdomen. She blinked her heavy eyelids open to find her dads' sympathetic faces lit by the obnoxiously white clinical lights.

"Shush, flower. It's okay." David cupped his warm hands over hers, his lip quivering, glasses perched at the end of his nose. "You're going to be fine. You had to have emergency surgery."

Surgery?

She turned to Lukas, hoping to find the punchline on the curl of his lips as they let her in on the joke. But as she breathed in the stench of hospital disinfectant, a sharp stab of pain almost made her vomit, and he hurried away to fetch a nurse from the station.

Faye flinched as a hand touched her shoulder. She blinked, and the white walls of the hospital dissolved before her, replaced by Carla's concerned dark eyes. The howl of the wind outside blew away the lingering memory, but her chest still heaved with panic.

"Faye." Carla's eyebrows pinched together, and she pushed the sunglasses up her face, resting them on her head. "Are you okay?"

She hated how her lip wobbled. She should've stayed

home, curled up in the safety of her bed, doing crossword puzzles while *Gilmore Girls* played in the background. Who was she kidding?

"I need to use the bathroom," she said instead, a habit formed after her operation. Checking put her at ease, even if the constant reminder of her ostomy exhausted her.

Confusion passed over Carla's features, and Faye hated it. She hated how the illusion was shattered. She wasn't carefree and young or brave and fearless like the women she admired. She couldn't crush the patriarchy like the suffragettes or pave the way like Marsha P. Johnson. She was plain Faye Donovan, a woman whose own body couldn't even function properly.

Carla plucked her phone from the dashboard. "Let me make a call. We'll be at the hotel quick as a wink."

"Hotel?"

She flashed Faye a big grin as she put the phone to her ear. "Two minutes away and very close to the port."

Before Faye could breathe with relief, Carla jumped to life. After a quick conversation, she dropped her phone in her lap and started to drive again. The sky darkened around them, streetlights illuminating the chaos outside. Trees battled to stay upright, losing leaves to the relentless wind.

Carla came to an abrupt stop outside a terrace of white buildings with cracks running up the plaster. A lone sock squirmed like a fish, caught in the iron balconies connecting the upper floors together, while the red neon "Raul's" sign hanging above the door blinked steadily, rocking in the wind.

Faye's heart kicked up a notch. Carla wanted her to stay here? It didn't look like a hotel, more like an underground den.

Accepting she had no other choice than to trust her, she followed Carla through the black door and into a cramped hallway. A turquoise-and-orange geometric carpet assaulted her eyes, clashing with the yellow wall paint.

Carla rang the tinny bell on the tiny wooden reception desk. Moments later, a man entered through a swing door, his face brightening when he spotted Carla. Rough stubble coated his chin, his black hair pulled into a tight bun at the back of his head.

He greeted Carla in Portuguese, then glanced at Faye and switched to English, which offended her a little. But after a full day of travel, screaming toddlers, crowds, and stoma worries, she was too anxious and exhausted to care.

"I like your hair tied back, Carla," Raul commented as he slid Faye's room key over the desk.

"I like yours, too." Carla played with her ponytail. "It's the dog's bollocks, I hear."

She glanced over her shoulder, encouraging Faye to join, but Faye folded in on herself. Witnessing their painfully obvious crushes made her want to bury her head in the reception desk's plant pot. It'd been a long day, and she could almost taste the solitude of her room. She fidgeted from foot to foot, eager to be alone.

After a few more uncomfortable exchanges, Raul

winked at the two of them and disappeared into the bar. Finally.

Carla helped Faye carry her luggage into the lift, the cramped space and creaky mechanical chains not doing anything for Faye's frayed nerves. At the top, she bid Faye a cheery goodbye, arranging to pick her up early in the morning once the port had reopened. But that was a worry for tomorrow.

Exhausted, Faye lugged her suitcase through the wooden door of her room, almost collapsing with relief as it closed behind her.

She'd made it. Well, kind of.

She dumped her luggage on the single bed and flicked on the antique wall-lights, bathing the small space in warmth. A poky wooden drawer had been crammed in next to a desk, but it was clean, and something about the room's minimalist decor brought a sense of comfort.

Faye emptied her bag in the cramped bathroom, struggling in the tiny space, then changed out of her aeroplane clothes and into her loose pyjama bottoms. The faded orange carpet scratched at her feet as she unpacked her essentials, but she was too tired to care. Her earlier optimism had been swept away with the gusts of wind.

She caught her reflection in the long mirror beside the door and frowned. She still wasn't used to it. The bulge at her abdomen. How the bag pushed back against her clothing. How nothing she wore ever truly hid it. She always knew it was there—but at least the ugly red protrusion wasn't visible.

A year ago, when Faye was curled up in her bed, begging her dads for more pain medication, she'd thought she'd do anything to treat her Crohn's disease. But this… Having an ostomy wasn't what she'd had in mind. How could she expect someone to want to be with her when she couldn't stand her own reflection in the mirror?

Her phone jumped to life on the desk, the group chat buzzing with messages. Faye pulled them up, smiling at her dads' names on the screen.

Lukas: *Told you you'd be fine! Enjoy yourself*
And don't stay hidden in your room

Faye shook her head, nibbling at her lip. The way her dad knew she would hole up in the hotel irked her.

David: *Just got out of class. Proud of you, sweetie. Send us some pictures when you get a chance. Miss you so much already 😭 😭 😭 😭 😭 xxx*

Lukas: *That's 50p for the excessive emoji jar*

David: *Five isn't excessive*

Lukas: *You said five cats were too many*

David: *The limit does not exist!!*

Faye chuckled, scrolling through their conversation as

they danced around *Mean Girls* references and came to the conclusion that having five cats wasn't much different from having four.

Faye: *I love you both so much. And of course, the more cats, the merrier*

She closed the app, taking in the four fluffy bundles curled together on her lock screen. Biscuit, Mochi, Angus, and Taco had helped her through the last few months, too, comforting her in that powerful way only animals could. She loved animals; animals were more trustworthy than people. That was one of the reasons she'd studied to become an ecologist. She wanted to protect them. To make a difference where it would matter.

Now, she couldn't even do that. She'd had so much time off work that she'd had to move back in with her parents. Any sense of achievement had been overshadowed by her ruptured bowel.

That's where the Sandy Springs course came in. No more feeling sorry for herself or locking herself away. She needed that enigma, needed to push herself. Not just for her sake, but for her dads. She'd put them through enough.

She blew out a breath, forcing herself to meet her gaze in the mirror. If she wanted that special quality, to be one of the enigma women, she needed to stay out of her comfort zone. She couldn't let her dads down already.

After swapping her pyjamas for light blue jeans and giving her make-up a top-up, she grabbed her rucksack and headed down to the bar. She could show her face, do a few sudokus, and then head back upstairs. No biggie. If it was terrible and creepy, she was only a lift away from the comfort of her bed. She couldn't stay up too late anyway, because Carla was picking her up in the morning. Her escape plan gave her enough courage to push open the bar door.

Like the rest of the hotel, the room had a cosy, snug feel. Pine-scented candles flickered on the tables, Portuguese music playing low through the speakers. Apart from three men chatting casually in the corner with Raul and another woman nursing a wine at the bar, it was quiet.

Faye approached, catching the eye of the impeccably dressed woman. Her dark chocolate eyes skimmed over Faye in a way that heated her cheeks. She was maybe late-thirties, with short blonde hair curled around her face, one side tucked behind her ear to reveal several hoop earrings and two sparkling studs. A fashionable burnt-orange pantsuit fitted her body perfectly.

Faye found it hard to look away. When she realised she'd been staring, she swallowed and uttered her best "*Boa noite*", with a nod.

The woman's lips lifted, and Faye followed the movement of her mouth. "*Boa noite*." Her rich voice wrapped around Faye like liquid gold.

Raul approached with a big grin, scratching at his stubble. "What can I get for you?"

Faye forced her gaze on him and ordered a non-alcoholic beer that she didn't really want. Ever since her surgery, carbonated drinks made her bloated and embarrassingly gassy, but she needed something to sip on to calm her nerves, and she didn't know what else to get.

She took a seat on the worn—but surprisingly comfy—chair in the opposite corner to the men, almost spilling her beer. Wiping her clammy hands on her trousers, she forced her attention to the gold-framed paintings hanging on the walls. Anything to distract herself from the woman at the bar.

"Right. Sudoku," she whispered to herself, clicking her pen and opening her book to the half-completed page she'd started on the plane. But the numbers danced on the paper, failing to hold her focus.

She tipped back the bottle, letting the ice-cold drink soothe her throat. But it couldn't stop her heart from thumping in her chest.

In her peripheral vision, Faye swore that the dark gaze had turned in her direction. The heat in her cheeks spread lower, curling in her belly. The woman oozed confidence in the way she was combing her with her stare, as though she didn't mind whether Faye noticed or not. Strong women were definitely a weakness of Faye's, prompting the decade-old question: did she want to *be* them or be *under* them?

Her attention snapped back to the woman like an elastic band. The way her blonde hair curled and curved in short, textured waves around her face, as if it'd been effortlessly styled. Her carved cheekbones and smooth porcelain skin. Then that curved mouth that Faye wanted to trace with her fingertips.

Definitely the latter, then.

She bounced her leg, distracted, and dug her pen into the paper, creating a deep groove. It'd been a long time since her body had reacted like this. Dating with a chronic illness seemed impossible. Especially after her last attempt at dating ended with her being ghosted. The combination of long distance and intense Crohn's flare-ups meant it was only a matter of time before her ex, Molly, had got fed up.

Now, dating with her stoma just seemed even more of an impossibility.

A sour feeling twisted through her gut. *Oh... That's why that woman is looking at me.* Her hand drifted to her stomach. Maybe she hadn't hidden her bag as well as she thought she had. Why else would an attractive woman be paying her attention?

Movement caused Faye to raise her head. The woman's delicate ringed fingers were playing with the stem of her glass. Then she raised it for a sip and stood. She was leaving.

Guess that's that, then.

Disappointment crept up Faye's spine, but when those long, elegant legs strode past the exit, her chest tightened.

The woman was heading straight towards her.

TWO

Diana

Diana swirled the golden liquid in her glass, inhaling the floral aroma, trying to pinpoint the various notes. She pursed her lips. Truthfully, it was a little too sweet for her liking. Probably not worth the headache. As she edged ever further away from forty, even the smallest taste of alcohol left her with a throbbing temple in the morning. But she had to pass the time somehow.

She'd opted for a private transfer to the port, unable to stomach the idea of squeezing onto a sweaty bus with a handful of strangers. Unfortunately, they'd still arrived a moment too late. Even Diana's fifty-euro offer couldn't convince them to let her cross the choppy water to the island.

Diana tapped at her phone to light up the screen, but still she had no messages. She'd asked her daughter to let her know when she arrived at Sandy Springs, but their chat sat idle, with Diana's last three messages unanswered.

It wouldn't be the first time she'd received the silent treatment from her daughter, but she'd hoped that her agreement to attend this three-week course at Sandy Springs together meant they were finally turning a new page.

So far, no dice.

A raucous bellow of laughter came from the other side of the bar, and Diana narrowed her eyes. She'd already fended off the men's advances with a sharp bite when they'd spotted her sitting alone. The oldest of the group, a round man with a quickly receding hairline, reminded her of her ex-husband, Jason. The way his deep voice carried over the room, his exaggerated arm movements, and his preference for crinkled polo shirts were enough to induce a sickening wave of déjà vu.

Even though they'd been divorced for over a decade, it never failed to amaze her how quickly those memories could resurface. Remembering dates, deadlines, and other professors' names—that took real brainpower. But her ex-husband's cutting words still lingered in her mind, taking up valuable space.

"You've abandoned me, and you've abandoned your daughter."

Diana sighed and took another sip from her glass, letting her gaze pass over the collection of pictures and signs decorating the bar. Rain hammered against the small windows; the candles placed on the empty tables flickered, filling the room with the scent of pine. A tasteful collection of mismatched chairs and sofas placed around the room gave the space character. Plus, the wooden bar-top was smooth and not sticky. Sitting here beat checking—then rechecking—her emails in her tiny room, even if the wine was sub-par.

Unable to fight the itch scratching at her any longer, she grabbed her phone and pulled up her inbox. No matter how many times a day she checked, there were always fresh emails waiting for her. Her heart quivered when she caught sight of one from Harvard, announcing who was taking over her socioeconomics classes. She tightened her grip on the phone as she read the name—Selena Borgo, her eager French colleague who was always nipping at Diana's heels like a perfectly groomed miniature poodle.

Bloody hell.

She fired a quick text off to her agent, Leanne, and sighed, rubbing her forehead. This Sandy Springs course better be worth the leave she'd taken from work. In Diana's field, she couldn't afford to sit and admire the view. Especially when Selena Borgo was breathing down her neck. What had started as a visiting post at Harvard had the potential to become something more permanent. Diana wanted to be first in line when that happened.

The door squeaked open, and a woman entered, big

doe eyes nervously flitting around. The room held its breath while her eyes steadied on Diana, weighing something.

She wore a simple blue hoodie and jeans, but something about her shifted the energy in the bar. Her make-up accentuated her natural cheekbones, a slender nose, and full lips, her dark hair falling long and straight past her shoulders. A few loose strands framed her face imperfectly. Simple, yet oddly striking.

The woman brushed her hands over her torso, perhaps a nervous tell, before making her way over. Then her clear turquoise eyes, winged with thin black eyeliner and eyeshadow that shimmered under the warm light, locked with Diana's. The well-rehearsed Portuguese greeting she offered caught Diana by surprise.

"*Boa noite,*" Diana returned, catching how the woman's cheeks warmed.

As she leaned on the bar, her soft scent—petrichor and vanilla—filled Diana's senses. She let her gaze drift over her clean baby-blue hoodie and oversized jeans as she sipped at her wine, trying to guess the woman's order. *Gin. Something fruity, maybe.* Diana collected data all the time, observing people. She couldn't help it.

"Do you have anything non-alcoholic?"

That surprised her again. As did the woman's accent. She hadn't expected her to sound so English, so…Northern. She followed her with her gaze as she took her drink and sat on the other side of the room in an orange armchair. A light buzz coated Diana's skin, from the wine

or curiosity about the woman's presence—maybe both—
and she stroked her thumb over the cool stem of the glass.

Her phone buzzed across the wooden top with a reply
from her agent.

Leanne: *I knew it! Selena would jump in your grave if she
thought it'd give her a leg up*
You know what you have to do, right?

Diana: *I'm not stalking her social media to dig up dirt*

Three dots bounced on the screen. She imagined Leanne's
lips pressed together. Fingers moving at lightning pace.
Black, springy coils falling over her eyes.

Leanne: *She's squeaky clean. I've tried*

Diana: *I don't want you to do that*

Leanne: *If you're not the lion, you're the dead antelope*
*And get writing that damn book! We have to move quick
while publishers are still interested*

Diana's agent hadn't been overly thrilled at the prospect
of her taking three weeks off instead of working on her
follow-up to *Bridging the Gender Gap*. It'd been the first
of her books to really take off, landing her interviews,
inviting her to speak at prestigious conferences, and
unlocking doors to teaching at the best universities in the

world. Leanne was always her biggest cheerleader, but Diana found it hard to articulate why she'd been so far behind on her manuscript. Whenever she sat down to write, nothing came out. It was as though she had nothing of interest left to say.

Leanne: *I need something substantial to work with by the end of the month. Can you do that?*

Diana sighed, letting her gaze wander until it landed on the pretty woman in the corner. She was scribbling something in a small book. *What is she writing?* Her presence stood out like a sore thumb—as she imagined she did too, in her orange pantsuit. She assumed the storm had something to do with the woman's late arrival.

She sucked in a deep breath and exhaled, trying to dislodge some of the pressure building in her skull. If she couldn't shake this writer's block, she was going to get left behind. Selena taking over Diana's classes wasn't an act of altruism. It was competition. And there was no way she'd allow Selena to be the lion eating her sorry carcass.

Diana: *Give me these three weeks to write. I'll sort it*

Leanne: *That's more like it. Agent mode, signing off. As your friend, I do hope this course brings you and Molly closer together*

Diana: *Me too. Speak soon*

She placed her phone down and rubbed her temples. Hopefully, the change of environment and interaction with different people would spark something. These next few weeks were going to be challenging. But if she could put together a decent proposal, everything would be fine. She could write while Molly attended the guidance sessions on the island. It wasn't as if Diana needed a self-help course.

Something small and shiny caught her eye, and she bent to pluck it from the wooden floor. A debit card belonging to a *Faye Donovan*. Diana smiled to herself, the name playing on her lips. It suited her. She must have dropped it earlier.

Raul had pulled up a seat to join the noisy men, so Diana had to be a good Samaritan and give the card back to Faye. Hopefully, the distraction would keep her from rechecking her emails or glancing at Selena's Facebook page to see if she'd made an announcement about taking over her position. That woman didn't need any excuse to gloat.

She sipped from her glass, letting the alcohol give her a boost and push her to her feet. Twining her fingers around the wine-glass stem, she glided across the room.

"I think this might belong to you," she said, holding the card up between two fingers.

Faye glanced up at her from under thick black lashes. "Oh, god. Thank you."

Diana gave her the card. "You're welcome."

"I can't believe I did that." She shook her head. "This has been such a disaster."

Diana observed her for a beat, the sleek, straight hair and the impeccable make-up. She hardly embodied a walking disaster. "Did the storm ruin your plans, too?"

"You could say that. So far, Portugal hasn't exactly welcomed me with open arms."

Diana nudged her chin at the book in front of Faye. "And sudoku doesn't help?"

Faye let out a soft laugh, her fingers brushing the page. "Not really. I'm stuck on this one."

"I'd offer my assistance, but sudoku isn't in my wheelhouse."

She shrugged. "That's alright. It's not everyone's cup of tea."

"But it's yours?" Diana eyed the pencil markings in the margins and couldn't stop the edges of her lips from lifting. What twenty-something-year-old spent their time doing extra-hard sudoku at a bar?

Faye gave a sheepish smile. "That probably sounds quite sad to admit."

"Not at all. I find that rather endearing."

Those blue-green eyes met hers carefully. Like she was trying to decipher the truth behind her statement. Something simmered low in Diana's chest, but before she could touch on it, a roar from the men behind them broke their gaze. Diana turned to the group, rolling her eyes as they tried to fit as many pretzels into their mouths as possible, spitting crumbs over the table.

"You can sit if you want," Faye said quietly, casting a glance at the table.

Diana needed to head to bed. She had to catch the boat in the morning, and that proposal for Leanne wouldn't draft itself, but something about the woman intrigued her. So she sat in the yellow chair opposite, crossing one leg in front of the other.

Faye flipped the sudoku book shut and tucked it into her rucksack.

"So," Diana began, "is this your first visit to Portugal?"

Faye dipped her head, hiding behind those thick lashes. "Yeah. You?"

Diana had been once before. Almost two decades ago, with Jason, to celebrate their daughter's birthday. They'd spent most of the week arguing after Jason had gotten a horrific sunburn. He'd spent the rest of his time sulking under a parasol, complaining about the lack of English beer at the hotel. "A long time ago," she said, relaxing into her seat. "How did the storm ruin your plans?"

"I was supposed to be getting the boat across to the island," Faye said, fingernails picking at the beer label. "But all the crossings were cancelled."

The island?

She wondered what had attracted Faye to a course designed to 'reset your life'. Though put together, her nervous energy didn't go unnoticed. But she was young, smart—if her sudoku abilities rang true—and brave enough to make the journey alone. What was she concealing?

"I suppose we'll be sharing the crossing tomorrow, then," Diana said.

"You're going too?" Faye eyed her, her voice dripping with scepticism. "To Sandy Springs?"

"Correct."

Faye opened her mouth like she wanted to say more but clamped it shut.

"What is it?" Diana prompted, her eyebrow quirking.

Faye traced the beer label, picking at a folded edge. "Nothing. I'm just…surprised. Surprised that someone wearing a pantsuit like *that* would be interested in a self-help course on a remote island." She bit her lip. "Not that I'm judging you. I try not to do that. Sorry. I'm rambling. It must be all the beer." She shot Diana a goofy grin, angling the bottle so she could read the "non-alcoholic" half-peeled label on the front.

Diana couldn't help but return the smile, finding her awkward bumbling charming. Plus, she was pretty sure there was a compliment hidden in there. Truthfully, parts of Diana's life had wandered astray—her relationship with her daughter, her love life—but her collection of pantsuits had never let her down. She smoothed her fingers over the material as if to say thanks. "The human mind favours categorising as a survival method. So I suppose we can't help but form opinions of others based on initial judgements. We'd exhaust ourselves otherwise." She let her gaze fall on Faye. "Though it's important to remember first impressions can be deceiving."

Intriguing, even, she added silently. Like the way Faye couldn't look at her for longer than a few seconds.

"It's not just humans," Faye said, drawing circles in the condensation on the table. "There's so much of the animal world that gets overlooked or put into boxes. Everyone thinks birds are stupid 'cos they have such tiny brains, but they can count. Pigeons can do as much maths as monkeys."

"Really?"

Faye nodded, meeting Diana's gaze for the first time in a while. Heat lingered. An invitation. A warning. Then she glanced away. "Chickens, too. Did you know there are about thirty-four billion chickens in the world? That's, like, four to every human. It's a shame so many are killed every year. I kinda wish they'd evolve to better defend themselves."

Diana considered this. "So, chickens with big bear claws?"

Faye laughed, and Diana found herself leaning closer.

"Yeah. Or shark teeth. Or venomous feathers."

"Interesting." Diana's mouth curled as she pictured wild, giant chickens chasing Selena around the faculty lounge, nipping at her skirt.

"I considered breeding my own species of super chickens to release into the wild, but I don't think I'd have time to perfect it until I'm retired." Faye sipped her beer.

"I'd also be worried they might hurt each other by accident."

Diana chuckled, a little lost for words. There was something about the passionate look in Faye's blue eyes, like she really believed she could save all the chickens in the world, that made her pause. A lightness she hadn't touched in years.

A loud cheer broke out from the other side of the room. Raul and the other two men applauded the Jason lookalike as he emptied two bags of pretzels into his mouth. He pumped his fists in the air, but when his overfilled hamster cheeks reddened, the celebrations turned to panic.

The chair clattered to the floor, drinks spilling over the table. His eyes jumped around the room, his hands grasping his throat.

"I think he's choking," Raul said, slapping the man on the back.

In a blink, Faye appeared at Raul's side. She wrapped her arms around the portly man and pulled inwards in three quick successions. On the last squeeze, the dislodged piece of pretzel sailed through the air and skidded across the wooden floor in a trail of saliva. The men cheered like the man had won World's Biggest Moron, slapping him on the back and chattering in Portuguese.

Diana rose to join the commotion, her brain still trying to piece the event together. Raul thanked Faye profusely, throwing in curses and crossing his chest, while the other men crowded around the choker, offering him a drink of beer to soothe his throat.

Honestly. Diana tried not to scold them like naughty schoolchildren.

"Is everyone alright?" she asked, trying to bring the anxious energy in the room down a notch.

Raul placed his hands on Faye's shoulders, his relief obvious. "*Sim. Sim.* But only because of you. Thank you. *Obrigado.*" He slapped the man on the back again, earning a grunt from him. "Daniel, *seu porco ganancioso,* eh?"

Faye laughed, but her hands were shaking. When her eyes landed on Diana's, she explained, "He called him a greedy pig."

Diana's lips twitched. Raul wasn't wrong. Then she took Faye's elbow. "You acted fast. That was impressive. Are you feeling alright?"

Faye nodded, her focus falling to where Diana held her through the fabric of her jumper. "Just feeling the adrenaline."

Heat seared under Faye's gaze, but Diana didn't drop her hand. "Do you want some water?"

"Please."

"Let me." Raul fetched some water and ice to their table, hovering while Faye drank. When she set down her glass, he produced a bottle of the wine Diana had been drinking and placed it in front of her. "Free drinks! For you."

Faye inspected the bottle.

"Do you drink?" Diana asked, hoping she wasn't being intrusive.

"Not really. No."

Raul brought over two more wine glasses and poured a generous helping into all three without asking. He raised his in a cheers, and Diana reluctantly clinked their glasses.

"You don't have to drink it if you don't want to," Diana assured her when Raul left to rejoin the others.

"I am trying to say yes to more things, but…" Faye's gaze locked with hers. Diana couldn't read the emotion swirling in her irises, but then a small smile played on Faye's lips, and she lifted her glass. "I guess I'm in if you are. It'd be sad to drink it alone."

Diana considered it. Maybe she should start saying yes to more things, too. She wasn't past having a few harmless drinks. It couldn't hurt, and it might help unlock some ideas for the manuscript hidden deep inside her brain.

"It would be my pleasure," she said, and she clinked her glass with Faye's.

***

Darkness cloaked the bar as Raul switched off the lights. "Right. Come on, everyone. Let's go. *Todos embora!* I mean it this time." The slight slur to his words wasn't convincing, and he had to grab the shoulders of the men slumped over the bar to guide them towards the exit. He turned to the two women giggling in the corner, two empty bottles between them. "You too, ladies. Don't make me manhandle you as well."

Diana scoffed. "Try it, and we'll set the chickens on you."

The two of them cracked into fits of laughter, and Raul shook his head, muttering something in Portuguese under his breath. "Ladies, *please*. You have an early boat to catch."

Something in Raul's glassy gaze pulled Diana back into functioning mode. She stood, tugging Faye with her. "He's right. Time to go."

"No," Faye groaned. "I don't wanna go yet. This is the most fun I've had in ages."

Raul blew out the last of the candles, and with only the streetlights to illuminate the bar, everything took on a hazy tone. A bang on the window made the women jump. Faye grabbed Diana's hand, their bodies drawing together like two magnets. When the men pushed their faces against the glass, pulling stupid expressions, Diana shook her head. Then the warmth in her palm registered. The dusting of Faye's breath against her neck. The curve of her body pressed into her side. A new fuzzy feeling spread from Diana's fingertips to her cheeks, filling her body with heat.

That must be the fifth or sixth glass of wine.

She steered Faye towards the door, said goodnight to Raul, then pressed the button for the lift as they waited by the reception desk.

Maybe it was because Faye was unsteady on her feet, or maybe it was something else—something she didn't want to read into right now—but Diana didn't let go of her hand. She sat down on the wooden desk, listening to the whir of the mechanical chains and Raul banging about through the adjacent wall.

"I had so much fun tonight," Faye said softly.

Diana turned her head, struck by the look of awe in her eyes. "Me too," she answered honestly. The night with Faye had passed quickly—too damn quickly—and for those few hours they'd left the world behind. But now they'd stepped out of the bar, already her dizzy mind started to snag onto tomorrow. Setting her alarm, catching the boat, seeing Molly.

Faye moved closer, sliding herself between Diana's legs.

Her breath hitched.

Faye's body pressed warm heat to the inside of her thighs. She tilted her head back to meet her gaze, Faye's scent pulling them closer together. Vanilla, and something sweet, like summer rain.

All she could focus on was Faye's mouth—the lipstick faded but still colouring her lips a darker pink—instead of the sensation fluttering between her legs. This wasn't supposed to happen tonight. But somehow, she didn't want to stop it either.

"I really like this mole." Faye brushed Diana's cheekbone. "This one here."

Diana inhaled at the delicate touch.

Faye wet her lips, and Diana's stomach rolled at the movement. The urge to close the gap intensified, the air thickening and squeezing them together. Her heart beat louder, the alcohol muddying her brain.

The lift dinged, and Faye jumped backwards, stumbling over a potted plant. She righted herself and slipped through the opening doors, pressing herself against the back wall with an adorable lopsided grin. Diana straightened her pantsuit and followed her in—her breathing heavier than she'd like—and the doors slid shut. Her pulse pounded in her ears, louder than that of the creaky pulley system as they climbed. There wasn't much room in the lift, even less so with the tension charging the air. She focused on the faded orange carpet, the peeling chrome on the railings, and not the pretty woman's gaze burning into her.

Finally, the doors opened with a hiss. Neither of them moved.

Diana's eyes snapped back to Faye. Her soft blue irises, swirled with delicate hints of green, blended into a breathtaking turquoise. Diana's throat tightened. Then a strong tug behind her sternum made her take a step forward, but Faye beat her to it, closing the distance between them.

Faye's soft, warm mouth enveloped hers. Diana melted into the touch, her hands cupping Faye's face and pulling her deeper into the kiss. They hit the back of the wall. Liquid heat coiled in Diana's belly, winding tighter when Faye gasped softly into her mouth.

She threaded her fingers through Faye's hair, brushing against her scalp, drinking in every breathless noise she gave her. Diana appreciated the notes of the wine now, recognising the pleasing tang on Faye's lips. Sweet hints of something fruity, giving her an all-consuming desire to lean in and have another taste.

She could get intoxicated on that alone.

She brushed Faye's silky hair over her shoulders, then drifted lower. Her hands caressed her small waist. Then her hips.

Faye jumped back, knocking into the railing with a huff. "Sorry. Sorry, I—I can't. I… fuck—" She shook her head, her chin dropping. Before Diana could say anything, she ran through the doors and down the hallway, her clumsy steps echoing in the quiet.

Diana stayed in the lift a minute longer, observing her perplexed reflection. Her chest, still heaving. Her blonde hair, dishevelled.

What the hell just happened?

THREE

Faye

Faye fidgeted on the bench by the port, the hard wood digging into her bum. She narrowed her eyes at the sudoku page clenched in her fist, trying to focus on the numbers rather than the tumbling terror in her stomach. The pungent smell of fish did little to help, the scent sticking in her nose as she inhaled. She cringed. Then, remembering the way she'd left things with Diana last night, she cringed even harder, folding in on herself.

Very smooth.

Carla's fierce banging on her hotel room had startled her into one of the worst hangovers of her life—and Faye had had a few, not to mention the one where she'd woken up locked inside a takeaway after taking a nap under the table.

She shook her head, trying to distract her brain from playing a montage of the top twenty most embarrassing moments of her life. But the surprise in Diana's eyes topped them all. She groaned and took a swig from her electrolyte drink.

Not only had Faye aggravated her stoma from all the wine, but she'd also missed her crossing to the island this morning. Poor Carla had tried her best to get Faye ready in time, but it was difficult to explain to someone she'd just met how she couldn't simply open the door and leave when an eruption matching Vesuvius threatened her abdomen.

Also quite difficult to explain to attractive women kissing her and running their hands over her hips.

For god's sake. Nights like *that* with women like Diana were as rare as unicorn dust. Why couldn't she just be cool and confident about it?

Because have you seen yourself recently?

Despite the extra care she'd taken matching her eyeshadow to her pink summer playsuit, nothing helped offset the awful bags under her eyes and the pale, pained look on her face. She felt as though she'd slept under that takeaway table for a week, while a heavy metal band practised in the room above her, smashing drums and screaming. At least Diana wouldn't see her like this.

Her fear of what-ifs meant she'd packed her brand-new lingerie. Some silky, some lacy, all designed to keep her ostomy bag secure and tucked away—but she'd still panicked. It wasn't like Faye had never had sex before, or that she didn't want to. When Diana pressed her against a wall and put her mouth to good use, there was nothing she wanted more. It was fear of the unknown.

Faye wasn't sure if she could do the same things she used to. Even if she could, Diana might be repulsed. It was silly, really. Diana, and the way she carried herself… that sexy, well-spoken English accent, the totally pullable short hair, those soft lips… Why would Diana be interested in her? Admittedly, in the moment, the alcohol had helped Faye overlook that question.

The sobering reality was that she couldn't plan for some things. No matter how organised she was.

Like last night. Faye groaned. *Piss off, brain.*

She picked at her cuticles. Where was Carla? She'd disappeared some time ago, chatting and giggling at her phone screen, and Faye hadn't seen her since. Maybe she'd gone to see Raul.

Lifting her gaze, she took in the sea, the waves rolling and bobbing the boats anchored at the port. Her head ached at the temples, and she took a big gulp of her drink. A fat seagull landed on the concrete next to her, tilting its little head and hopping forward expectantly.

"Sorry, mate," Faye said. "I haven't got any fish for you."

He took one more look at her, head twitching as though expressing his distaste for her life choices, then leapt into the sky. He dove around the port, showboating his large wings before landing on a nearby bin to pull a stale bread bun from inside.

Faye opened her mouth to lecture the bird, knowing the bread would only bloat him and fill his stomach with empty calories, but the earth-shattering rumble of a horn made her cover her ears.

Fucking hell.

When the pain lowered to a bearable level, she aimed her gaze at the perpetrator. A small man with a full head of dark hair stood on the deck of a white catamaran. His face split into a full grin, and he waved at Faye. Some of her frustration dissipated, and she forced herself to wave back.

Then Carla appeared beside her.

Oh. He was waving at *her*. She ducked her head, heat warming her neck, and considered climbing into the nearby bin to let the birds feast on her instead.

"Here you go, sleepyhead." Carla handed her a cup of fruit juice and nodded towards the catamaran. "Time to go."

Faye's excitement about her trip had long since evaporated, but Carla plucked her up by the elbow and steered her towards the boat, anyway.

Faye couldn't admire the boat, which seemed far too large for transporting the two of them. She couldn't chat either. As they chugged out of port, she pinned her gaze towards the horizon, the fierce wind and choppy motion of the boat doing little to calm the anxious knots in her stomach. The bright sunlight made the ache in her skull deepen and pulse. Once again, she wished for her broken sunglasses.

The boat slapped over the waves, and she leaned over the edge, prepared to vomit. Salty seawater sprayed in her mouth and wet her face. Her stomach surged.

Note to self: never drink wine again.

"Duarte, abranda!" Carla called to the captain, but the wind stole her words.

Footsteps clunked against the deck. More words Faye couldn't hear. She clung to the railing, trying to keep her insides where they should be. Thankfully, the boat soon slowed. The thuds lessened. But her guts still swirled in circles. *If I don't puke, it'll be a miracle.*

After a few more minutes, with the boat humming along at a steady pace, Carla helped Faye sit. A chill washed over her cheeks, like the colour had been pulled right out of them. Her make-up must be ruined.

"Need these?" Carla asked, producing a pair of sunglasses shaped like pineapples. "You can borrow them." They weren't Faye's style, looking like something David might keep in their dressing-up box, but she wasn't in a position to be picky.

"Thank you," she said, breathing with relief as the world darkened around her.

A seagull bombed overhead with a loud caw that sounded an awful lot like laughter.

"You haven't touched your juice." Carla lifted her cup. "It will help."

"What is it?" Certain fruits gave her flare-ups, and

after the beating she'd put her body through last night, she had to be careful. Not to mention Duarte's speedy boat-ride testing her gag reflex.

"Mango. Fresh from the island."

That should be fine. If only her stomach would stop spinning. She didn't want to seem ungrateful, so she sucked on the straw, humming as the smooth liquid slid down her throat.

"Thanks. It's kind of you to bring me this." She chanced a look at Carla, relieved that the juice had stayed down. "I'm sorry again for missing the crossing."

"No more apologising." Carla wagged a finger, peering at Faye through her enormous sunglasses. "I should have warned you that Raul is a bad influence." She shrugged, letting out a sigh. "But he does have the best hangover recipe."

So she had been to see Raul. *Interesting.*

"What is this face?" Carla asked.

Oops. Faye dropped her eyebrows into a neutral expression, then took another sip of juice. "You two seemed close, that's all."

"Eh, nothing serious." She waved her hand, the sea breeze tickling the loose strands from her ponytail. "He's still young."

Faye bristled at that comment. Lukas had said something similar when Molly ghosted her. *'You're young, you've plenty of time for love.'* As if the future held anything other than empty promises and vague platitudes.

Molly had been the straw that broke the camel's

back. Their relationship had started online, like the others: fun, flirty, then a couple of dates. Texting and video calls to shrink the space between Manchester and London. And for a while, it had worked; Faye could keep her pain hidden. Then reality hit. Texting became silence. Calls went unanswered. Eventually, Molly became just another person Faye no longer spoke to, like her school friends. The worst thing was she couldn't blame them; she hadn't been a lot of fun to be around. But Molly vanishing without a reason hurt.

Faye could only blame herself. There was a pattern. The sicker she got, the more distant people became. Chronic disease scared people.

"Can you see it?" Carla's voice pulled her back to the hum of the boat. Faye followed the point of her finger to the curve of the island coming into view.

The towering trees, steep cliffs, and golden, sandy beaches gave her an injection of life. She was nearly there. Sunshine, mindfulness, and—the biggest sway in her agreement to come here—an ecologist's dream of endemic species. Noctule bats, shearwaters, and parakeets—animals she hoped she'd be lucky enough to see—stirred new excitement in her veins.

The island promising answers. The island prompting change.

Relief blurred the edges of her nausea. Resetting her life was within reach.

Thank god, she was almost there.

The boat slowed as it docked, and the hot sun beat

down on Faye's back. As soon as she stepped onto land, she let out a huge breath of relief. *Solid ground feels great.*

The toot of a horn drew her attention to the dirt path cutting up the hillside. A small buggy with off-road tyres sped towards them, kicking up sand in every direction. A woman with cherry-red hair waved from behind the wheel. She crunched over a collection of debris that must have gathered during the storm, almost catapulting herself from her seat.

Faye recognised her from the website—the big smile, curvy body, and bright hair—and nerves surged in her belly again. She wanted to make a good first impression with the two women who ran the course, but already she was late and stinking of last night's booze.

The buggy skidded to a stop, and the woman hopped out, wearing a yellow-and-white dress and chunky white sandals. "Hey! You must be Faye. I'm sorry about the weather delaying you, but welcome to Sandy Springs." She held up a hand in greeting. "I'm Ella. Ooh, nice sunglasses."

"Nice to meet you." Faye remembered the stupid pineapples on her face but didn't have it in her to explain. "Thanks."

Carla linked arms with Duarte as he appeared next to them. The top three buttons of his shirt were undone, revealing thick curly chest hair. Carla nodded to Faye. "She's a good one. Faye is the dog's bollocks."

Faye certainly didn't feel like it today, but she offered her best attempt at a smile. "Thank you. I'd never have made it if it wasn't for you."

"We're going to play poker now," Duarte said, with a big grin. Carla elbowed him. "I mean… we're going…fishing."

"Make sure you check his sleeves, Carla." Ella winked before turning to grab Faye's suitcase and lift it into the back of the buggy. She climbed into the driver's seat. "You can sit up here with me. I won't bite."

Faye slid in next to her, catching the scent of aloe vera, and Ella sped off, the wheels spinning and kicking up sand as they raced up the trail. Over her shoulder, Carla and Duarte grew smaller. A small ball of sadness tightened in her chest. She'd made a nice bond with Carla, but she was on her own again.

What about Diana?

Pfft. Diana would probably run for the hills when she saw Faye again. Another wave of embarrassment flooded her. Hopefully, she wouldn't bump into her today; Faye had no idea what to say.

Ella veered off the wooden slats a few times to avoid fallen branches, making the seat vibrate and shudder. Faye's insides surged, acid tainting her throat. She swallowed it down, gripping the railing.

"Sorry." Ella shot her a worried glance. "We've not managed to clean up the after-effects of the storm yet. Romeo is supposed to be clearing the main path. I'm not sure where he's gone."

Not a moment too soon, Ella pulled the buggy to a stop outside a white wooden cabin with blue shutters.

Fresh pollen mingled with the salty air, and Faye breathed it in. Pink bougainvillaea twisted up the walls, and purple lavender bloomed in traditional ceramic beds by the door.

"Here's your home for the next three weeks," Ella said. "Due to all the disruptions from the storm and the late arrivals, we're holding the introductions at two in the reception hall. It's a short walk down the track, by the courtyard. You have a couple of hours to acquaint yourself."

"Thank you." Faye tried her best smile. Whatever it took to get inside quicker. She just wanted to lie in the dark for a while with her headphones in.

Ella handed over her suitcase and placed a key in her hand. "If you need anything—and I mean anything—I'm your girl. Just let me know."

The opening and slamming of a cabin door further up the track made them turn their heads. Feet crunched the gravel, and then the familiar fall of tight blonde curls made Faye's stomach drop.

The woman looked just like Molly.

Her hangover was playing tricks on her.

She averted her eyes, not wanting to engage with any more strangers today—especially when her insides ached. And definitely not with anyone who mirrored her ex-girlfriend.

"Faye?" The high-pitched voice made her gaze snap upwards.

Her name, wrapped in that familiar London lilt from late-night phone calls, sent a chill racing up her spine.

Molly?

Faye pushed her ridiculous sunglasses up her face to get a better look, squinting under the light. Wide blue eyes stared back at her, and a surge of warring emotions rose in her stomach.

This isn't happening.

Nausea won out, overpowering the rest. She darted to the purple flora, falling to her knees to spew her guts into the flowerbed.

FOUR

Faye

Faye spat into the flowerbed and wiped her mouth with a tissue from her pocket. She didn't want to turn around and see the looks on the women's faces, but she had nowhere to hide. Humiliated didn't even come close.

Ella leaned over her, casting a shadow that swallowed Faye's withering frame. "Are you alright?"

Faye's mind stalled. Malfunctioned. Another wave of nausea, and her head swayed. The sour and putrid stench of her mess overpowered the sweet flowers. Should she leave it? Cover it up like a cat? *Oh my god.*

"Do you want help getting up?" Ella offered her hand, and Faye accepted, moving off her grazed knees onto unsteady feet.

Worst-case scenario: Molly is here, witnessing you throw up into a flowerbed with stupid sunglasses on your head. Best-case scenario: it isn't her, and you're overreacting, acting completely unhinged in front of a stranger trying to enjoy their holiday.

Her feet rooted in place, all the earth's magnetism pinning her there. She wished the ground would split open and suck her through the cracks. As if she'd ever be so lucky.

With heavy limbs, she forced her body to turn as adrenaline fired through her veins, swirling the sickness in her throat again.

Molly wore white denim shorts and a cute crop top, her belly-piercing catching the light. Her blue eyes widened, but the surprise didn't mask the sharp edge behind them.

It's her. Oh god, oh god, oh god.

"Faye?" Molly's voice came out. "What're you doing here?"

"Do you two know each other?" Ella asked.

When neither of them answered, Ella cleared her throat and backed up towards the buggy. "I'll give you two some privacy." She hopped in and started the engine, calling out behind her, "See you at the introductions!"

Left alone, Faye swallowed the acidic remnants of the fruit juice trying to push its way up her throat. *Say something.* Anything.

This was supposed to be her reset. Her "stop moping

and get your shit together" moment. To help her discover her enigma. She wanted to be moving forwards, not backwards.

But she still couldn't find her voice.

"You look different," Molly commented. Her gaze fell over Faye's outfit, making her skin prickle.

Faye didn't know if she was referring to her clothes, her stricken hangover-face, or the fact that she'd gained weight since her surgery. Either way, the "different" didn't fill her with confidence.

Molly hadn't changed in the year since she'd last seen her. Her soft blue eyes held the same puppy expression, her small, round face only enhancing the adorable image. Faye knew how misleading that image could be, though. That puppy had bite.

She wrapped her arms around herself. "You…look the same," she managed, her voice quiet and pathetic. It was supposed to be a compliment, but from the way Molly's eyebrows pinched together, she didn't seem to take it as one.

Molly glanced over her shoulder, but no one was there. She scratched at her neck. "I'm going to the beach." She lingered on Faye for a moment too long, enough to make the prickles on her skin turn into a burning wildfire. "I guess I'll see you around."

Faye watched, dumbstruck, as Molly strutted down the hill and out of view.

Out of all the retreats in the world, she had to be here.

She dragged her case inside her cabin and closed the door. The image of Molly, wide-eyed and rooted in spot, smacked her between the eyes with another splitting headache.

She sank to the cold tiles, her back to the door, tears spilling down her cheeks. Powerless and exhausted, she let them fall.

Her ex-girlfriend was here. Seriously, Universe? Last she knew, Molly was on track to graduate as a lawyer. Before Faye had muted her on social media, she seemed to be having a great life without her.

She bit back a sob. Everyone seemed better off without her. Why didn't they keep in touch otherwise?

Her guts twisted, and she gagged, but there was nothing left to come up.

Tipping her head back against the wall, she rubbed her eyes. Then, feeling something wet on her midsection, she glanced down. *Great.* Now, her bag was leaking as well.

What a shitty day. Pun intended.

She did sob then. Big, ugly wails left her mouth as she dragged herself into the bathroom to strip off her clothes, bag, and peeling baseplate. She couldn't even appreciate the room's cleanliness or the large charcoal tiles; she just climbed into the shower and turned the water up hot.

Tears slid down her face, melding into the stream of water pelting her head and shoulders. Today was a disaster. Her brain replayed every miserable moment back to her, and she cried harder as embarrassment, shame, and disappointment leaked into her bones. She watched the water swirl down the plughole, wishing she could get sucked inside too and live in the drains forever.

***

Faye stared at her reflection. The little catnap had eased some of the puffiness around her eyes, but it couldn't work miracles. She swivelled, checking her new dress hid her bag adequately. She'd applied extra stoma powder to dry her skin and more adhesive to cope with the extra humidity. She wouldn't be making the mistake of rushing again.

Introductions would start in thirty minutes, but she was more nervous over who she might bump into on the way—Molly, her curly-haired ex-girlfriend, or Diana, the gorgeous older woman she'd kissed and then ditched like a hot potato. She needed to clear the air with both of them, but the very idea made her want to lock the door and board up the windows.

Faye wished she could tell her dads about what had happened and ask for advice, but her phone had lost all signal and abandoned her, too.

Get a grip, Faye.

Emmeline Pankhurst would never crawl under the bed and hide after a couple of setbacks.

She forced herself to meet her gaze in the mirror. Her

winged eyeliner made her eyes pop, and the pain in her head had lessened a little. This trip hadn't begun ideally, but she could still turn it around. A frown twitched on her brow, and she sighed.

Before she could talk herself out of it and make a nest in her bed instead, she grabbed her rucksack and headed out the door, flinching at the bright sun. She nipped back inside to pluck up Carla's ugly pineapple sunglasses and slipped them on.

Better than going blind. The way her day was going, she'd better not tempt fate.

Her sandals clunked against the gravel path as she headed down the hill. Blue skies stretched out above her, blending into the rolling ocean at the kiss of the horizon. She sucked in a big lungful of air. Then another. Feeling a little lift, she dared to smile. She really needed to stop being so dramatic.

She was on holiday, after all.

The courtyard opened before her, a stone-paved square with a beautiful view over the cliffs and ocean below. She recognised the fountain sitting at the front from the Sandy Springs website. This was where the guests did yoga in the mornings—another terrifying obstacle Faye didn't want to think about right now. But an image of her bending over and her bag erupting, washing away the other screaming guests like a tsunami, played in the front of her mind anyway.

Cheers for that one, brain.

Her eyes landed on the big "Welcome" sign hanging

from the wooden pergola. Leafy vines and colourful flowers twisted around the structure. She passed through the open door to the reception, following the arrows to the introduction hall.

She entered the silent room, and a dozen faces swivelled towards her. Heat flushed her cheeks, and she hurried to the nearest available seat, keeping her eyes trained on the wooden table. Incense burned somewhere, filling the air with patchouli. After a few awkward moments, she lifted her gaze and scanned the room. Motivational quotes and colourful paintings hung from the cream walls, which still smelled faintly of fresh paint. The staff stood by a large screen at the front, the guests avoiding eye contact with each other. Faye searched their faces. When she met Diana's dark eyes, her heart skipped in her chest. Then she spotted who she was seated next to, and her stomach fell to the soles of her feet.

Molly. Molly *and* Diana. Sitting next to each other. *Oh my god.*

Red-hot panic fired through her veins. *Why, Universe, why?* Before she started hyperventilating, a tall woman with blonde, wavy hair made her way to the front and clasped her hands together. Faye recognised her too; she'd done her fair share of research before coming here.

"Welcome, everyone. Let's get started so you can make the most of that gorgeous sunshine." She grinned. "I'm Riley, and I'm the manager here at Sandy Springs. I know there's a lot to take on board, but don't worry. We've got packs to give you at the end with all the information you need."

Faye swooned hard. Information packs? Yes, please.

"First, I'll introduce you to the team," Riley continued. "Then we'll walk you through what to expect on your journey here at Sandy Springs." She turned to her left and pointed to the curvy redhead. "Ella is my right-hand woman. Without her, this course would crumble to the ground. There's no problem she can't sort. If you have any issues in your time here, let her know."

Faye cringed, remembering how Ella had witnessed her awkward encounter earlier.

Riley introduced the rest of the staff, all smiling in their blue uniforms, apart from one man who wore a golden kaftan—Senhor Arenoso, the course founder and lead energy-alignment guru. Faye had read that he'd taken a step back from his responsibilities, but he still provided sessions and conducted the Fire Ceremony at the end of the course. This was where guests would be awarded with their spirit familiars.

A fancy presentation followed the brief introductions, detailing their days, workshops, and extra-curricular activities for the upcoming weeks, including trips to the island ruins, surfing, and painting. Most days started with yoga, followed by sessions with their guidance counsellors. Spread throughout the week were energy-alignment courses with a guru—Faye hoped she landed Senhor Arenoso.

Unfortunately, she missed a lot of the details, her focus sneaking back towards Diana and Molly. Molly leaned on her elbows, cradling her face in one hand and looking as though someone had told her Christmas was cancelled. Diana's mouth wore a hard line, giving nothing away. Faye wondered what had happened in the time since they last saw each other. Thankfully, Molly and Diana weren't talking; Faye would find that weird.

Diana's gaze flicked to her, catching her staring, and all of Faye's insides pulled taut. Remembering the feel of her lips on Faye's and that slick, silky tongue in her mouth sent a shiver of pleasure between her legs. She glanced away at the screen, but the words blurred.

What did Diana think about last night? She needed to talk to her and explain. Maybe then—

Her brain couldn't finish the other half of the sentence. Someone like Diana would never be interested in her. People her own age weren't interested, let alone someone as smart and put together as Diana.

Her earlier arousal withered and died. She'd missed her chance, but she could still apologise. It'd definitely make the next few weeks less awkward.

Riley switched slides, and Faye's attention moved to Molly. As for what to do about her ex-girlfriend, she was more unsure. Diana was the easier fix of the two; she'd be brave and speak to her once the introductions finished. She needed to know where Diana's head was at.

She tried to focus on Riley, but anxiety flooded her veins, making her palms damp. What did she say? Something about the ruins? Her attention kept pinging back to Diana. Her low-cut baby-blue blouse showed a delicious amount of pale skin, and Faye found her eyes dipping lower, trying to undo the buttons with her gaze.

Everyone brought their hands together, and she startled at the applause. She blamed her hangover for her poor concentration, but she knew it was the presence of the two women sitting across from her.

People stood, collecting their information packs on the way out. Faye avoided eye contact with Ella, afraid she'd pry for details about her earlier awkward encounter, and stepped out into the sunshine. A quick scan of her surroundings found Molly trudging back up the path and Diana standing alone by the fountain. Faye blew out a breath. Diana's hair tousled in the breeze. Her shorts freed the elegant line of her calves, her sandals revealing manicured toenails. Something about her made Faye want to drop to her knees and kiss her feet.

That powerful enigma. Diana had bucketfuls of the stuff.

She forced out another breath and crossed the stone paths towards her.

"Diana." Her voice came out tentative, not confident like she'd practised in her head, but Diana turned towards her regardless.

Fuck. Here we go.

Someone tapped her on the shoulder, then stepped into view with a huge grin.

"Hey. I'm Quin." Faye noticed the they/them pin attached to their bag strap. "Do you wanna buddy up for the walk to the ruins tomorrow?" They ran a hand over the long black Afro curls falling over their eyes. "Sorry. I'm Quin," they said again, bouncing from one leg to the other like they'd drunk five litres of coffee. "I can't remember if I said that or not."

Faye blinked, a little taken aback by the bundle of energy in front of her. "I'm sorry. Buddy up?"

Quin nodded, their bouncy coils flying. "Yeah. Riley said we should find someone to pair with for the walk tomorrow. Didn't you hear?"

Faye shook her head. "No. I guess I missed that."

"Apparently, the path disappears when the tide comes in. I'd hate to get stuck out there; I'm scared of the dark. What are you scared of?"

Faye didn't know where to start. "Sorry. I need to…" She sidestepped them, trying to catch Diana's attention, but the fountain was unoccupied. *She left. Dammit.*

"I like your sunglasses," Quin continued, their black brows rising. "They're…unique."

"Thanks." Faye glanced over her shoulder, but other than a group of seagulls pecking at cracks in the masonry, there wasn't another soul around.

"Sorry. Am I bothering you?" Quin stilled. "My dad says I'm too much. That I'm like a frog in a sock, bouncing around and not knowing which way is up."

Faye caught the chink in Quin's expression as their hands slid into the pockets of their grey shorts. Faye was being rude.

"No, you're not bothering me. Sorry, I'm just…hungover."

Quin's loud crack of laughter made her wince, and they smiled sheepishly in apology. "I'll try to talk quieter then. My bad. Do you fancy exploring the beach together?"

Faye's bed called to her, but she remembered her dads' words about hiding away in her room. She wasn't used to someone being so forward, but she could hardly look a gift horse in the mouth. Though Quin's chatter crawled inside her skull, getting to explore the island would make a nice distraction.

"That sounds nice."

They strolled across the courtyard, the warm sun on Faye's skin giving her an encouraging push—towards the opportunity to make a friend, or towards Diana, she couldn't tell. She walked a little faster, hoping her new start waited around the corner.

FIVE

Diana

Diana stood on top of a nearby cliff, hoping the fresh sea breeze would help clear her brain fog. But the salty, seaweed smell did little to comfort her. She didn't care much for the sea. Where some people saw a friend and a confidant, she only felt the echoes of everything the sea had seen. The lulling waves wore their mask, trying to entice her, but Diana sensed the secrets hidden in their dark depths. It was a front, a show; she wouldn't let it work its voodoo magic on her.

But the ephemeral tendrils seeped out around her, demanding her attention. Fresh, powdery doughnuts. Her mother's tinkling laughter as she brushed sugar from

Diana's round cheeks. "*You have more on your face than in your mouth.*" Her mother's voice echoed around her, and her blurred face came into view. Blonde hair pinned back to reveal kind blue eyes, crows' feet, and laughter lines etched deep into her skin. Diana's heart squeezed.

They didn't have a lot of money growing up—her father worked on a local farm, and her mother stayed at home—but they still visited the seaside every summer. Her mother loved the sea, and the two of them would spend whole afternoons playing along the shore with her father watching from his towel on the sand.

In her seaside recollections, her father played a background role, carrying their luggage and sitting with his feet up. A figure rather than an active face.

Until the spring of Diana's tenth birthday, when everything changed.

Goosebumps rippled along her skin, despite the burning sun overhead. No matter how many years passed, the huge gap her mother left in her life still ached. She never got to say goodbye.

Diana sighed and checked her phone signal. Still nothing. She knew she'd only miss updates from Leanne and work emails, but the inability to check made her skin itchy. What if she missed something important? She took one last look at the ocean waves, cursed them for their secret-harnessing powers, and then spun around. They tried to lure her back, but she dug her feet into the gravel, pushing forward.

She blamed the alcohol lingering in her veins for her

depressive recollection. Though her headache had passed, a sadness hovered—or maybe that was more to do with Molly's unwelcoming reception.

Frosty would be an understatement.

She joined the path back towards the courtyard, glancing over the cliff at the blips of people in swimwear enjoying the beach below. When Molly was young, Jason wanted to take her to the east coast and couldn't understand Diana's reluctance. But that was Jason all over. If something didn't directly benefit him, he wasn't interested.

She wished she'd had her mother to help guide her back then. Diana had been nineteen when she fell pregnant with Molly. Her father had been furious—he wouldn't have a grandchild born out of wedlock—and he'd kicked her out of the house, straight into Jason's arms. Had her mother been there, Diana hoped she would have reacted differently. Truthfully, she didn't know what she'd have said, or if she'd be supportive of Diana's bisexuality. Diana hadn't spoken to her father in years.

She stopped to catch her breath when she reached the courtyard. The hill climb and trip down memory lane had tired her. A food van selling a mix of freshly fried fish and potatoes made her belly rumble. She offered the woman behind the counter a tired nod before walking past. Even the scent of fish brought back more memories of her childhood at the seaside; she couldn't stop her brain from digging up all these repressed feelings.

I blame the wine for that, too.

The memory of Faye's lips seared her, sending an electric current over her skin and halting her in place. Faye had tried to get Diana's attention earlier, before someone jumped in. She probably wanted to explain why she'd bolted mid-kiss. Let Diana down gently. The tingly warmth dissipated, taking the memory with it.

But honestly, Diana could spare the heart-to-heart. Life was complicated enough. She didn't have time for romance—not that Faye wanted that anyway—with the pressures of work and her crumbling relationship with her daughter.

Molly's scowl popped into her vision. *"You were late. I wouldn't have been surprised if you didn't show up at all and abandoned me here."*

She'd definitely inherited Jason's temper.

Frustration tangled with guilt. Molly didn't see the storm as a worthy excuse, nor the effort and sacrifice Diana had made to make this trip a reality. She and Molly had been housed opposite each other, which had been ideal for her, but less so for Molly, given how she'd reacted.

Sometimes she felt she couldn't do anything right for her daughter.

Goats wandered over to the stone wall, bleating at her from the field and butting their dirty white heads together. Deciding enough time had passed, Diana headed back up the trail towards her cabin.

Their relationship had been rocky for a couple of years now, ever since Jason's third wife entered the scene and Diana's career took off. She'd spoken to Molly about the opportunities to travel and teach, and Molly had encouraged her to go. They'd spent hours on the phone from all over the globe, catching up about Molly's time at university and sharing Diana's anecdotes. But cracks had started to show with the distance. Molly spent more time at home instead of studying and began echoing Jason's accusations of selfishness and control. Diana only wanted the best for her daughter, but somehow that always got twisted. It got harder to defend herself when Molly stopped returning her calls.

She never regretted having Molly—she was the best thing that had happened to her, and definitely the best thing to come out of her struggles with Jason in her early life—but playing the bad guy in Jason's narrative just got…tiring.

She arrived at Molly's cabin and knocked, listening to the scuffles behind the door. As the setting sun sank behind her, golden light filtered through the tree leaves, casting shadows on the ground. When no one answered, she knocked again. "Molly, love. It's me."

The door swung open, and Molly raised an eyebrow, unamused. "Who else would it be? The bogeyman? Although that's not far off," she muttered.

Diana bit her tongue. Hitting her back with a snarky remark would only shut the door in her face. She offered a smile. "Can I come in?"

"I suppose. There's nothing else for me to do here." Molly stood aside, and Diana passed her.

The cabin was a replica of hers, white and clean with a double bed in the corner and wood-framed nature pictures decorating the walls. Molly's open case lay on the floor, and Diana chose not to comment on the mess of scrunched-up clothes inside—or the clutter of make-up and hair products already crowding the dresser. Even as a kid, Molly had left toys and dolls everywhere.

"Seriously, Diana." Molly crossed her arms. Diana tried not to flinch at the cold formality of her first name. "There's no phone signal. No Wi-Fi either. What was the point in coming here?"

"We discussed this. It's so you can clear your head and think about your next steps. And so we can spend some time together."

"I'm not helpless. I'm twenty-two, for Christ's sake. I don't need you to tell me what to do." She stomped across the tiles. "I should've never agreed to this."

"I'm not telling you what to do." Diana sucked in a deep breath, looking at one of the framed pictures of waterfalls on the wall. "I'm trying to help you find some direction."

"To be like you, you mean," Molly snapped.

Diana flinched. It hurt, hearing Jason's words leave Molly's lips, but she tried not to show it. "That's not true. I'm worried about you. When you dropped out of your final year of university, well—"

"You act like I need rehab or something. It's so dramatic." She shook her head, her curls falling around her face. "I changed my mind. My degree sucked."

"I'm trying to help. This is important. Your decision was so sudden…and since then you've not been yourself."

"Like you'd know," Molly huffed, mumbling something under her breath that Diana didn't catch.

She sighed. "Come on, Mol. You're acting as though I've checked you into a prison cell. We're together in sunny Portugal, on a beautiful island with blue skies…"

Molly softened a tad, her pout slacking.

Diana took a step towards her. "Why don't we make the most of it? Give me a chance."

Molly relaxed her arms, then the tease of a smile curled her lips. "I guess I do look good with a tan."

"Okay, good." Diana tried not to mind that that was the part Molly focused on. "Now, do you fancy getting some dinner together? I saw a little van selling food in the courtyard."

When Molly hesitated, her heart flopped.

"Actually, I just wanted to get an early night. With the storm yesterday and then that bloody cockerel this morning, I got no sleep."

She nodded, trying to hide her disappointment. "Alright, love. I'll see you in the morning."

Molly waved bye and shut the door behind her. At least this time she hadn't slammed the door in her face. But as the sky continued to darken, burning orange at the horizon, loneliness enveloped Diana like a blanket. She sighed into the humid air and walked the short distance to her cabin.

SIX

The next day, the group followed the path towards the ruins, where blue and purple oleanders bloomed from bushes along the hillside. Sweat beaded Faye's forehead as her feet carried her up the incline, Quin chattering in her ear. She breathed in the fresh air—the sea salt and the pollen—catching a whiff of Quin's woody aftershave too.

Somewhere in the mostly one-sided conversation, she caught Quin's hope to see turtles.

She stopped for a moment to rest her aching muscles. It'd been a long time since she'd done anything strenuous, but at least her hangover had passed. "Did you know that sea turtles use the moon and stars' reflection on the waves to find their way back to the ocean?"

"Wow. You're like the coolest person ever." Quin readjusted their vest strap across their rich, russet-brown skin. "Like an encyclopaedia."

Faye laughed. "Are they cool?"

"Umm. Maybe not. But my dad says an investment in knowledge pays the best interest. So maybe?"

Faye's focus drifted ahead of her, where the rest of the group were following the path up towards the ruins. She'd only known Quin for a day, and despite them being a couple of years younger than her, their presence comforted her. With all the uncertainty going on, having a friend eased her nerves, and Quin didn't mind when she didn't have much to say.

She shifted the heavy rucksack on her shoulders, starting to feel an ache in her back from the weight. In her professional Pankhurst style, she'd prepared for every possible type of bag-related emergency.

Which reminded her—she still needed to speak with Diana.

Diana was walking at the back with Molly. Apparently, they'd "buddied up", which must've been a result of the introductions yesterday. She couldn't help glancing behind her, pretending to admire the view, but really she wanted to get Diana alone. The last thing she needed was an awkward "how do you know each other?" in front of Molly. Hard pass.

Raised voices behind them pricked Faye's ears. But before she could turn round to nosy, Molly stomped past, her blonde ponytail swinging.

Strange.

Sensing her opportunity, she glanced at Quin, hoping they wouldn't mind walking alone for a few minutes. She wanted to avoid messing up any more relationships if she could help it. "Hey, can you excuse me for a minute? I'll catch up to you."

Quin uttered a "sure, no problem", casting Faye a curious glance as she slowed her pace. Two older men overtook her—Quin inviting them into a conversation about turtles—and Faye joined Diana at the back. Her heart kicked up a gear, and all of her earlier eagerness swept away on the breeze. *How did people start conversations again?*

"Hey."

Hey? Women like Diana deserved more than a "hey". More like a sonnet, or an anthology of sonnets.

"Nice to see you again," Diana replied.

Did she mean that? Or was she being ironic because the last time Faye saw her, she'd kissed her and run away?

When Diana met her gaze with a soft smile, those deep, chocolatey browns reflecting the sun, Faye knew she meant it. Her attention fell on her black-and-white striped jumpsuit with its bandeau neckline, revealing smooth collarbones and a delicate neck. She relaxed a little, letting their steps fall into rhythm, the murmur of the group's conversation drifting around them.

"Planning on staying for a few days?" Diana asked, nodding to Faye's oversized rucksack clunking against her back.

She laughed nervously. "Yeah…you never know what you might need. Prepare for the worst and never be disappointed." She chewed her lip. *Come on.* "I wanted to talk to you."

"You don't need to, Faye."

That caught her by surprise, and she squinted at Diana in the sunshine, having left Carla's sunglasses at home.

"We had a lot to drink, and you changed your mind," Diana went on. "That's okay."

"What? That's not what I was going to say." Their eyes locked. Diana's eyebrow rose slightly. "I don't regret it," Faye continued. "Only the way we ended things." Below them, frothy waves lifted up to kiss the rocks. "I'm sorry for running out on you. I had a shit year… My body changed, and it was the first—"

"Alright, everybody!"

A fierce whistle pierced the air. Faye stumbled on a rock as the group stopped walking and almost pushed one of the older men over the edge. She mumbled her apologies, but he grumbled and moved away.

Ella and Riley stood at the front, the ruins rising behind them. Stone steps embedded in the hillside, leading up to the tall, towering stonework. Green vines snaked between the cracks, blending history and nature together.

"Welcome to the ruins," Riley started. "The historic home of the royals and Princesa Inês Teresa's final home.

Like a lot of you, she came to escape. Her controversial split from her betrothed caused an uprising on the mainland. Some say she watches over the island, helping heal the heartbroken souls that wander upon it, as repayment for how the island healed her. We hope you feel some of that energy on your journey." Riley and Ella shared a loving glance, and Ella linked her pinkie finger with hers.

Those two are so cute.

A small sliver of envy wrapped around Faye's heart. She wanted that. The little touches two people shared. That instinct of two bodies leaning towards each other like sunflowers, soaking up the warmth. The kind of love her dads had.

In her experience, she'd just end up in the shadows spinning in circles, like a dog chasing its own tail.

Riley and Ella led them up the steps, and Faye fell in step beside Diana. When they walked under the stone arch, she turned to take in the view. The sea sparkled below, white-crested waves cutting through the blue until they washed up the cliffs. Birds chirped all around them, dipping and diving over the water.

Wow. Is this place available to rent?

The crumbling structure only added to nature's impressive presence. Sure, it didn't have a roof or windows... but Faye had seen worse student accommodation.

As the others ventured farther into the remains of the building, talking among themselves, Faye started her assessment of the grounds on autopilot, starting with the outside.

Her attention was drawn to the greenery flowering through the holes in the stonework before moving further out. She recognised some plants—the blue hydrangeas, the orchids—but was unsure about others. A particular pink plant with bell-shaped petals caught her eye, growing out of one of the cliff faces, and she leaned closer. It reminded her of purple foxgloves. She wished she'd brought her botanical book with her, but she'd opted for a spare change of clothes instead, in case of a bag emergency. She searched in her pockets for her phone, but she'd left that on charge at the cabin too. *Dammit. So much for Pankhurst preparations.*

She leaned closer to the flower, gently stroking a petal with her finger. Waxy but soft. *God. How could I not bring my book?*

"What's wrong?" Diana asked. "You look concerned."

Faye didn't know how long she'd been watching her, but she gave the petal one last brush before straightening up. "Not concerned. Annoyed I forgot my phone, so I can't take any pictures."

"What are you looking at?"

Faye hesitated, mulling over how best to explain. She decided to keep the answer simple. "I think it's one of the endemic bellflowers, but I can't say for sure."

Diana leaned closer to get a better look, and her perfume caught on the breeze, filling Faye's mind with flashbacks of their night at the bar. "It's certainly unusual."

She nodded, trying to focus on the plant instead of the other emotions stirring in her system. "The island is full of unusual and unique species. Bats, parakeets, bullfinches. It's incredible, really; I love it." She admired the ruins, the flora growing through the holes and the cracks in the stone. "You can't stop nature. It's too fierce. I admire that."

Silence filled the space between Faye's breaths. Feeling Diana's gaze on her warmed her cheeks.

So much for keeping it simple.

"You seem to know a lot about it."

"I'm an ecologist." Faye couldn't help but smile. It still felt incredible to say out loud. But then her face fell. She'd been off work for so long because of her emergency operation, it didn't feel completely accurate anymore. "You're a professor, right?"

Something like surprise caught Diana's features.

"I remember," Faye explained, hoping it didn't come off creepy.

Diana nodded, letting out a small sigh as she considered the bellflower again.

Faye wanted to know exactly what that sigh meant. There were many things she wanted to know about Diana. Not all of them appropriate. Well, not even half of them. But there was something that interested her, something beyond a physical attraction. Because, yes, even though the woman had the most perfect cheekbones Faye had ever seen, instead of flocking to the building like everyone else, she'd paused to look at the little details that often get overlooked.

Faye liked that a lot.

"Well, if it helps, you can use my phone. I'm not sure it has the best camera, though."

Faye grinned. "Thank you. That would be great."

She snapped a few photos of the pink flower and the stems. Then she combed the grassland and cliffside to see if she could spot anything else, trying not to overthink the fact she had *Diana's* phone between her fingertips. Bellflowers sprouted from a sandy patch on the rocks, so she moved closer, hyper aware of Diana's presence behind her.

"What makes them endemic?" Diana asked, her sandals crunching on the path.

"A lot of factors. The volcanic soil. The island is secluded. Plants love that sort of thing. Some people, too."

I sound like a bumbling idiot.

But Diana nodded. She wet her lips with a flick of her tongue.

Faye remembered the feel of that tongue in her mouth, and her stomach somersaulted. Maybe there was still something between them. Or maybe the altitude had turned Faye's brain into mush. Hard to tell.

But then movement out of the corner of her eye made her turn her head. Molly stood under the archway, observing them with a frown.

Is she jealous?

Molly's stare narrowed, then with a huff, she disappeared back inside.

Strange…

Diana stood up and dusted her hands. "I should go in now. Thank you for showing me these."

"No problem." Faye watched as Diana joined the others under the archway, her gaze lingering on the jumpsuit swaying with her hips. She didn't usually find herself checking someone out with such fascination, but there was something extremely addictive about the woman's slow, controlled movements. "Literally any time," she said to herself.

She supposed she should join the others too and see how Quin was doing, but she didn't want to look too eager following Diana. She looked out over the sea, counted to twenty, and then left to join the rest of the group. They were dotted around the different parts of the structure, tilting their heads back to observe the large bell tower. Quin was chatting with Sanjay, one of the older men in the group, standing beneath a huge tree whose branches had grown through one of the open holes and formed half a roof. Ella and Riley gathered inside, in the sunlight pouring through the holes and lighting up the grassy floor.

"What do you think?" Ella asked when Faye neared.

"It's beautiful." The damp, earthy smell tickled her nose. "Musky, but beautiful."

Riley nodded. "The ruins are an undeniable beauty. Even in the rain—especially then." The two of them shared a glance, and Faye's jealousy flared again.

Her gaze passed over the crumbling stone and the moss growing up the rocks. "What room would this have been?"

"The princess's chambers." Riley pointed up at one of the windows. "The princess would spend every morning looking out at the view, writing her poetry, and then reciting it to her servants in the afternoon."

"Really? What did she write about?"

"Love. Heartbreak. Feminism. The poems she wrote either brought people together or tore them apart. She had a power through words like no one else."

Sounds like Princesa Inês had heaps of the enigma, too.

"Didn't she write something famous about the moon?" Ella asked. "'Do not swear by the moon, for she changes constantly'?"

Riley's eyebrows drew together. "I don't think that's one of hers…but it's pretty." She gave Ella a kiss on the forehead, and they linked hands, heading out the back "door"—an empty hole—to chat with some other guests.

"Shakespeare."

Faye smelled Diana's perfume before she appeared beside her.

"Pardon?"

Diana gazed up at the window in question. "'O, swear not by the moon, the inconstant moon.' It's Shakespeare."

Faye wet her lips and swallowed, thrown off by the woman's sudden presence and her reciting poetry in that rich tone. "A big Shakespeare fan?"

"Not particularly." Her mouth ticked. "But I admire that quote."

"I'm not a Shakespeare fan either."

Diana took a few steps, examining the structure. Her playsuit teased at the curves underneath, and Faye loved how the material fell over her figure with every step.

"Do you believe that?" Diana asked.

"Believe what?" Faye hoped she hadn't missed something by admiring her too hard.

"That Princesa Inês acted like a Cupid of the island, using poems to unite and divide whoever she saw fit?"

She breathed in Diana's intoxicating scent, the space between them shrinking. "It's not as far-fetched as some things, so sure, why not?"

Diana's eyebrow quirked. "A romantic, are we?"

Faye shifted her feet. "Perhaps."

"It shows." A slow smirk spread across Diana's face, one that dripped gooey heat from Faye's sternum into the pit of her stomach.

A rustle in the foliage interrupted her thoughts. Green and white flashed across the open doorway. A series of sharp, distressed chirps grew louder until a bundle of feathers tumbled through the space and cowered in the corner, flapping.

Faye's heart sank. A bird flailed in the white net, its wing caught in the holes. Each frantic movement further entangled itself.

The rest of the group appeared at the doorway, and

Faye jumped into protection mode. "Wait outside," she said. "We need to give it space to calm down." She dropped to a crouch, trying to appear less threatening, and cooed at the bird. "Hey. It's gonna be okay. We're going to help you take that nasty net off."

The bird twitched, letting out another distress call that pulled at Faye's heart. She took in the bright green feathers and orange beak. Some sort of parakeet. The net obstructed some of its head, but when it angled towards her, she caught a flash of pink, like a little pink crown. *A Pink Polari parakeet.*

She released a breath. To have seen one of the rare birds endemic to the island was incredible. But not like this. She inspected the net. It appeared new and clean, not like an old fishing one the bird had accidentally tangled itself up in. Someone had done this on purpose.

"What's going on?" Riley peeked through one of the holes in the wall.

"A Pink Polari parakeet is caught in a net. Looks like it injured a wing."

"Oh, Jesus. Let me alert the wildlife centre." After a few steps, Riley's walkie-talkie crackled to life, and Portuguese rolled off her tongue.

The darkness inside the structure seemed to help the bird. It sat in the corner, breathing heavily but no longer fighting against the net. Faye spotted the brown patch above the beak. A female.

"Will it be alright?" Diana asked in a low whisper, raising the hairs on Faye's arms.

"I hope so. They're close to becoming endangered."

That was putting it lightly. Birds in high demand in the pet trade, like the Pink Polari, were targeted for their colourful feathers. Poachers were known to clip their wings, making it impossible for them to escape and putting them in excruciating pain. As if that weren't bad enough, they were starved and kept in such bad conditions that many wouldn't survive the journey to be sold.

The idea that people could do this to other living things made Faye want to destroy them in a blaze of fire. She looked at the poor little bird and the net entrapping it. Could it be a coincidence? Or were there poachers on the island right now?

"Come on, everyone," Ella called. "Let's make our way back and give the bird some space."

The group dispersed, talking quietly among themselves. Quin popped their head through the doorway and raised two questioning thumbs-ups.

"I'll catch you later," she whispered, and Quin nodded, shooting finger guns back at her.

"Are you coming?" Diana asked.

Faye's muscles burned from crouching, but she shook her head. "I'm gonna stay with her until the wildlife team gets here."

"How do you know she's female?"

"See the brown patch above her beak there? That's the cere."

"You really know your stuff." Diana slowly got to her feet, smiling when her knees audibly cracked. The way she moved with such care and fluidity so as not to scare the bird made Faye's heart squeeze. "Good luck, Faye. See you tomorrow."

They shared another look before Diana joined the others. The feeling of her gaze lingered long after she'd left.

"Guess it's just you and me for a little bit," Faye whispered to the bird.

She didn't realise until much, much later, that she still had Diana's phone in her pocket.

SEVEN

Diana

Diana fiddled with the gold watch around her wrist. *How has it only been fifteen minutes?* Blinking under the white spotlight in Marco Marcos' office, it felt like weeks had passed. The small room carried the scent of mango and ginger, perhaps remnants of the empty smoothie resting on the bald man's desk. She scanned the motivational poster behind him. "Thoughts are not facts." Perhaps not, but it didn't change the fact that Diana thought this was a waste of her time.

She wasn't the one who needed counselling. She had a successful career and a best-selling book, for Christ's sake. Molly needed some direction, not her. She just wanted to catch up on her work—but evidently, the guidance sessions were non-optional.

Marco Marcos steepled his fingers, each knuckle thick with dark hair. "So, Diana, tell me more about your reason for attending Sandy Springs."

She folded her hands in her lap. "For my daughter. I wanted her to try something new and find what she wants to do."

He peered down the bridge of his nose, square glasses tilting with the movement. "And you?"

"I thought it would be a good opportunity to spend time together."

He nodded, scribbling something in his notepad. "Do you do that often?"

The clock ticked loudly on the wall, marking her misery. She hoped he wouldn't notice the hesitation. "Not so much nowadays."

"Would you like to expand on that?"

Not particularly. But judging by the intense dark eyes on her from across the room, she didn't have much choice in the matter. "Molly and I haven't always seen eye to eye. Since I left my ex-husband, it's been a slow decline. It doesn't help that I know what sort of nonsense he fills her ears with." She shook her head instinctively as Jason's voice swirled around her.

"You've abandoned me, and you've abandoned your daughter."

Diana loved being a mother. But that was all Jason

wanted her to be. The idea that she could be successful in other areas of her life—or, heaven forbid, more successful than Jason—was taken as an insult. A threat. His ideologies were still stuck in the Stone Age.

Diana had imagined marriage to be a partnership. Two people working *together* to better themselves and create a life *together.* But when she progressed and was offered a grant to study her master's, she went from inspiring to selfish overnight. Jason's tide turned, and she realised she was all alone.

Yes, she had colleagues, and Leanne, her agent, but when her phone quietened, loneliness festered. Not that she'd admit that to Marco Marcos, who seemed all too eager to scribble down her life's failures. He frowned and vigorously erased something he'd written, wobbling his chair in the process.

My phone.

Faye still had it. Diana realised last night when she went to check her emails. She needed to find her after this.

The woman's face flashed before her eyelids. The way those striking turquoise eyes lit up as she spoke about the different species on the island. Her long brown hair cascading over her shoulders. The unique Faye essence that flowed from her. There was something special there, something unique she didn't quite understand.

Diana had wanted to continue their conversation from the hike, to understand what Faye meant by regretting the way things had ended at the bar. But she'd become distracted by Faye and how she viewed the world.

The delicacy in how she treated living things.

"So your relationship with your husband didn't end amicably?" Marcos asked, pulling her from her thoughts.

She repressed the urge to scoff. She wouldn't call coming home to find her belongings waiting for her on the drive exactly "amicable". Her fingers found the strap of her watch again, tracing the cool metal. She didn't want to get sucked down that rabbit hole.

"Alright." He eyed her and tapped his pencil on the pad. "I see we have work to do."

***

Diana exhaled, turning her neck left and right to release some of the tension in her muscles. Her head throbbed at the temples, a consequence of fighting the repressed memories trying to surface in response to Marco Marcos's questions. She'd been naïve, perhaps arrogant, to think she'd get off lightly on the mind-probing. With the storm disrupting them, Molly's unfavourable reception, and Faye's surprise kiss, her time here so far had been unpredictable. Not exactly the relaxing mother/daughter holiday she'd imagined. She'd barely had time to consider her proposal for Leanne.

The afternoon sun hung high in the sky, coating her skin with warmth. Molly had requested she give her some space today, so she figured she should get her laptop and start drumming up some ideas.

Remembering Faye had her phone, she decided to find her first. Except she didn't know where Faye was staying. Diana assumed they'd all be in a similar area, but she couldn't say for sure.

After a wander up the path provided no answers, she returned to the courtyard and sat beside the fountain, admiring the trickling water show. Occasionally, people walked past and greeted her. She recognised Louis and Charles from their course, an older couple who were using the retreat as their honeymoon. Personally, a self-work course wouldn't have been on Diana's list, but who was she to comment? It wasn't as if she'd ever had a honeymoon with Jason. After years had passed and it started to feel more like a nag than a celebration, she accepted it was never going to happen.

She frowned, hating that Jason had popped into her headspace again. That man had occupied enough of her life already. She pushed herself to her feet and walked towards the stone wall, breathing in the fresh sea breeze. People milled about on the sand below. Once again, envy nipped at her.

She wished she could let go like they could. Not calculate and overthink every decision. Not let her emotions get the better of her, turning happy memories into something negative. For a brief moment, she wondered if Molly did something similar with her.

I hope not.

A sudden wave of guilt swept over her. Was that what she'd let her mother's memory become? The feeling weaved between her vital organs, pulling tight and pushing bile up her throat. Her mother didn't deserve that.

She took the path down to the cliffs, passing the spot where she'd watched the waves a few days ago, and kept walking. The windy gravel path became steps spotted with sand. When the steps disappeared onto the open beach, she stopped, her pulse hammering in her neck.

This is stupid. It's just a beach.

It was just a beach, but it felt so much more than that. The weight kept Diana in place.

You have a doctorate in socioeconomics. You can do this.

Glancing up, she caught eyes with one of the sunbathers shaking sand from their towel. She probably looked like a peeper, standing there at the edge of the beach. She imagined Selena's face lighting up at that news. *Former Harvard Lecturer Arrested.*

So she stepped onto the sand, her sandals sinking. Grains slipped between her toes, and she scrunched her nose as they scratched her skin. She kept her gaze on the ocean waves, counting as they rolled towards the shore, her hands solid fists at her sides.

She scanned the beach, looking for Faye, forcing her feet forward. Unable to spot her in any of the groups, disappointment curled in her belly. Was that just because of her phone?

Of course, it was.

With nothing else to do, Diana continued walking, following the curve of the shoreline. The soft whoosh of the waves teased her memories, but she pushed forward, focusing on the itchy feeling between her toes instead. She followed a flock of birds as they soared over the waves and landed on the cliffs. *I bet Faye knows what type of birds they are.*

She bit her lip. *Stop thinking about her!*

She needed to focus on her relationship with Molly, on clearing her writer's block, on getting back to the top of her game so she could deal with anything Selena threw at her next. Not whatever this curiosity was with Faye.

But then she noticed someone with long brown hair crouched beside the cliffs. Her heart did a stupid little flutter, and she bit harder on her lip. It'd been so long since Diana had had any sort of time to consider a romantic interest that her body had gone completely overboard.

Never mind that Faye was the first woman to kiss her in a year—and she was at least ten years older than her.

She laughed to herself. Leanne would think she'd lost her marbles.

I just need my phone. That's all.

She smoothed out her blue dress and then started over towards Faye, her tummy squirming with nerves. No—Diana didn't get nervous. She was just curious.

Faye wore black denim shorts and an oversized lilac T-shirt, hair hanging straight over her shoulders. She looked up from her binoculars and her face broke into a smile, making Diana's heart do a funny little flip.

"Come here," she whispered. "Quick." She handed

Diana the warm binoculars and pointed towards the sea, guiding her arm until she faced the right direction.

Diana's breath hitched as Faye's vanilla scent filled her senses. "What am I looking at?"

"See those birds in the water?"

She blinked. All she could see were the deep blue waves bobbing up and down.

"You might need to adjust the focus." Faye's soft fingers touched Diana's, and she gasped, heat sparking at the contact. "There."

Diana blew out a breath and adjusted the dials until the image focused. Three brown, ordinary birds bobbed along the waves. "I see them. What are they?"

"They're Balearic shearwaters. Endangered. Quite rare to spot. It's breeding season, so I was hoping to see them nesting in the cliffs or caves down there. Spotting a group is a good sign, though."

Diana fought the grin tugging at her mouth. Hearing Faye talk about the—frankly—quite boring-looking birds was oddly endearing. She handed the binoculars back, noting how Faye grinned when the birds came into focus.

It was that passion, that unable-to-contain-it passion, that Diana missed. The fuel that made her stay up until the early morning, reading research papers and writing until her fingers ached. That passion had driven her to write her first book. Not to make money or to stay relevant.

"Amazing," Faye breathed. "I love seeing them out here. You know they could be extinct in sixty years?"

"That's awful."

"It really is." She packed her binoculars back into her enormous bag and slung it over her shoulder. What else did she carry in that thing?

"What are you doing out here on your own?" Diana asked.

Faye gave a small shrug. "It's not a big deal. I'm kinda used to it."

That pulled at Diana, making her pause. "Where's your friend?"

"Quin? They've gone to the reception, to call home."

"I didn't know we could do that." Maybe she could call Leanne and the university to check on things.

"There's Wi-Fi there." Faye raised an eyebrow. "Didn't you read your information pack?"

Diana chuckled. "No. I can't say that I did." They headed back along the shore, waves inching towards their feet. The old familiar scent of the sea beckoned her. The sun at her back.

This isn't so bad. She wasn't thinking about her mum at all.

"I didn't peg you for a rulebreaker," Faye murmured, the teasing tone lifting hairs along Diana's neck.

She soaked in the feeling, letting the moment elongate before meeting Faye's gaze. "Didn't anyone tell you that first impressions can be deceiving?"

Faye's eyes sparkled with mischief. "Yeah, actually. A woman I met in a bar told me that."

Diana hummed. "She sounds wise."

"Yeah? You should've heard what she said about

mutant bear-claw chickens taking over the world, or some nonsense."

Diana grinned. "I believe that was you."

Faye laughed. "Oh! Here." She reached into her bag and pulled out Diana's phone. "I meant to give this back."

"Thank you. I hope the pictures were helpful."

"Yeah, thanks. I was pretty chuffed. The flowers *were* the endemic Sazorina bellflowers. I checked in my book."

The horizon stretched before them, heat blurring the tips of the ocean waves. Her feet throbbed in her new sandals, but there was no way she was going to walk barefoot. "Have you always been so interested in plants and animals?" Diana asked.

"Yeah, I guess so. You never know what people are thinking. Animals and plants don't really lie." A slow smirk pulled at Faye's mouth. "I mean…squirrels can pretend to bury nuts in places to keep other squirrels guessing, but people, in my experience, are rarely ever honest. It's hard to know where you stand."

Diana nodded. "The human psyche is complex. New research reveals a different theory all the time." She frowned, the pressure from Leanne to write descending for a moment. "The field is always evolving."

A light breeze tickled the hair around Faye's face. "Do you think it would be easier if people always told the truth?"

"Hmm. Yes and no." Diana pursed her lips, letting the question swirl around her brain. "Even if humans became incapable of lying, the obligation to speak the truth doesn't force confessions. We could still conceal information, choosing what we want to disclose. But always telling the truth would make things more black-and-white. We'd quickly discover which friends are true friends and which are not. Societies might benefit from the trust, particularly the government, but such honest bluntness might cause a lot of instability and trauma too." She frowned. Molly and Jason were already loose-lipped with their words, and that was bad enough.

"I guess so. But I hate not knowing, not having answers." Faye paused to pluck a smooth stone from the sand, running a thumb over it before dropping it back to the beach. "I try to be honest, so it sucks when someone isn't quite who you thought they were, you know?"

"Sadly, I do." The sun dipped lower in the sky, glinting off the edges of the waves as they rolled up the shore.

"Look at the petrels."

Diana's breath caught as Faye leaned across her, pointing to a group of birds soaring above. Her vanilla scent pulled her back to that lift. Her sweet wine-tinted breath. Her unapologetic hands and hot tongue. Her stomach dipped; their bodies suddenly too close to be considered friendly.

The birds flapped and dove before vanishing out of view, and Faye turned to her, eyes sparkling like she'd witnessed something magical.

Diana felt the same, but admittedly for different

reasons.

Whatever this was, she couldn't entertain it. She didn't have time; she had more pressing matters to attend to. These three weeks were for Molly and for her proposal—not to lure her libido out of hibernation.

So why could she think of nothing else than the taste of Faye's lips?

She composed herself, squashing her expression into something neutral. The two fell into step with each other again, a cool breeze lifting hair along her bare arms. Sunbathers and swimmers had dispersed with the sinking sun, leaving stretches of perfect white sand. The beach soon gave way to the dusty steps, leading them back to the courtyard and cabins.

They continued to chat as they climbed, taking turns to admire the natural beauty of Sandy Springs. Conversation flowed easily, but Diana's mind kept snagging on their earlier topic. In particular, the sadness of Faye's statement. She wanted to know who had hurt her, but her curiosity would only open more doors she shouldn't look behind.

The courtyard was empty save for a few birds resting on the wooden canopy. The fountain trickled in the quiet as Diana sidestepped a few bees buzzing around the flowers.

"Oh my god. Goats!" Faye ran to the far side by the stone wall, clicking her tongue and cooing into the field.

A few white goats raised their heads, trotting over to see the commotion. Faye held out her hand and giggled as they nibbled at her fingers.

"Ooh, you're lovely," she cooed, scratching the head of a smaller one with patchy fur. She glanced at Diana, who was still standing some distance away. "Don't you want to say hello?"

Diana raised her hand, scrunching her nose at the smell of urine and hay. "Hello."

Faye laughed. "Not a fan?"

"My dad worked on a farm," she said, as if that would explain her reluctance. When the words left her mouth, she frowned. That time of her life wasn't something she liked to talk about. "The smell never comes out of clothes," she offered, hoping it would be enough. "And this is a nice dress."

"It is. And I can't say their odour isn't…pungent." Faye gave the goat one last scratch behind the ears before returning to her. "But working on a farm is cool. Did you spend a lot of time there?"

"I used to. I don't like to think about it." When Faye stayed quiet, giving her the space to continue, her voice quieted. "As a kid, I loved it. Running around the fields in the summer, playing in the barn with the farmer's children. We'd have the best games of hide-and-seek." She smiled. Once, she'd hidden in one of the horse's empty feeding sacks for an hour without being found. Her mum had pulled hay from her hair all night. The feeling soured, and she blinked the memory away. "After my mum passed…I never went back."

The words sounded loud in the quiet. So loud, Diana

wished she'd never said them. The ache in her heart flared, the way it always did when she thought about that time of her life.

But then Faye took her hand. "Diana, I'm so sorry."

"It's alright." She swallowed the lump in her throat. "It was a long time ago."

Why she'd decided here, of all places, to dig up her family trauma was beyond her. Especially with someone she barely knew. She blamed Marco Marcos for his mind-probing.

But Faye looked back at her with those kind blue eyes, and for some unfathomable reason, on this dusty path on an island in the middle of the Atlantic, she felt safe.

"How old were you?" Faye asked.

"Ten."

Faye squeezed Diana's hand tighter. The act of sympathy would usually make her pull away, but with Faye, it did the opposite. Something about her authenticity, that unique Faye-quality she harnessed, pulled her closer.

"That must have been awful. I'm so sorry, Diana."

Diana gave a small nod of acknowledgement. What more was there to say? *Yes, it was awful. It flipped my life in a way I never thought possible at that age. Then my father made my life an utter misery.*

So she opted to conceal the rest, letting the heavy silence sit between them, as it often did when the topic of death reared its ugly head.

Faye indicated the cabin to their left. "Is yours far?" Diana hadn't even noticed they'd stopped walking. "This one is mine."

"Oh… No, I'm over the hill." She collected herself, giving Faye's hand a small squeeze before releasing it.

The abrupt end made the mix of feelings stir more. But their time was over. Diana had her proposal to start. Excavating her traumas wasn't going to help. Nor would distracting herself with Faye.

Faye fished in her bag for her key, and they took a couple more steps towards the door. A light breeze made Diana cross her arms.

Faye turned at the door, her key in the lock. "I…I feel like I should share a truth, since you shared one with me."

Diana's heart beat hard, steady but loud against her ribs. "Alright. If you wish."

They hovered for a moment; the crickets chirped with the bleating goats.

"I think you're the most beautiful woman I've ever met."

The boldness of the statement hit Diana square in the chest. Surprise flickered across her features, confusion chasing it. But the softness in Faye's voice and the steady glint in her eyes left no room for argument.

She swallowed. "Faye—"

"It's okay. You don't have to say anything." Faye gave a small smile, her eyes dropping to her feet.

Why the sadness? Why the sudden change from bold

to brittle?

Diana reached for her hand, needing her to look at her, needing to understand. Heat sparked at the touch. The soft gasp leaving Faye's mouth was enough to draw her attention to her puckered lips.

She wanted to feel them. To taste them again.

This wasn't a good idea. But the longer she remained in the doorway, the harder it became to think about anything else.

It'd been so long since anybody had told her she was beautiful. Even longer without there being an underlying motive behind it. But Faye wasn't like that.

A beat passed, with Diana lost in the soft swirl of Faye's irises. The tug in her belly deepened, heat spreading up her neck. Then she pushed her up against the door, pressing her lips to hers.

EIGHT

Faye

Faye gasped into Diana's mouth as her back hit the door. Her kiss was bruising yet soft, her fingertips holding Faye's jaw then threading into her hair. Faye moved her own hands before her brain could catch up, sliding them around Diana's waist. Curling into the material of her dress. Want coiled low in her belly, hot and fierce, intensifying with every movement of Diana's fingers. When her warm tongue slipped into Faye's mouth, she nearly lost it, releasing a groan that rumbled deep in her chest.

The soft, breathy sound that left Diana in response was enough to buckle her knees. She wanted to hear it again. And again.

She let Diana guide her inside the cabin, shutting the door behind them with a flick of her wrist. Faye might have voiced her awe at the ease of the gesture, but the soft lips landing on hers again with a hungry need overrode everything else.

For a few moments, anyway.

Because as Diana's hand slipped from Faye's neck to her waist, fear jolted her back to earth like a cold glass of water thrown over her head.

You can't do this.

She wanted to. The heat pooling between her thighs was more than obvious. In fact, every cell in Faye's body had been set alight in a way she hadn't experienced before. She wanted nothing more than to give in to her completely. But as Diana's fingers brushed against her hip, the urge to push her away set off like a flare.

I can't do this.

But it was Diana who pulled back, her dark eyes wide and full of something Faye couldn't name. She took a step away from her, her fingertips flying to her mouth like she could erase the kiss.

All the heat coiling in Faye's stomach drained out the bottom of her feet. Her heart pounded, making her dizzy.

Is this how Diana felt after I ran away?

"I'm sorry." Diana shook her head, her fingers still resting on that succulent mouth. "That was wildly inappropriate of me."

Faye had her own reasons for panicking, but that

hadn't been one of them.

Wildly inappropriate?

"What do you mean?" The words left her mouth before she'd really considered whether she wanted the answer. Judging from the way Diana's eyebrows pinched together, it could only be bad news.

"I'm forty-one, Faye, and you're…mid-twenties?" Gravel crunched outside as a buggy flew down the track. "I shouldn't be here."

The panic from earlier solidified into a steely resolve. Adrenaline pumped through Faye's system. "Why not? I'm not one of your students, Diana."

"But you could be."

"But I'm not."

She met Diana's gaze, cogs turning behind her pupils. Her skin tingled the longer she looked at her.

After what felt like an age, Diana said, "No, you're not." She tucked her hair behind her ears. "I'm sorry. I've been…out of sorts lately. I didn't mean to make this situation uncomfortable."

Faye crinkled her nose at her choice of language. So formal and distant, not at all like the woman who had just kissed her against the door and set her body on fire.

She swallowed, trying to gather the courage to look into Diana's eyes. "Is this about what happened at the bar?"

Diana's eyes flickered, and then the emotion was squashed, hidden beneath her calm expression. The words hung in the air, Faye's chest aching with anticipation. But instead of answering, Diana rubbed her temples, gesturing to the bed. "Do you mind if I sit? My feet are killing me."

"Uh, yeah. Sure." She straightened the white duvet, waiting for Diana to sit before taking the seat next to her, the mattress dipping under their weight.

"You'd think the break from heels would be a comfort, but these new sandals are rubbing my feet raw." Diana smoothed her dress with a smile that felt a little forced, then crossed one leg over the other.

Faye couldn't help admiring her straight spine and slender neck. Good posture was a secret kink of hers. Yet as Diana turned to face her, she couldn't help feeling like a student about to be scolded in the headmistress's office.

Although...that might not be such a bad idea. Diana in a low-cut white blouse and senselessly short skirt, twirling a cane between her fingers... How enthralling it would be to be disciplined by her. A fresh wave of arousal pulsed between her legs.

A cane? Really, Faye? Jesus.

She swallowed, digging her nails into her palms, trying to divert the blood flow someplace else. *Focus.*

"That night at the bar," she said, folding her hands in her lap. "I panicked. See, ever since I can remember, I've had...issues."

God. I make it sound so weird.

She blew out a breath. She didn't want to waste time on the wrong people, but somehow the right words were never easy to find. "It made me different. Now I'm even more different." She grimaced, nails digging into her skin and trying to untangle the knots in her throat. "I'm not good at saying things," she said, further proving her point. Why couldn't she just speak the words? What was so damn hard about it? No wonder everyone thought she was a freak. Now Diana would too—

A soft hand steadied hers, and she stopped scratching. The nervous habit often left her with bloody cuticles and sore skin, but the warmth radiating from Diana's touch gave her pause. She looked up from Diana's manicured toenails and focused on the white wall instead.

She tried to breathe like Riley had instructed in their yoga classes. *In through the nose...and out through the mouth.* The chaos in her mind sank to lower levels, and when she opened her eyes, she found Diana watching her. That curious expression assessing while her thumb stroked soft circles on Faye's wrist.

Just do it.

"I have an ostomy. A stoma," she blurted, loud enough that it made the woman jump. So loud that everyone on the island probably heard. "That's why I freaked out before. I was—still am—afraid of what people might think. I mean, it's not exactly sexy, having a flapping bag of poop attached to my body."

A flapping bag of poop? A perfect mental image for the extremely hot and sophisticated woman sitting on your bed. A puff of laughter escaped her. Then, seeing the surprise on Diana's face, she laughed again. If the scarring image didn't scare her off, Faye's maniacal laughter surely would. She tipped her head back, water forming in her eyes. At this point, she didn't know if it was from the laughter or from the sheer stupidity of her confession. It might have been a mixture of both.

Only she could have the most beautiful woman in existence kiss her and then immediately drive her away.

But Diana's mouth cracked into a smile, and a rumble emerged from her throat, unlike one Faye had ever heard. Rich and deep and sexy in a way that it had absolutely no right to be.

When the laughter subsided, Faye's stomach aching and tears wetting her cheeks, she brushed them away with her free hand, realising that Diana was still holding the other.

Diana didn't pull away.

That almost made her cry real tears. The ugly, snotty kind that left her skin blotchy and red.

Luckily, Diana spoke first.

"Thank you for telling me. It makes sense now, why you reacted that way." Her thumb continued to brush Faye's hand. "I'm sorry if I've ever made you uncomfortable."

That word again. "You haven't. I'm the one who kissed you first, remember?"

Diana's mouth ticked up at one side. "I do."

The movement of her mouth—that plump, soft mouth—tugged at Faye's belly, reminding her of the woman's proximity to her *and* her bed. She suddenly realised that Diana was in *her* bedroom. And that she'd kissed *her* up against the door.

Somehow it felt like a fever dream. But no, that actually happened.

Did that mean… Diana had a crush on her, too?

The word crush felt childish and inadequate. But to call it anything more would be getting ahead of herself. Faye didn't want to do that again.

But as Diana's thumb circled her hand, raising the hairs along Faye's arm and sending a tingle to her sternum, she couldn't help the feeling swelling in her centre.

"Have you had it long?" Diana's smooth voice pulled her gaze towards her. Her straight nose, heavenly sharp cheekbones, and her pointed chin, which, Faye just realised, had a small dimple in it. Diana raised an eyebrow when Faye didn't answer, and added, "Your stoma?"

"Right." Heat flushed Faye's neck. Diana had definitely caught her hopelessly checking her out. "It's been six months and twelve days. Not that I've been obsessively counting or anything."

Diana nodded thoughtfully. "That's a big lifestyle change."

"Yep. Especially when I had no time to prepare for it."

Bright white lights flashed through her vision. The hospital's monotonous beeps had crawled inside her skull like angry crickets. The pain in her abdomen flared up on instinct, and she put her hand over it, crinkling the plastic weight in its place.

"It was an emergency op," she said, blinking away the images. "I was diagnosed with Crohn's disease when I was eleven. Since then, I've been in and out of pain and had loads of different treatments. It's weird. Sometimes, it seemed there was nothing wrong. I'd go weeks, sometimes months, without a flare-up. I could play with the kids on the street and go to the after-school gardening club. I remember the other kids talking about watching caterpillars grow until they formed their cocoons, and I thought that was the coolest thing ever. I didn't want to miss a thing. I'd cross my fingers and pray, hoping the pain wouldn't come back. But sooner or later, it always did."

She smiled, thinking of a younger Faye sitting at her pink desk with her diary and glitter-gel pens, making sure she ate and drank the right foods. Afterwards, she'd line up her stuffed animals to pray with her to increase the odds of being heard. She wasn't sure when she stopped praying, or believing in God, but remembering it now stirred a forgotten ache in her chest. Of wanting to be heard. Wanting to be normal.

"On bad days, I'd take my duvet and pillows and curl up on the bathroom floor. But this particular time was worse than normal. A lot worse. The pain never left, and I burned hot all over. I probably should've called my dads sooner, but I didn't want to bother them." A flash of pain ghosted through her at the memory. "The next thing I know, I'm waking up in the hospital. I'd blacked out from the pain."

Diana squeezed her hand, grounding her. She hadn't meant to say so much, but once the words were out, they'd tugged at a string, unravelling so much she'd kept inside.

"My bowel was so badly inflamed it had perforated, and the tearing caused a severe infection. They had to remove a significant part, so they gave me this." Her hand brushed the bag. "My dads say I'm lucky to be alive." Her throat thickened, and she swallowed. "Sometimes it doesn't feel that way."

Tears pricked her eyelids. She'd never admitted that out loud. Never dared let her thoughts linger there too long. She had to be positive and happy for her dads, to stop them worrying. David had taken so much time off work, and Lukas had cancelled his art tour. Faye hated how it had affected them. She hated being the "abnormal" one. The failure.

Diana moved her hand to catch Faye's tear, smoothing it across her cheek. The gesture was so soft, so gentle, that more tears followed.

"That sounds very painful and tiring." Diana looked at her, those brown eyes so full of care, it touched someplace deep in Faye's chest. "What is the pain like now, since your operation? Do you still get flare-ups?"

Faye shook her head. "As far as my Crohn's goes, the pain has more or less stopped."

It had always been an option for her to have surgery, but the lifestyle change had felt too drastic. Too different. Too *abnormal*. She didn't think she'd be able to cope with it. Until that decision was made for her. Which could be considered both a blessing and a curse.

"That's one good thing to come out of all of this, then," Diana said.

Faye chewed her lip. She'd never thought of it that way before. She'd always focused on the negative changes having an ostomy brought. The positive ones had never crossed her mind.

The surgery had caused her a lot of pain and discomfort, sure. But since then? She couldn't remember the last time she'd had a curl-up-on-the-bathroom-floor day or had to run to the bathroom constantly, day and night. She'd had other challenges and frustrations, with leaks and anxiety, but as far as the pain went? None.

"I suppose it is." She let out a huff of laughter. "Thanks."

"What for?"

"For listening. Not running for the hills. I was…nervous to tell you."

"You were?"

"Well, yeah. I don't really tell people. I guess I choose to conceal."

Diana nodded, something else seemingly swimming behind those irises. "Thank you for being honest. I value that." Then she frowned, the line between her eyebrows creasing. "I owe you the courtesy of doing the same."

Nervous heat stirred in Faye's abdomen. She hoped Diana couldn't sense her fluttering pulse as her fingertips stroked her wrist again.

Diana wet her lips. "I find myself drawn to you."

Faye's heart skipped a beat, jumping up into her throat. She couldn't squash the smile spreading across her face.

"But I have other priorities," she added, cutting that hope down fast. "My work schedule is hectic. I have a looming deadline I'm unprepared for, and personal relationships I need to repair. I fear that my fascination with you is my brain trying to hardwire a distraction. I can't afford to do that, so it's best we're on the same page about this." She patted Faye's hand and then moved her hand away, resting it on her own thigh. Faye grew cold with the absence. "Pursuing something wouldn't be fair. I'm sorry."

Diana stood, picking up the wrap that she'd left folded on the bedframe, and headed towards the door. Faye didn't want her to leave yet. They were finally getting somewhere. If she let this moment pass, she knew she'd regret it.

Adrenaline from her confession pushed her to her feet. She cut Diana off at the door, pressing her own back against it so that they faced each other.

The memory of Diana pushing *her* up against it only a few moments ago sent another flutter through her stomach.

"I'm not a kid, Diana. I don't need to be your priority. I'm under no illusions that anything with you would be just short-term; we're only here for three weeks. Which actually makes this the perfect arrangement."

The way Diana's mouth quirked sent a thunderous

pulse between her legs. "Arrangement?"

"The island is all about opening yourself up to possibilities, new pathways, new experiences, right? Maybe this is what we both need." Faye raised her chin. "As long as we're on the same page about where we stand, what's the problem?"

Faye didn't expect her offer to be so forward, nor for Diana to watch her silently, those dark eyes assessing her.

Shit. Have I overstepped?

"We're both attracted to each other," she went on. "We've nothing to lose. It seems a wasted opportunity not to have a little fun. When was the last time you did that?" She wet her lips, trying to ignore her heart thumping against her ribcage. "Don't write me off yet."

Diana's eyes crinkled, her gaze passing over Faye agonisingly slowly, reawakening the throb in her pelvis. She leaned forward, her lips a mere few centimetres from Faye's ear, so that her breath tickled her neck. "I'll consider your arrangement." She pulled back. "Goodnight, Faye." Then she sidestepped, reaching around Faye's waist, her hand caressing her lower back, to reach the handle.

They were so close now. Just a breath separating them. Faye's body burned as she thought about closing the distance and pushing Diana backwards onto her bed. To feel her lips on hers. To feel them in other, more sensitive places. For her to stay.

"Don't take too long," she said.

"Oh? I didn't realise this was a limited offer."

What did you go and say that for? Panic licked up Faye's spine.

"I just think…there's no time like the present."

Is that the best you've got?

"Hmm. I think your debate skills need work. Your closing argument could be more convincing." Diana released a wicked smirk. She opened the door, the salty air feathering the fabric of her dress.

Faye stepped out of the way.

More convincing, huh?

As Diana turned to say goodbye, she cupped her face, planting a kiss on the woman's perfect mouth. Slow and soft. Enough to turn Faye's own legs to jelly. The sensation churned further, pulling her deeper into the kiss as Diana kissed her back, her hands firm at her waist.

Diana pulled away sooner than she'd have liked, her body protesting in response.

"That's better," Diana said, a little breathless—which Faye took as a win.

She watched her walk away until she disappeared over the hill, hoping she'd put that swing in her hips just for her.

NINE

Faye

Faye sat on a comfy chair in Senhor Arenoso's hut, the material sticking to the back of her thighs. The sun blazed, pouring through the large glass windows. She let out a breath as a rare breeze slipped through, caressing her neck and fluttering the stray hairs that had escaped her bun. Today, the Portuguese weather had truly outdone itself.

Senhor Arenoso hummed a tune as he stirred the tea. How he could drink anything hot in this weather, while wearing a long, hefty kaftan, was beyond her. She couldn't wait to get back to her room, strip off, and bathe in the beautiful breeze of the AC.

But for now, she took a sip of her cool water, admiring the course founder's space. The dark wooden panels paired with the abundance of leafy plants crowding the floor and ceiling gave the room a rich, earthy aroma, tangling with the sharp scent of the ocean as it drifted through the open windows.

If Faye had her own place, she'd like to do something similar. Unfortunately, that hadn't worked out. The idea of moving out again, without the safety net of her dads, packed her full of dread.

She fanned herself with her hand. It was the perfect day to cool off in the sea, but the thought of going in with her bag filled her with so much anxiety, she'd rather sweat to death. She plucked her T-shirt from her skin, wishing she'd opted for her lighter tank top. But it showed too much of herself, and Faye wasn't ready.

Telling Diana about her ostomy had given her a boost, but sadly, not as much as she'd hoped. Diana was one person, but the rest of the world was full of actual shitbags. So Faye had chickened out, swapping her bikini for normal underwear and a baggy T-shirt which now draped her like a heavy weight. Old habits die hard.

She wished she'd said something to Diana this morning in their yoga session. A cool and casual quip, a little flirty but not overbearing. She dragged her nails over her skin, wishing her earlier confidence hadn't disappeared during the night. She didn't want her quietness to come across the wrong way. Maybe she was overthinking it, but overthinking was what she did best. *Prepare for the worst and never be disappointed.*

The clinking of a spoon brought her attention to

Senhor Arenoso as he retook the seat beside the window and crossed his legs. He smoothed his thick moustache.

"*Bem vinda*, Faye. Are you sure I can't offer you a hot drink?"

"No, thank you. It's too warm for me already." She gave him a smile as sweat beaded the back of her neck. "Water's great."

His gaze passed over her thoughtfully. "It looks like you're settling in well. How are you finding things?"

She hesitated. Senhor Arenoso was already aware of her ostomy situation, and she'd hoped to be assigned to him for these sessions—his reviews were outstanding—but unease still settled in her chest. There was something so disarming yet unsettling about being in his presence, and she second-guessed what to say.

She took another swig from her glass, hoping it would ease the lump in her throat, and went for something simple. "The island is beautiful. I love being in nature."

"I suppose your field of work gives you an appreciation for what others don't see."

"Definitely. It was a big sell for coming here. The number of endemic species at Sandy Springs is amazing." The Pink Polari parakeet popped into her head. Her frightened panic as she'd tried to escape the net tangled in her wings. She needed to ask Riley for an update on how she was doing. "It's a shame to see others disrespect that."

He nodded, tracing the rim of his mug with a ringed finger. "Humans are often afflicted with a selfish ego. So distracted by what they think they want, as opposed to what they need. When we become distracted by these things, we neglect our inner self."

Faye considered this. Wants and needs so easily went hand in hand. Sometimes she wasn't sure how to separate them.

He seemed to catch her line of thought. "What do you think will make you happy, Faye?"

Talk about being put on the spot. She gripped her glass tighter. Happiness, true happiness, was something she hadn't felt in a long time. She'd had fleeting moments, which came like passing streetlights, brightening her life for a second before dipping into country-lane darkness, but nothing that stayed.

Pre- and post-surgery, after every flare-up or hurried dash to the bathroom to check for a leak, a thought always stuck with her. "I just want to be normal," she said, low and quiet.

He let out a hum. "It's a funny word, isn't it? *Normal.* What does normal even mean, in a world as diverse as this?"

She tangled her clammy hands in her lap, hoping he didn't expect her to answer that.

Luckily, after a moment's quiet, he continued, "Ever since we take our first breath, the world starts evaluating us, assessing where we fit into its boxes. It starts small—our heart rate, our weight—and builds into lists that seem as tall and dense as forests. Have lots of friends, but don't be *too* social. Excel at work. Build a career. Buy a house. Have children. To be 'normal' means to be with the majority. To be accepted. And there's nothing wrong with that, if that fulfils you here." He placed a hand over his chest, his rings reflecting the sunlight. "But if you're following these parameters to please others and satisfy *their* needs, you will never be happy. Something will always be missing when ignoring our true self."

He paused, letting the words hang in the air between them. His voice softened. "Have you ever wished you were someone else?"

Faye traced the pocket on her shorts with her finger. It felt wrong to admit, but she nodded, anyway, unable to form the words in her throat.

"May I ask why?"

"I've always felt different… Wrong." The humidity in the room tripled in size, sinking into her lungs, pressing onto her shoulders. "A disappointment to my dads." Tears pricked her eyelids. "I wanted to be better. For them."

"Have your parents ever expressed their disappointment with you?"

"No, but this couldn't have been what they were expecting when they adopted me."

"Perhaps not. But to assume that that equals disappointment is a damaging assumption." He stroked his chin. "When we confuse our assumptions with the truth, we can create problems for ourselves that never existed. When that inner world starts to colour our outer world, it distorts our reality too. Assumptions can be very damaging. A slippery slope created by our own doing." His eyes flicked to hers, steady and warm. "You have a big heart. I feel it. The way you care for the world is admirable. But what I feel is missing is that same love and care for yourself. Would you agree?"

Well, shit.

Something deep inside her chest flinched. But she knew she had to answer. "I… Yes."

"Admitting these things doesn't come easy. But it's a very important step. Thank you for sharing that with me." He inclined his head, and Faye noticed his thinning hair rounding in the middle. "Many people spend their lives looking over the garden fence," he continued, "wanting to be someone else, wishing for greener, thicker grass. All the while, they're missing the riches at their own feet."

He leaned forward, the scent of sandalwood following him. "Part of your time here is to identify your core needs so that you can embrace all of your uniqueness. When we love ourselves for who we are, accepting our differences and imperfections, we can celebrate life again."

His words stirred something primal in Faye's soul, and she wanted to grip it and bottle it so it couldn't get away. If this was what having the enigma felt like, she could get used to it.

"Aligning your state of mind with your soul, connecting with your higher self, and reuniting with your familiar guide are all part of embracing your personal journey here."

My familiar guide. With all the distractions these last

few days, that detail had almost slipped her mind. Completion of the course awarded guests with their spirit familiar, their own personal guide to support them in their next steps. Faye had always wondered which animal she connected with the most, and why they'd hidden in the shadows for so long.

She could've used some guidance.

Senhor Arenoso opened his arms. "When we filter out the other voices and listen to ourselves, we can find true, unblemished happiness. True transformation starts within." He let the words settle before asking, "Shall we begin the guided meditation?"

She grinned. "Let's do it."

***

The scorching concrete burned Faye's soles as she drove herself up the hillside. The slope clawed her backwards, each step like sinking quicksand. *Damn this heavy T-shirt.* Her mind ached too, drained from the conversation with Senhor Arenoso, though all she'd done was sit and listen to him.

She paused, lungs heaving, and took a long gulp from her electrolyte drink. It was easier to get dehydrated with an ostomy, so she had to be careful. The last thing she wanted to do was piss it off and end up in the hospital.

Long, sandy beaches stretched out below her, with shearwaters and gulls ferrying overhead like mini planes.

Her heart stuttered as she spotted someone by the cliffs who resembled Diana. But when she blinked, there were only the shadows from the jagged rocks. She turned to the white sands dotted with people lounging under yellow parasols, then to the bobbing bodies breaking the waves and enjoying the cooling relief of the sea. A smidge of envy settled in her chest, amplifying that familiar feeling of wishing to be someone else.

The feeling usually went unacknowledged, but this time, she plucked it from her thoughts, giving it a heavier weight. It was true she wanted that enigma, the confidence and strength to push herself, to be unapologetically her…to make a difference. But loving herself? That was easier said than done.

Faye didn't mind a bit of hippie ideology here and there. The flower-power era was pretty cool in the sixties, but honestly, she could think of better gifts than loving herself—like a working intestine, for one.

A trickle of sweat dripped down her neck. She was too tired and hot to think about all this now. She needed to lie down.

As she pushed her feet back into the hard ground and took a step, someone called her name. But it was the shrill whine accompanying it that made her stomach drop.

Not now.

"Faye! There you are." Molly strode towards her, blonde curls bouncing on her shoulders. A baby pink dress hugged her petite frame, stopping mid-thigh, showing off her milky skin. Matching pink pumps completed the ensemble, making her look like she'd been plucked from Barbie's Dreamhouse.

"Hi, Molly." Faye forced a smile.

A cloudless blue sky hovered above, the fizzing heat radiating from the cliffs. There was an awkward beat where no one said anything. Faye didn't have the energy to attempt a conversation. Maybe if she kept walking, Molly would get the hint. She smiled again and moved to step past her, but Molly's voice pulled her back.

"Warm today, isn't it?"

Faye relaxed the frown pulling at her mouth. "It is. Are you going for a dip?"

"No, no," Molly replied hastily, like the idea was preposterous. "Actually, I was looking for you. My session made me think about some things, and I think we should talk."

Faye stiffened. "What do you want to talk about?"

"We should clear the air." She flipped her long hair over her shoulder with a playful shrug. "About us."

"Oh." Faye had been so consumed with her situation with Diana that she'd almost forgotten about Molly. All her past anxieties crashed over her like a tsunami. The rejection. The fear. The failure. "I can't right now."

Molly's eyebrow twitched. "Somewhere to be?"

Shit. "Yeah. I'm..." Her mind drew a blank. She squirmed like an ant under a magnifying glass, frying under the heat of Molly's stare. Then she spotted Riley at the top of the path, peeling off towards the painting studio. "I'm meeting Riley," she said, with more conviction than was necessary. "So I can't right now. Maybe tomorrow."

She scampered up the path like a dog with its tail between its legs. What had she said that for? She didn't want to have that conversation tomorrow. She didn't want to have it ever.

She felt like she was walking weirdly and straightened her posture, hoping Molly wasn't watching her. *God, I hope I don't have a sweaty back.* She cursed under her breath, replaying the conversation in her head. Panic mode engaged.

She couldn't avoid Molly forever, but she also couldn't stand and listen to a list of reasons why she wasn't good enough. Though they'd only seen each other a handful of times while they dated long distance, Molly had ended things without so much as a text. Actions spoke louder than words, and she refused to be squished underneath Molly's pink pumps like a bug again. Molly probably wanted to gloat, anyway. To tell Faye about her new girlfriend and her perfectly working intestines.

"Challenge those thoughts," Senhor Arenoso's words echoed in her head. *"Assumptions can be very damaging."* The guided meditation they'd done together aimed to pinpoint those assumptions when they arose, but still, she was surprised that she'd actually noticed her thoughts.

She didn't have time to celebrate the feat because in order to challenge them, she had to face them.

And that meant having the damned conversation with Molly. *Ugh.* Faye would rather roll in a field of nettles.

She heaved out a breath as she reached the painting studio. A stack of easels rested beside the door, and there was the rustle of movement inside. The wood cabin had been painted white, with big, rectangular windows giving a spectacular view of the beach.

Faye ducked her head inside. "Hey, Riley."

Riley looked up from a pile of canvases, using her arm to shield the sunlight. She broke into a grin when she spotted Faye in the doorway. "How're you doing?"

"Good. Good." Faye sucked in a deep breath, trying to calm her racing heart. A lone ceiling fan spun above their heads, doing nothing to combat the heat. "I just wondered if there was any update on the Pink Polari parakeet."

Riley finished setting out the fresh canvases on wooden easels situated around the space. "Next time I head over, you can join me if you'd like?"

"That'd be great." Faye hesitated, chewing her lip. "You sure it's not too much trouble?"

She brushed her hands over her beige cargo shorts, creating finger smudges. "Not at all. Someone with your expertise will be helpful."

Faye nodded, not entirely convinced. She wasn't sure what she could offer after being out of the field for months. Nevertheless, the opportunity to get away from Sandy Springs and the awkward conversations with Diana and Molly had come at a perfect time.

"Okay, cool." She forced a smile. "Thanks, Riley."

All she had to do now was make it to her cabin without bumping into either of them or melting into a hot, sweaty puddle.

TEN

Diana

Diana crossed one leg over the other, leaning into the wooden bench hidden beneath the pergola and its canopy of flowers. The air closed thick around her, pressing her dress against her skin with sweat. At least the courtyard, being high up, brought a nice breeze from the cliffs, carrying the tickle of pollen to her nose.

Diana refreshed her phone with a swipe of her finger. Since Faye had mentioned the Wi-Fi at reception, she saw no harm in seeing what she'd been missing. She still stiffened with every passerby, though, like her phone was contraband.

The spotty Wi-Fi did little to ease her frustration.

She huffed, tapping the screen impatiently. She was better off not knowing than watching the buffering sign spin in lazy circles.

An awful realisation pinged into her brain—what if nobody had actually contacted her?

Feeling another flush, she undid a button on her dress.

She felt out of control without her day-to-day tasks, endless students needing assistance, and colleagues peppering her with questions. With Faye's proposal swirling around her head and unwelcome memories bombarding her, she needed a little reality check.

Finally, her emails jumped up the screen. She exhaled. 108 emails. But instead of relief, a frown pulled at her mouth. She clicked on her message notifications.

Leanne: *How's the tan coming along?*

Met any Portuguese hotties I can spend my lunch break daydreaming about?

Any progress with the proposal?

Diana stared at the last message for a little too long. Guilt crept under her skin, winding tighter and tighter until a dull ache spread through her temple. She wasn't any closer to an idea for her follow-up book. Honestly, she hadn't even thought about it.

She'd achieved what her father and Jason said couldn't be possible. People listened to her and engaged; her ideas and theories had pushed socioeconomics in ways others hadn't. She'd travelled Europe, Asia, and America, landing prestigious teaching positions at the best universities in the world. Yet now, at the precipice of it all, her brain was failing her.

Although Leanne was her friend, her job came first. If needed, she'd let Diana go in search of the new hot talent. She couldn't blame her for that.

Maybe Diana was already old news.

She'd always been a firm believer that age didn't encumber her but improved life as she got older. But now she had her doubts.

The throb in her temple deepened as she clicked back onto her emails, sifting through spam and stationery sales. She skimmed a mountain of university updates and replied to her students before landing on one from her boss, the subject in bold.

New internal position. She scanned the details, her chest tightening. A permanent position. At Harvard. In socioeconomics.

She shifted on the bench, its hard wood digging into her spine. A sunburnt couple chatted as they walked past hand in hand through the courtyard, like two lobsters, folded beach towels pinned under their arms. She gave them a tight smile before looking at her screen. The words stared back at her.

It would be a lot to juggle. The book tour, writing, increased classes, more marking…Molly. And she'd travelled the world teaching. Giving that up and settling down in one place itched at her, though she couldn't put her finger on why. But a permanent job at one of the best universities in the world was hard to pass up. Hard to pass up and extremely competitive. And she'd just taken three weeks off, which meant Selena would already be chomping at the bit. *Great timing.*

"What are you doing hiding in the shadows?"

The cheerful voice made her head snap up from her phone. Faye grinned back at her, another oversized white T-shirt drowning her tall frame. She could barely make out the hem of the denim shorts poking out underneath— shorts that revealed long, slender legs.

"I'm not hiding."

"Good." Faye quirked an eyebrow, her eyes drifting to the patch of skin above Diana's cleavage. "'Cos you're quite the standout in that dress."

Diana couldn't stop her lips from lifting. Faye's surprising confidence always seemed to defuse her.

Faye's focus dropped to her phone. "Everything okay?"

"Work stuff." She lifted her shoulders, trying to ease the tension slinking into her muscles.

"Bet your students are missing you."

"I doubt it." The image of Selena Borgo strutting up and down Diana's class, speaking in her fancy French accent, made her sigh, annoyed that the woman had gotten under her skin. "They're well looked after."

Faye took a seat beside her, and Diana breathed in the mix of vanilla and perfume and something else that she was beginning to recognise as inherently Faye.

The rumble of tyres against gravel grew louder, and then Ella appeared on the buggy, red hair flying out behind her. She waved as she drove past, then parked at the reception, hopping out and singing a tune to herself. When she disappeared through the door, the quiet lingered, birdsong carrying on the wind.

"I was checking my emails," Diana said. "My boss has announced a new permanent position." She shook her head, feeling foolish for voicing it out loud. "But…I don't know. It's made me more confused about what I want."

Faye didn't jump in; she just listened, her careful eyes observing her.

"I've always been driven," Diana continued. "I've known what I wanted. Each paper was a burning idea I needed to write out of my system. My book was the same. Nothing else mattered until I'd finished it. Teaching those ideologies felt right—a natural progression. I never doubted myself. But now? Doubt is all I'm sure of."

"Is that why you came to Sandy Springs? To get a break from it all?"

She brushed a hand through her hair. "I told my agent I would use the time to work on my proposal for my next book."

"It sounds like you're a little burnt out."

"Burnt out," she repeated, with curled lips, like it was a slur. She caught concern in Faye's soft eyes. In the sunlight, the green and blue danced together, forming a new colour Diana had no words for.

"When was the last time you enjoyed a day without

ticking items off a checklist?" Faye asked. "When you did things that made you happy, for fun?"

Diana frowned as she combed her brain. "I'm not sure."

Deciding to study alongside raising Molly had been her decision. She'd pushed for her education. Earned it. Worked hard to get where she was. But a sickly uncertainty swirled in her gut. The long nights, the endless meetings, the pressure to keep performing and doing and creating. When did she start doing that for someone else, and not for herself?

She turned her phone over in her hand, suddenly feeling its weight. She had an urge to throw it over the stone wall and let it tumble down the cliff.

Faye leaned back into the bench. "You don't seem like the type of person who takes breaks. Am I right?"

Diana nodded, but her mind was still somewhere else. Maybe that's why she felt so detached lately.

"Maybe you should take a break these few weeks." Faye nudged her playfully. "I think that was kinda the point of being on a remote island."

Diana let out a breath that wasn't quite laughter. "I can't really argue with that." When she looked back at Faye, something in her chest fluttered.

Faye's gaze held hers. Steady. Grounding. Kind. "You don't need all the answers right now," she said.

"No. I suppose not."

Faye's eyeliner had smudged at the edges, her cheeks tinged pink from the heat. But as Diana let herself admire her for a moment longer, the finer details shone through. How her small nose perfectly balanced her square jaw. How beneath the make-up, she was jaw-droppingly gorgeous.

Until now, Diana had never noticed how unaware Faye was of her own beauty. The subtle way her hand rested over her abdomen. The baggy T-shirt. How she made herself small. She hated how she hid herself away.

Her gaze dropped to Faye's mouth.

A tingle spread from her sternum, dropping down into her navel. Excitement buzzed around her. A feeling she hadn't experienced in so long, it felt foreign. Like an out-of-body experience, lifting her up and out of her skin.

So why did she feel guilty? Like she should be doing anything but exploring this?

"I should probably go," she said, hating the way disappointment flashed over Faye's features.

"Okay. Catch you later." Faye smiled and stood to leave.

Diana watched her go, wondering why she'd said anything at all. There was no denying her attraction to Faye, yet her mind pushed back at the first sign of feeling something.

Maybe because this trip wasn't supposed to be about you, but about Molly.

With that reminder, she headed back up the trail to the cabins, the sun hot on her back. Faye's conversation played on her mind, her stomach warring with opposing feelings.

Why shouldn't she feel excited over the prospect of someone being interested in her? Not in her position or her connections, but in *her*, Diana Thompson?

Yes, this holiday was for reconnecting with Molly, but there was no reason Diana couldn't do something for herself, too. Her lips quirked at the idea. Why not have some fun? She worked hard. She deserved a break. Faye was right.

Part of her wanted to turn back around, to find Faye and tell her the truth about what was on her mind. Her heart skipped in her chest at the implication of getting to know her better, setting something alight that fired through her whole system. Then the cabins popped into view, and newfound clarity washed over her.

Maybe Molly needed a bit of fun, too.

So she dipped into her cabin, taking the bottle of Dom Pérignon from the fridge in the kitchenette. She'd received it a year ago from her boss, after exceptional student grades, and had been saving it for a special occasion. Might as well toast this change of mindset. Even if Molly wanted none of it, Diana did, so she was going to drink it.

She knocked on Molly's door, bottle in hand, and waited, bouncing on her toes. The muffled slap of sandals against stone echoed on the other side, and then it opened.

"Hey, Mol. Fancy a glass of this out on the back?" She waved the bottle in the air.

Molly eyed the offering like it was poison before giving a small shrug and leading Diana through her cabin, out onto the private balcony. Two potted plants flanked a small wooden table and two chairs. A black railing separated the patio from the pink and yellow wildflowers growing in the spaces behind the apartments. The sea rolled and frothed in the distance, peeking through the gaps between the buildings. Though not completely private, the area was sheltered from most of the neighbours. Absolutely worth the price upgrade, in Diana's opinion.

"What's the occasion?" Molly asked as she sluggishly fetched two glasses from the kitchen and placed them on the table. She slumped into her chair, and Diana tried her absolute best not to frown at her dressed in her pink pyjamas.

Molly should be out there exploring, meeting people, taking advantage of this place. Not lounging inside in her sleepwear. Was this what she'd been doing since dropping out of university? She pushed the thought from her mind, trying to focus on the carefree feeling from earlier and not the stern-professor mum-mode she so easily slipped into.

Have fun.

She blew out a breath. "No occasion. Just thought it would be nice."

Molly eyed the bottle warily, like it had a coiled-up snake hidden inside. "Seems a bit hypocritical, don't you think?"

That landed like a punch to the gut.

"An alcohol-free course and you sneak a bottle of ridiculously expensive champagne in?"

"It's not a big deal." Diana shrugged. "It's not like we're flaunting it in front of the staff."

Every muscle in Molly's face seemed locked into stone. Cold, carved, and unmoving. Then her mouth broke into a wide grin, revealing the small gap she'd inherited from Diana's mother. A rare, genuine smile. "You're a bit of a rebel. I like it."

Diana laughed, offering her the bottle. "Do you want to do the honours?"

Molly took a while to loosen the cork, and Diana had to nip her hand to stop herself from interfering. Finally, she popped it, sending the fizz flowing over the glasses. Molly shot her a panicked look. "Oops. Sorry about that."

Diana bit her tongue at the sight of a hundred pounds' worth of top-quality champagne pooling on the stone ground. "It's fine."

"Trust me to spill the most expensive champagne I'll ever drink." Molly handed her the glass, sticky liquid dripping down the stem and onto Diana's fingers.

"It was just a gift from my boss. Don't worry." She caught the dip in Molly's expression at the mention of her work and sat a little straighter. "But we're not talking about work. Or your future. Or any of that stuff."

Molly's eyebrow lifted. "No?"

"No. I brought this too." She dug in her pocket and placed a pack of cards on the table. "Remember how we used to play rummy?"

"God. I haven't played that in forever." Molly laughed, and for a moment, her eyes held that same flicker of excitement she'd had when she was a little girl. When she still wore frilly socks, and her favourite band was One Direction. "Sounds fun, though."

Fun. Yes, that was what they needed. Diana couldn't remember the last time they'd really had fun together. Guilt nipped at her, but she pushed it away, gripping the stem of her glass and lifting it to Molly's.

"Cheers," she said.

Their flutes clinked; they took a sip. Then Molly dealt the cards.

Diana savoured the crisp sharpness of the champagne as it rolled over her tongue, and her mind wandered to Faye. It was official. This trip, she was taking a break.

It was time to truly enjoy herself.

ELEVEN

Faye

Faye tried not to frown as she observed her reflection in the mirror. She turned to the side, pulling the top of the waistband of her support lingerie above her belly button so it fit snug over her bag, hiding it. The black lace ran like silk under her fingers, but it couldn't completely distract from the bulge in her abdomen, no matter how many times she adjusted it.

She sighed, pulling at the material, even though there was nothing more she could do. It was hard to feel sexy in the underwear when she felt like a reject from the Bridget Jones franchise.

She turned away from the mirror and padded across

the cool floor to the bed. She lay back on the soft cotton and blew out a breath, finding a comfy position that didn't push her bag against her abdomen. *Just relax.* That was what her good friend Google said. So, freshly showered, her skin smooth against the fresh sheets, she was ready.

Get comfortable. Think sexy thoughts.

Diana's dark eyes flickered into her vision. No surprises there.

She stretched out her legs, spreading them like a stranded starfish. It had taken a long time to heal after such invasive surgery... Then a whole while longer to even think about anything sexual. Not that she'd had a partner at the time or any hope for one. Part of her had thought her clit might shrivel up and die from neglect.

But Sandy Springs had changed that. Diana Thompson had changed that. As soon as she'd slinked up to her table, wearing that sleek burnt-orange pantsuit, those inquisitive eyes combing her with confidence, her libido had jolted back to life.

She closed her eyes again, the memory of Diana's gaze passing over her. Flutters rippled across her clit, and she pressed against it with her fingers. The way Diana looked at her made her forget all of her anxieties. As though she wasn't just the woman with the bag, but something else. Something desirable. She wanted to focus on that as much as possible. Now the bag was tucked away, hidden by the black lace, she pushed her fingers a little harder.

"Fuck," she muttered, already feeling herself

dampen through the material. Little sparks of pleasure fired outwards, and her toes twitched.

Her gaze darted to the door. *Did I lock it?*

Yes. You did.

"Shut up, brain." She circled herself, her muscle memory wakening, and gave in to the feeling. Hums of pleasure left her throat, and she swallowed them back.

But she didn't need to be quiet. It wasn't like her dads were in the next room. For once, she could fully enjoy herself.

She reached for the little gold bag beside her, feeling a low pulse throbbing between her legs. Could she? What if it hurt?

She hesitated over the sharp corner of the zip. The ache in her pelvis convinced her to just open the bloody bag, and she pulled out the small vibrator.

Faye needed to know everything down there still worked…for science.

No. Not for science. For her. *She* missed coming. *She* missed having orgasms. If she wanted anything to progress between her and Diana, she needed to be comfortable with touching herself first—and she was going to enjoy it.

Before she could talk herself out of it, she clicked the vibrator on with her thumb and traced it over her pelvic bone, reacquainting herself with the feeling before letting it drift lower. The vibrations tickled at first, but when the toy reached her clit, it stopped being funny.

She gripped the soft sheets with her free hand,

circling the other over her underwear. "Fuck." Pleasure burst in waves, and she struggled to keep her grip.

She fumbled as she lowered the setting, a fuzzy haze coming over her vision. Now she'd had a taste, she was determined to keep going. As soon as the vibrator touched her clit again, she moaned, pushing into it. Without prompting, Diana's mouth flashed before her eyes. The memory of her tongue in her mouth. Her back against the door. *God*, she wished she were here.

She groaned as the pulses electrified her, flooding her fingers through her underwear. *Yes.* She needed this. She needed it so bad. Why on earth had she waited so long?

She circled her clit, imagining Diana's elegant fingers instead. She barely had time to form the thought before she peaked, letting out a high-pitched cry as she came. The toy pushed harder against her, the vibrations carrying her up and up before dispersing. Lungs heaving, she tossed the toy aside, gazing up at the ceiling.

"Oh my god." She laughed dreamily to herself, letting her hand fall between her legs. She'd finished so quickly, and she was completely drenched. She didn't even need to make use of the crotchless feature on her underwear.

In fact, she hadn't really noticed her bag at all.

"Amazing." Her voice came out low and dry in her throat, and she laughed again.

Her laughter vanished when three raps on the front door echoed through the room.

What the hell? She glanced at the clock. *22:43*. Faye was no party animal, but who would be knocking on her door at this time?

If she ignored it, maybe they'd go away. She sank further into the mattress, the cool AC making the ends of her hair dance.

What if it's an emergency?

She bit her lip. Surely an emergency would require more banging and more urgency than three neat little knocks.

What if it's Diana?

That stirred a whole other feeling low in her abdomen as she indulged in the fantasy. God, she was really overthinking this.

You could just open the damn door and see.

She scrambled to her feet on wobbly legs, threw on the white, complimentary dressing gown hanging on the back of the door, and blew out a breath. The door edged open, and her excitement and nervous energy sucked out of the gap like a gust of wind.

There was no one there.

She leaned her head out, catching a glimpse of legs disappearing out of sight.

"Hello?" she called out, clutching the robe closed over her chest.

A few seconds later, someone rounded the corner, and her heart fluttered.

"I thought you were sleeping," Diana said, her shoes clacking on the stone. Her blonde hair flicked out around her temples, over-tousled. In the darkness, her eyes shone like the midnight sky, sparkling with a familiar gleam Faye recognised after that night at the bar. *Has she been drinking?*

The thought flew out of her mind as Diana's attention was drawn behind Faye, through the wide-open door, to her bag of sex toys on the bed.

Oh my god. Her cheeks flushed pink, and she tried to block the view with her body, but Diana gripped her waist.

A teasing smile ticked up her mouth. "I thought you were sleeping…but you weren't, were you?"

Faye swallowed as Diana's other hand found the fold of her dressing gown, and she walked her inside the cabin. The heat from her face spread down into her navel, low and thick, burning hot. She could barely breathe.

She wet her lips. "No, I wasn't."

"No?" Diana traced a nail down her chest, parting the material of the gown to reveal more pale skin.

Faye gasped as she brushed a finger down her sternum, leaving blazing heat in its wake. A ping of pleasure struck her clit.

"Then what *were* you doing?" Diana angled her head, soaking in Faye's bare skin, her plump lips inches away.

The sound of Faye's breathing was too loud, but she couldn't help it. "Thinking about you."

Diana's eyes snapped up, pinning Faye with a new hunger. One that made her clit ache and beg for attention.

She asked, a little breathless, "Have you been drinking?"

"I might have enjoyed a glass or two." Diana gave a light shrug, her eyes never leaving hers. "But that's not why I'm here."

"Then why are you here?"

In a swift movement, Diana seized the folds of her dressing gown, walking her back to the bed until her thighs touched the mattress. She held her there, Faye's chest heaving underneath her hands. Then her lips captured hers.

Faye gasped into her mouth, tasting a sweet hint of alcohol. Diana held her firm, kissing her slow and deep. Almost as though she was giving her the opportunity to push her away. When she didn't, her lips grew more desperate, more possessive, mixing harder kisses and nipping at her bottom lip. Faye gripped her waist, loving the feeling of her hips, and pulled her closer. She groaned as Diana's tongue slipped into her mouth, tightening her hold as hot, silky need rolled and curled in the depths of her belly. She moved against her, her clit pounding, magnetised by the woman's every move.

Diana tugged her forward by her dressing gown. "Can I take this off?" she asked, her breath tickling Faye's cheek.

Faye thought it would've been a hard decision. That her mind would jump in, firing flares and alarm bells. But in a split second, as easy as breathing, she nodded, letting Diana slip the dressing gown from her shoulders.

An appreciative hum left Diana's throat as she drank Faye in, eyes flickering. Lingering. Assessing.

Faye's breathing turned shallow, her pulse firing loud in her ears with anticipation. But she didn't hide. The adrenaline firing through her system was solely focused on the woman in front of her. She just wanted to be buoyed in this feeling, to keep Diana looking at her like that.

Like she was the only person in the world who mattered.

Am I dreaming?

Did I come so hard I knocked myself unconscious?

If she was dreaming, she didn't ever want to wake up.

Diana's gaze swept over her in open approval. "Beautiful."

The word left her mouth in a soft whisper but packed a punch to Faye's gut. The way she said it like a fact. Like it couldn't be taken back.

Diana kissed her again, and Faye clung to her dress, trying to pull her closer. She broke away too soon but remained holding Faye's waist, hands firm, like she owned it.

"We'll start slow." She leaned down to place a kiss on Faye's neck.

But Faye didn't want slow. The last six months had all been building to this moment, and it had peaked overnight. She didn't want to wait any longer.

"I'm not fragile."

Diana didn't break stride, her breath tickling her skin. Her sharp tone contradicted the softness of her touch. "Everyone has limits, Faye. We're going to start slow. No exceptions."

Well, fuck.

Diana kissed her neck again, shutting her up. Then she drifted lower, to her shoulder blade, lips soft but firm. Her collarbone. Neck. Jaw. Despite her commanding mouth, her touch was curious, gentle, as her hands skimmed Faye's hips.

She cupped Faye's breasts, pinching her nipples just enough to make her moan. Her whole body fizzed with Diana's caress, every part aching to feel the softness of her lips. All she could do was remain there at Diana's mercy as she glided to stand behind her, hands steady on her waist, leaving a trail of fire.

If she hadn't already come, she'd be in trouble.

"I want you to tell me what you like. What you want," Diana said. "If anything hurts or makes you uncomfortable. Communication is very important to me." Her lips found Faye's back, soft, teasing, before her teeth sank into her flesh. Faye groaned, her head tipping back.

"Too much?"

"No. I like it."

Diana hummed, caressing Faye's jaw before tilting her head to expose her neck. "What about here?"

"I *really* like it," Faye said, her whisper somehow still too loud for the room. The pressure of Diana's finger vibrated underneath her voice box, then Diana replaced it with her mouth, and Faye groaned, slick wet heat slipping between her thighs when she sucked hard at the sensitive skin.

God, she needed this. She needed this more than she dared to admit. Could she really say what she wanted? Was it that simple?

She swallowed hard, turning so she could look into Diana's eyes. "You wanna know what I really want?" She waited, letting their heavy breathing fill the silence. "What I want is you. Now. Here. No more waiting."

A beat passed before Diana's lips curled into a gorgeous half-smile, and she closed the gap between them. Her mouth commanded Faye's, hot and forceful, as they sank onto the mattress, making Faye's stomach dip and dive.

She happily let Diana guide her to the headboard. When Diana leaned over her, holding back her full weight, Faye tried to grind their pelvises together; the ache so strong, it was painful. She wanted to feel all of her. Taste all of her. But she wasn't calling the shots. She could hardly stand the distance between them as she squirmed underneath her.

She wasn't going to last five minutes.

Diana pulled back with a playful tsk. "Do you not remember what I said?"

Faye wrapped her legs around her, hooking her in place. "Sorry." She let out a soft, breathy laugh. "But have you seen yourself?"

"Have you seen you?"

Faye had to look away. "You can hardly compare the two of us." She caught sight of her black underwear, holding everything in place. "You're an absolute goddess, and I'm just—"

"Stop comparing yourself to other people."

Diana was right; she was seriously killing the mood. They hadn't kissed for thirty seconds, and it was thirty seconds too long. She could self-deprecate another time.

"You're incredibly smart, Faye. Beautiful. Strong. Don't wish that away."

"Fine." Faye tightened her legs around Diana's waist. She'd agree to anything to kiss her again. "But you know what I want. Please." She pulled Diana's face to hers, locking her in a kiss. The taste of her sweet tongue in her mouth made her whimper, pushing her to the edge.

When they parted, both panting, Diana whispered, "But do you know what *I* want?"

Her soft breath against Faye's lips made her shiver, and she shook her head. A million different scenarios fired through her brain, making it impossible to think. She wanted all of them. At once. Her clit was going to explode. She didn't know where this energy had burst from, but she wanted to take full advantage, afraid it might slip away if her brain started to wake up.

Diana kissed her again, slow and soft, her teeth pulling at Faye's bottom lip. "I want you to show me what you were doing. Before I rudely interrupted you."

Her throat tightened. "You want to watch me touch myself?"

"Is that a problem?"

"No." The only problem would be if Diana stopped touching her. When her voice took on that low, husky tone, she was pretty sure she'd do anything she asked.

Diana untangled herself from Faye's legs and stood. Faye missed her weight immediately. She leaned against the stack of plump pillows behind her, while Diana moved to the foot of the bed, her eyes glued to Faye like she was a work of art.

God. Another roll of pleasure swelled in her centre, and she groaned, touching her throbbing clit. Even this dance with Diana was intoxicating. The way she demanded her attention. How that fuelled Faye, made her drunk on the feeling.

The best thing was that she didn't care about her bag. Her brain was focused on doing, not thinking, and that was fucking magical.

She pressed her fingers harder through the soaking material, loving the way Diana followed every movement. The power it gave her.

"Let me see you," Diana rasped, voice dark and velvet-smooth.

A deep throb pounded in Faye's pelvis, and she opened her legs wide. Diana's focus fell between her thighs, and she rubbed herself in circles, letting out a little whimper. She was so turned on, she could feel herself pulse underneath her fingers.

"Did you keep that closed the whole time?" Diana nodded at the fasteners on her underwear.

"I was so wet, I didn't need to open it."

She caught the dip in Diana's eyes, how her teeth dragged over her bottom lip.

"Thinking of you tends to have that reaction," Faye murmured.

Diana's mouth curled into a slow, sexy smirk. "Show me."

Faye fumbled for the vibrator in the bedsheet and wasted no time in finding the same setting as earlier. When she brushed it against herself, her whole body convulsed. "Oh…,*fuck*."

Her eyes squeezed shut as she rolled her hips. Only one thing fired through her mind on repeat. *Diana. Diana. Diana.*

She forced her eyes open, needing to see her, needing to check this was actually happening. The sight of Diana at the foot of the bed sent another bolt of pleasure through her core, and her hips bucked.

"I'm…not…gonna last long," she managed between gasps. "I want to…feel you."

She was losing focus. All she could think about was how the most attractive woman she'd ever seen was standing a metre away and *not* touching her.

"Diana," she pleaded. Her voice bordered on a whine, but she couldn't bring herself to care. "I need your fingers. *Please.*"

The slight quirk of Diana's lips, cracking through her serious, sultry expression, almost pushed her over the edge. But Diana didn't move. How could one woman hold that much power?

For a horrible second, Faye thought she was going to deny her. Then something flickered across Diana's face, and she glided to her side of the bed. Faye's core tightened as she approached, dress swaying around her hips, the scent of her perfume tangling in her senses.

In one movement, she popped the fasteners on her underwear. A jolt of pleasure pinged through her pussy. Then slowly, Diana slid her fingers up her slick entrance and around her swollen clit.

"Oh, fuck!" Faye grasped her shoulders.

"You're so wet," Diana hummed, leaning over her. "This is what you want?"

A rush of pleasure erupted through her as Diana slipped her fingers inside.

Diana raised an eyebrow. "I can't hear you, Faye."

"Y–yes." Lust robbed her of her voice as it claimed her completely. "Please, Diana. Fuck me."

As soon as the words left her mouth, Diana pumped her fingers lightly, every reaction tracked by her steely gaze. Faye squirmed, a moan tearing out of her throat. Satisfied, Diana fucked her harder, her fingers gliding easily.

Faye clawed at her, pressing her head into the pillow. The sensation of Diana's fingers inside her, the delicious friction, tightened and swelled in her centre, pushing her over the edge.

"F–fuck! I'm—" She cried out as the feeling crested and burst, flooding all of her senses. Unlike before, the intensity didn't die. She grasped at Diana as her legs trembled, her muscles quivering, hot pleasure firing through her until she was completely spent.

She lay back on the bed, head dizzy, chest tight. The feeling lingered, fogging her brain. As the ceiling swirled above her, she could hardly breathe.

Now that *was an orgasm.*

It was only when Diana tilted her fingers upwards, and she gasped, that she realised she was still inside her.

She looked into her eyes, drinking in the different shades of gold and brown as they combed her naked body. Realising Diana was still fully clothed, she wound the material between her fingers, giving a light tug. "This hardly seems fair."

Laughter quirked Diana's mouth. "We're taking it slow."

Faye didn't have it in her to be irked. She'd go at whatever pace Diana wanted. To do anything with her was nothing short of miraculous.

She reached out and tucked Diana's hair behind her ear, just because she could, letting her thumb caress her cheekbone, then her favourite mole. She thought she knew the answer to the question swirling in her brain, but she had to check.

"Does that mean you've accepted my proposal, then?"

TWELVE

Faye

"Don't forget about your breathing," Riley called out from the front of yoga class, where she sat cross-legged by the fountain, her blonde hair falling in long waves past her shoulders. "In…and feel your spine lengthening."

Faye sat up a little straighter, noticing the slump in her posture. She sucked in a lungful of air, spreading her shoulders and trying to ease the restless feeling in her bones.

"Out…and gently open your hips. Feel the sensation of your breath as it enters and leaves your body."

Faye pressed her hands into her knees, feeling the light burn through her muscles as she stretched a little wider. She was surprised by how much she was enjoying her morning yoga sessions. All that time lying in bed hadn't done her joints any favours, but she was already noticing subtle differences as her body worked *with* her for a change.

Though her body was still feeling heat in other places.

She opened one eye again, peeking at the back of the gorgeous woman's head a few places in front. Diana looked like she'd been doing this for years. *Has she done yoga before?* She'd have to ask.

Excited butterflies fluttered through her belly as the events of last night played through her mind. Diana showing up at her door, hair messy and eyes love-drunk… The graze of her fingernail down Faye's sternum. The expert way she'd made her fall apart around her fingers.

God. It was better than she'd dared imagine. And they were still going slow. Whatever that entailed, sign Faye up for seconds and thirds.

She adjusted her legs as thick heat curled low in her belly. She should be concentrating on her breathing, but instead of Riley's voice, Diana's echoed low and husky in her ears. *You're so wet.*

She was—and soon she would be again if she didn't get control of herself. She opened her eyes, trying to focus on anything else. *Pat, pat-pat, pat, pat-pat.* Quin tapped their fingers against their knees next to her as they danced in fluid sequence. In front of them, a thick-set man's last tuft of hair twitched in the breeze as it clung to his scalp.

"*In…*" Riley called. "And…*out.*"

Faye wondered what they were all thinking about. If other people were in a constant battle to *just breathe* like she was.

Was Diana, too?

Is she thinking about last night?

Her soft, wanting mouth. Her hot, silky tongue, and how Faye couldn't wait to feel it between her legs, so Diana would *really* know how wet she was—*no! Stop it.*

Luckily, Riley clapped her hands together, snapping Faye from her filthy daydreams.

"Well done, everyone. Now for our final pose." She grinned, dimples popping in her cheeks. "You'll have to trust me on this one."

They lay on the floor, legs and arms extended by their sides in a position mirroring Faye's existential crisis from her uni days. Afterwards, she stood with Quin in line, waiting to put their yoga mats back into the wooden cubbies.

Lying back on her mat, attempting to release the tension from her body, had only stirred her feelings up further.

You're like a horny teenager, she chastised herself.

She shuffled forward in line, trying to ignore the sensation between her legs as Quin chatted away about Drew Barrymore films, ranked from worst to best.

"I can't understand the hate on *Charlie's Angels*. It's shit, yeah, but it's *good shit,* you know?"

"I've never seen it."

"Dude!" Quin grabbed her arm. "That's criminal. It's like the fifth-best Drew Barrymore film."

"Maybe we can have a movie night sometime. You can show me around Cornwall."

"Oh my god, yes! We can make a list of every film that inspired all of this queer. Interestingly, Drew Barrymore features in a lot of them. Although…Drew Barrymore is banned in my dad's house. So maybe we'd be better at yours in Manchester."

Faye hoped Quin meant that. Her past tried to worm into her brain, promising that when the retreat was over, so was their friendship. She wanted to say this friendship with Quin was different, but she had to prepare for the worst.

Quin grabbed her again, eyes wide. "OMG, we can make a list of the best movie snacks, too. Popcorn is a classic, obvs, but Skittles are seriously underrated."

Diana turned around, catching Faye's eye, and something inside her snapped like an elastic band. Everything else fizzled out for a moment. Faye loved the movement of her mouth, how it turned up slightly at the corners. Loved how she had the privilege to notice such small changes in her expression. Then Diana brushed past her as she left, leaving a tingle where her warm fingers had traced her waist.

That should not be as arousing as it was. But the tingle sank low into Faye's belly, filling up her senses until she could feel nothing but Diana.

"Uh, hello? Pringles or Maltesers for number three?"

Quin slotted their blue mat into the cubby, then raised their dark eyebrows. "Well, well. What's got you all hot and flustered? And I don't think it's Drew Barrymore."

"I'm not flustered. It's just hot."

"Yeah…and me making my G.I. Joe's scissor was just a phase." They stepped out with Faye from under the shade and raised their arm to block out the morning sunlight. "Come on. What are you smiling about? Or should I say who? Don't think I haven't noticed you making eyes with Mrs Robinson over there."

"Quin." Faye laughed, her nonchalant demeanour cracked. "Diana is not Mrs Robinson."

"Aha! So she does have a name…" When Faye shot them a look, they grinned. "Fine. But this isn't over. Just make sure you don't ditch me completely for the waterfall tour tomorrow."

"I won't." Although the thought of seeing Diana in a bikini made Faye's pulse quicken. Despite the fact she'd laid herself bare last night, Diana hadn't so much as lifted her pretty yellow sundress. That drove her even wilder.

Yes, yes, taking it slow…I know…

But Faye itched to explore Diana's body, to discover the smaller details and quirks that others hadn't. Like the way she tousled her hair when she thought no one was watching, or how her eyes held so much emotion it felt like seeing right into her soul.

The intensity of it all. And this was only the beginning—they still had over two weeks to go. Faye couldn't stop the smile stretching her face.

But then Molly stepped into view, cutting in front of Quin. "Can we talk?"

The light feeling filling her body fizzled dry like wet fingers on a hot flame. *Not this again.*

Quin wiggled their eyebrows behind her, mouthing, "And now Blondie too?"

She couldn't compose herself to react. Panic set in, the earlier heat flooding to her face. What should she do? She could hardly run off again.

Molly was going to be at Sandy Springs the whole time she was, so she needed to do this sooner or later. Their sessions with the support counsellors started in thirty minutes, too, so at least there was an end in sight.

Harness that enigma.

She breathed in deeply, and on the exhale, said, "Yeah, sure," with far more enthusiasm than she'd intended. "I'll catch you later, Quin."

They flashed their finger guns, then headed towards the reception, probably to try to connect to the dodgy Wi-Fi and report back to their dad.

Here we go.

Faye wiggled her toes in her sandals before picking her gaze up from the stone slabs. Most people had left the courtyard, heading down the steps to the beach or back to their cabins. Riley was conversing with a man by the fountain. Faye wondered if she'd pick up on a distress signal if she gave one—though judging by the man's crossed arms and the huffs escaping his chest every few seconds, it looked like Riley could use a distress signal of her own.

Stop looking for a way out, Faye.

The half an hour until their support counsellors suddenly seemed far too long. What were they going to talk about for thirty minutes? They'd barely exchanged a sentence in a year.

"Shall we take a seat?" Molly indicated the bench where Faye had found Diana yesterday.

Faye frowned. She didn't want to taint the space with something that was definitely not going to be fun.

But Molly didn't wait for an answer. She walked towards the bench, hips swishing in another pink dress, in a way that didn't have any effect on Faye whatsoever. She blinked as that hit her. At some point, whatever minuscule hold Molly still had on her—the tatty tendrils Faye was still holding onto for no other reason other than masochism—had been cut.

She breathed a little easier as she took a seat beside Molly on the hard wood, keeping a nice distance between them. Maybe getting closure wouldn't hurt? But could she handle the brutal truth right now?

Molly turned to her. "I might as well just come right out with it."

Oh. Faye wound her fingers under the hem of her shorts, trying to swallow back the nerves threatening to surface.

"I'm sorry for what I did. For ghosting you. That wasn't cool."

Faye's automatic response of *it's fine* stopped at her

lips as the memory resurfaced… Lying in bed in darkness, checking and rechecking her phone, wondering what she'd done to push Molly away. Rereading the unanswered messages, overthinking every word, telling herself she wasn't good enough. That she would never be good enough for someone to love.

It wasn't fine at all.

She forced herself to meet Molly's blue eyes, seeing herself reflected in them. She sat a little straighter. "What you did really hurt me. And I know we were only together for a few months—you might not even count it a relationship—but I thought you cared about me. For you to just disappear without reason or explanation, well, yeah, it wasn't just 'not cool', it was extremely shitty."

Now the words were out there, a tight ball in her chest loosened. *That actually felt good.*

Molly nodded, folding her manicured hands in her lap. "I know. I'm sorry." The hush of the waves rolled in the distance before her voice softened. "I just didn't know what to do."

At the change of tone, Faye glanced at her, noting her pinched eyebrows, her bottom lip threatening to wobble. She looked away, following the zigzag path of an orange butterfly while she waited for Molly to continue.

"Have you ever woken up and felt like you couldn't breathe?" Molly asked. "Like you're in someone else's life and not your own? Everything was wrong. I realised I was going into the final year of a degree I didn't want, and I had no idea what I *did* want." She shot her a shy look. "You were included in that. So I quit. Everything. Overnight. Packed up and went back to my dad's house. I didn't want to speak to anyone. I couldn't. I was too embarrassed. How could I talk about it when I didn't really understand it myself?"

Molly's words hung in the air as Faye tried to process them. She understood how it felt to wake up and feel like her life wasn't her own. Despite everything, she didn't want Molly to be sad. She'd always assumed she'd just found somebody better than her.

"Assumptions can be very damaging." Maybe *Senhor Arenoso had a point.*

The butterfly landed on a flower tangled around the pergola before fluttering away over the cliffside.

"I'm sorry to hear that, Mol. I wish you'd talked to me. Maybe I could've helped you through it, but..." She sighed. "I guess it doesn't matter now. I do appreciate the apology, though."

"It does matter." Molly reached for her hand, and Faye flinched. "Don't you think there's a deeper meaning to this? I mean, what're the chances of us being here at the same time?"

A slow swell of nausea rose in Faye's throat. "What? What are you talking about?"

"Us, silly. Surely, this is a sign for us to try things again."

She pulled her hand away. "I...er—I don't think that's a good idea."

"Why not?"

Faye's mind fuzzed. A few months ago, she might've welcomed this reconciliation. Anything to feel like a real human who someone desired. But as she sat here with Molly, she knew it wasn't what she wanted anymore.

"So much has happened since then, Molly. We can't just jump back into things. As much as I appreciate your apology, it doesn't change what happened."

"Right. Yeah, of course." Molly tucked her hands into her lap.

"Maybe we could try being friends, though?"

"Wow." She scoffed. "Friends?"

"Why not?"

Molly huffed again. "And what, have little tea parties where we tell each other the latest gossip and braid each other's hair?" Then a small smile crept onto her face, and she glanced at Faye.

Faye shrugged, feeling a grin on her lips as well. "Sounds good to me. If we throw some cupcakes in there."

"Vanilla ones?"

"Oh, I don't know, vanilla is quite, you know, vanilla."

Molly really smiled then, revealing the cute gap between her teeth. "Then I take back what I said before. It must be the island doing crazy things to me."

"Maybe it's Princesa Inês Teresa writing you some poetry." Faye imagined the princess at the window of the belltower, calling out to them below. She grinned, remembering Diana reciting Shakespeare, and how she'd glided around the ruins like she owned every stone. She had the same presence in the bedroom. Another flash of heat jolted through her, and she crossed her legs.

Molly scrunched her face like she'd just bit into a lemon. "Princess who?"

"From the…oh, never mind." Faye bumped her shoulder with hers. "Really, though. How are things now?"

"I'm here, so about as good as I imagine you are." She laughed, flipping curls behind her shoulder. "But now I don't have the university stress, it's a little better. I never liked law. I only did it because I thought it'd make my mum happy."

The mention of her mum caught Faye's attention. Molly had never spoken about her much, and Faye had only met her dad, Jason, the once, and he'd left a lot to be desired. He didn't even look up from the TV to greet her because a football match was on.

"Have you seen your mum recently?" Faye asked. "I remember you didn't speak with her a lot."

Molly sighed. "She's trying. That's why we're here. To work on our relationship and 'give my life direction'." She punctuated the words with her fingers and a roll of her eyes.

She's here? Have I seen her already?

"Speak of the devil," Molly muttered, casting a sideways glance as someone stepped into the courtyard.

Faye looked up, locking eyes with Diana. She had her hands tucked into the pockets of a mint-green playsuit, the hint of a smile playing on her lips.

What...?

Faye glanced around the stone paving, the fountain, the steps, hoping to see someone else—anyone else—but when she came up empty, her gut twisted.

Diana's gaze passed between them, curious, before she decided to approach, that flirty swish in her step.

No. This isn't happening. Nausea tumbled in Faye's gut, dipping and diving and threatening to erupt. *It can't be her.* All the colour drained from her face when Diana stood in front of them. If Faye weren't already seated, she would've passed out.

"Hey, Mum," Molly said, casually. "Wanna walk there together?"

THIRTEEN

Diana

Something was off. Diana knew as soon as she saw them sitting together. But what exactly was off, she couldn't put her finger on.

Faye wouldn't look at her. The usual rosy shade tinting her cheeks and chest was now a sickly white. She turned to Molly, searching for any clues in her expression, but she was the opposite. Relaxed. Comfortable. Oddly so.

What is going on?

"Everything alright?" she asked, keeping her voice level.

"Yeah. We should go, or we'll be late." Molly

jumped up from the bench, casting a glance behind her. "You coming?"

Faye nodded, but her face said she'd rather do anything else. They headed towards the reception where the offices were held, something unspoken thick in the air.

Had something happened?

Diana was too afraid to ask.

But then Molly filled in the gaps for her, and her eyes almost fell out of her head.

"Mum, this is Faye. We kinda used to date."

The bundled ball of nerves in her stomach jumped into her throat. *Used to...date?*

A beat of silence stretched too long as Diana glanced at Faye. Her guts wound together, twisting into something ugly and sickly. Did Faye know that she was Molly's mum?

Seeing the same horror reflected on Faye's face, she knew the answer to that. Of course she didn't—but god, what a mess.

When did they date? How did Diana not know about this? What else had she been missing in Molly's life?

She hummed a response, a mixture of mild interest and intrigue. "Were you together long?"

"Mum," Molly gasped. "You can't ask that. Honestly." As Faye pushed through into the reception, Molly hissed at her, "We didn't exactly end things amicably."

They waited by the wooden desk, time seeming to slow down as Diana's brain fought to catch up. She needed more information than this.

"Funny how we bumped into each other here after all this time," Molly chirped, looking at Faye in a way that made Diana want to throw up. "Don't you think?"

"It is quite…improbable," Diana replied, chancing a glance at Faye. She looked how Diana felt. Sick. Like she might collapse at any moment. She'd been planning to see her later, to pick up where they'd left things last night, but now…

God. She really might vomit if she thought about it too hard.

She could just imagine Jason's reaction. *Not only have you abandoned your daughter, you've traumatised her as well.*

Her heartbeat kicked up a notch as she pictured Selena reporting her to the local news. *Respected professor involved in family sex scandal.*

Thankfully, the man with the hairiest knuckles Diana had ever seen walked through the doors; she'd never been so happy to see Marco Marcos, even if his name suited a tacky kids' TV presenter rather than a doctor.

"Ah, you're here." He straightened his glasses. "Are you ready to start?"

"Yes." She nodded, waiting until he'd unlocked his office and headed inside before turning back to the others. "I'll see you later." Her gaze locked with Faye's, and a swirl of conflicting emotions tumbled in her belly before she looked away.

Don't throw up. Don't throw up.

She closed the door behind her, taking a deep breath in as she contemplated knocking her head against the wood.

So much for having a little harmless fun. She'd just made everything severely more complicated.

And if Molly found out?

All the progress she and Molly had made would be lost. Not just lost, but blown into teeny, minuscule pieces never to be fixed again.

How has this happened?

"Everything alright?" Marco Marcos asked, his deep voice jarring her upright.

Diana stepped away from the door, remembering where she was, and dusted her hands over her playsuit. *Be professional.* She offered him the sincerest smile she could muster, though her hands were still shaking. "Absolutely fine."

He pursed his lips, then offered the seat opposite with a practised gesture.

Diana sank into the cool faux leather. On the inside, she continued to sink lower and lower, wishing she could disappear completely.

She couldn't have spent the night with one of Molly's exes. Life couldn't be that cruel.

She suppressed the urge to roll her eyes at herself. Life absolutely *could* be that cruel.

"She's gone, Dee," her dad's words echoed in her ears, and suddenly she was small again, sitting in the oversized armchair in the living room. The room still smelled like fresh bread from that morning.

She'd been pencilling her mum a picture of colourful flowers, the kind she always admired in the fields, albeit more lopsided. Their neighbour, Mrs Waddington, had told her it was a lovely idea, so she'd sat in the corner, creating picture after picture until her fingers ached, until her neighbour had returned home to let her two terriers out for a wee.

But now Mrs Waddington had gone, and her dad stood in the doorway like a hulking shadow, groaning as he dropped his bags beside the door.

"Gone where?" she asked, in a small voice.

He groaned again as he slipped his coat from his broad shoulders and hung it over the door. His long days working the farm meant he was always carrying aches and pains somewhere.

Diana held a breath as he crossed the room, pulling a pack of cigarettes from his pocket and lighting one. The orange tip glowed, highlighting the thick scruff on his chin. He grasped her shoulder, giving it a little shake.

"She's gone with the angels now. With Grumps and Granny Sue."

"No." Tears she'd been fighting all day filled her eyes. "Tell her to come back."

His hand stilled as he took another drag, the stinky smoke curling around them. "That's not how it works, Deedee."

She scrunched her nose, tears escaping freely. She hated the nickname. She hated how teasingly he used it after her mum asked him not to. *Deedee Dumdum.* She hated the smoke and how it would stick to everything like a parasite, lingering long after the cigarette had been stubbed out. Mum always made him smoke outside or in the kitchen when Diana was home. But Mum wasn't here.

It was all wrong.

"It's just the two of us now, Deedee."

Diana moved her shaking hands from her face, and the bright lights of the office brought her back to the present. A lone tear slipped down her cheek, and she brushed it away with her fingers.

Wordlessly, Marco Marcos offered her a box of tissues. She tugged one from the top and dabbed under her eyelids. Her chest tightened as the flood of emotion continued to rock inside her. How she waited up every night, hoping there'd been a mistake and her mum would walk through the door. How she took on the role of housekeeper while her dad worked himself into the ground, smoking like a chimney.

Her life had changed irreversibly that day. The weight of it still floored her. It was too much for a little girl to carry.

"I never got to say goodbye." She sniffed, embarrassed by her confession.

Marco Marcos stilled, kindness falling over his features as he waited for her to continue.

"My mum died when I was ten. Brain aneurysm. One day she was there, the next…she was gone."

"I'm sorry. That must've been very difficult for

you."

Diana wiped her nose. "I've been thinking about her a lot. Since being here." She sighed, feeling a lump rise in her throat. "There was so much I never got to say to her."

"It sounds like you're still holding onto a lot of that pain."

Her eyes snapped up from the beige carpet. "Have you ever lost a parent, Marco?"

He wilted a little under her gaze. "No, I haven't."

"Then how would you know how it feels?"

Another wave hit her hard, and she put a hand to her forehead, feeling a headache coming on as another memory came to her.

Her dad slammed his empty glass down on the counter, plucking the photograph from her fingertips. "You need to stop with all this blubbering now. It's not helping anyone."

She'd wiped her eyes on her sleeve, flinching when her dad's voice boomed through the kitchen again.

"And stop dirtying your frock. What would your mum say to that?"

"Sorry, Dad."

"We have to move on now." He snapped the album shut and picked it up. "This is for your own good."

Diana bit hard on her lip as his heavy footsteps sounded through the house, drawers slamming open and closed. If he hid the album in his bedroom, she knew she'd never find it. Diana never went in there anymore. The safe space where her mother used to read to her, wrapped up in the softness of fresh sheets, had become a dark, stinky pit the sunlight never touched.

She'd not seen any photos of her mum since that day.

She touched a finger to her lip, finding blood where she'd been biting down. She let out a sigh. "I'm sorry, Marco. I know you're only trying to help."

"That's alright." He readjusted the glasses on his nose before taking them off and cleaning them with a tissue. "Grief that's not dealt with can manifest in many ways. We can push it into corners and sweep it under rugs, but it'll always be there unless we grieve for what we lost."

"I have grieved her. I grieved her every day until—"

Her dad's furrowed brow popped into her vision, cigarette smoke teasing at her nostrils.

Revisiting those memories, her body had curled in on itself. The home she'd once loved, filled with homemade apple pie and her mum's happy hums from the kitchen, became a bear's cave where she was stepping on eggshells. The best days were the spring and summer months, when her dad worked long, gruelling shifts. She'd always rise after he'd left for work and go to bed before he arrived home—the best way to avoid conflict. But those quiet winter months filled her with dread. He always found something to criticise. The laundry wasn't white enough, and the soup was too bland. Diana couldn't wait to get out of there. But she'd go on to trade one suffocating man for another; she just didn't know it yet.

Sometimes, when the nights were lonely and her

mind a pit of jabbing thorns, she feared that what Jason said about her was true. Could she have been a better mother herself if her own hadn't died? What would her own mother say about this situation with Faye? Would she scold her or offer her advice?

Diana had finally let loose a little, followed her instinct, tried to have some fun, and where had it got her? With herself in boiling hot water and someone threatening to close the lid.

What am I going to do?

"You grieved her until what?" Marco prompted gently.

She shook her head, but she could feel the words about to spill like the torrent of emotions flowing out of her. "My dad hid all our photo albums because I wouldn't stop crying. We never really spoke about her after that."

"How did that make you feel?"

"Terrible." A tear streaked down her cheek, and she wiped it away with the tissue. "Sorry."

"You have nothing to apologise for here."

"I'm not sorry, I just—" She pressed her lips together, frustration replacing the sadness swelling inside.

"People deal with grief differently. That's not to say there's a right or a wrong way, but you were just a child, Diana. You needed more support."

"I'm fine."

He scribbled some notes on his pad, then looked up at her. "Have you ever thought about writing a letter to your mum?"

"I don't think the Post Office deliver where she is, Dr Marcos." She cringed. "God, I'm sorry. I don't mean to be so rude."

A hint of a smile twitched his mouth. "Don't worry." He threaded his knuckles together. "Writing a letter can be a powerful tool. Expressing the feelings and emotions you've buried can help you move forward. It can bring closure, getting to voice all the things you never got a chance to say."

Diana nodded, letting his words sink in. "A lot's happened in thirty years."

"If anything comes to mind, and you'd like to voice it, I'm here to listen."

She didn't have the strength to laugh. There was so much swimming in her mind. The pain from her mother's death, the confusion and stress with Faye and Molly, the pressure of her career hanging in the balance. How was there room in her brain for anything else?

But she met Marco's kind gaze, breathed in deep, then started talking.

FOURTEEN

Faye

Faye did exceptionally well throughout her entire guidance session not to puke. Between assuring the sweet elderly Beatriz that she was alright and taking breaks to gather herself in the toilet, she'd still left the counsellor's office with the world swaying underneath her feet.

Diana was Molly's *mum*.

What?!

It didn't make any sense. Everything seemed…wrong. It didn't add up. How could Molly and Diana be related? They were nothing alike.

The thoughts continued to rock side to side in her brain, following the motion of Riley's buggy as they rounded each corner. Faye had been hoping to snag a trip to the wildlife centre, but now Riley had offered one, it didn't feel like the right time.

Senhor Arenoso said the familiar guides helped navigate them on their path, but Faye figured this one might perplex even some of the most respected familiars. What was she supposed to do in this situation? Pretend it never happened? Her whole body wilted at the thought of last night never happening again. It wasn't as if she and Molly were anything serious. Faye's health issues and Molly's reluctance to travel meant they'd only met up enough times to count on one hand. Would it be so bad if she and Diana continued things? Especially if it was only for these few weeks anyway?

Ugh. She just wanted to bury her head in the sand and wake up from this strange dream.

"You're quiet," Riley commented, giving her a sideways glance. "Everything alright?"

The seat vibrated underneath her as they drove over a pile of stones. "Just feeling a bit off." She clung to the overhead grip to steady herself.

"Is it my driving?"

"Compared to Ella's, this is like flying first class."

Riley laughed as the path thinned out and the trees towered above them. "She does drive like she's outrunning a zombie horde."

The wind blew a few stray hairs from Faye's ponytail, and they tickled her face. She turned back to the greenery, breathing in the fresh air. Her insides still warbled with every thought.

Diana.

Molly.

Stop it.

The jagged mountains in the distance rose up to kiss the blue sky. She closed her eyes, wishing she could magic herself to the top. Maybe the change in altitude would give her some clarity.

Poor Beatriz, Faye's counsellor, had seemed confused by her reluctance to open up. It wasn't like she didn't want to; she just had no idea how to form her thoughts into words.

The older woman had shot Faye a curious look over her notepad. "Telling someone new about your ostomy is a big step. How did it make you feel?"

Faye folded her hands in her lap. At the time, telling Diana had been a relief. Like stepping out into a cool, misty rain on a hot summer's day. It had almost felt as though she'd stressed over nothing, the way Diana had listened, how she hadn't pulled away. The calmness in her gaze. Her soft hand holding Faye's, smoothing the ridges Faye had scratched into the skin.

"It felt good," she told Beatriz, unable to look her in the eye.

"Each time should get a little easier and increase your confidence," Beatriz had said. "Would you like to walk me through it?"

But remembering the moment now made her queasy. Diana would probably never look at her that way again.

She swallowed. "Sorry. I need to go to the bathroom." Holding one hand over her bag, she dashed out of the room. She didn't like to use her bag as an excuse, but she couldn't say for sure if she could end the session without Beatriz ending up covered in her morning croissants.

Riley pulled the buggy to a stop, jarring her from the memory. "We have to walk from here, but it's not far."

Faye stepped out, unsteady on her feet, and grabbed her backpack from the back seat. The path they'd been following had narrowed into a thin trail disappearing into the forest. An earthy scent hit Faye as soon as they stepped among the trees.

"How was your session this morning?" Riley asked.

She stumbled over a thick root and righted herself. "It was fine."

Riley sighed. "I know I'm the *manager* of the course." She marked the word with her fingers, bumping Faye's shoulder. "But I'm told I'm a good listener too. I know all this soul-searching can be a bit of a rollercoaster, but you've got the support around you to help make sense of it, okay?"

Faye swallowed the lump in her throat. She didn't want to cry in front of Riley. But she was being too nice. "Thanks. It's just been a lot today."

Sunlight dappled through the leaves, casting zigzag shadows across the dirt.

Riley nodded, looping her fingers under the straps of her backpack. "If all you need is to be quiet and process, too, that's fine. I don't want to push you. I just want you to know you're not alone. I know how that feels."

The sincerity in her voice almost made Faye start weeping on the forest floor. It was strange for her to come to trust people in such a short space of time, but the kindness Riley showed her seemed to just flow from her in waves.

Luckily, a wooden structure came into view, and Riley turned into a tour guide.

"It doesn't look much," she said, "but over the last year we've rehabilitated over a hundred birds and returned them to the wild."

"That's impressive."

Which was more than could be said about the tiny centre itself. Inside, the cramped space felt even smaller. Caged enclosures sunk into the walls from floor to ceiling, with a desk in the middle of the room piled high with feeding equipment, papers, and empty boxes. A small woman appeared from a back room, wearing a stained yellow top and a blue apron tied around her middle.

Her wide customer-service smile relaxed into a real one when she spotted Riley at the door. "Ah, am I ever happy to see you." She pulled her black hair loose from its messy ponytail and retied it, looking exactly as dishevelled as before. "Ana couldn't make it today, and there are lots of little mouths that need feeding."

"I'm here to help."

"Me too," Faye added. Maybe keeping herself busy and being around animals would be the perfect solution for her spiralling thoughts.

"You don't have to do that, Faye," Riley said, though judging from the other woman's scowl, she didn't seem to agree.

"I want to." Faye smiled, meaning it for the first time all day.

They set to work. Faye cleaned the cages and bowls, refilling the water, while Riley and Catarina started the feeds, scattering seeds and nuts, and then handfeeding the few hatchlings. She quickly fell into the routine of being back at work, and an ease fell over her, her thoughts and worries drifting to the back of her mind.

She liked taking care of things. It filled her with purpose. That was why she'd wanted to be an ecologist in the first place. To try to make a difference somewhere. Seeing the little bullfinches and parakeets, some with bandages and splints, others missing feathers or carrying grazes and cuts, peering at her with their little curious eyes, caused that feeling to flare again.

After they'd made their way through the patients, they took a seat in the small staff room, where a fridge hummed in the corner next to an espresso machine.

It wasn't until Riley and Catarina were elbow deep in various bits of paper that Catarina jumped up to make coffee. She offered Faye one, but she declined. She'd only just stopped feeling jittery from the day's events. Best not to add caffeine into the mix.

"Sorry to throw you in the deep end, Faye," Riley said as she pushed a stack of papers to one side. "This was supposed to be a tour and not a work shift."

"I don't mind. I enjoy it."

"That's a relief," she said with a grin. "Last thing we need is to be slapped with a forced-labour claim."

Catarina's eyes widened, hair messed like she'd been dragged through the forest from the back of Ella's buggy.

"I'm joking," Riley assured her.

"My heart can't take it." Catarina filled two cups with the hot brown liquid and passed one to Riley. "We're one slip away from going under."

"I'm working on it."

"And we've had even more admissions this month."

Riley frowned, glancing at the stack of papers before returning her focus to Faye. "Anyway, would you like to see how your parakeet is doing?"

"Absolutely." She followed Riley out of the room, leaving Catarina huffing and puffing over the paperwork.

The noise from the lone fan spinning above them did little to detract from the sweet cacophony of cheeps coming from the cages.

"The centre is run by volunteers," Riley explained, waving a hand over the mess organised into different piles. "We're trying to get some funding from the government, but at the moment, most of the income comes from donations and from Sandy Springs. I'd love to get more people involved and educate them on what's happening, but Senhor Arenoso says I shouldn't have too many irons in the fire."

Faye noted the three empty cages at the bottom; the

place was almost at full capacity. What would happen to the animals needing care when they were full?

Under her feet, the cheap linoleum was bubbling and curling at the corners, and its black shade was dotted with flakes of mint-green paint that had peeled from the walls.

Riley stopped in front of a door marked 26B. "Anyway, this is your little gal, right here."

Faye peeked inside. The parakeet was resting in the corner, her little green chest rising and falling, her wing strapped to her side with a clean, white bandage. "Has she broken it?"

"Luckily not. The vet said it was just a sprain. With some rest, she should be back to normal in no time."

Faye straightened up, noting the rows of other parakeets in similar conditions. "What's going on here, Riley?"

Riley's expression soured as she followed Faye's gaze. "There's been an uptick in admissions the last few months. Parakeets especially. Pink Polari ones even more so."

"Poaching?"

"I'm worried that it's getting worse. People want the next hot thing as pets. Pink Polaris' colourful crowns seem to be it. But they don't understand how damaging and cruel these poachers are to these birds."

"Do you have CCTV?"

"Only at the main resort and the ports. Duarte monitors who comes to and from the island, but we don't have a lot of control over private boats mooring out of sight. The locals are aware of it, but without help from the government, I'm not sure what to do."

"Let me help."

"I can't ask you to do that. You're a guest here."

"It can be part of my rehabilitation. A trial run for getting other people involved."

Riley smiled, but it didn't touch her eyes. "The course is all about you focusing on *you*, Faye. I'm not going to encourage any distractions from that."

"This is part of what I do, Riley. Please, let me help."

"I appreciate the offer. I really do, but I can't accept it."

The doorbell jingled, and a happy voice called out, "Did someone ask for a delivery?"

Carla and another man stood in the doorway, two heaped boxes in their arms. Carla grinned when she spotted Faye. "Ay! The dog's bollocks. What are you doing here?"

Faye couldn't help grinning back. "Just visiting. You?"

"Just delivering. People, supplies, food. I do it all."

Catarina rushed in to collect the boxes, mumbling something under her breath which Faye couldn't understand. The man gave her a kiss on the cheek and then followed her and Riley into the office, fast Portuguese flowing between them. Faye just caught "late" and "always".

Some good that Duolingo was.

Carla waved a hand. "Catarina and Bruno are like an

old married couple." She laughed. "Actually, they *are* an old married couple. Don't worry about them. So how are you?"

"I'm okay." At least, she had been. The question pulled the rug from under her, and everything Molly and Diana came flooding back.

"Just okay, huh? I heard a little differently."

"What? From who?"

Carla gave a playful shrug. "A…friend."

Faye knew that look. "A friend named Raul?" What did he know? When Carla's cheeks flushed pink, Faye nudged her. "Or is he more than just a friend?"

"I can't kiss and tell here." Carla nudged her back, waggling her eyebrows. "Come play poker with me, and I'll tell you everything."

"I'm not really the gambling type."

"*Mentiroso.*" An alarm buzzed on Carla's watch, and she switched it off. "Bruno, *precisamos de ir agora.* Come on!" She turned back to Faye and tapped her nose. "I can pick you up. It'll be fun."

"Maybe." Faye didn't know anything about poker, but she was still trying to say yes to things.

Bruno appeared, giving Faye a nod with his balding head.

"*Maravilha.* See you later, Dog's Bollocks!" And then they were gone, the bell jingling behind them and a new course of energy swirling around Faye.

Though Dog's Bollocks wasn't a nickname she'd ever intended acquiring, somehow, she didn't mind.

In fact, she needed to start living up to the nickname. As she continued watching the door, the chatter of Riley and Catarina in the background, her mind started to clear. She knew what she wanted, what she needed. She wasn't going to sit back and let the world pass her by. She'd done her fair share of that already.

The situation with Molly and Diana wasn't ideal, no. But what journey is plain sailing? She couldn't stay on the dock for fear of rocking the boat.

Faye had to get on board and be her own captain.

FIFTEEN

Faye

The next day, the air blanketed them, thick and humid, as they trekked through the forest. Riley and Ella led the group through the lush vegetation, while Faye and Quin lingered at the back. Chitters and chirps rang out from the trees above, birds flying overhead from canopy to canopy. It would've been paradise for Faye if Diana hadn't been avoiding her all day.

Faye's confidence from psyching herself up in the mirror dwindled with every step. She repeated Carla's words to herself—"*You're the dog's bollocks*"—but even that started to lose its effect.

She'd already dealt with tricky situations on the

island; what was one more? But she knew deep down that she liked Diana more than she cared to admit. This couldn't end yet. Not like this.

The sight of Diana walking at the head of the group with Molly made Faye frown again. She needed to talk to her, and for that she needed to get her alone. But how?

Quin bumped her shoulder, pulling the navy baseball cap further on their head, their black coils bursting out in every direction. "So, when are you going to spill the beans on Mrs Robinson?"

Faye shushed them, though she knew Diana couldn't hear. "There's nothing to spill—and please stop calling her that."

"You do know I have a sixth sense for sexual chemistry? I was blessed by the gay gods. That's why my hair is so curly."

"You're full of it." She looked down at the soft mulch underfoot and adjusted the backpack on her shoulders. Ahead, the river they'd been following curled around the corner out of sight. The waterfall must be close; that made her even more nervous.

Quin shook their head, putting extra bounce in their step. "Nuh-uh. That's how I know something's up with Blondie over there, too. You guys having a three-way?"

"Quin!"

The older couple in front of them, Henrietta and Marvin, turned their heads. Faye offered a weird half-wave, and they spun back around, whispering something to each other.

She gave Quin a stern look. "You're gonna be starting rumours in a minute."

"Is it a rumour if it's true?"

"It's not true." She grimaced. "That's just…gross."

"Don't knock it 'til you try it."

Her voice had a bite to it. "They're mother and daughter."

"Oh." Quin's smile slipped for a moment, then they shrugged. "Fair enough, then."

Large ferns and blue hydrangeas popped up beside the path, adding a burst of colour to the endless green. Faye brushed the leaves with her fingers but couldn't shake the feel of Quin's gaze on her.

"What?" she asked. They raised their black eyebrows, and she sighed. "Fine. But it's a bit of a weird one."

Quin grinned. "That's what I was hoping."

After Faye had explained what had happened, from that first night meeting Diana at the bar, and how Molly had approached her wanting to get back together, Quin sucked in a breath. "That's quite the soap opera. No wonder you're stressed."

"Yup."

"And do you know what you want to do?"

"Yeah." Her eye landed on Diana again. That had never been in doubt. "I just need time to talk to Diana about it."

"I'm sure I can help with that. I'll be your wing-pal. The gender-nonconforming Robin to your Batman."

The path curved into an incline, winding around a rising cliffside, and Molly grumbled something from the front.

"It's not much further now," Ella said. "I promise it's worth it."

Molly huffed, her face brightening when she spotted Faye at the back of the group.

Please don't come over. Please don't come over.

But Faye's familiar must've been sleeping at their desk.

Molly stopped, waiting for Faye and Quin to catch up. Diana turned around too, but when she caught eyes with Faye, she turned back to the front.

I hope she doesn't get the wrong idea, Faye thought.

"I feel like we've been walking for days," Molly whined, flicking her hair over her shoulder.

Faye shrugged. "I enjoy it."

Which was a chronic understatement. Faye loved the outdoors, the fresh air, the feeling of blood pumping around her body. All she needed was a bat detector and a clipboard, and she'd be in her element. She'd missed being outside so much.

Molly cast her a glance. "Don't you think it'd be better to just use those buggy things and save us all some time? I could be back sunbathing by now."

"You can't rush it. It's all part of the experience."

"I don't get it." She brushed her arm against Faye's. "You know, we could've buddied up for this. Got to catch up properly."

Faye shot a look at Quin that said, "Help me".

Quin cleared their throat. "Anyway, we were just talking about cheese."

"Cheese?" Molly didn't hide the repulsion on her face.

Is this their idea of being a wing-pal?

"I like fun cheeses," Quin continued, undeterred. "Babybels, Cheesestrings, those cute little triangles of cheese, you know? But Faye prefers aged cheese, like a good Cheddar or Gouda. Ain't that right?" They shot her a grin.

I'm going to kill them.

Before Faye had a chance to consider pushing Quin back down the hill, the sound of rushing water filled her ears.

"You hear that?" she asked, picking up her pace. "We must be nearly there."

She passed Henrietta and Marvin, hoping they hadn't overheard any of their conversation, and caught up with Ella and Riley as they crested the top. Just below, water flowed between the rocks, cascading down into a deep blue lagoon. The pool split into two sides. A larger, deeper one for swimming, and a shallower stretch sheltered by large boulders. Plants sprouted from every surface, growing up the cliffside and colouring the whole area in a vivid green.

She watched Diana take in the scene. Did she see natural beauty like Faye did? Or a time-wasting excursion like Molly?

Though they were only a few feet away from each other, it felt like miles. She wanted to close the distance between them, to kiss her like she had in her bedroom, to help her understand there was nothing going on between her and Molly, and really, there never had been.

Faye knew that this was all temporary, but she couldn't bear to waste another second of it. Not when that person was Diana.

Riley clapped her hands. "Right, let's head down, and we can take a dip."

A light mist coated Faye's skin as they descended the path, the rushing water soothing to her ears. Even Quin was quiet beside her, while others posed for photographs by the railing.

The waterfall spilt over the mossy rocks in a wide silver curtain, mist rising and tangling through the dense ferns at the bottom. The group peeled off to leave their bags on the dry land, and people started undressing. The sun peeked through a hole in the canopy, casting a stream of golden light onto the water.

Riley wasted no time removing her vest and shorts, revealing a blue swimsuit. Ella needed a bit more convincing, but then the two ran hand in hand—Ella shrieking all the way—and jumped in together with a big splash.

The others were more tentative, dipping in toes first or taking time to take photos of the waterfall crashing into the pool.

Faye and Quin waited on the pebbly beach, Quin's

backpack still hiked up high on their shoulders.

"You not going in?" Faye asked.

"I don't think so." They bit their lip, watching Riley and Ella floating on their backs. "Ever since…well. Ever since my top surgery, I just get nervous undressing in front of people. Not that I ever enjoyed it before, but…"

"I understand." A group of green parakeets swooped low over the water, wings flapping. "Ever since my surgery, I feel the same."

Quin turned to her. "Your surgery?"

"Yeah." Nerves pinched her stomach. She wanted to tell Quin more, but the words stuck in the back of her throat. What if they ditched her like her other friends had?

You told Diana. You can tell Quin, too. Come on.

"I have an ostomy bag. I'm still getting used to it, and even telling people is hard, never mind them seeing it." She blew out a breath, trying to hide her shaky voice.

"I had no idea."

"Really?" She didn't know if they were just trying to make her feel better.

"Not a clue. But you shouldn't let that stop you."

"I could say the same for you."

They were quiet for a moment, just the rush of the waterfall crashing and people shrieking as they entered the lagoon.

"Yeah," Quin said. "It's just so easy to say 'Don't care what people think.' Doing it is different, isn't it? I hate people staring at my scars and seeing the looks on their faces."

Faye nodded, relief settling. "But those who mind don't matter, and those who matter don't mind."

"Is that a Senhor Arenoso quote?"

She shook her head, a smile curving her mouth. "Dr Seuss."

"Sweet." Quin took her hand and gave it a squeeze. "You're full of secrets today."

"That's it now. I'm pretty boring."

"I don't think so." They grinned. "You're a pretty cool encyclopaedia."

She laughed, then, feeling a surge of bravery, inclined her head towards the water. "How about we start by dipping our toes?"

"I think I can handle that."

With linked hands, they kicked off their sandals and crept towards the water, the hard stones digging into the soles of their feet. Quin squeezed her hand harder as they stepped into the shallows, and Faye screamed.

"Jesus! It's freezing."

Quin giggled, tugging Faye deeper into the pool. The water prickled goosebumps up her legs, and she shivered.

"How are those two swimming in this?" she asked, eying Riley and Ella swimming in the depths.

"Probably don't notice it 'cos they're so hot for each other." They nudged her. "You could have that too, you know."

Faye's gaze found Diana, paddling at waist height on the other side of the pool. A ruched red swimsuit fit snugly to her body, the open back revealing the neat cut of her shoulder blades. Faye's pulse kicked up a notch.

Molly stood on the pebbles not far away, arms crossed, like Diana's personal bodyguard. Any possibility of getting Diana alone dropped by the second.

"I got this," Quin said. "Let me take care of Princess Peach."

Before Faye could argue against it, they'd started making their way over to Molly.

This should be interesting.

She sucked in a breath. Whatever Quin was saying seemed to be going surprisingly well, and after a few moments, they led Molly away to the small pool on the other side of the rocks.

How the hell did they pull that off?

Not wanting to waste any time pondering Quin's tactics, Faye waded towards Diana, flinching as the cold lapped up her legs and thighs. Any higher, and her shorts would be soaked through. Diana turned as she approached, her expression giving nothing away.

Nerves coiled in Faye's belly as she stood beside her, leaving enough room so as not to draw unwanted attention.

You got this. Channel that 'dog's bollocks' energy.

"How are you doing?" she asked.

A bit of a lame start, but a start, nonetheless.

Diana looked straight ahead, where a few more daring people had joined Ella and Riley in the water. "It's a lot to comprehend."

When she didn't elaborate, Faye jumped in. "I just

want you to know I had no idea—"

"I know." Diana said it softly, but so resolutely, her reply didn't fill Faye with ease.

"It's not ideal, I know, but that night we spent together?" Faye lowered her voice, wanting to reach out and touch her, for her to look at her at least and see how much she meant this, but Diana continued watching the swimmers. "I've not felt that way in such a long time. And I know you feel it too."

Something flashed across Diana's features before it was neatly tucked away again. The emotions stirring in Faye's chest climbed higher and higher. She needed to get everything out. "I don't want this to end. Not like this. I know we live different lives in different places. I'm not expecting us to run off into the sunset when this all ends, but why not enjoy the time we've got together, like we agreed?"

"It sounds simple when you say it like that."

"Me and Molly haven't spoken in a year." Diana's dark gaze locked with hers, and Faye's emotions spilt over. "There was more connection between you and me that first night at Raul's than the whole time I've known Molly. Don't let it go to waste, Diana. Don't let me be something you regret. Please."

Shrieks from the waterfall drew their attention. Louis and Charles had jumped into the deep together after encouragement from Riley. Louis flicked his long hair back while Charles scrambled back to the safety of the rocks, cursing.

Faye turned back to Diana, heart fluttering when she found her already looking at her. Those deep, chocolate eyes only pulled her deeper, and she almost forgot where she was until another splash burst her bubble.

Was that Quin and Molly?

Diana still hadn't said anything. Faye took that as her cue to give her some space. She took a step backwards, the water rippling around her. Her heart in her throat. She let her gaze drift down Diana's swimsuit, lingering on the expert way it lifted her cleavage. "You look incredible, by the way."

Then she turned, wading through the water, releasing a shaky breath from deep in her lungs. Holy shit, that was intense. But she did it. The ball was very much in Diana's court now.

Now get me out of this freezing water.

She shivered as she stepped back onto the pebbles. Another scream came from the other side of the boulders, along with flailing arms and a flash of blonde hair.

If Faye didn't know better, she'd think Quin was trying to drown Molly. What the hell?

She pulled a towel out of her backpack and dried her legs. As she tied it around her middle, she chanced a look at Diana.

She was still in the water, fingers drawing ripples around her hips. Golden light shone on her, illuminating her beauty. As though she could sense Faye's gaze, her focus flicked towards her. Then Faye saw it. The smallest movement of her lips. The hint of a smile.

And it lit Faye up like a firework.

She itched to run to her, dive right into the deep with no reservations, and kiss that gorgeous mouth. Instead, she soaked it in, letting the feeling buoy her until she was rising high above the trees.

Then she smiled back.

SIXTEEN

Diana

Sunday was the day of rest at Sandy Springs. There were no classes or sessions, and the instructors hoped the extra time would inspire reflection on the week's events and learnings.

Diana couldn't believe only a week had passed. The noise in her head could have filled an entire school year. The ghosts of her past had teamed up with the hauntings of her present, making her toss and turn throughout the night.

Now, as she looked up at the ceiling, following the swirling patterns across the bright white, she wished she had something to wake up for.

A meeting. A class. Even a dental appointment.

Her phone lay switched off in the bedside drawer. Her itch to check her messages and emails still resurfaced, but she needed a break. She'd always thought she was being productive, keeping on top of things, but now, she wasn't so sure. The endless stream of communications exhausted her. It was no wonder she couldn't write a damn thing worth reading. Her life had become that of a tired librarian, and Diana a dusty old book left on a shelf.

Was that why she was so enamoured by Faye?

Someone had taken an interest in her for herself, with the simple idea of getting to know her, and not through a phone screen.

But it was more than that. Faye had a depth more profound than anyone else's she'd known, a compassion and kindness the world seemed to have forgotten. And she was clever—and beautiful—cautious and nervous in a way that evoked a protective nature in Diana she found hard to explain. A need to show Faye just how powerful she really was.

"Don't let me be something you regret."

Faye's words had struck a chord. But the situation was delicate—whether she and Molly were a serious item or not.

Diana rubbed her eyes. It was too early for this.

She flung back the covers and sat on the edge of the bed, rolling her neck left, then right, stretching the muscles. Early sunlight glowed beneath the blinds, while the rest of the room lingered in hazy darkness. Forcing herself to stand, she straightened the covers, tucking the sheet under the mattress like her mother used to do.

She still needed to write that bloody letter to her mum, too—but one thing at a time.

She shed her silk nightgown onto the tiles and stepped into the shower, letting the hot water soothe her skin. Methodically, she washed, but the routine didn't ease her mind.

After shaving and moisturising, she studied herself in the mirror. New lines were etched into her skin where they hadn't been before. She blinked, and someone resembling her mother looked back at her. Same cheekbones, same mouth, but instead of blue eyes, Diana's deep brown were steady and still. She waited, hoping to find some answers hidden somewhere, but nothing changed.

Maybe Senhor Arenoso had a point about these familiar guides steering them, and this course had come around at the right time.

Letting out a humourless laugh, she let her head drop. *Listen to me.* How had she ever thought she had it all together? Before Sandy Springs, she'd been a successful academic, an author, an esteemed colleague. Now, she didn't know what she was going to do once she stepped back on home soil. Really, she didn't even know *where* home was anymore. She could argue that since her mum died, nowhere had felt quite right.

She'd considered taking a job at Oxford many moons ago, but she couldn't remember the details now. Was that why she'd opted to travel instead of taking a permanent position?

How long had she been running?

She brushed her hands over her face. Maybe she should go speak to Faye? But it was too early, and besides, she didn't know what she was going to say. Maybe seeing Molly would help?

Ugh. I don't know.

Nervous energy buzzed in her veins. She took a seat by the window and attempted to read the book she'd brought for the plane.

When the light stretched further across the floor, and the book still lay unread in her lap, she deemed it an acceptable time to go see Molly. She needed a familiar face and decided against Faye's, knowing if they were back in that room again, anything could happen.

She knocked on Molly's door, hoping she'd let her sleep enough to avoid a lecture. Molly'd always enjoyed her sleep, even when she was a baby. Diana's friends had said she'd got off easy having a baby that slept through the night, but they'd never experienced her teenage years.

A groan came from the other side of the wood, and Diana's ears pricked.

"Mol? Are you alright?"

She tried the door, but it was locked. Another groan. Then footsteps.

Molly opened the door, her face white as a sheet. A layer of sweat stuck her hair to her head, and she squinted under the light. "I think I'm dying," she whined.

"Oh, sweetheart." Diana put the back of her hand to her forehead. *Sweltering.* "Can I come in?"

She nodded, and Diana guided her back inside, Molly groaning all the way to her bed.

"What happened?"

"I've been running back and forth to the toilet all night." She collapsed onto the mattress, curling into a ball. "It's that water," she mumbled. "I'm gonna kill Quin."

"Sounds like you've caught a bug. Here, I'll look after you."

Yes. This she could do.

She filled a glass with cool water and encouraged Molly to drink. Then she wet a flannel and laid it over her forehead. "Try to get some sleep."

Molly gave a tiny nod, and her eyelids fluttered closed.

Diana set to work, cleaning the toilet and sink, and then, unable to help herself, she rearranged some of the clutter. Afterwards, she took a cloth and wiped down the kitchen and the counters, leaving it all spotless.

Satisfied, she turned to Molly, her heart squeezing at the sight of her ghostly complexion. She rewet the flannel and pulled out a chair to sit beside her, brushing the hairs away from her face.

She used to do the same for Molly when she'd curled up in that pink princess bed of hers as a child, her blue elephant plushie pressed against her face. She'd have done anything to protect her little girl from the ways of the world.

Time passed so quickly. One minute, Molly had been running up to her after dance class, pink bows in her hair, then the next, she was ignoring her texts and calls.

Molly dropping out of her studies was something Diana couldn't understand, but maybe she didn't need to. Molly knew herself best. Who was Diana to judge?

She sat with her while the sun moved the shadows across the room. Every so often, Molly would spring up and dash to the toilet, then grunt as Diana forced her to drink more water.

When Diana's back and bum were numb from sitting, Molly stirred, blinking at her. "You're still here?"

"I am. What do you need?"

"You've been here all day?"

"Of course. If you need me, I'm here."

Molly groaned, but Diana wasn't sure if that was from the illness or the sentiment. "You should go. I'll be fine now."

"It's okay. I've got nowhere else to be."

"Honestly. I just want to sleep."

"If you're sure? I'll come check on you in a little while."

Molly closed her eyes again, and Diana pressed a kiss to her temple. At the door, she hesitated.

"I'll be fine. Go," Molly said. "And thanks, Mum."

"Get some rest." Then she stepped out into the late afternoon sun.

She blew out a breath. Now she was outside, mum-mode switched to standby, her stomach growled. A soft beat carried up on the wind. Music?

She walked towards it, the twang of guitar strings and rhythmic clapping getting louder. *Surely where there's music, there's food.*

A collection of small round tables gathered around the outskirts of the courtyard, where people were watching dancers. Diana assumed it was a private event, but then she spotted Louis and Charles in colourful Hawaiian shirts, clapping along to the beat. She scanned the crowd for Faye, anticipation dwindling when she came up empty.

She wasn't sure what was going on, but she spotted a small cart selling food near the reception and hurried over. The aroma of garlic and spices filled her nostrils, and her mouth watered seeing the bounty of seafood, rice, and cooked vegetables.

Once holding her steaming bowlful, she stood awkwardly, trying not to spill any down her dress. But the fresh fish melted in her mouth, the creamy rice enough to make her close her eyes in delight.

The music kicked up a notch. The guitar player grinned as he stepped into his solo, and everyone clapped him on. Dressed in traditional bolero-style jackets and embroidered shawls, the dancers spun each other in circles, stomping their feet.

"Why don't you take a seat, Diana?"

The voice made her jump. She'd been so enthralled by the dancers, the woman must've snuck up on her.

"I'm not staying. Thank you, though."

Ella collected two bowls of food and thanked the woman in Portuguese, then indicated her table with her head. "Come on. You can sit with me and Riley. We're at the cool table." She started walking, giving Diana no choice but to follow.

Diana sat in one of the empty seats, exchanging a polite smile with Riley. She hoped this wouldn't be an impromptu session disguised by the music and dancing. She really just wanted to eat and relax a little.

After scraping every last bit from her bowl, she set it down and gave her full attention to the dance floor. Their enthusiasm was infectious, the snaps and stomps of their feet hypnotising. The dance reminded Diana of a waltz somewhat, with their posture and the high arms, but it was looser, bouncier.

Ella leaned in to whisper. "Aren't they great?"

"They're wonderful."

"Do you like dancing?"

"From time to time." She'd never been much of a dancer. Growing up with her father the farmhand had definitely set her apart from other faculty members. She'd saved some money to pay for lessons after she found out it was common for professors to join in the various balls and dances around campus. But she still avoided it whenever possible.

The band brought the song to a close with flair, and the dancers took an exaggerated bow.

"Now you've seen the dance…" A tall man with slicked-back hair stepped forward, and the band played a steady beat. "…And you've had time to learn the steps—it's your turn! *Venha*!"

I should've seen this coming.

Diana turned to Ella. "You stitched me up."

Ella gave a playful shrug, mischief glinting in her eyes. "Dancing heals the soul."

"I…shouldn't. I've just eaten."

A familiar laugh jolted electricity through her. "I'm sure one dance won't kill you."

She spun round to find Faye behind her. She wore a baby-blue linen two-piece, her dark hair loose.

Ella winked at Diana as Riley led her onto the courtyard.

Damn it. I really have been set up.

"So whatcha say?" Faye asked, holding out her hand.

Diana wanted to say she couldn't—she *shouldn't*—but her body betrayed her. She placed her hand into Faye's. With a tug, Faye pulled her up, threading their fingers together like it was completely normal, and joined the others populating the stone flags.

"It's very easy," the man said, taking up the locked-arm position. "We sway face to face, back to back, turn, and repeat. Listen to my calls, and I guide you. *Excelente*." He clapped his hands, and the band jumped back into song, the guitar, harmonica, and drum finding a lively rhythm.

Faye grinned as she took the lead. The group gathered in a circle, each couple following the directions, some better than others. Riley led Ella in a well-practised sway, spinning her effortlessly as they flew through the steps. Louis and Charles also fitted right in, despite their colourful Hawaiian shirts being the opposite of the traditional Portuguese attire.

Diana glanced at the others around them, but no one was paying them any attention. She relaxed a little, leaning into Faye's warmth and letting her guide her.

"Spin your partner!"

She gasped as Faye twirled her. The grin on her face wider than she'd ever seen it. The new confidence in her pulsated through every movement, and Diana couldn't help but grin back.

"You're like a dog with two tails," she commented.

"I'm feeling good. Can you blame me?" Faye spun her again, bringing them back together. "Dancing on a beautiful island with a beautiful woman in my arms? What's not to be happy about?"

"And clap. One-two, three!"

They were a little clumsy, a little mistimed, but the group followed the man's instructions before resuming their rhythmic sway.

"As much as I'm enjoying this…" Faye slipped her hand lower, and she dipped her lips to Diana's neck. "I want to get you out of this dress."

Her words slid like smooth silk between Diana's legs, taking her breath. She pressed her lips together, hiding the feeling from showing on her face, but she couldn't deny the effect of this more forward approach. The shy and passionate Faye was hot. This confident and forthcoming Faye was, also, hot.

Faye pulled back, leading them around another couple, not taking her eyes off Diana. "I think it's only fair," she continued, the flicker of something mischievous in her eyes.

"Fair?"

"You upheld your part of the proposal." She leaned in closer again, her breath tickling her neck. "Let me uphold mine."

"*Now stomp your feet!*"

Diana laughed at her partner's exaggerated movement, absorbing the pure joy radiating out of her. This woman and the woman she'd met at that bar were so different. Was Diana evolving at the same rate? Or was she just spiralling?

Either way, a unique, carefree happiness spread through her veins, the kind that can't be manufactured or faked, the kind that warmed her from the inside. The feeling shook her from her paralysis, and this time *she* spun Faye, taking the lead.

Faye's eyes widened before dropping into that look Diana understood well. She loved when Diana took control.

And good job, because Diana loved that too.

"You're quite persistent," Diana murmured. They jockeyed left and right, the movements becoming familiar. Her old dancing lessons resurfaced, and she locked their arms the way she'd been taught.

Faye's make-up was flawless, a thin black winged

eyeliner making those blue eyes pop. She raised an eyebrow. "If you're not interested, I'll leave you alone. You can enjoy your holiday, and I'll enjoy mine. But I don't think that's what either of us wants, is it?"

Diana's brow furrowed. The way Faye could see through the barriers she constructed around herself made her misstep. She righted herself, hoping Faye hadn't noticed, but this woman noticed so much of what Diana didn't always want her to see.

She spun Faye again, trying to distract herself from the ache in her pelvis. When they came face to face, Faye's lips slightly parted, and so close to hers, the thought of kissing her overrode everything else.

Their movements fell out of sync with the others, the band becoming a background blur as Diana's thumping heart took centre stage.

Then the music drew to a dramatic close. The band took a bow, and everyone around them burst into applause, while Diana and Faye stood frozen in the centre of the courtyard, eyes locked together.

SEVENTEEN

Diana

As the door to Faye's cabin slammed closed behind them, their mouths collided. Hands that had been structured and formal for the dance now roamed and pulled at any hot flesh they could find. Hard, hungry, and heavy.

Diana kissed Faye back with equal need, as though every second had been building until they could be alone in this room again.

She could already feel herself soaked through her underwear. She needed to pace herself. *Take it slow.*

She pressed Faye to the wall, letting her weight hold her there while her lips softened to trace her jaw and neck. Her teeth grazed the sensitive point she'd committed to memory, and Faye groaned.

"Fuck. I love it when you do that."

Diana responded by doing it again, a little harder, and Faye dug her nails into her back.

Her stomach pulled, a fresh wave of arousal flooding between her thighs. She shifted, doing her best not to squirm under the pressure building. If she were ten years younger, she'd not have so much resistance, but fine-tuning her control made everything much easier to manage.

Faye ran her hands over her back and then gripped her waist. Diana let her curl her fingers under her dress for a moment before directing her attention elsewhere. Her collarbone. Her neck. Her ear.

She savoured each sound, each whimper; every shred of evidence of Faye's pleasure deepened the ache sitting low in her navel. When she pulled back, Faye's eyes were hooded, a deep indigo as they combed Diana's face.

"You're so fucking hot," she said.

Her mouth ticked at the edges. The compliment warmed her—all the more as it came from Faye. To avoid thinking about it too deeply, she kissed her again, this time deep and slow, her fingers tangling in Faye's hair.

Faye pulled back suddenly. "Just give me five mins to empty my bag. I'll be right back."

"Of course. Take your time." Diana watched her until she turned around in the doorway to the bathroom, flashing her a red-faced grin.

God. She's cute.

She let out a shaky breath to collect herself and straightened her dress. She looked at herself in the mirror, fluffed up her hair, then took a seat on the edge of the bed. Her heart continued to race; her skin tingled like an electric current ran through it. She wasn't sure why she was so…nervous.

Diana didn't get nervous.

She shook her head, letting her gaze pass over the room as the clang of cupboards being opened and closed came from the bathroom. Faye's space was tidy. Either she'd anticipated this might happen and prepared for it, or she naturally kept things organised. The stack of books beside the bed were in colour order, making a rainbow of fiction mixed with non-fiction nature books and her sudoku. Her make-up and extra medical supplies were arranged on the dresser, tidied into patterned zip-bags. The only thing out of place was a pair of large pineapple sunglasses.

Before she could go and inspect them, the door clunked behind her, and she turned. Faye was resting against the door-jamb, wearing black lingerie. The patterned lace rose over her belly button, and a matching bra held her cleavage.

Wow.

Diana didn't hide the look on her face as she drank her in. She wanted Faye to know just how beautiful she was. She wanted to show her.

She rose, closing the distance between them, and brushed her fingers over the lace. "You look incredible, but I hope you know, you don't have to hide your bag from me."

Faye let out a nervous laugh. "It makes me more comfortable like this. Keeps things secure, you know?"

"Alright. Good. And you know we can take—"

"If you say take things slow one more time, I swear I'm going to lose my mind." There was a teasing tone to her words, but it sure sounded like a challenge.

"Come." Diana headed back to the bed and took a seat, tapping the space next to her. "Sit."

Faye did as she asked, moistening her lips. Nervous? *Good.*

"I'm not sure what your previous love affairs have been like." Diana took her chin gently, turning her to look at her. "But I take my time. I don't rush." She brushed a thumb over her mouth. "I'll give you what you need. My tongue? My fingers? But you have to understand, the best things in life are worth prolonging. You need to exercise some patience."

Faye nodded, her chin still cupped by Diana's hand. "Good."

"I'm not trying to be a brat," Faye said. "It's just hard for me. Before I met you, I had no desire for any of this stuff. I just felt so…unsexy. Now it's like that part of me has woken up. I want you so badly, it hurts."

Faye's words landed square in Diana's chest. So raw. So…vulnerable.

Faye opened her mouth to talk again, but Diana silenced her with her finger. "Lie back," she commanded.

Faye shuffled to the headboard, propping herself against a pillow.

Diana's eyes dipped. "Let me see you."

Understanding dawned on Faye's face and, slowly, she unfastened the clips securing her underwear, popping them one by one. Then she spread her legs, letting Diana see all of her glistening wetness.

"Perfect." Diana swallowed, her own arousal curling in her centre. "Now turn around. Get on your knees. Let me see that pretty pussy from behind."

Faye pushed herself up, head down, giving Diana the perfect view of her slick entrance.

Diana positioned herself on the bed, tracing two fingers through her wet heat.

Faye shivered. "God, Diana, you're killing me." When Diana's fingers stilled, she added, "I'm not complaining, by the way. I'm having a great time absolutely losing my mind over here."

Diana couldn't stop the smirk on her face as she applied more pressure, circling Faye's clit and hearing her reaction. As more wetness flooded her fingers, she dipped closer, replacing her fingers with her mouth.

Faye gasped and groaned into the pillow as Diana explored with her tongue, slipping deeper into her. One taste of her tangy sweetness, and she was addicted, kissing, lapping, and sucking at her, Faye's moans deepening the ache in her own pussy.

"God, you taste good."

She spread her wider, teasing at her with flicks of her

tongue. Faye whimpered, her legs trembling beneath Diana's hands. As much as she wanted to stay there all night and let Faye finish on her tongue, she wanted to see her face while she did so.

She pulled back, pressing her hand flat to Faye's clit. Faye groaned, rubbing against the contact, breathing heavily.

"Turn around."

Faye grumbled again. "Diana, I—"

"You'll do as I say if you want to come."

Faye fisted the sheets before flipping over, her stare burning into her. Her quiet defiance only pleased Diana more. Her thighs continued to tremble, and Diana leaned over her, taking her lip into her mouth. Faye grasped at her, pulling her closer, and she deepened the kiss, slipping their tongues together.

Faye bucked underneath her. "Fucking hell."

Diana broke the kiss and slid down Faye's front to rest between her legs. She pushed them apart, leaving her fingers on her thighs, her face just inches away from her. "I want to be able to see your face." Her eyes flicked from Faye's wet heat to meet her gaze. She pressed a kiss to her sensitive spot before sweeping her tongue over her. Faye reacted immediately, and Diana did it again, this time a little slower. "I've been wondering if your orgasm tastes as sweet as the rest of you does."

She let her mouth do the rest of the talking, building slow circles around Faye's clit, soaking in every reply she gave her. God, she loved the feel of her. The taste. She noted every detail. How Faye's brows were furrowed slightly, her lips parted, her eyes dark with unhinged desire. How her soft moans mixed with chesty sighs. And how every one made Diana's clit swell.

Deciding she'd teased her enough, she quickened her pace, and Faye writhed on the bed. She traced two fingers up her soaked entrance, sensing she was close, and slipped them inside.

"F–fuck—Diana—"

Her stomach rolled, hearing her name leave Faye's lips. She flicked her tongue right where Faye needed it, her fingers giving that extra friction to push her over the edge.

Faye cried out, legs trembling and locking around Diana's head. She continued to roll over her clit, dipping lower and replacing her fingers with her tongue. Warm liquid flooded her mouth, and she groaned at the sweet taste, gripping Faye's thighs and pulling her closer. She looked up to find Faye watching her through half-closed eyelids. When their gazes locked, Faye groaned again, her muscles contracting underneath Diana.

Diana passed her tongue lazily over her, evidence of her orgasm coating her cheeks, then propped herself on her elbows, taking her in.

Faye followed her movement, still breathing heavily. "That was intense."

Diana planted a kiss on the inside of her thigh, caught between quiet disbelief and pure satisfaction.

"I don't think I've mentioned this before," Faye

started, voice gravelly. "But you're so fucking hot." She gave her a goofy half-grin. "Seriously, though. How is it legal for someone to be that attractive?"

"You flatter me." Diana pushed herself up further. "But I'm not finished with you yet."

Faye sat up too, gripping the material of Diana's dress and wrapping it around her fingers. "If you think I'm going to let you out of here without taking this off again, you're sorely mistaken."

The hesitation must've shown on Diana's face before she could squash it. Faye's smile faded. "What's wrong, Diana?"

Now the question had been put to her, the fear became real. Tangible. Sticking to the roof of her mouth like glue.

What *was* wrong?

She'd always been able to separate sex from relationships. If she hadn't got the stress relief from somewhere with all her work pressures, she'd have imploded. But the encounters were routine. Emotionless. Controlled. One-night stands that Diana never thought about again.

But the woman in front of her was different.

There was something else there that Diana didn't want to touch. An essence so bright and colourful, she feared what opening herself up to it might do. She needed to be in control. If she were in control, she would be fine. Keeping it close, closed, kept her safe.

But the essence still flickered regardless, unbothered

by Diana's fear.

Diana didn't really know what to do with that. Whenever she thought about it too hard, it sparked a prickling feeling up her spine like she was being watched without her knowledge.

Because they both knew their arrangement was temporary. So why was she giving it all so much weight?

She focused on the kind, curious eyes searching her face. Her voice came out soft, embarrassingly so, and she tried not to grimace as the words left her lips. "I haven't let anyone touch me for a long time."

"Oh." Faye loosened her grip on Diana's dress. "I'm sorry. I shouldn't have been so pushy."

"It's okay. You didn't know."

Faye traced a finger over the lace running over her abdomen. It was quiet for a moment. Then she asked, "Why didn't you say anything?"

She could have. She'd had ample opportunity, and Faye had been so honest with her. But it was hard to explain when she didn't know the answer herself.

"I'm not sure." When Faye looked up at her, she forced herself to dig deeper. "I keep to myself a lot of the time. It's comfortable, and I don't tend to spend time outside of my comfort zone. As new as this is for you after your operation, I suppose, it's also relatively new to me, too. Something I'm realising right now."

The admission started her pulse racing, and she adjusted herself, taking a seat beside Faye. All her earlier confidence had been eaten away by fear. She wasn't the pantsuit powerhouse people expected of her. Not really. Not anymore. Maybe she never had been.

But Faye cupped her hand, bringing it to her lips and kissing it. "Thanks for being open with me." She held her hand in her lap, tracing delicately with her thumb. "It's fine if you don't want to undress or receive from me. The last thing I want is to make you feel uncomfortable after how at ease you've made me feel."

Was that what she wanted? No reciprocation? The slick heat still gathered between her thighs told her otherwise. The very idea of Faye touching her got her pulse quickening again, but for other reasons. It was just…frightening.

Most of Diana's hook-ups were happy to take what she was offering and leave it at that. It suited her fine. Faye wasn't like that. She was passionate and brave, wanting everything, wanting to dive in headfirst and deal with the repercussions later. Some of that fearlessness Diana had lost somewhere after her divorce.

"I do enjoy that side of sex too," Diana continued, meeting Faye's gaze. "I just…"

"You want to take it slow," Faye finished, her eyes brightening. "Oh! *Riiiight*. I totally get it now."

"What?"

"That's what your whole 'taking it slow' thing is about, right?"

Diana opened her mouth to protest, but her brain hijacked the words. She'd always thought of taking things slow as something she enjoyed, but maybe it *was* a way to protect herself. *Interesting.*

"Honestly?" She gave a small smile. "Maybe."

"Well, just to be crystal clear. The ball's in your court. Do whatever makes you comfortable. I'll let you take the reins on that one." She wet her lips. "As for me, well, I'll tell you if anything hurts or whatever. But I'm here for all of it. Fast, slow, do whatever you want to me."

Desire pulled low in Diana's belly, awakening that burning hunger only satisfied by touch. Her attention fell to Faye's cleavage, her abdomen, her open lingerie, revealing her pink and wet from their previous encounter.

"Fuck." Faye's voice stuck in her throat. "I love it when you look at me like that."

Diana held her gaze a moment longer. Then she propped herself up, positioning herself over her. Faye opened her legs, welcoming it, and Diana bent to nip her lip.

"You better get used to it," she murmured.

She kissed her hard, letting their bodies melt together. Faye ground her pelvis against her, just the thin material of Diana's dress separating them, and hot jolts of electricity pulsed at the contact.

As they pulled back for breath, Faye combed her fingers through Diana's hair, tight enough to tug at her scalp. Those deep blue eyes stunned her, touching something in her chest.

"I don't think I ever will get used to it," Faye said.

As Diana's heart raced with a mix of conflicting emotions, she didn't know if she ever would either.

So she did the only thing she knew. She kissed her again, and again, her fingers slipping into her with ease, slick, wet and still sensitive. There was nothing slow this time. No resistance. Diana kissed her hard. She fucked her harder. She wanted her spent and soaking and calling out her name.

She was tired of thinking and thinking and thinking. She let her body do all the talking. Silencing those voices in the back of her head. Ignoring the way her heart bloomed for the woman in front of her. She had it under control.

She had it all under control.

EIGHTEEN

Faye

Faye focused on the feeling. The air in her lungs. The energy it gave her. She breathed out, letting the calming voice of Senhor Arenoso guide her through the movements. She repeated the process one more time, then opened her eyes, the darkness evolving into the earthy space of Senhor Arenoso's hut. The light feeling in her chest spread outward, and she sighed.

"How do you feel?" he asked.

"Good. Really good."

His moustache lifted as he smiled. "I can sense a real difference in you."

She wanted to say it was the guided meditation and

soul-searching she'd been doing, but surely body-defying orgasms were great at unblocking chakras too?

For two nights in a row, Diana and Faye had spent the evening together, tangled in the sheets and talking until the early morning. She tried not to mind that Diana would sneak back to her place instead of sleeping over, but lying in bed with the scent of her everywhere kept her awake, thinking, wondering, dreaming.

This is temporary, she reminded herself, trying to stop the fluttering feeling gathering in her heart.

"I can feel the difference," she replied, hoping he didn't notice the pause.

He nodded, pushing a fresh glass of water towards her. "You should drink."

She took a few grateful sips, then let her gaze drift to the sea. She really did love it here. The soothing lull of the waves, the birds chattering as they ferried overhead, the hot sun warming her skin. Being on the island was exactly what she needed to get back to her old self—well, better than that, it was exactly what she needed for a *new* and improved Faye. One who traded sudoku for socialising. One who felt good in her body and shed the comfort of her bed for new adventures.

That had nothing to do with Diana.

Alright, maybe it did a little bit.

She couldn't find it in her to mind. Endorphins pumped through her veins, lifting her higher. Mission accomplished—or at least, mission definitely on the right track. How could anyone argue against that?

After saying goodbye to Senhor Arenoso and slipping on Carla's pineapple sunglasses, she stepped out into the Portuguese sunshine. The light glistened off the waves as they rolled onto the shore, with people already enjoying the water. Her skin itched to join them and feel the cool relief herself, but she checked her watch.

She didn't want to be late for her date.

Flutters gathered in her belly at the thought of seeing Diana. She picked her head up as she approached the courtyard, the bustling noises filling her ears. A blended aroma of seafood, garlic, and fresh bread carried on the wind. The square was covered with various stalls and people browsing the market. Through the blur of people, she spotted Quin sitting by the reception, scowling at their phone. They looked up as she approached, quickly tucking their phone into their cargo shorts.

"Hey. Everything alright?" she asked.

"Yeah." They held out their hand, and Faye pulled them to their feet. "Just my dad."

"What has he said?"

"Nothing new."

"Quin." Her voice softened. "You can talk to me, you know."

They scratched their head, avoiding her gaze. "He just…doesn't understand me."

"What do you mean?"

"He thinks I'm confused. About being non-binary. He doesn't get it. When he found out about my top surgery…he threatened to disown me. Sandy Springs was kinda my last chance to 'sort my life out'."

"Quin, that's…" She looked at them. Still. Quiet. Then she pulled them into a big hug, breathing in their woody scent. When Quin wrapped their arms around her too, she squeezed harder. "I'm sorry your dad makes you feel bad about yourself. But you shouldn't change who you are. Not for anyone. Not even family. Have you thought about not talking to him while you're here?" she suggested. "It seems like whenever you do talk, he puts you in a bad mood. And a break might do you some good."

They moved out of the way as two young kids skipped past with melting ice-cream cones.

"Thanks, Faye, but we're trying to meet in the middle. He's my dad…and it's one of the agreements to check on my progress. I can't really get out of it." Quin sighed, pulling a hand through their Afro. "Anyway, I fancy catching one of Riley's painting classes, if you want to join?"

Faye filed the conversation for later. "I can't today. I have plans this afternoon. But I could tomorrow?"

"Mrs Robinson?" They raised their eyebrows. "Hell, yeah. Up top."

"I'm not high-fiving that."

"Come on. Don't leave me hangin'."

Faye rolled her eyes but slapped her hand against theirs. "You wanna meet up later?"

"Absolutely. Give me all the goss. I want to know everything. And I mean *everything*." Their voice softened. "Hey. I don't suppose you've seen Blondie lately, have you?"

"Molly? Diana said she hasn't been feeling well. Why?"

Quin bit their lip.

"What did you do, Quin?"

"I didn't want her to get ill. I was just trying to be the best wing-pal ever and might have got carried away." They ran their fingers through their hair again. "Is she alright? What did she say? Oh god. I didn't mean to poison her. I don't want to go to prison."

Poison her? "Hey, it's fine." Faye grasped their shoulder. "She's just been sick. Diana thinks she caught a bug or something. What happened?"

"I…uh…" They scratched the back of their neck. "I told her the water had healing properties and if she drank it, she wouldn't wrinkle."

"Quin!"

"I know. I'm sorry. But it worked, didn't it? You have another hot date."

She shook her head, relieved they hadn't done something more stupid.

"I swear I didn't know it would make her ill. Although you should've seen the way she guzzled it down."

They both cracked a smile before bursting into laughter. "You're terrible."

"Or am I a terrific wing-pal?"

"Maybe a bit of both."

Quin glanced over Faye's shoulder, their grin widening, and she turned to find Diana on the other side of the courtyard. Diana looked up from a stall selling handwoven blankets, and their eyes locked, sparks shooting across her skin.

"Don't let me keep you," Quin said. "Come find me later."

They gave Faye a wink and left, heading towards the painting studio. Diana slinked towards her. The slight breeze tousled her hair, and her silk navy-and-white blouse and shorts combination swayed around her hips. Her skin held a bronze tint from days in the sunshine, and a pair of oversized square sunglasses covered her eyes.

"You look amazing," Faye said, openly admiring her.

Diana's lips pulled up into that signature Diana smile, and Faye's belly flip-flopped.

The woman was perfection.

"Nice sunglasses," Diana commented. "Very…fun."

"Oh, yeah." Faye tugged them from the top of her head, inspecting the pineapples. "Mine broke the first day here. As soon as I stepped off the plane. So I'm borrowing these."

Amusement pulled at Diana's mouth. "Shall we go?"

After purchasing some fresh fruit and a few cakes from the market, they made their way through the throngs of people and headed up the gravel path towards the ruins. Faye figured she might as well make the most of the time Molly wasn't around; as much as she loved spending her evenings with Diana, it did feel a little like she was dating a vampire.

Well, not *dating*, obviously. But whatever this summer fling, impending heartbreak was categorised as. Fuck buddies? Diana was more sophisticated than the term implied, but nothing seemed quite appropriate.

She pushed those thoughts aside and tuned into the present, as she'd practised in Senhor Arenoso's sessions. The waves crashing in the distance, the soft slap of their feet against the path, and Diana's intoxicating scent drifting in on the breeze.

Faye snuck a glance at her, admiring her strong cheekbones and pointed chin. Her hair curled in short flicks around her face, one side tucked behind an ear, revealing a collection of gold hoop earrings that caught the sunlight.

"Do you have any other piercings?" Faye asked. She heard the undertone behind her question and scrambled, trying to force the image of intimate piercings out of her head. "I always wanted my belly button pierced when I was younger, but I can't do that now."

"Because of your stoma?"

"Yeah. It can cause infection and complications. It's just not worth the risk."

"I'm sorry."

"It's alright. There are worse things than not having my navel pierced." She laughed. "I think it was more to do with Britney's influence than anything else, anyway."

Diana chuckled. "I didn't picture you as a Britney

fan."

"Who isn't a Britney fan?" They fell into step on the worn trail. "You can't tell me you don't sing along to the classics. I can totally see you tearing up 'Hit Me Baby One More Time'."

Diana laughed again, and the feeling lifted Faye like she was walking on the clouds. "My singing is certainly not something you want to hear."

"It is."

She glanced at her. "Why? It's awful."

"I don't mind. I think it's a nice thing. Whenever someone sings, they're happy. It's like a human phenomenon that slips through without us realising it. At least that's what my dads say." She shrugged. "But they're also hardcore Britney fans, so who knows?"

They rounded a few bushes, which were covered in flowers, their white-and-pink petals turning towards the sun.

"What are your dads like?" Diana asked.

"David's a history teacher and Lukas is an artist. They drive me crazy, but they're great. David might be coming to celebrate the Fire Ceremony at the end of the course." Before she could ask if Diana would have anyone joining her, as per the Sandy Springs tradition, a bundle of orange darted across the path. "Oh my god! Look. It's a cat." She fell to her knees, letting out little kisses and chirps.

The cat peered at her from under a bush, the swishing of its tail twitching the leaves.

"Come on, kitty," Faye encouraged, creeping a little closer.

The cat slinked out from under the greenery and tentatively sniffed her hand. After another sniff, he rubbed his soft head against Faye's knuckles, and she beamed. *Friends. Sweet.*

She turned to grin at Diana, who was watching the encounter from a safe distance with curiosity. "Come say hello."

With the same cautiousness as the feline, Diana moved closer. "Do you do this with every animal you meet?" she teased, bending next to her.

"Pretty much."

The ginger cat switched his attention to the new arrival, taking his time to assess the status of friend or foe. When he relented, brushing against her, Diana let out a little laugh of delight. How could she be so adorable and so hot at the same time?

The cat scampered off, and they both rose to their feet.

"Do you have any pets?" Faye asked as they carried on along the path. The sun hid behind the clouds, allowing them a brief respite from the warm rays.

Diana shook her head. "No. But there were cats at the farm my dad worked at, and I used to play with them sometimes."

Faye grinned, imagining a young Diana chasing cats around the barn. "I love cats. I have four."

"Four?!"

"Yup. Biscuit, Mochi, Angus, and Taco."

"I don't know why I'm surprised. It makes perfect sense."

"Yeah, you'll have to…" The words died on her tongue. Diana couldn't meet them sometime. Even if it were something she wanted to do, she was going back to America, and Faye back to England. She'd be naïve to think otherwise. She swallowed the lump in her throat. The harsh truth stung like someone had torn off the world's largest wax strip on the back of her legs. "You'll…er, have to get a cat. When you're home. Cats are great."

Cats are great? She repressed the urge to scoff at herself. *Smooth recovery, Faye.*

The hill curved upwards, the ruins poking their stone heads out of the trees in the distance. Faye directed her attention to the different flowers and plants on the way, pointing them out to Diana. She needed distraction.

As the incline steepened, she pushed through the burn in her muscles, the path turning to stone steps taking them higher. She actually enjoyed the feeling. The pain. The breathlessness. Her body proving it wasn't always a complete failure. She always erred on the side of caution, always doubting, always preparing for the worst. But how far could she go without giving up? The fresh sea air encouraged her to go further, stand taller, be more, and so she did, relishing the ache in her legs until they reached the top.

She wiped her forehead, pulling the water from her

bag and gulping it down. She didn't realise she'd left Diana behind until she joined her a minute later.

"If that was a race, I guess I lost," Diana said, turning to look out over the view.

"Sorry." Faye managed between breaths. "I got a little carried away." She tried to hide the tightness in her chest and the dizziness between her ears. It hurt, but the sense of accomplishment pumping through her veins overpowered the pain. "That felt good." She felt Diana's gaze on her and turned to meet it. "What?"

But Diana just smiled, making her way into the crumbling castle. Faye's focus fell on the slow swish of her hips as she followed, the silk flowing around Diana like water.

Inside the ruins, Diana tilted her head back to look at the tower, the windowless hole where Princess Inês was rumoured to sit.

"Would you live here?" Faye asked.

Without breaking her gaze, Diana answered, "On the island or here in the ruins?"

Faye imagined Diana's apartment. Judging by the woman's exquisite taste in clothes, it had to be grand. Large open windows, marble counters, expensive furniture. Why she was choosing to spend any time with Faye was mindboggling. *She probably has nothing better to do.*

The sick feeling tainted her mouth again. *Stop ruining this, brain.*

She placed a hand on the cool stone, trying to ground

herself. "Would you live in the ruins," she clarified.

"It's a little…sparse for my liking."

Faye pushed off the wall, letting her eyes wander the empty space. "Oh, I don't know. A lick of paint, some light reconstruction work…I think it'd scrub up nicely. Realtors would go bananas over the view alone. So what if it's missing a roof?"

"I suppose the archways are still surprisingly intact."

Faye ducked inside, waving her arms like a fairy godmother. "A giant bookshelf here, an even bigger sofa by the window, some cosy, fluffy rugs. I'm not sure about the empty space over there, though."

Diana joined her, pursing her lips. "A bar would be nice. Then I can sit and drink my cosmopolitan while you do your sudoku."

Though said in a playful way, her reply warmed Faye's cheeks, sending sharp tingles across her skin. She tried to hide her body's response, playing into the game. "A good addition. Might I request a butler or three so the lady's hands don't get tired holding her glass?"

Diana hummed. "Most thoughtful. To repay your graciousness, the lady will demand a cluster of cats to fill these empty halls."

"A cluster? That would be exquisite!" Faye laughed, surprised by Diana's willingness to indulge the fantasy. She took her hand and pulled her into the centre of the empty space. The ground, hard from the lack of rain, was almost like that of a sleek ballroom—if you ignored the debris in the corners and the stench of earthy moss. She wrapped her arms around Diana's waist. "Did you know they call a group of cats a clowder?"

"I did not," Diana said. "But I'm not surprised that you know that."

"I'm full of useless animal facts, my queen." She spun Diana, a little less graciously than their time dancing in the courtyard. "But thou dazzle me with thy kindness."

"You're very cute." The corner of Diana's mouth lifted. "But I thought you didn't enjoy Shakespeare?"

She remembered. Warmth filled Faye's chest. She laughed. "I don't enjoy him. But that's what I imagine rich people in his day spoke like."

"Probably not Princess Inês."

"Probably not."

Diana tugged their bodies closer, caressing Faye's hips. The subtle smirk curling her mouth made Faye want to kiss it off her gorgeous face.

She knew that look. Surely, Diana didn't want to fool around here, did she?

Her thoughts became tangled, lost in Diana's touch as she explored her with her strong hands, taking her time, her steady gaze assessing every reaction. Faye's breath became ragged, anticipation already slicking wetness between her thighs. Whatever game they were playing was over. Faye only had one thing on her mind. Keep teasing her like this, and she'd be begging Diana in no time.

Diana brushed hair away over Faye's shoulder and leaned closer. The warm breath of air tickling Faye's neck turned her on further, and she wound her fingers into Diana's blouse.

Diana pressed a kiss to her pressure point before dragging her mouth over the sensitive skin. Faye let out a whimper, and Diana sucked just hard enough to weaken her knees.

"Do you think the princess would approve of this?" Diana whispered.

Her clit pinged, arousal dripping where she needed Diana the most. She swallowed. "I…I think she would, yeah."

Diana kissed her hard, all traces of softness and teasing gone. Faye welcomed it, gasping into her mouth, her hands threading through her hair. Her whole body held taut, winding tighter with every touch and feel of her soft lips.

Any fears or hesitation she'd had vanished. She needed this. She needed Diana. Nothing was going to stop her.

Somehow, they ended up against the wall, their hands squeezing and caressing, leaving no part untouched. Faye groaned, trying to grind her aching pelvis against Diana's. Her clit pounded so hard, she thought she might pass out if she didn't relieve it.

Without breaking their kisses, Diana gripped Faye's shirt, loosening the buttons one by one with her slender fingers. Then she pressed her lips to Faye's chest, her sternum, lower with every inch of exposed skin. She cupped her breasts, teasing her nipples through the thin fabric of her bra, and Faye tilted her head back. Why not indulge? Why not enjoy it? Their time was limited, so why the hell not?

There was a crackle in the distance. Or maybe it was fireworks conjured up by her brain.

Completely dizzy with want, she cupped Diana's chin, bringing her mouth back to hers. She ached to touch her, to feel her, to see if she was as hot for her as she was for Diana, but she kept her hands on her waist, letting her mouth do the talking.

But then there was the crackle again. Louder. And this time, a deep voice following it.

Oh, shit.

Faye didn't want to stop. Her body begged her not to. But Diana must have heard the noise too, because she broke their kiss, pushing her against the wall. Another wave of arousal washed over her. The close proximity. Diana's gorgeous, plump mouth. Those talented fingers resting against her sternum, and what she knew she could do with them.

Their chests heaved together as they listened, breathless, for anything besides the birds chirping in the woods behind the ruins.

When nothing followed, Faye nipped Diana's lip between her teeth, eager to continue.

"Não há nada aqui."

A loud crack echoed through the building, and they froze.

"Onde?"

The gruff voice was looking for something. Faye's Portuguese lessons were finally coming in handy.

"*Eu disse-te.*" The man huffed. "*Aqui não há nada.*"

"What are they saying?" Diana whispered, and Faye shivered, still aroused by her proximity.

"He's looking for something." A lightbulb flared in her mind. "Wait. What if he's after the birds?" Without giving it much thought, she followed the voice, using the crumbling structure to shield her from view.

The sound came from the woods behind them. She waited, feeling Diana come up behind her.

"What are you doing?"

"Just having a look."

A blur of black moved between the trunks, and Faye called out, "Hey!"

The man snapped his head up and sprinted in the other direction, back down the hill. Adrenaline still pumping from Diana's touch, she didn't think; she just ran. Clearly, this man was up to no good. Why would he run otherwise? Something had to be done, and for the first time in a long time, she knew she was the person to do it.

She leapt over the roots, weaving between the trees, her open shirt flapping. There wasn't really a path, and the bushes and branches reached out, making it difficult to navigate.

Luckily, the man also had the same problem, and she started to gain on him. She kept her eyes pinned to his back. Unassuming khaki shorts, a black T-shirt, and a rucksack that clunked with every step, helping Faye keep track as they weaved through the undergrowth.

"Hey!" she called again. "Wait!"

But then her foot caught on a tree root, and she stumbled. A branch whipped her across the face. She spun and cried out, her tired legs burning, unable to right herself. Maybe she'd overdone it with the hike earlier, or maybe Diana's touch had jellified them too far. Whatever the case, she tumbled downhill, thorns and branches digging and pinching at her, until she finally rolled to a stop.

She groaned, her face throbbing. Spluttering blood from her busted lip, she rolled onto her back, the taste metallic and sharp in her mouth. The blue sky looked down at her with pity, as the thump of the man's footsteps grew quieter in the distance.

NINETEEN

Diana

Diana squinted as the sun poured through the windows and raised her arm to cover her eyes. Riley was gesticulating wildly as she walked the length of her studio, but her words didn't reach Diana's ears. Though she hadn't left Faye's side until she was completely satisfied she would be alright, she couldn't stop the image of her bloody and dirt-stained face popping into her mind. They'd gone to Riley afterwards, Faye adamant that the man she'd chased through the woods had something to do with the poaching on the island. While trying to find Faye's borrowed pineapple sunglasses, lost somewhere along the way, they'd uncovered a messy annotated map of the island and a penknife with the initials *DS* carved into the wooden hilt. Riley admitted the behaviour was suspicious, and she'd have her team look into it, but Diana had also seen the way her cool eyes had fallen on them both, curious, questioning.

The two of them had hardly been subtle that night, dancing in the courtyard, but were the two of them *that* obvious?

She swallowed, trying to steady her breath and focus on Riley. She hadn't heard a word she'd said. She glanced at Molly, perched on a stool to her left, engrossed and nodding, paintbrush in hand. The others in the small class mirrored Molly's enthusiasm, leaving Diana feeling like a misbehaving schoolchild.

Since when had she been so easily distracted?

She knew the answer, of course. Ever since that beautiful brunette had walked into the tiny little bar by the docks—nervous, and windswept by the storm—and her striking eyes found Diana's.

The same woman who had continued to push and pull Diana like the moon captured the tide. Who continued to surprise her and challenge her, threatening to tug at the bonds of control Diana worked hard to keep close. She'd loved the nights they spent together, when the world outside fell away, leaving them caught in this dance of Faye panting and cursing and Diana eating up every second of it. But every second more chipped at her resolve, and she was afraid of what that might do.

Riley's gaze flicked to hers. She hoped she hadn't

missed something important. But then Riley brought her hands together, her attention moving to the rest of the students.

"With all that being said…" She grinned, popping a dimple in her cheek. "Painting is so much more than studying all the different techniques. It's about emotion. Passion. About finding something inside that can only be expressed through colour at the end of a brush. You might just surprise yourself with how cathartic you find the process, and what you might discover." Her eyes landed on Diana again before moving away.

Was that intentional? Or was Diana becoming paranoid now, too?

She pressed her lips together. Riley was probably worried about the poacher situation. Why would she care who Diana was sleeping with? The only person who would care was sitting to the left of her, and there was no way she was ever going to find out.

She uncrossed and crossed her leg, lengthening her spine. She had it under control. Everything was going to be fine.

When she tuned back into the room, the swish and scrape of brushes filling her ears, she realised she needed to start doing something—but what exactly was she supposed to be doing?

Her eyes flicked to the whiteboard, where Riley must've scribbled some tips during her speech. Reading the title, she tried to hide her scoff.

Painting from the heart.

This was the precise thing she'd wanted to avoid. Unlocking that trapdoor and diving into all the parts of her life she didn't want to think about had already roped her into deep and meaningful sessions with Dr Marcos. Anything "from the heart" threatened more complication—and she still needed to write that bloody letter to her mother. Though what good it would do, knowing her mum would never read it, she didn't know. It sounded like unnecessary torture.

From the heart. She chewed her lip. Her paintbrush hovered over the canvas. The swishing movements of those around her, clearly not suffering the same predicament as Diana, only irritated her further.

She dipped into the blue paint. Why was this so difficult? Why couldn't she think of anything?

She closed her eyes. The darkness morphed into the familiar sight of dark lashes framing dreamy pools of turquoise and green. The most beautiful colour, which, try as she might, Diana could never replicate with a brush. Nor that perfect, soft mouth parting as her eyelids fluttered closed, words spilling like prayers from her chest. *"Oh, yes—Diana. Like that. Just like that."*

Heat flushed between her legs at the memory. Crossing and uncrossing them did little to dull the ache in her pelvis, and she cursed. *Is this what a midlife crisis feels like?*

She'd clearly defined anything that had to do with Faye and her heart. So why was Faye's face the first thing she thought of?

That wasn't from the heart, she argued. It was from a more promiscuous and demanding body part that pulsed between her legs.

When Riley had questioned Faye about the man in the woods, Faye had insisted "*she had a feeling*". She was so sure, trusting her gut instinct, and Diana could hardly argue with that. Perhaps because the young woman was so determined and passionate, or perhaps because the same feeling, although for different reasons, echoed in her own body. A feeling that whatever was happening between her and Faye had the ability to consume her in ways she hadn't thought possible. Call it gut instinct. Call it sheer human stupidity. The feeling lingered all the same.

You're getting weak in your age, a voice with the same bite as Jason's warned her.

She scoffed, not hiding the sound as well this time, judging by the curious glances from her classmates. But she wasn't going to start listening to any voice resembling that grumpy, narcissistic fart's. She hadn't listened when they were married, and she wasn't going to start now.

Annoyed by the reminder of her balding ex-husband, she squeezed the paintbrush between her fingertips, finally pressing it to the canvas.

A blue splodge marred the white, a blemish on an otherwise pristine surface. She spread it from side to side, then in circles, expanding the mess outwards. The swirls made her think of Faye's eyes again, and her hand stilled. Faye held so much power in the way she looked at her, like she'd hung the stars in the sky herself. It disarmed her, flattered her, touched a place that Diana kept locked away. But Faye, in all her innocence and passion, had breezed past her barriers without her realising.

She dipped the end into the paint again, adding more blue, more circles, until they no longer resembled Faye's captivating irises, but ocean waves. She pressed harder, and her strokes darted across the white, frenzied and choppy. She could feel the froth lapping at her ankles, hear her mother's joyful cries as they galloped towards the sea. It didn't matter if Diana's dress got wet or how loud she screamed, her mother held her hand. She was safe.

Taking a step back, she narrowed her gaze at the blue monstrosity in front of her.

God. She hated the sea.

Except she didn't, not really. She hated everything it reminded her of, everything she'd lost. Ever since her mother's hand had been ripped from hers, along with her warmth and love, she hadn't felt safe. Not with her father. Not with Jason. Not even with work.

That realisation rocked her, and tears pricked her eyelids. But she wasn't about to start sobbing in front of people, so she gritted her teeth and continued painting.

When Riley called the end of the class, Diana's wrist and fingers ached. She released the paintbrush from her iron grip and flexed her joints.

"Don't worry if you haven't finished yet," Riley said, tucking her long blonde hair behind her ears. "You can come and work on your masterpiece in any of your free afternoon slots. If you've finished, leave them here to dry, and you can collect them later. Don't forget to sign them!"

"Whoa. Mum." Molly stepped towards her. "That's awesome. A bit scary but…awesome."

Diana pressed her lips together, hoping she wouldn't pry further. She didn't want to talk about the giant wave-turned-monster blocking out the sun or the thick darkness filling the sky. She wasn't even sure people could see what she intended through all the hurried strokes and blurs of colour—not that it mattered, anyway.

So she misdirected, leaning over towards Molly's work, where a giant sun took centre stage, beaming its golden light on a girl lying on a doughnut-shaped lilo. Her daughter had a talent for the paintbrush; the layers of colours shimmering on the water were truly impressive—but painting from the heart? She wasn't sure if she'd hit the mark. One thing not up for debate was the complete contrast to Diana's doom and gloom.

A gnawing feeling itched at her, making her want to cover up her painting or flip it over. She didn't want others to see it—to see her—but luckily Molly continued talking.

"I'm always happier in the sun. You were right about that. Everything feels better here, doesn't it?" Molly glanced at her, and Diana gave her the most genuine smile she could muster. "I think everyone's heart wants them to be happy. And I think being in the sun makes me happy."

It wasn't quite the jaw-shattering revelation Riley

had perhaps expected of them. But Diana wasn't going to scold Molly for opting out of the soul search. From the way she'd admired Diana's work, and had chatted with the others in the class, her daughter did seem…lighter. Ultimately, that's what Diana had hoped this excursion would bring. In comparison, Diana's world was still spinning too fast, her quick pulse making her unsteady on her feet.

"Great work, ladies." Riley appeared behind them, nodding as she studied their work. "Wonderful use of light and shadow, Molly. You're a natural."

Molly glowed.

What would "painting from the heart" mean to Faye? Would she find herself as surprised as Diana at what might emerge? Or would she not hesitate to show herself?

"This is very emotive, Diana." She turned to find Riley studying her work. "I can feel it jumping from the page."

Diana brushed her hands over her apron. "Thank you."

Riley lingered a little longer, and she cringed, wondering what she saw. Just as she opened her mouth to say something, a quick knock sounded, and Ella appeared at the doorway, in a burst of energy.

"Hey, everyone! How was your class?" A black swimsuit hugged her curves, her lower half hidden by a pair of beige cargo shorts that were the mirror of Riley's.

Riley left Diana's side to greet her girlfriend with a

kiss on the cheek.

"Now, who is up for some surfing?" Ella asked. "If I can ride a wave, there's hope for everyone. Right, babe?"

Riley nodded. "It's true."

As a murmured discussion sprang up in the class, Molly huffed.

"Absolutely not," she said. "The island water is poisonous. I should know." She shot a glare across the room towards Quin, who quickly packed up their bag and rushed out.

"I wouldn't recommend drinking saltwater anyway, love," Diana said.

"I'd much rather sunbathe. What do you say?"

"You want me to join you?" She tried to hide the surprise in her voice.

"Why not? We might as well while we're here, right?"

Warmth filled her chest. Though not the most direct invitation, it was progress. Maybe coming to Sandy Springs had been the right move after all.

Just disregard the Faye factor, and everything is fine.

They left their paintings to dry and followed the rest of the class, stepping out into the humid air.

"Where would you like to go?" Diana asked.

Molly looked out at the horizon. "We could go to the beach. Then we'd have five-star entertainment watching people failing to surf."

The beach.

She'd already braved the sand this trip, walking along the shore with Faye, so why did the thought still make her stomach twist into knots?

She cursed inwardly. Her emotions had been much easier to control before she stepped onto this infuriating island. The topsy-turviness of it all was making her seasick.

But she wasn't going to let this get in the way of her and Molly bonding, so she nodded. "Sounds wonderful, love."

They walked along the pebbly steps, passing Senhor Arenoso meditating outside his hut. Molly happily filled in the silence with chatter about the class, and Diana tried to focus on the new ease that was growing between them, instead of the irrational fear creeping up her throat.

You have this under control.

But when sand crept onto the path, she stopped at the edge of the vast, sandy beach, her sandals sticking like glue. Molly continued walking, her curls bouncing. She paused, glancing behind her.

"Are you coming?" she called.

You have this under control.

"Mum." Her voice was louder. Closer. But she couldn't see. The darkness and the monster had merged into one, the painting becoming real. "Are you alright?"

A hand grasped hers, and she focused on her breathing, as Riley had guided them in yoga classes many times before. *In...and out.* After a few rounds, she opened her eyes, the brightness blinding her.

Molly squeezed her hand. Concern creased her brow.

Diana pulled in another deep breath. "I'm…fine. Come on."

Molly tugged her forward. Her feet sank into the soft sand, and she breathed out shakily. If Molly thought she'd lost her marbles, she never commented, but kept leading them further towards the sea.

Molly picked a spot away from other beachgoers and set down her bag. Letting go of Diana's hand, she pulled out her pink towel and laid it on the sand. She sat at one end, patting for Diana to take the other.

The crash of waves reached Diana's ears, and she watched, hypnotised by the movement. How could the sea be so soothing and so terrifying at the same time?

"Mum," Molly pressed. "What's going on?"

Patience never was her daughter's strong suit, but she supposed she'd made her wait long enough. She brushed the towel with her fingertips.

"I've never really spoken about your grandma much, have I?"

Molly's nose wrinkled. "Granny Jane?"

Not that old crowbag, Diana wanted to say, blinking away the unwelcome image of Jason's mum, the tight-lipped vulture. "No. Your other grandma. My mother." She swallowed the lump in her throat. "Charlotte."

"Charlotte?" Molly echoed. "I don't think I ever knew Grandma's name."

That landed a blow to Diana's chest. She'd been so afraid of her mother's memory, she'd prevented Molly from ever knowing her. That stung.

She tensed her jaw, pushing the emotions back under the surface. "Yes. I'm sorry I've never really spoken about her. I…it's painful for me."

"Is that what your painting was about? But…I don't understand."

Diana could see the cogs turning in Molly's head, trying to piece it together.

"The seaside used to be my happy place." At Molly's look of encouragement, she kept going. "Every summer, we'd go to the beach, and they were some of the best summers of my life. Mum and I would spend hours combing the shores for pretty shells and stones to decorate our sandcastles." She breathed deeply, letting the memories fill her. The cold English sea beneath her feet, Sarge splashing them as the dog catapulted through the waves. Her mother's laughter as she tipped her head back, tugging Diana after the giant furball. *"Come on, Di. First one to catch him gets an ice cream!"*

"When she died, everything changed." She blinked back the tears that threatened. "We never went to the beach again. At first, I was so upset. It was something we'd always looked forward to every year, but now…well, I'm glad. It's one of the few places my dad didn't taint with bad memories. But in a way, that makes it harder too. I miss her."

Her voice broke on the last word, and a treacherous tear slipped down her cheek. Her chest ached, the crater she'd kept covered for years hissing and spilling out hurt into every fibre of her being.

"I sometimes wonder how different my life would have been if she hadn't died. If I'd have been a better person or a better mother. I tried my best, Molly. I know that might not always have been good enough. I—"

"Mum," Molly said forcefully. "You are good enough."

The words hung in the air for a moment, silencing Diana's racing thoughts. She drew in a few shaky breaths. *In...and out.*

Molly rested her hands on the sand. "I had no idea you felt like this. You're always so...put together."

A bark of laughter left Diana's lips. "I can assure you, I'm not. My time here has been particularly testing."

"I like this side of you. Tell me about it."

Had she said too much? Diana shifted position. She could hardly mention the knots Faye had her tangled up in. The fear and excitement that being around her brought. But having this conversation with Molly was therapeutic. *Sorry, Marco Marcos.*

"It seems I haven't fully grieved my mother," she admitted. "And your grandad and I haven't spoken in a long time."

"What? Why?"

Diana sighed, looking out to the sea. The surfing class were gathered by the shallows, each figure carrying a board by their sides. "Our relationship is complicated. There are a lot of things that have gone unsaid throughout the years. I understand he was also grieving when my mother died, but I was only ten and…"

The slamming of the photo album rang in her ears. "*We have to move on now. This is for your own good.*"

She shook the sound away. "I wish I could show you some pictures of her."

Molly smiled. "I'd like that." At the conflicted expression on Diana's face, she asked, "What's wrong?"

"I don't know where they are. Grandad hid them from me."

"He did *what?*" The anger in her daughter's tone jolted her. "Mum. He can't do that. That's not fair." She grabbed Diana's hand. "I'll go get them. I'm sure we can find them together."

The determination in her eyes reminded Diana of a younger version of herself. The comparison warmed her, but then she admitted what she'd been afraid to voice. "I'm not sure they'll still be there, love."

"He can't throw them away. He can't do that. They must be there somewhere." Molly huffed. "We'll turn that house upside down if we have to."

A joyful holler echoed across the beach, and they turned their heads. Ella and Riley had each caught a wave, spray flicking up behind their boards. The others looked on as they slid onto the shore, their expressions a mixture of eager and fearful as the demonstration turned into their own practice.

Diana was thankful to be on this side of the beach.

They watched in peaceful quiet as the group swam out on their boards.

Molly laughed as a woman rose to her knees and immediately plopped into the sea with a splash. "It was a good idea. Coming here." She kept her gaze on the scene at sea, but her voice softened. "Thank you."

"You're welcome."

"Actually...I've been thinking about possibly moving abroad. I feel much happier in the sun."

Diana's mum-mode activated. What would Molly do for work? What about finishing university? How would she afford it? She forced herself to relax. Maybe Molly's painting had more depth than she realised. She shouldn't be so quick to judge. "I think you should do whatever you think would make you happy."

She felt Molly's gaze on her. "Okay. What has happened to you? No talk of me completing my studies and getting a degree? Have you been poisoned too?"

"What?"

"You're different here. More fun. Less uptight."

"Excuse me?"

Molly shrugged. "I'm just saying. The island life looks pretty good on you, too, Mum."

Unsure how to respond, she just smiled, and they relaxed into watching the surfers. A weight in Diana's chest lifted. Sitting on the sand like this, she couldn't help but think Charlotte would be proud.

But what would she think of Faye?

As the swirling blue waves morphed into those enchanting irises once more, she hoped the monster from her imagination would stay just that. But as they sat under the sunshine, conversation flowing freely, she knew there was an unsuspecting tsunami lurking that was powerful enough to sweep it all away.

TWENTY

Diana

Diana tapped her pen against the blank page. The emptiness stared back at her. She willed her hand to move, to connect her brain to the paper, but the longer she stared, the less convinced she was anything was going to happen.

Tap-tap. Tap-tap. She needed to start somewhere. With only one week of the course remaining, she could hardly put it off any longer. *Tap-tap. Tap-tap.*

With a sigh, she wrote. *Mother.*

Then she crossed the word out. Too cold. Too formal. Dr Marcos said she needed to write from the heart. She resisted the urge to roll her eyes. What was it with these people and their obsession with the major organ?

She pressed the pen to her chin, her gaze drifting to the dresser. Her heart skipped, remembering a needy, naked Faye spread atop it just a few nights ago. She'd gripped the top of her soft thighs, while Diana's tongue and lips drew out the most delectable moans Diana had ever heard. Faye had barely been able to recover before she'd craved her again, bending the woman over the dresser this time and fucking her within an inch of her life, not satisfied until Faye had tightened around her fingers, her name falling from her lips with a strangled cry.

They'd nearly broken the mirror that night, managing to catch it just before it shattered across the floor. She could have covered the expense comfortably—explaining why Faye was peppered with glass shards in places clothes normally covered wouldn't have come quite so easily.

She should be more careful. But as the days passed and the hunger in her chest only intensified, Diana had become a little reckless. Any resemblance to 'taking it slow' had receded so far, she wasn't sure if it had ever existed. As soon as the two were alone, the feeling was insatiable. Nothing felt as good as making this woman fall apart. Whatever construct she'd created to keep her level, to keep her control, was so close to slipping… Once it was gone, Diana wasn't sure what she'd do.

She should've known better than to play with fire. She should've, and yet she couldn't bring herself to regret it. But maybe that would change when their time came to an end, and they parted ways. Never kissing her again?

Never tasting her, quivering and sensitive and all Diana's?

Because in one week, she would have to say goodbye. In one week, it would all be over.

She removed the pen from her mouth, realising she was biting it. *Focus. Write the letter.*

"Okay." She breathed. "Just start."

Charlotte, she wrote, then after a beat, crossed that out too. She never called her that. Why would she start now?

So with a sad sigh, she wrote, *Mum.*

Something about the choice felt juvenile, but she *was* only a child when she died. Getting hung up on semantics was only delaying her further, but if Diana was going to write a letter to her mother, she also wanted it to be perfect. "Mum" was the chosen starting point, but looking at the stained paper, she crumpled it with a huff and tossed it in the bin by her feet. She'd have to start again.

She blamed her new addiction for the distraction, but really, she'd sat here all week facing the same problem she'd faced recently in her academic life. She didn't know what to write.

A chipper knock at the door flushed all those feelings away, and she rose, fluffing her hair in the mirror before answering it.

"Hey." Faye stepped inside, all energy and warmth, wearing her green University of Manchester T-shirt, her long hair twisted up messily. "You're not gonna believe this." She set her rucksack by the door and kicked off her shoes, mouth moving a mile a minute. "I just got back from the reserve, and little Pinkie is doing so well, they're planning to release her back into the wild in a few weeks."

Diana smiled at the affectionate nickname she'd given the parakeet. "That's wonderful news."

"It is." Then her expression sobered. "Still no update on the poaching, though. Riley says they can't go around accusing people, but I mean, why not? If people have nothing to hide, they shouldn't mind." Her attention fell to Diana's purple robe. "Whoa…You look incredible."

Diana squashed the smile threatening to rise. "I'm only wearing my shower robe."

"Exactly."

The way Faye's eyes roamed her hungrily set that sensation rising. The need to touch her, undo her, have her fingers bringing her to a climax hard enough to forget her own name.

She raised an eyebrow. "Keep looking at me like that, and you know what happens."

"God, I hope so." Her gaze held steady.

Diana had grown fond of that look. Whenever she was alone, anytime she tried to focus or relax, the memory of those eyes completely possessed her. That look did more to her than she'd care to admit out loud.

She knew the sensible explanation. Faye provided that toxic kick of dopamine and oxytocin, and Diana's love-starved body couldn't get enough. The question she didn't have an answer for: was she addicted to the feeling or to the woman?

It's just sex, she told herself. *You have this under*

control.

She stepped closer, her pulse ticking up. Her hands ached to touch her. The smooth, pale skin the sun didn't see. Her perky breasts and soft arse. The perfect waist and hips, all curves and lines she wanted to trace with her tongue, and often did.

Diana liked to tease her. She savoured the tension, the hardening nipples. Breathy pleas, cursing and demanding more. Teeth sinking into supple flesh, kisses soft and tender, everything building until Faye was wet enough to combust at the first feather-light touch of her fingers.

But tonight, she didn't want to wait.

She cupped the back of Faye's neck, the spot more accessible with her hair twisted up in its messy bun. She traced the line along her square jaw with her other hand, thumb delicate as it brushed the healing line marring her perfect bottom lip. Faye's breath hitched as their gazes locked, Diana's own heart thudding like a drum. Then, unable to ignore the pull any longer, she captured Faye's lips with hers. Her heart fluttered at the warm mouth eager to welcome her, the hint of berry lip balm drawing her deeper. Faye licked her silky tongue into her mouth, and the ache between her legs cracked like lightning.

The shift was instant. She slipped her hands under Faye's T-shirt, Faye's own hands tangling in Diana's hair, their mouths rough and hungry, no longer asking for permission but demanding it. Their bodies knew where to go now, how to touch, when to exchange hard kisses for soft ones.

It was messy, raw, real. Diana loved it.

She pressed Faye to the wall with a grunt, sliding a knee between her thighs. Faye moaned into her mouth.

"I'm running out of new places to fuck you," Diana murmured, feeling Faye shiver underneath her fingertips.

Faye released a shaky breath. "I didn't realise this was part of a checklist of yours." Her lips curled, teasing, full, perfect. So perfect, Diana couldn't resist placing a kiss on the corner where the cut was.

"I didn't hear you complaining while you made a mess on my dresser." She trailed her mouth across Faye's jaw, to her pulse point, and Faye arched underneath her. "Or when you nearly pulled the showerhead right off the wall."

"No complaining here. Just an observation."

Diana kissed her sensitive spot, just hard enough to draw another gasp from her mouth, then pulled back, taking in the breathless woman in front of her.

Cheeks pink, mouth puckered and swollen from kisses, her nipples hard and pressing through the thin T-shirt.

"My observation is that you're not wearing a bra." She cupped Faye's breasts, thumbs pinching the peaks until she cursed.

"I know how much you like it."

Those eyes looked back at her. Unafraid. Daring. Pupils blown wide. The moment stretched, something unspoken passing between them. Then Diana palmed her breasts again, harder, keeping her eyes fixed on hers.

Faye sucked in a hiss, teeth dragging across that full bottom lip.

"Do you need to change in the bathroom first?" Diana asked, rolling a nipple between her fingers. She pressed her free hand between Faye's legs, and Faye let out a whimper. "Or can I show you what I've been thinking about all day?"

"The s–second one."

Diana slipped her hand inside her shorts, her stomach tightening when she found her completely soaked. "God," she growled. "You're not wearing underwear?" Molten heat slipped between her thighs. "So wet." She circled Faye's clit, swollen beneath her fingertips. "Always so wet."

"All for you, Diana."

Faye said it so easily. Like the words wouldn't punch through Diana's ribcage and lodge straight into her heart. But unloading what that meant, why her entire body stilled, would have her last sliver of control completely slip away.

She packed those thoughts to the back of her mind and tugged Faye's shorts down her legs. Faye kicked them off, and her mouth found Diana's again, hard and fast, like she couldn't wait any longer.

"I need you so badly," she gasped. "Please."

Diana gripped her waist, pushing her back until she hit the dresser they were becoming so acquainted with. Faye perched on the edge, already spreading her legs wide, and Diana pushed up her T-shirt, the black lace support belt covering her stomach just visible, and fisted the fabric tight so Faye's nipples strained against it.

Diana couldn't think of anyone ever looking more perfect.

She slicked her fingers through her folds, and Faye arched. "Fuck, god, D—"

Faye didn't finish the rest of her sentence. Diana sank her fingers into her, pumping hard and fast. The dresser rattled, but Faye was louder, her nails digging into Diana's waist. Her breathy gasps forced Diana deeper, and she tilted her fingers to hit that spot that made Faye weak. She wanted to feel her tighten around her, to feel that rush of pleasure soak her. To feel her come completely undone, and for Diana to be the reason.

All for you.

Faye fell back with a groan, supporting herself with her arms, her legs wrapped around Diana's back. Diana held her with one hand, the other fucking her with long, fast strokes, feeling her begin to tremble.

"Look at me," Diana commanded, and Faye's eye fluttered open. "That's it. Watch me. You love it when I fuck you, don't you?"

The woman could barely nod, her core contracting underneath Diana's hand. Her gaze dropped to Diana's chest, her eyes widening slightly.

"And so bloody pretty while I do it too."

Faye groaned, fisting Diana's robe in her hand and pulling it. "Your r–robe. Fuck—" Diana kissed her, and she shattered, whimpering into her mouth as she came. Diana kept the rhythm, toes curling at the sensation of squeezing around her fingers. She savoured every moan, feeding on every sound Faye gave her until she couldn't take anymore.

As Faye loosened her grip on Diana's robe, Diana slowly pulled out her fingers, taking them to her mouth. Faye watched the movement, still quivering, trying to steady her thighs with her hands.

Diana hummed at the sweet taste—but it wasn't enough.

She dropped to her knees, hooking underneath Faye's legs and pulling her flush to her eager tongue. She drank in the intoxicating taste of her—the hit instantaneous—but needed more. She kissed and lapped at her, getting lost in her wetness, burying herself between her thighs until Faye gripped the back of Diana's head, pleading with her not to stop.

So Diana indulged, her tongue working circles over Faye's clit until she cried out again, tugging at Diana's scalp.

Almost suffocated by the squeeze of her thighs, Diana spread them apart, mesmerised by the glistening wetness. How long could she get caught in this cycle, she wondered, before one of them tapped out? Was it possible to overdose on a person?

She swept the length of her again before pressing a kiss to the inside of her thigh and finally coming up for air.

The sight of Faye, shiny with sweat, hair dishevelled and falling out of her bun, had the corners of her mouth twitching.

"I think you might have killed me if you'd have started again," Faye said. "I'm pretty sure my clit has fallen off."

Diana shook her head, unable to hide a smile, and offered a hand to help Faye up.

"No. No. I need a minute after that last one." Faye let out a happy sigh and stretched her legs. "I swear they just keep getting better and better."

"You did seem especially fond of my robe today."

"It's hot. I mean, I'm pretty sure you could wear a potato sack and still look sensational."

She raised an eyebrow. "Sensational, huh?"

"You deserve all the adjectives, Diana. Resplendent, splendiferous...pulchritudinous."

"*Pulchritudinous?*"

Faye grinned. "My dad used to do 'archaic word of the day', and it's a pretty fun one. But yeah, that purple robe is pulchritudinous; the perfect choice for a queen."

"I'm glad it pleases thee so." She brushed her hand down the robe, feeling its silkiness, and smiled, remembering their day at the ruins. The play pretend and silliness, the fun side Faye so easily brought out in her.

Even Molly had noticed it too.

Best not think about that now.

Faye made to sit up, letting out a mixture of groans and laughter as she did so. "Although your robe did start to open up at one point. I tried to tell you, but well, my words weren't really working. I didn't see anything, though." She smoothed the fold with her fingers, and Diana's breath hitched as she grazed the bare skin of her chest. "Just this. Here."

Faye traced the fabric of Diana's gown, almost as if she couldn't look her in the eye. Even deep in the throes of passion, seconds away from combusting, she still wanted to respect Diana's privacy. That touched her in a place so delicate, it was hard to bear.

"Can I ask a question?" Faye said, her attention still on Diana's gown.

"Of course."

"Are you naked under here?"

Diana's heart kicked up another notch. "Yes."

Faye groaned like the answer was painful, but she didn't press. "That is…good to know."

Diana knew how much she wanted her; she saw it in Faye's eyes, felt it in the way she kissed her. But Faye hadn't pushed, not once, since their conversation.

If Faye had been brave enough, with all her concerns about her stoma, Diana could be brave too.

Could she?

Faye finally looked at her, those big blues soft and full of emotion. She caught her reflection in them, wondering what Faye saw, then closed the distance, capturing her with a kiss. Slow. Deliberate. Like they had all the time in the world, and it wasn't slipping through their fingers. Desire pulled low in her belly, curling deeper when Faye kissed her back, just as soft. Like Diana was something she was afraid to ruin.

But maybe she already was ruined.

"Undress me."

Faye pulled back. "What?"

Diana cupped her face, looking deep into her eyes, hoping she could see how much she wanted this too. "Undress me."

The words caught in the air between them.

"Are you sure?" Faye continued searching, and the kindness in her gaze made Diana want this even more.

"I want to feel your hands on me. I want you to know how much my body craves yours."

"Fuck." Faye's throat bobbed, and Diana wanted to follow the movement with her tongue, her teeth. To mark her, leave an imprint of herself that could never be washed off.

Faye loosened the tie around Diana's waist, slowly, as though she was waiting for her to change her mind. The thin material opened, and Faye dragged her gaze over the bare skin revealed, with a mixture of curiosity and hunger that had Diana pulsing. Faye slipped a hand underneath one of the folds, caressing Diana's collarbone as she gently it eased over her shoulder. Then she repeated the movement on the other side, letting the gown drop to the floor with a whisper.

The room filled with the sound of their breathing.

Something so simple had wetness already gathering between Diana's legs. She'd never felt more naked—or more alive. Laying herself bare for someone, giving them something she normally kept locked away.

"Oh my god. You're a fucking masterpiece, Diana."

Faye pressed her lips to Diana's chest, the warmth making her tingle—or maybe it was the soft hands, skimming her as though trying to memorise every detail. Faye was gentle at first, caressing her waist, the swell of her hips, then she stood, pushing off the dresser, her hands firmer, confident, as she guided Diana back to the bed.

Diana had forgotten just how good it felt to surrender to the feeling. Control kept her safe, absolutely, but it restrained her from really letting go. How might it feel to give herself to Faye? She couldn't lie and say it was just about sex anymore; it was more than that. And as Faye leaned over her, eyes commanding her, she wanted to give herself. She wanted to give herself so much, if she stopped to think about why, she might cry.

Her back hit the headboard, and all those thoughts vanished, her mind driven solely by her throbbing clit and how badly she needed Faye to touch her. For her to know how much she wanted her too.

"I want to kiss every part of you." Faye's breath tickled her stomach as she followed through on the promise, peppering her torso with kisses until she reached her nipple. "Your boobs are perfect."

Diana hummed as Faye took her nipple between her lips, teasing her with her tongue. Slowly at first, testing, then harder as she sucked more of her breast into her mouth. With her free hand, she caressed the other breast, rolling her hardened nub between her fingers.

"Harder," Diana commanded, her clit pulsing with every flick of Faye's tongue against her nipple.

Faye obeyed, sucking and nipping with her teeth, sending hot jolts of pleasure between Diana's legs. Her breath hitched as Faye trailed a hand lazily down her waist, a teasing thumb resting just above her clit.

Faye pulled back, and those striking eyes floored her. Was she asking for permission, or wanting Diana to see how much this was affecting her, too?

"Don't stop," Diana said, her voice low in her throat.

Faye dipped her hand lower, brushing her slicked folds. "Fuck, Diana. You're so wet." She slid into her and pumped her fingers.

"Yes. Like that." Diana opened her legs wider and fisted the sheets. She could've been embarrassed at how she sounded—so wet, so *needing*—but she couldn't find it in her to care.

Faye groaned. "You feel amazing."

Diana's pussy clenched, orgasm already blurring the edges, and Faye groaned again, fucking her deeper. Heat filled her, curling tighter and tighter, threatening to burst. She was close, so close, and yet part of her wanted to stay suspended, Faye's fingers drawing her towards climax, over and over. That way, she wouldn't have to overthink or worry about the end of the week; she could just enjoy the feeling, this connection, for everything that it was.

"Diana," Faye said, "Look at me. I want to see you too."

Diana hesitated. She'd already given too much. Parts of herself that were hard to get back. But like everything else, somehow, she couldn't deny Faye. She opened her eyes, and when they landed on the gorgeous brunette, her stare dark and holding so much behind those irises, the building pressure inside finally gave way, sending blinding hot pleasure surging through her.

"Oh god, Diana, I can feel you. Come for me."

She bit her lip to muffle her cry, her orgasm striking with such force she could barely contain it. Faye's fingers continued to work inside her, drawing out the feeling, the waves crashing over her until her lungs burned.

Faye slowed, gently removing her fingers and placing kisses over Diana's thighs.

Diana drew in a shaky breath, a little embarrassed by how long it was taking to pull herself together. In a dizzying haze, she still drifted somewhere up in the ceiling. She forced her focus to the woman still skimming her hips, struck by the tender way her hands caressed her skin.

"Wow. You're incredible," Faye said.

The words hit harder than she wanted them to. Had she ever had a person look at her like she were gold? Like she were treasure? Diana had told herself many times she didn't need this. While coworkers and friends wasted time dating, she'd focused on more important things. She'd taken care of herself; she always did. She'd never yearned for someone to hold her or shower her with compliments. People had agendas and disguises. People left and lied and hurt.

So why now, in the arms of a woman she'd only known a few weeks, did it feel like she finally understood what she'd been missing?

Panic flared hard in the depths of her brain, her chest tightening.

You have this under control.

"I love all your freckles," Faye said, joining Diana at the head of her bed, her warm body pressing into hers. She traced her fingers over the scattering of little brown spots decorating Diana's abdomen. "But this one has always been my favourite."

Diana's breath hitched as her thumb brushed her cheekbone. The adoration in Faye's eyes was so genuine, it pulled at something deep inside. Hard to look at. Hard to look away. The touch so gentle, it hurt.

The hollow ache in her chest deepened.

"Are you alright?" Faye's voice was quiet.

Diana blinked, and a tear slipped down her cheek. Faye caught it with her thumb, her eyes searching, wanting to ask more, but perhaps too afraid to.

Heat singed Diana's neck. What must Faye think of her? Emotional and weeping after climax like some dusty old widow. But she felt too much; the ache opened into a chasm large enough to bury her inside it.

Realising she hadn't said anything for some time, she gave Faye a small smile. When that didn't ease the worry etched between her brows, she cupped her face and pulled her in for a kiss. Soft and slow, hoping her lips could speak the words she didn't know how to voice. Faye tangled her hands in her hair, deepening the kiss with such want, it made her groan.

The need stirred again, possessive and hungry, and she tipped Faye onto her back, her hand already slipping between her legs. She groaned again, finding her just as wet as she knew she was herself, their kisses becoming messy and bruising.

You have this under control.

But the more she tried to tell herself that, the less she believed it.

TWENTY-ONE

Faye

Faye turned one way, and then the other, examining herself in the mirror. A short-sleeve green plaid shirt fell over her shoulders, and her black boyfriend-style shorts hugged her hips.

How has Carla roped me into this?

The woman was nothing short of persistent every time she bumped into her around the island. But she was the first person who had been kind to her here, and she supposed she owed her one for the sunglasses—but still, why couldn't they go for a nice walk instead?

Listen to yourself. Would Emmeline Pankhurst say no to a poker game?

I bet she would know the rules.

It wasn't as though she had much else planned tonight. Quin had their scheduled chat with their dad, and Diana was spending time with Molly. Faye needed a distraction to stop her brain from counting down the days.

She and Diana had been avoiding that conversation. They'd spoken about life at home, Faye going back to work, Diana possibly having a career change, but breezed over any details concerning the two of them.

It made sense. Why would they talk about "them" when there was no "them" to speak of? There was always an expiration date, but that little bud of hope had dared to sprout in Faye's heart, and she didn't know what to do with it. She'd wanted to come to the island and find herself again, open up to the opportunities life had to offer, but maybe she wasn't ready for this. Not with someone like Diana.

A night apart would probably do them some good.

But she didn't mean that, not really. Every moment she could spend in Diana's company wouldn't be enough.

It was more than the way she touched her. It was the other parts she'd had the pleasure of uncovering. How she'd press her fingers to her lips after she laughed, like she hadn't meant for the sound to escape. How she didn't even blink at Faye's ostomy. How she treated her like she wasn't fragile. How easily she mixed the delicate with the dastardly. The woman was a weapon.

Faye's mouth dried at the memory of her bare skin. Of slipping off the purple robe and revealing all her curves and freckles. How good it felt to touch her, to feel her. She couldn't help but hope it meant something to Diana, too.

She noticed those quiet moments where Diana went inside herself. She wanted to peel back those walls and understand—but what if she had it all wrong? What if Diana knew Faye wanted more and wanted to let her down gently?

Ending this between them was going to feel like being catapulted off a cliff, whichever way it happened. So no. She didn't want to accelerate the suffering or ruin what little time they had left.

Still, the question lodged deep in her brain: would saying goodbye undo all the progress she'd made?

Two cheery toots of a horn pulled her attention from the mirror. Carla had arrived.

"Ay, Dog's Bollocks!" she called, waving like a wind turbine about to blow off its hinges. Her long dark hair, usually contained in a ponytail, flowed in loose waves down her back. It was strange to see her wearing jeans and a T-shirt rather than the blue uniforms the staff wore on the island.

"How is Faye?" Carla asked as the buggy pulled away.

"Good. I love it here… I can definitely see why Ella came and never left."

Carla chuckled, the wind blowing her hair like a terrible shampoo advert. "Princesa Inês working her magic, huh?"

The memory of Diana's mouth on Faye warmed her neck. The breath tickling her ear. *"Do you think the princess would approve of this?"*

"What about your bag?" Carla asked, unaware of the heat unravelling in Faye's navel. "How are things?"

She brushed her abdomen, and the bulge that was always present. "A little better. It's getting easier to tell people…and Senhor Arenoso said some things that helped me see the situation a little differently."

"Mm-hmm. He is a wise man. A handsome one too." Carla nodded with a little too much appreciation, and Faye wrinkled her nose. "But not all things are solved with a three-week course. Some take time and practice."

"I guess so." Faye spun the question back on her, hoping to avoid any questions about her love life. "So how is Carla?"

"I'm enjoying myself. Work is good." She let out a joyful squeal as they hit a particularly gravelly section of road, the seat vibrating. "It will be even better once we win some money tonight, eh?" She bumped shoulders with Faye.

"I don't even know the rules," Faye admitted. "And won't you get in trouble? If Riley finds out?"

"Why? We're all friends. It's not like I'm taking you to an underground den in Lisbon." She grinned, her silver septum piercing catching the light. "Stop worrying so much."

If only it were that simple.

The sun sank over the horizon, its pink and orange hues washing the sky like a watercolour. In the distance, Faye swore she could see the twinkling lights of the mainland. A mainland she didn't want to think about.

"How are things with Raul?" she asked, turning to Carla. "You said you were going to tell me *everything* if I came to poker with you."

"We have lots of fun together." Carla adjusted her hands on the wheel. "But we work a lot, and…he's young."

That pricked Faye's skin, but Carla went on, "A few times he's mentioned me living with him so we could see more of each other, but he was just being kind. He didn't mean it."

"Sounds like you're assuming to me." Faye's pulse sharpened as Carla glanced at her. "You're assuming that because he's younger than you, he's not taking it seriously. But what if he is?" She folded her hands in her lap, nails picking at the skin. "Both of you would miss out on something great, not because you didn't want it, but because you miscommunicated."

Carla clicked her tongue. "Huh. I guess I hadn't thought about it like that."

The bud of hope rooted inside Faye dared to grow. Was that what she was doing, too? Still assuming how Diana felt? But their situation was different; it was always clear what they were getting into. They had an arrangement: a bit of fun on the island and then part ways. It was embarrassing to admit that it had all changed for Faye.

But what if it had changed for Diana, too?

She bit her lip, anxiety smothering the hopeful feeling before it had chance to spread. If she wasn't sure, she couldn't assume either. Not if she ended up regretting it for the rest of her life.

Damn Senhor Arenoso. He is a wise man.

"It's scary, taking that risk," she said. "But I suppose that's what life is about, right? No risk, no reward."

"Yes!" Carla pounded the steering wheel. "See. You're going to be an excellent poker player. I knew it."

Carla spent the rest of the journey explaining the different hands to Faye. Which hands beat what, what the "flop" was, and how an older woman called Filamena had the best poker face in the group.

When they arrived at the dock, a shiver rolled up Faye's spine.

"I thought you said we weren't going on a boat?"

Carla laughed as she switched off the engine. "Not a moving boat. Don't worry. Your stomach is safe tonight." She hopped out of the buggy and headed towards Duarte's boat, which was swaying against the walkway with a gentle creak.

Faye grabbed her backpack and followed, reciting the poker hands in her head. Was it a flush or a straight that was better? She checked her watch; she should be fine without emptying her bag for a few hours. How long did poker games usually take?

Carla led them onto Duarte's boat and into the cabin, which housed a wooden table and chairs, an overflowing coatrack, and a rusty coffee machine that looked like it might've been saved from a sea wreckage. She opened another door that led downstairs. "After you."

Faye frowned. "I thought you said this wasn't an underground den."

Carla chuckled, patting her on the back. "Come on." She steered her down the wooden steps. Immediately, cigar smoke hit the back of Faye's throat. She blinked to adjust to the darkness.

Five pairs of eyes looked back at them as they entered. The area was lit by a solitary overhead bulb. If the lack of light was for ambience or simply the captain's carelessness, she didn't know, but she recognised Duarte, with his headful of dark hair and the enormous grin on his face. Some of the other faces were familiar, but she couldn't place them.

"*Olá a todos*!" Carla greeted. "We have a guest. Put out that dirty smoke."

The men on either side of Duarte grumbled but did as she asked, extinguishing the cigars in an old tin can acting as an ashtray.

"You've met Duarte already, but maybe you don't remember, because your head was hanging over the side of the boat." Carla cracked out laughing, then pointed to the man on his right—a taller, less smiley version of the captain, but with just as much dark hair. "That's Tiago, but—"

"*Toranja*," Duarte interrupted, earning a scowl from his brother and laughter from the others.

Carla sighed, as if the very effort was draining. "But sometimes they call him *Toranja*."

"Grapefruit?" Faye asked. "Why?"

"Trust me. You don't want to know."

Bruno, Catarina's husband from the nature reserve and Carla's coworker, sat on Duarte's left. Faye had seen Bruno a few times, but he'd never offered more than a grunt. In the corner, a long, gangly man called Romeo perched on a chair, floppy brown hair falling over his eyes. Faye guessed he was around twenty, although the fluffy fuzz covering his chin and cheeks made him look younger. Filamena, the only other woman, didn't pay either of them much attention. She huffed as she shuffled the cards, tucking her short white hair back into her *lenço*—a red floral wrap tied at the nape of her neck. Deep-set wrinkles carved ridges into her skin, but her eyes were a clear and sharp honey.

The stark difference between the grinning Romeo and the annoyed elderly lady made Faye relax a little. As far as underground dens went, this wasn't bad.

Carla broke Faye's twenty euros using Duarte's tip jar—it was mostly empty, which Faye put down to the man's wild sailing—and handed her the change. She counted out their stack of coloured chips, and the two of them joined the others at the table.

Filamena let out another sharp huff, strong enough to

blow the shack down, and Carla announced the buy-in bet—twenty-five cents. The chips started moving across the stained green felt, and Filamena dealt the first round. Faye plucked up her cards, sticky to the touch, and the numbers on the suits stared back at her. She couldn't remember one thing that Carla had said.

"Do you like goats?"

Faye turned to Romeo.

"What?"

He held his phone out to her. "Goats. Look." A video was playing, showing his long limbs as he tried to encourage a white goat to jump through a hoop. He swiped to the next video. A goat stood on a raft, chewing on a hat as it bobbed along the ocean waves. A woman screamed in the background.

"Oops." He swiped again, and a loud bleat came through the speakers.

"*Para com isso*." Tiago pushed him with his big hand. "She isn't interested in playing with your billy goat."

The men laughed, and Romeo turned beetroot red, shoving his phone into his pocket.

The next cards were dealt. Duarte raised the bet, then his brother and Bruno matched it. Feeling overwhelmed from the low light, the buzzing from a microwave in the corner, and the suffocating testosterone in the room, Faye folded. She didn't want to lose all her chips so soon, so figured she'd play it safe for a few rounds and observe.

Perhaps poor Romeo should've done the same. By

the end of the fourth round, his pile was almost empty. His lack of wins didn't seem to bother him, though. He spoke in hushed tones in between rounds, showing her more pictures under the table. Apparently, he was trying to train the goats for a show on the mainland, but judging by the failed attempts at tightrope-walking, which had ended with his face full of goat poop, it wasn't going very well.

In the time waiting, Faye studied the others as they sat around the table, treating it like a field survey at work. But instead of noting patterns in species' behaviour and ecosystems, she studied the way the players interacted with each other.

Duarte and Tiago's sibling rivalry was obvious, as they each tried to outbet the other. Their taunting extended to Romeo, who was often the butt of the joke, until Carla told them to cut it out. Filamena was very hard to read, perhaps because she didn't speak English, and the Portuguese she did speak was so fast, Faye couldn't comprehend.

By the time moonlight glowed through the small window above their heads, the buy-in bet had doubled, and Faye had come to know all the different winning hands. She looked at the steady pile of chips in front of her; she wanted to give the Portuguese a run for their money.

"Raise," she declared, tossing a chip into the middle.

Filamena barely blinked as she checked, her facial expression the same shade of mildly annoyed as it had been all night.

Faye channelled Filamena's indifference as the jacks in her hand stared back at her. "Raise," she said again, catching the men's surprised glances in her direction.

Filamena cursed in Portuguese, folding, quickly followed by Bruno and Duarte. Tiago's eyebrow twitched, and he mumbled something that made his brother laugh, then met Faye's gaze across the table. The hairs on her neck stood on end.

"Raise." He pushed two more chips into the middle.

Carla turned over the last card. A five. Faye showed no reaction but added another chip to the pile. Tiago did the same, and then, on three, they revealed their cards.

"*Toranja*." Duarte chuckled, smacking his fist on the table. "*Ela topou-te!*"

Faye had a full house. Tiago had a flush.

He scowled, studying the cards so hard, a deep line formed between his brows.

A rush of adrenaline swam through Faye's veins as she scraped the winnings towards her. Carla winked, and Romeo clapped her on the back.

Okay, now I get it. Winning is fun.

The next few rounds passed quickly. Carla won, Filamena cursed some more in Portuguese, and tension built between the brothers as they continued to compete against each other. Bruno seemed unbothered—or perhaps he was used to the rivalry—but Filamena snapped at them, pointing her finger when they got too rowdy.

"*És mesmo azarado, otário.*" Tiago grinned, taking

the winnings from the middle and the last of Romeo's chips.

The other men laughed, calling him further names, but Faye caught the hurt on his face, the way his cheeks burned red as they continued to poke fun at him. She imagined they did this most weeks, and she wasn't going to sit and do nothing. She eyed the table, noting how most chips sat beneath Tiago. She was determined to win some back for Romeo.

She waited, keeping a close eye on the man opposite for his tell-tale twitch—the glance at his chip pile. He'd raise the bet, goad Faye into the challenge, but she'd fold, letting him win. People always underestimated her. She was going to use that to her advantage.

The cycle of folding continued, until one hand, she didn't. She only needed one more spade for a flush.

It was risky. Tiago could have the same but a higher set of numbers.

"Raise." She placed a handful of chips into the growing pile.

No risk, no reward, right?

Tiago tutted, shaking his head. "Oh, *miúda*. What will I do with all your money?" He met her call and raised again, his oily face shining under the warm overhead bulb.

Irritation flared at his use of *little girl*. She dug her nail into her hand as the last card was dealt, using every last drop of composure to hold her face still. A five of spades.

She tore her eyes back to Tiago, catching his glance

at his skyscraper of chips. This smug arsehole thought he was going to win.

"Last round of bets," Carla commented. "Play nice." She tried to keep her voice upbeat and teasing, but even she couldn't squash the tension filling the room.

All attention fell on Faye, and with all the essence of enigma she could muster, she pushed all her chips into the centre of the table. "All in."

Romeo inhaled sharply. Carla's gaze snapped to her. Even Filamena's stony expression faltered for a moment, something akin to pride raising her thin eyebrows.

But Faye kept her focus on the man across from her, trying to ignore the way her heart thudded. The seconds stretched painfully. Then he pushed all of his chips into the middle, the skyscraper towers crashing down onto the table.

"Brother," Duarte scolded, slapping him on the shoulder. "What are you doing?"

"What's it look like? I'm going to win."

"You never learn, do you? This is my money you're gambling with."

He gritted his teeth. "I said I'll pay you back."

He cursed in Portuguese, the two of them raising their voices until Filamena cut them off.

"*Silêncio.*" She shook her head, glaring at them, fierce Portuguese falling from her lips.

Whatever Filamena had said, the men snapped out of it. Tiago crossed his arms, and Duarte's usual friendly demeanour had vanished.

Carla cleared her throat. "Okay… Let's see what you got."

The room grew quiet. Just the buzz of the old microwave in the corner, and the soft slap of the waves against the boat.

Faye held Tiago's gaze. Even when he waved for her to go first. Even when he raised his eyebrows. She didn't blink, didn't waver, and then, with a shit-eating grin, he spread his cards on the table.

A row of spades looked up at her—a flush.

She glanced at her hand, then at the mountain of chips in the centre. It wasn't a landslide amount by any means, maybe one hundred euros, but it was definitely enough to repay Romeo.

And besides, she really wanted to wipe that smirk off Tiago's face.

She let her lips drop enough to cause Tiago's eyes to crinkle. "Ah. I have a straight."

He pounded his fist on the table, the chips clinking. "Yes! See. I told you—"

She cleared her throat, laying her cards down. "A straight flush that is."

He glared at the pretty row of spades in disbelief.

"I believe that means *miúda* wins." Faye grinned. "And you're bust." She turned to Carla, who was stacking her chips in neat piles. "You're right. I am good at this." She stood to reach a few flyaway chips that had rolled away, and Tiago burst from his chair.

"Aha! *Ela está a fazer batota*. She's cheating!" He

pointed at Faye's abdomen, spit flying from his mouth. "I knew it."

She glanced down, spying her bag outline underneath her T-shirt. "I'm not cheating."

But he stood up, undeterred. "Look. She has something under her shirt. Extra cards."

"Tiago," Carla warned. "Sit down."

The aggression from the man might've scared her, but instead, she fought the urge to roll her eyes. Being at the table with him all night felt like being trapped in a hungry gorilla enclosure. "I don't need to cheat to beat you. This is my ostomy bag."

He scowled. "*Quê?*"

She lifted her T-shirt. "It helps me go to the bathroom. That's all. No cheating here."

Tiago's lip curled, more spit flying from his mouth. "That's disgusting."

The room stilled for a beat, but adrenaline steadied her voice. "No, it's not. But the way you're unable to speak without splashing everyone with your saliva, frankly, is."

Romeo chuckled, but Tiago's glare cut to him, and he looked away.

"Sit down." Duarte touched his brother's arm, but he shook it off. "She beat you fair and square. Take it like a man."

"Or better yet, like a woman," Faye said. "Maybe then you wouldn't have to perform this egocentric caveman act to try to recover your pride."

"Okay, okay." Carla waved her hands. "I think everyone needs to take a chill pill. *Acalmem-se. Sim?*"

Despite the game being very much over, no one made to move. Tiago's heavy breaths were giving the old appliance a run for its money.

"That was amazing," Romeo murmured, leaning into Faye. "What are you going to do with your winnings?"

"I'm going home on Monday. I don't really need it." She lifted a shoulder. "I thought maybe you could use it to get some more training equipment for your goats."

"Really?" His eyes brightened. "That would be amaz—"

"For *goats?*" Tiago snapped. "You have to be joking. I need that money, and you're going to waste it on grass-eating fleabags?"

Duarte seized his brother's shoulder. "Enough. No more. No more money either. Not until you pay me back for everything you lost."

Tiago banged his fists on the table like an oversized toddler, knocking Faye's chips over. "I will pay you back."

"This is what you keep saying, but all you do is take. The tip jar, Pai's favourite coat, my fishing knife?"

"*Calem-se!*" The room settled into silence. Filamena rubbed her fingers against her wrinkled forehead as though she were trying to iron out the creases—or trying to remember why she'd put herself through this ordeal. With a sigh, she unleashed angry Portuguese on the two brothers. Judging by their reddening faces and Carla's sheepish expression, they'd been given an earful. Shame the woman couldn't translate.

Filamena dragged her tired eyes towards Faye. "And you. Well played." Faye's ears pricked up at the clear English. "You certainly had the Santos boys fooled, but I knew you'd be one to watch."

Faye closed her gaping mouth. "Uh…thank you."

Filamena stood, adjusting her *lenço*. "That's enough fun for one night. Carla, Romeo, Bruno, always a pleasure." She tugged on each of the brothers' ears. "You two behave yourselves. No more stealing, *Toranja*."

The group laughed, but Faye's head spun. A lot of information had been dealt out in the last few minutes. Carla and Romeo helped pool her winnings together, exchanging the chips for the money in the pot. Tiago watched begrudgingly, his eyes burning a hole in Faye's face as Duarte gathered her notes.

"Great game." Duarte grinned. "I do love watching my brother lose. But it is better when it's his own money. Here."

She accepted the notes from his hand, catching the engraving on his ring. DS.

DS. Duarte Santos. The same initials she'd found on the penknife in the woods.

Her eyes darted to Tiago. He continued to glower at her, but Faye's amusement had twisted into something else. Could this be the man she was chasing? Her attention flicked back to Duarte. Or was it something to do with the captain?

"That fishing knife you mentioned… What did it look like?" she asked.

Tiago stiffened.

Duarte used his fingers like a ruler. "About this big—with my name carved on the tip." He cut an annoyed glance at Tiago. "It was a gift from my father."

A cold chill spread up her spine.

"It's you," she said with a little too much force, turning to Tiago. A glimpse of fear flashed behind his eyes—the guy really needed to work on his poker face.

"I haven't done anything."

The group glanced at each other in confusion.

Faye turned to Duarte. "Have you heard about the poach—"

But she didn't get a chance to finish her question. Tiago bolted, knocking Filamena off balance as he rushed out the door. His footsteps thundered up the wooden stairs.

The others stood in shock. Faye's pulse skyrocketed.

"He's–he's the poacher," she stammered. Disbelief rooted her motionless. "It's him!"

She couldn't let him get away. Not for a second time. The adrenaline kicked in, and she sprinted up the stairs, onto the dock, and out onto the beach. The midnight sky did little to help her, but the sound of footsteps guided her to the left.

"Hey!" she shouted. "Why are you running? Afraid I'm going to beat you again?"

She didn't really know what she was saying, but she

did want to beat him. And not at a stupid card game, but with her hands and fists.

A burning river of lava had replaced the blood in her veins. She couldn't stand people who took advantage of others—and especially people who took advantage of animals. She forced her muscles harder, but she was already slowing, her breathing too loud in her ears.

Dammit. She was unfit. Her lungs ached; her feet sank with every step, like she was running in glue. If he got into the woods, there was no way she'd be able to find him in the darkness.

"You're–a—you're a…coward!" she yelled into the night, hoping to antagonise him at least a little.

Faye didn't notice someone coming up behind her until they passed her, their quick pace putting her to shame. She squinted at the silhouette, tall and looming in the moonlight. Romeo?

There were sounds of a scuffle, a dull thud, and men's voices. She could make out a tangle of bodies on the sand. When she caught up, Romeo was kneeling on Tiago's back, his arm twisted behind him.

"*Sai de cima de mim seu perdedor!*" Tiago tried to roll free, almost tipping Romeo onto his side.

Faye sat on his wriggling legs, hearing more voices heading towards them. "The only…loser here…is you, Tiago." She sucked in a lungful of air and gave Romeo a pat on the back. He beamed at her. Faye matched his smile with her own.

"I love animals," Romeo said.

A laugh escaped her, extra loud in the quiet. "We did it." She nudged Romeo. "We actually did it."

"Stupid kids." Tiago struggled underneath them, kicking up sand. "Get off me."

Faye bit back a *Scooby Doo* reference about "meddling kids" as the others gathered around her, confusion on their faces. In the moonlight, Duarte was white as a sheet. Faye brushed the sand off her legs, checking her bag was still attached. Winner.

"Carla, call Riley. She needs to get here ASAP."

TWENTY-TWO

Faye

Faye hadn't stopped smiling for days. Maybe it had something to do with wrangling one of the poachers, subsequently exposing a network of baddies trying to exploit the island. Maybe it had more to do with the beautiful woman wrapped between her thighs, making her feel things she didn't think were humanly—or scientifically—possible.

Another one of those blinding orgasms ripped through her, taking her breath and her vision along with it. She clung to Diana, biting her nails into her shoulders as her tongue continued to roll over her clit. Pleasure blanketed her, warm and fierce, and she moaned, bathing in the feeling, the pressure of Diana's lips against her enough to keep it rippling to the tips of her toes.

Faye exhaled happily, her chest tight. "Well…Good morning to you, too."

Diana hummed contentedly, placing a wet kiss on her thigh. "Indeed." When her eyes flicked up and met Faye's, another ping of pleasure jolted through her.

How was that even possible?

It should be concerning how much she reacted to her. When her rich, honey-sweet voice took on that husky tone, Faye was pretty sure she'd steal children's lunch money if Diana asked her to. And don't get her started on that mouth.

The ungodly crimes she'd commit for that mouth.

The soft shape of her lips had to have been sculpted by goddesses. It was the only way to explain the silly somersault her stomach did whenever her mouth pulled up in the corner. Lips smooth and wide, their deep pink the most beautiful colour Faye had ever seen. Those lips could easily replace the Mona Lisa's in the Louvre, with people crowding around for hours in the hope of seeing them move. Nothing compared to her smile—the *real* Diana smile—when laughter poured out of her like a shaken-up can of pop. Electric and unstoppable, unfiltered in a way that made Faye feel like she was standing in that museum where no one else was allowed entry and her pockets were lined with gold.

A little nip on her thigh made her gasp, and that tinkle of laughter vibrated against her skin, sending her stomach loop-the-looping.

"Did you hear me?" Diana asked. "Or have your other senses become numb from overstimulation?"

Faye stretched with a laugh, the burn pulling through her muscles. "The second one. You might have to be my guide Labrador for a few minutes while I recover."

"Is that my new spirit familiar, hmm? Labrador? I had hopes it might be something a little more exotic."

Faye brushed a stray hair behind Diana's ear. "Do you think anyone has ever actually gone blind from coming? At least temporarily."

"I'm not sure." She pushed herself up, her gaze passing over Faye's body. "But maybe we could concoct our own study?"

"So now you *want* to be my Labrador? *Interesting.*"

Diana shook her head, but Faye caught her smile. "Anyway, I said I was going to hop in the shower." She stood, and Faye couldn't help but ogle her round—and milky-white—arse, and how it jiggled gloriously with every step. "You're more than welcome to join me. In fact, it's encouraged."

"Give me a minute to recover, and I'll be right in."

"Well, don't take too long. We have to be at yoga in twenty minutes."

"Of course, my queen."

Diana disappeared into the bathroom, Faye glued to

every slow sway of her hips until the door closed.

Diana really was a masterpiece.

She stretched her legs, fighting off a yawn with the back of her hand. The early morning would catch up with her later, but with both of them struggling for time in the evenings—Diana spending time with Molly, and Faye with Quin—they had to make some time somewhere. She rolled onto her side, shamelessly inhaling Diana's scent on the pillow. She wished she could've stayed the night.

Faye wasn't complaining. Though the doubting part of her brain would disagree. She didn't want to explore the reasons why they hadn't slept in the same bed. They'd stay up for hours talking until the early morning, but then Diana would make it clear that they needed to go back to their respective cabins. Faye didn't want to read too much into it. She wanted to be respectful. But the selfish side of her, the one that wanted to know everything about Diana, from the way she took her coffee to her favourite colour Power Ranger, ached for the things she wouldn't ever know. Did she snore? Did she curl up on her side or sleep on her front? And how soft would she look when sleep overcame her, and she didn't have to worry about anything at all?

Faye wanted to ask her, wanted to tell her that she didn't want this to end when the week did, but every time she opened her mouth, the words wouldn't come. That little doubting voice whispered in her ear, telling her she was going to ruin everything. And now the Fire Ceremony was tomorrow, and they were leaving the day after. Two days.

Her heart squeezed at the thought of saying goodbye. Of going back home at all. She missed her dads and her four cats, but trying to go back to her old life before she knew Diana would be like trying to breathe underwater.

A low hum, mingling with the patter of water on tiles, infiltrated her thoughts. Was Diana…singing?

Faye turned her head to the bathroom. Then her voice came again. *"Tell me why..."*

Wait. The biggest grin took over Faye's face. Not only was Diana singing in the shower… She was singing Backstreet Boys in the shower?

She had to press her hands to her chest, afraid her heart was going to burst. The feeling was too much, touching places it had no right to. The most gorgeous, smart, impeccably dressed woman she'd ever met had a guilty pleasure for nineties boy bands?

Are you kidding me?

Then a high-pitched scream cut through that feeling like a knife, and she sprinted into the bathroom, the steam hitting her face.

Diana had pressed herself back against the tiles, the stream of water hitting her feet.

"What's wrong?" Faye asked. "Are you alright?"

"Yes." Diana swept her hair back, releasing a breathy laugh. "There was just a big spider."

Afraid of spiders, too?

Faye bit the inside of her cheek, trying to squash the surging feeling in her heart, but it was too powerful, too full. "Would you like my spider-removal service?"

"If you wouldn't mind."

She picked up the glass from the sink and stepped inside the shower, water droplets sprinkling her skin as she trapped the spider, then escorted the trespasser outside through the window.

"Thank you," Diana said.

"You're welcome." She leaned against the tiles. "You're kind of adorable when you're scared."

"I wasn't scared. Merely caught by surprise."

"Sure, sure. He was probably just a Backstreet Boys fan."

Diana tried to hide her smile. "I don't know what you're inferring."

"Mm-hmm." She let her gaze drop over Diana's body, her soft stomach, full breasts, the contrast of her pink nipples, sharp and hard. She was going to say something clever or make a joke, but everything emptied out of her mind.

"Are you going to join me?" Diana's voice made her eyes drag up. "Or just continue to gawk from over there?"

Wordlessly, she moved towards her, her hands finding Diana's waist as she stepped into the stream of warm water. She kissed her, pressing her against the wall, and the sensation rippled over her body—wanting Diana, needing her, being unable to separate the two, no matter how hard she tried. She nipped at her lip, lowering her hands to tug their bodies closer together.

Diana groaned, putting her hand to Faye's chest. "As

much as I'd love to, we don't have time."

"Are you sure? That sounds like a challenge to me." She flexed her hands, which were still cupping Diana's arsecheeks. "I'm already wet, I bet it wouldn't take longer than a minute."

She caught the flicker in Diana's eyes, then gasped when her hand pressed against her clit. She moaned at the fingers gliding through her folds.

"A minute, you say?" Diana murmured, slipping inside her easily. Faye arched, letting Diana turn her, then bend her over, her fingers pushing deeper. "Then that's all you've got."

She started fucking her hard and fast, and Faye whimpered, supporting herself on the wall with one hand, the other reaching behind her to grab Diana's waist.

Diana twirled Faye's hair into a makeshift ponytail down her back, holding it with her free hand. "I wish I had my strap," she said breathlessly. "God, the things I want to do to you." She pulled on Faye's hair, tightening her grip, thrusting inside her, drawing her closer and closer to the edge.

Each drive of Diana's fingers was thorough, punishing, and deliciously building pleasure in her centre. "F–fuck, Diana. I'm close."

Faye whined when Diana stopped fucking her for a second, pulling her upright and guiding her foot onto the shower shelf. She pressed into her back, nipples sharp, and kissed her neck, the water drizzling over them, and spread Faye wider with her fingers, rolling her thumb over her clit.

"This is what you wanted, isn't it?" she said, half-whisper, half-growl. "Then show me just how bad you need it."

"P–please, Diana. I want to come for you so badly. I can't get enough of—fuck!"

Diana filled her again, deeper, hitting a sensitive spot that she hadn't been able to reach before. It wasn't long before Faye was cursing, the coil in her core winding tighter and tighter until it snapped. She cried out, the air ripping from her lungs as she came hard around Diana's fingers, her legs barely holding her own weight.

Diana held her upright while her body trembled, the shower sprinkling them with droplets. Faye relaxed into her, the tightness in her chest easing, but her breathing still shallow.

Diana pressed a kiss to her shoulder, and her spine tingled. "We might have run a little over, but it was totally worth it to feel you fall apart like that."

"I'm glad you think so."

Diana hummed her approval, adding another kiss. "But we really have to get ready now."

Faye begrudgingly untangled herself from Diana's warmth and turned to face her on shaky legs. She blew out a breath as she leaned back against the tiles, feeling the exquisite ache everywhere. Diana started washing herself, and even that she found mesmerising. The way her hands moved, the fingers that had just brought her to such a brilliant climax now busying themselves doing something mundane. But none of the ordinary things were mundane with Diana.

A different ache pulled at her. The one craving all life's simplicities without a time limit or flights heading in different directions looming over their heads.

Her eyelids pricked, and she looked down at her feet. God, her hormones were all over the place. Thankfully, the mix of water and steam hid her swell of emotion, and she gathered herself.

She plucked at her support belt, the material clinging to her like a sloppy second skin. She wanted to take it off, but a sudden shyness fell over her. What if Diana didn't mind her bag when it was mostly hidden away? Would she feel differently if she saw Faye without her cover-up?

It might've been her post-orgasm brain talking, but Faye didn't want to hide anything from Diana. She wanted her to know all of her before they left.

"Do you mind if I take my support off?" she asked. "It'd be nice to shower without it."

"Of course I don't mind."

The answer was so quick and so sure, emotion swelled inside Faye again. To stop herself from opening her big mouth and declaring something too big for the shower cubicle, she slipped off her garment, moving it away with the flick of her toe.

She looked down at herself, completely bare, her skin-toned bag snug to her abdomen. She didn't want to look at Diana. What if she saw something, a flicker of uncertainty—or worse, disgust—that burst this entire bubble?

She closed her eyes. The blackness soothed her, the hiss of water filling her ears. Another voice joined the cacophony in her head. *Stop assuming.*

Her overactive brain loved to fill in the blanks with worst-case scenarios, but those assumptions were draining, exhausting, and usually wrong. Even if Diana *was* repulsed by her, Faye deserved to know. She had nothing to apologise for. She wasn't about to start hiding again. Not for anyone, even Diana.

She felt hands on her, guiding her into the stream of water. A snap of a bottle opening and a squirt, then the return of hands, firm and gentle as Diana lathered body wash over her, starting with her shoulders.

She opened her eyes to find Diana washing her with such fondness and care, it almost floored her.

"You're beautiful," Diana said, her gaze flicking to Faye's as she caressed her bicep, drawing her fingers down her forearm.

"Thank you." She swallowed, an unease creeping into her throat—because it was strange to actually feel beautiful for once. "You are too. I told you that when I first met you, and I think it every day. You're the most beautiful woman I've ever known, Diana."

Diana's fingers stilled on Faye's wrist, just for a millisecond, but Faye caught it. The hesitation. Did Diana not believe it? Faye wanted to tell her every single day. To kiss her, to *love* her, and—God, she was going to say something *really* stupid if she didn't change the subject.

"So is it just Backstreet Boys you like?" she blurted. "Or is it all boy bands?"

Amusement crinkled Diana's eyes, and she burst into laughter. That pure, magical laughter that made Faye feel like she was standing on mountain tops.

Diana caught some water in her hand and began washing the soapy suds off Faye's arms. "I might have a soft spot for some of the classics. Boyzone, NSYNC, Five, Backstreet Boys—"

"Sounds like you were a *lot* of a fan. A bit of a groupie."

She gave a small shrug. "I might've queued outside HMV for twelve hours to get a signed copy of *Millennium*."

"No way." She pictured a teenage Diana fangirling, and the grin hurt her face. This new information flipped a switch.

She wanted *this*. Uncovering guilty pleasures, hearing Diana sing in the shower, spending mornings and evenings and any time in between with someone who made her feel the best version of herself.

She wanted Diana.

All fear of rejection drained away. Standing in front of Diana, laying herself bare, she'd never felt more sure of herself. The distance would be tricky, but Faye wasn't rooted anywhere. She could compromise. It was worth it to take a chance on this.

Their gazes locked, and confirmation flared through her veins.

"Diana, I—"

A quick banging noise made them both swivel their heads. Was that Diana's door?

"Hello?" a familiar high-pitched voice called out as the front door opened.

Faye stiffened. *Shit. Molly.*

A little detail she'd forgotten—along with locking the door.

"Oh, Christ." Diana stepped out of the shower and grabbed a towel. "Just a minute!" she called, her voice squeakier than usual. She turned back to Faye. "Just…stay there." She flipped the shower off, threw Faye a towel, then scampered out of the bathroom.

Holy fuck. Faye's heart jumped into her throat. She wrapped the towel around herself and stepped onto the shower mat, glancing around. Of course there was nowhere to hide. Who designs hidden compartments in a bathroom? There was a window, but even if Faye could manoeuvre herself through the tiny hole without detaching her bag or flashing a bunch of strangers, the sound of her attempted escape would most definitely draw Molly's attention. The best thing was to stay put.

Water dripped down her spine, and she pulled the towel tighter around herself. *What is Molly doing here?*

What if she came to use Diana's shower because her bathroom had flooded? Maybe that could be Faye's excuse for being over here so early in the morning? Or maybe she should stage a fall in case she came in? Or maybe she could drape Diana's robe over herself and become the world's best human statue in the corner?

Oh god. I don't know!

The sound of voices filtered through the door. She tiptoed closer, barely breathing.

"…not like you to be running late," Molly commented.

"I overslept. Just give me five minutes to finish up in the bathroom, and then I'll be right out. In fact, why don't you wait at yours and I'll come and knock for you once I've finished?"

There was movement on the other side. "Okay."

She was leaving! Thank all the gay gods. Faye let out a breath of relief that was a moment too soon.

"What are those?" Molly asked, and Faye tensed.

What had she seen?

Diana's voice came next. Careful. Measured. A little *too* easy-breezy. "Oh…they're Faye's sunglasses. I think she left them at class. I'm going to give them back to her today."

Carla's stupid pineapple sunglasses.

Faye aged twenty years in the silence as she waited for Molly's response.

"Oh, right. I didn't think they were your style."

Giant pineapples aren't my style either, but beggars can't be choosers.

"I won't be long, love. Five minutes tops."

Faye didn't dare breathe. Then more movement. The closing of a door. Diana entered the bathroom, her earlier carefree demeanour replaced with fear and dread.

They didn't say anything for a moment, just their breathing and the steady *drip-drip* from the showerhead loud in the room.

"That was close," Faye said, breaking the silence.

Diana nodded. "Too close." She sighed, sweeping her wet hair from her face. "Right. Come on." She started busying herself, but Faye stood still, droplets still snaking down her chest.

The moment to talk had gone. And it was going to require more than five minutes of their time to have that particular conversation.

With a sigh of her own, she started to dry herself, trying to swallow the lump in her throat.

Because as much as there were challenges in their way, she'd omitted a rather important detail. What would they do about Molly?

TWENTY-THREE

Faye

Faye's nerves didn't settle until the afternoon. It might have been her imagination, but she swore Molly kept glancing her way during yoga class. Nothing could squash the unease growing in her chest—not stretching, not any of the breathing exercises, not even her last alignment session with Senhor Arenoso.

She cursed herself for not being more present, but she couldn't tune in to the deep timbre of his voice. All she could think about was how differently this morning could have played out. If Molly hadn't come in, Faye would've confessed her feelings for Diana. Would she be elated right now? Or nursing a bruised heart?

And what if Molly *had* walked in on them together? What the hell would've happened then?

The very notion made her skin crawl.

"Faye." His calm voice sliced through her thoughts. "You seem distant. Is everything okay?"

She opened her eyes, meeting his concerned gaze. "Sorry," she breathed, shaking her head. "I just have a lot on my mind."

"And the meditation isn't helping?"

She shook her head again. "Sorry."

"Nothing to apologise for here." He smiled, and Faye relaxed a little. "Would you like to talk about any of those things on your mind?"

She blinked, refocusing on the room. The green behemoth plants hanging floor to ceiling, the salty air drifting through the window and tickling her face, the calmness radiating from the man in front of her.

Faye didn't warm to many men easily. Her dads were the greatest in the world, and when it came to strangers, the standard was significantly lower. But over the passing weeks, a bond had developed between her and Senhor Arenoso. The safety in this room, the reminders of nature, the kindness and patience he showed everyone—and *everything*—around him. He made it so easy to be herself and to be honest.

In that moment, she realised it was more than Diana

she was going to miss.

It was all of Sandy Springs.

"I'm afraid of this ending." Her heart squeezed as Diana's beautiful face filled her mind. Their unguarded moment in the shower before reality shattered it. She had to talk to her, but her earlier confidence had dissipated after Molly's loud reminder of her presence. "I'm not sure how to say goodbye."

He nodded. "It's perfectly normal to be apprehensive about returning to the real world. There are many challenges to navigate on returning to work duties and family responsibilities, but it's essential to remember your Sandy Springs mindset. Easier said than done, I know." He offered her a genuine smile. "But goodbyes aren't always a negative thing. We need goodbyes to be able to transition. Whether we're transitioning from good or bad situations, the fear of *the change* is often the same. But without an appropriate conclusion, things remain unfinished, ambiguous…open. Saying goodbye gives us the chance to close one book and open another.

"This is partly what the Fire Ceremony aims to achieve. It's an evening of celebration, but it's also a marker to reflect on our journey. A chance to say goodbye to old habits that aren't serving us anymore, and welcome new ones with open hearts. A chance to be thankful for what brought us here, but at the same time to acknowledge that, for growth to occur, changes are needed. Sometimes getting what we want means letting go of something that we have."

Faye considered this. "I'm not good with change. Waking up one day and having everything be completely different was really difficult. Even if it did save my life…I resented my stoma for all the difficulties it brings. It's easier to focus on the negatives, but…I have to admit, my quality of living is better now. I still have bad days, but a lot fewer than before."

He steepled his fingers. "Adjustment can take some time. The discovery of your familiar, too, will help keep you grounded and guide you through these next steps."

Faye nodded. She eyed the owl pendant hanging around his neck. She'd hadn't given much thought to what animal she connected with most. She'd always adored them all.

Senhor Arenoso continued, and she lifted her gaze. "Consider what it is you want to gift to the flames at the ceremony tomorrow. It's a moment of regeneration, of taking the next steps on your path. You've come a long way, Faye. Whatever the changes bring, you're ready."

Her breathing steadied, and she forced a smile. "I'm ready." Even if she didn't *quite* believe it yet.

After her session, Faye met Carla in the courtyard. The woman's enthusiastic waving ignited a pang, knowing she'd have to say goodbye to her soon, too. She tried to ignore the sadness. There were too many feelings to contain in one box today.

But Carla wasn't in the mood for chitchat as she bundled Faye into the buggy and sped off towards the rehabilitation centre. Questions about why the woman was so eager to get there were answered with just a grin or by miming zipping her lips. Normally, this would make Faye nervous, but with everything else going on today, she just sat back and let Carla drive her there for the last time.

As the green trees blurred past, the mountains towering in the distance, Faye tried to commit them to memory. The abundance of colour, the jagged and smooth edges, the way the air filled her lungs with purpose. As though she could do anything she wanted—be anything she wanted. And it was coming to an end.

She scolded herself, trying to remember Senhor Arenoso's words. *"Goodbyes are good. Change is good."*

Pretty sure that was the gist of it.

So then why did everything feel so very bad?

Her old overthinking habits were back in full force, and she'd not even set foot off the island yet.

Carla pulled the buggy to a stop, the gravel crunching under the tyres.

They walked the short distance to the centre in comfortable quiet, listening to the chatter of wildlife up high in the trees above, with the sunlight projecting patterns on the forest floor. When the wooden cabin came into view, Carla flashed Faye an excited grin, putting her arm around her shoulders.

"Just so you know," Faye mumbled. "I don't like surprises."

"I think you'll like this one."

They stepped into the rehabilitation centre, the bell

jingling, and Riley greeted them with a beaming smile.

"Hey! I'm so glad you could make it." She eyed Faye, eyes sparkling. "Are you ready to send Pinkie back home?"

"What, now?" Excitement licked up her spine. "I thought she had a few weeks to wait?"

"She's ahead of schedule." Riley lifted a shoulder, grin stretching. "She's ready if you're ready."

"Of course I'm ready," she answered, but this time more convincingly.

They headed back to Carla's buggy with Pinkie in the carrier. The sun had baked the dirt track pale and chalky, gravel popping beneath the tyres. Carla drove along it, this time at a steadier pace, making her way as close as she could to the ruins, where the path surrendered. They entered the shaded forest at the bottom, walking further into the dense trees, the morning heat trapped and close. It was important to release the parakeet close to where they'd found her, in the hope she'd find her flock again. Over the next few days and weeks, the centre would keep a close eye on her using the tracker they'd attached. With a bit of luck, she wouldn't need any intervention.

Riley broke the quiet, her voice low as they hiked further into the woods. "Thank you again, Faye, for your part in discovering Tiago's involvement."

"It's my pleasure." Her footsteps sank into the soft earth. "Honestly, I would've felt awful leaving knowing it was still going on."

"It wasn't your problem to solve, but I really do appreciate it."

"How's Duarte holding up?" Faye asked.

Riley glanced at Carla, who wiped her brow with the back of her hand. "He's not good," Carla said. "Beating himself up like it was him who'd done it. I think he feels responsible for bringing his brother here."

"Maybe I need to have another chat with him," Riley said, twigs snapping under her feet. "I know he would have nothing to do with something like this."

"What will happen to Tiago?" Faye asked.

"He'll be tried and fined. Maybe even a prison sentence, depending on how deep it goes."

Good. The word settled solidly inside her. "I just hope the animals are safe now. Will the centre be alright?"

Riley hesitated, lifting her eyes to the gaps in the canopy where golden sunlight passed through. "Catching the poachers won't fix all of our problems, but it should help with the strain on resources at least." The sound of birdsong grew louder, closer, and Riley set the carrier down carefully, crouching on the forest floor. "This is my favourite bit about all of this," she whispered. "To see them back where they belong." She straightened, turning to Faye. "Do you want to do the honours?"

"Really?"

"You found her. It seems only fitting you release her again."

Faye knelt in the mulch, her finger hovering over the lock. She slid the metal clasp open and eased the door wide with a soft creak.

Nothing happened.

The parakeet stood still, head twitching and assessing. A breeze threaded through the trees, lifting the hairs along Faye's arms. Then Pinkie hopped forward, as though the leaves had whispered their encouragement. Then another hop.

They waited, the moment stretching, Faye's breathing too loud. Faye could understand the bird's hesitancy. "Come on, Pinkie," she whispered. "It's time to go home."

She admired the bird's pink crown, her bright green feathers, and the sprained wing that the volunteers at the centre had lovingly healed back to health. What an amazing thing to have witnessed up close.

The bird took another hop forward, head tilted towards the sky, and then with a flap of her wings, she burst free, a rush of colour flashing through the air. Elation flowed through her.

Pinkie did it!

Faye stayed kneeling, hands loose in her lap, listening as the forest settled back into itself. She scanned the canopy, searching for any sign of the bird, but she couldn't see without her binoculars. In the blink of an eye, that was goodbye. She sucked in a breath, feeling stupid for feeling sad. It wasn't a sad thing at all. It meant a second chance, a new start; it meant life.

The heat returned. Her skin was sticky beneath her shirt, but her chest weighed lighter, as though something significant had been set right.

Carla whooped, the sound echoing through the trees. Riley laughed and joined in, cupping her hands around her mouth. Faye grinned and let out a loud cheer from deep in her chest, shaking loose whatever heaviness clung there.

The treetops rustled above them. They tipped their heads back in time to see a flash of green bombing from the leaves. Dozens of parakeets poured into the air, wings cutting through sunlight as they swept the top of the forest in perfect synchronicity.

Faye's mouth fell open. She'd never seen so many all together. They cheered and clapped until they disappeared out of sight, the sound chasing the flock as they vanished beyond the trees.

Faye stood there smiling long after the birds were gone, her pulse racing—not with anxiety this time, but with something clean and bright.

Of course she needed goodbyes to move forward. Otherwise, she'd stay still, confined in a cage because she was too afraid to try. She wanted the new start, the regenerated version of Faye. She didn't want to be scared anymore. What was the point? It was only her who suffered.

Something slid into place. She was going to do it! After the Fire Ceremony tomorrow, Faye was going to be honest with Diana. She didn't want to take away from the significance of the ceremony; that would be wrong of her. But afterwards, once they'd given their thanks and received their familiars, she was going to be brave and honest and say what she wanted. Even if that meant saying goodbye for good.

But first, there was something else she needed to do.

***

Faye ran into the reception building. "Quin!" Quin's eyes grew wide as she approached, but she didn't slow down. "Come with me."

"What's wrong?"

"Nothing. Nothing's wrong. Just…you need to come with me."

"I can't." Their brows furrowed. "I have to ring my dad in five minutes."

"Quin. Do you *want* to ring your dad?"

"I have to. It's part of the rules."

"That's not what I asked."

They looked at their phone in their hand and slowly shook their head.

"Then please, come with me. We can tell him a storm wiped out the Wi-Fi or something."

"He'll check the weather forecast."

"Well then, a giant, clumsy parrot. Please. I really want to do this with you. And we have to do it now."

They raised an eyebrow. "You look completely unhinged. Do you know that?" Then they grinned, reaching out a hand for Faye to pull them up. "Fine. You got me. What is it you want to show me so badly?"

Faye threaded her fingers through Quin's, and they ran down to the beach, giggling like schoolchildren. They didn't stop until they were at the water's edge. The late sun was sinking, painting the waves with pink and orange streaks.

Faye kicked off her shoes, letting out a happy sigh as the sand sank between her toes.

"Is this the part where you sacrifice me?" Quin asked.

"Don't tempt me." She nudged them. "Shoes off, please."

"Oh, I see. You're trying to *seduce* me." They laughed but did as she asked, slipping out of their worn Birkenstocks and into the grains glistening beneath their feet.

Faye took Quin's hands, urging them to look at her. New energy continued to surge through her veins, making her unafraid, and she needed to share it. "Quin, you're one of the kindest people I've ever met. You make people smile without trying, even though I know you have your own shit to deal with. You've been there for me, been the best wing-pal ever, and…I'm really going to miss you."

"Girl, don't you start. You're going to have me ugly crying in a minute."

Faye squeezed their hands. "You're awesome, and I hate seeing the way you change whenever you speak to your dad. You shouldn't make yourself small for anyone. You shouldn't have to hide who you are."

Their eyes glossed over, and they looked away. "It's

not that easy, Faye."

Her heart squeezed. "Oh, Quin. I'm so sorry. I'm sorry that someone who's supposed to love you unconditionally lost the memo somewhere. But you can't change who you are."

"He's my only family. I don't have anyone else."

"You have me."

Tears spilt from their eyes then, and they wiped them on their arm.

Faye squeezed Quin's hand again. "This might sound crazy. But when this course ends, come live with me. I've been wanting to move out again, but I've been too afraid. We can make a new start together."

Their eyes flicked over Faye's, searching for any crack in her expression. "You mean it?"

"Of course."

They crushed her in a hug, knocking the breath from her, and spun her in circles. "Oh my god. This is going to be great. I'm going to be the best roomie ever, I promise. I make a mean veggie tortellini and—oh my god. We can have a Drew Barrymore marathon!"

Faye screamed as they continued to spin her, feeling dizzy when they finally put her back on the ground. "We have to mark it. Make it official."

"Sure!" They held out their pinkie, but Faye shook her head.

In a swift movement, she pulled off her T-shirt and threw it on the sand, standing just in her bra.

Quin looked at her quizzically. "I hope you're not

wanting to consummate this agreement, because you know, as hot as you are, it's purely friend vibes."

"Shut up, you." She nudged them. "It would be a sin not to have a swim in the Portuguese ocean before we leave. So what do you say?"

They hesitated, worry etching between their brows as they glanced around the beach. People were sunbathing in scattered groups across the sand, the water dotted with swimmers already enjoying the water. The white-tipped waves rolled back and forth, encouraging them deeper.

"Fuck it." They tugged their T-shirt over their head, revealing a bare chest with two faint surgical scars.

"Yes!" Faye removed her shorts, exposing her bag, and double-checked it was still snugly attached. Her bags were waterproof, but making sure the seal was done properly was important.

When they were both standing in their underwear, the sun warm on their backs, she held out her hand for Quin to take.

"We're saying goodbye to the island, but we're also saying goodbye to all the shit that's held us back. To everyone who's judged us and looked at us like we're freaks. We're leaving it all behind."

They nodded. "It doesn't end here. It starts."

"Exactly. On three?"

"Let's just go!"

So, with loud screams, they set off running into the waves, water splashing their calves and thighs before they dove into the deep, their laughter ringing out across the beach. Faye lay back, letting the ocean buoy her, the setting sun lighting her vision.

She was ready. For the first time today, she meant it.

For the ceremony, for Diana, for life after this…

I'm ready.

TWENTY-FOUR

Diana

Diana didn't have anyone flying out to celebrate with her. The only person she'd have wanted was Leanne, but she was in New York wrapping up a big book deal—not dissimilar to the one Diana was supposed to be writing. But it didn't bother her. This trip had never been about her—until it had been.

She sighed, then continued applying mascara in the mirror. Her time on the island had revealed some unsavoury truths. She wasn't happy with her life, not really. Some big changes and difficult conversations were needed when she returned home, not all of which she felt prepared for. But people rarely have the luxury to be ready. Life tends to throw us overboard, headfirst, straight into the deep end without asking questions or whether we have a carefully calculated plan.

She'd certainly never planned any of this with Faye. They'd successfully avoided the topic of the future; not that this was Diana's finest hour, but she still didn't know what she was going to do when the night ended. Her stomach flopped, claws hooking into her ribs.

Finishing things here, the way they were supposed to, would probably be doing Faye a kindness. Diana's life was busy and hectic. The idea of long distance had never appealed to her, and the numbers didn't lie—they were more likely to end in failure than success.

Yet the possibility of continuing this with Faye in the real world made the weight of all the pending changes easier to stomach. Faye had that effect on her. Like everything would work out alright if you just willed it hard enough.

But how could it? If Molly found out, all the progress they'd made on this trip would be torn to shreds, shattered beyond repair.

So why was it so damn hard to stop? The idea of saying goodbye to Faye forced those claws deeper and deeper into her ribs until she couldn't breathe.

A knock at the door snapped her spine straight. She blinked at herself, her reflection mirroring the sharp edges inside her.

With a deep breath, she morphed her expression into something neutral and answered the door.

Molly came into her cabin with a spin, curls bouncing, yellow dress fanning outwards.

"Well, don't you look nice!" Diana commented, remembering how Molly used to enter in exactly the same way home from school with exciting news of a school disco or a class trip.

"So do you." Molly beamed her gap-toothed grin. "You look like you mean business."

That hadn't exactly been Diana's intention when she wore one of her pantsuits. Nerves about the ceremony had been nibbling away at her, so she'd opted for something more familiar rather than a dress. Was she overdoing it?

Molly's eyes flicked to the envelope resting on the dresser. "Did you finish writing the letter?"

Diana's gaze followed, feeling the weight of her words penned inside it. "I did. Late last night."

Sleep had eluded her for many reasons. Yet this overwhelming urge to see this through had caused her to rise from her bed and put the pen to paper. A tired hand and six sheets later—front and back—she'd fallen to sleep in a matter of minutes.

"I'm proud of you." Molly crushed her in a hug. The gesture took Diana by surprise, but she wrapped her arms around her, breathing in her strawberry shampoo and planting a kiss on her head.

"Thank you. I'm proud of you, too." She pulled back,

keeping her hands on her shoulders. "Proud of you for really trying with this trip and spending time with me. I know you didn't want to, but I'm glad you did."

"I am too. I've seen a different side to you. More fun, less robot." Molly shrugged, laughing, as she laid her hand on the door handle. "Now let's end this thing in style."

Dusk fell over Sandy Springs in purples and blues, the last of the sun's rays streaking orange streamers across the sky. The steady beat of a drum carried on the sea breeze as they neared the courtyard, and the sound of clapping grew louder.

The courtyard, lit by blazing torches, had been completely transformed. Huge garlands of purple, orange, and white flowers hung from the wooden beams and lined the pathway into the centre, where a large stone firepit awaited lighting. Intricate carved logs ringed the fire for seating, each with a basket filled with bundles of herbs and plants on either side. A band played a steady beat under a canopy of flowers at the back as locals gathered across the stone flags, smiling and greeting the arrivals.

"Wow," Molly breathed. "This is amazing."

And it was. But Diana's pulse kicked up, overwhelmed by the sights and sounds, and all the hungry eyes. Her gaze passed over the crowd of strangers, faces dancing in the flickering light. She wished then that she'd invited someone she knew.

But then she saw her.

A beacon in green and gold, like someone had turned

up all the lights and shone them on her.

Faye laughed at something Quin said next to her, then her gaze lifted and locked with hers.

Everything else fell away. Like the courtyard had opened up for Faye to lead them in the Portuguese dance. Like it was just the two of them alone in Diana's room. Like the crowd had disappeared, and it was that first night again in the bar.

So much had changed. She felt so much weaker. She felt so much stronger. Her emotions continued to wrestle each other as she joined the others waiting by the fountain, where Senhor Arenoso took centre stage. A beautiful owl headpiece, with intricate beading, sat atop his head.

The drum continued to beat, hands clapping in time to the rhythm. Anticipation ate at her. These few weeks all boiled down to this moment. The mark of a new start, the end of an old one. Diana didn't know if she was ready, but time had officially run out.

Senhor Arenoso brought his palms together and bowed, and the music and clapping fell into a silence that hung too loudly in the space.

"Welcome, everyone!" he greeted, in a booming voice that echoed through the courtyard. "Thank you for joining us. Today marks the crossing of our latest group as we award them with their familiars and guide them into their next phase of life." He led the way through the parted crowd, commanding all the attention in the courtyard as he approached the firepit.

"Every second of this life is precious. Some people

forget this. Some wish the seconds away or waste them on things that don't bring them happiness. When we find the things that make our soul happy, we let fear take the reins. Fear of judgement, fear of change, fear of failure—but do you know what I say to that?" He received a flaming torch from Riley and beamed. "Live!"

He lowered the torch to the base of the fire, and flames burst skywards, drawing a collective gasp from the crowd. The fire burned bright and fast, popping and crackling and sending wisps of smoke into the darkening sky. Enthusiastic applause and cheers filled the courtyard.

Instinctively, Diana found Faye again. They smiled at each other, their own fire flowing between them, then Faye mouthed, "You look beautiful."

She let her gaze lower over Faye, dark hair long and straight past her shoulders, a beautiful green dress hanging on her tall frame, then mouthed back, "So do you."

A burst of adrenaline licked up her spine, and she wished then that she could tell her everything. How she made her feel—the good, the brilliant, and the terrifying.

But Senhor Arenoso's voice captured everyone's attention. "Fear is natural. But we can't let fear of life stand in our way. We have to have faith, take back control, make space for the changes in our lives." He gestured to the fire, his features darkened by shadows. "I invite each of you to give a gift to the flames. Fire is cleansing. It clears the old and makes way for the new. Say goodbye to something that doesn't serve you anymore. Anything you've been holding onto." He lifted his hands. "Let go and live life with love in your heart and peace in your mind. Let's celebrate this new step together!"

The crowd roared with applause, and the group lined up to take turns giving their offerings. The weight of the letter was heavy in Diana's pocket. She knew it was time.

She pulled it out, tracing the smooth paper with her fingers. The words inside flowed back to her like water running downstream.

Mum,

I miss saying that. Even at forty-one. I've been trying to write this letter for weeks. It's ironic how I had so many things I wanted to say to you, but trying to express them in words feels like an impossible task. Nothing is important enough, but every detail is important too. In a way, we're strangers now. I suppose I should at least reintroduce myself.

The group moved forward as Louis and Charles threw their offerings into the fire, the flames roaring. Diana thumbed the envelope. Once she'd started writing, she couldn't stop. She'd told her mum about Jason, her pregnancy with Molly, the disagreements with her dad, and how lonely she'd felt once her mum died.

There was so much of herself in these pages. So much she'd never said.

I was angry at you for leaving me. As an adult, I understand you didn't choose this for yourself. But I was still angry. I think parts of me still are.

She gripped the letter tighter.

I feel guilty, too, for denying parts of myself that remind me of you. Did you know I didn't step foot on a beach after you left? It hurt too much. I didn't want any more happy memories tainted with the pain of losing you.

She'd cried last night. Curled herself into a ball and let the feeling consume her. How did she have any tears left? The last thing she wanted was to break down in front of all these people in a grief-stricken epiphany. But the words kept coming back to her as the line in front continued to move, the rounds of applause barely touching her ears.

Never saying goodbye to you hurt. But it was more than just that moment. It was saying goodbye to everything you would never get to see. My life. My children. Saying goodbye to things I'd never know and never get to ask you. I was too young to really understand the finality of it all, the way it would stretch and touch everything. I've made mistakes, Mum. How am I supposed to know if you're proud of me? I tried my best, but I just want to know. Are you proud?

There were only a few people left. The heat of the fire intensified with every step, along with the weight in her feet.

In front of her, Faye pushed her hair over her shoulders. She stole a glance at Diana. Just the small smile—the flicker of a moment—reassured her, and she breathed in.

What was Faye thinking? What was she wanting to leave behind?

Faye plucked a green bundle from the basket and held it to her chest. After a few seconds, she tossed it into the flames and threw up her arms in celebration.

The flames danced, smoke spiralling upwards into the darkened sky. The next person added their offering, and Diana squeezed Molly's hand as she stepped up. A flower was incinerated, another round of applause, and then it was Diana's turn.

Hundreds of eyes were fixed on her, but the letter in her hand held her focus. The fire warmed her face as she plucked a blue flower from the basket—her mum's favourite colour—and placed it on the envelope.

I don't know how to end this. Much as how I didn't know how to start. I don't suppose there's ever a good way to say goodbye to someone you love, is there? One thing I do know is I'll do better. I'll talk about you. I want Molly to know who her grandma was.

She looked into the flames, alive and bright, and she knew it was time. Time to let go, to move forward, to say goodbye. She tossed the envelope into the flames, the paper blackening instantly. The roar of the crowd was deafening.

Goodbye, Mum. Thank you for everything.

The knot in her chest loosened, tension leaving her body. The words, along with the letter, had crumpled into ash, spiralling into the sky like snowflakes. She watched them dance in the darkness, flickering orange and slowly fading away. People she didn't know congratulated her as she passed, as well as familiar people from the course, and

Ella gave her an enthusiastic hug. Diana's gaze lingered on Faye for a fraction too long, but she couldn't help it.

Her bones were lighter, her muscles relaxed. She was…free. Fre*er*, at least. She couldn't remember the last time she hadn't felt life's pressures tugging at her ankles.

She slid in next to Molly and tapped her knee. "You okay, love?"

Molly beamed back. "It feels like we're supposed to be here, doesn't it?"

Surrounded by the warmth of the fire and friendly faces, the light feeling flowing through her veins, Diana could only agree. *You're meant to be here.*

She'd repaired her relationship with Molly, figured out some home truths, and learned a lot about herself. Not everything was crystal clear, of course, but as the group gathered together to watch the flames spitting and sparking, Diana let herself embrace the feeling, hoping that it would last longer than the wood took to burn.

Once the burning steadied, Senhor Arenoso stood again, ready to award the group with their spirit familiars.

He placed his hand on his chest. "When we slow life down and take a moment to reconnect with nature, amazing things happen. When we start to listen, start to feel, we discover parts of ourselves that were always there, hidden by the shadows. Our guides are not new to us. They're shut off from our hearts, disconnected from our true selves. When we tune into their energy and nurture that relationship, that bond is strengthened. Our guides are part of us. Embrace that, and we accept and love who we are. With that acceptance comes peace. With that, comes love." He smiled, his face lit by the flickering flames. "We are all connected. Everything."

The words resonated with Diana. She'd spent so long keeping people at a distance, the idea that she'd also shut off part of herself from the world didn't surprise her.

Her gaze fell on the glowing embers, and she breathed in the scent of the herbs and spices from the offerings. But then, Senhor Arenoso called her name. After a small push from Molly, she rose to join him, the warmth of the fire heating her as she passed.

"Palm up, please," he said.

She did as he asked, and his knowing gaze lingered, the owl headpiece towering above her, feathers spread wide.

"Diana," he began, his voice carrying throughout the courtyard. "Ambitious, dominant, independent. Strong and powerful qualities that can often steal the spotlight from some of your other, softer qualities. Remember, there's also strength in weakness and in trusting our gentle side. Don't smother that side in fear. She needs sunlight and space to grow." He touched her palm and closed his eyes, releasing a deep sigh. "Your guide has come to me. In all their light and mightiness." He produced a wooden totem, which he hung over Diana's head. Then he grinned, his dark eyes sparkling. "The dove."

She looked down at the wooden carving, with its intricately carved feathers.

"Doves are often celebrated as symbols of peace,

which is true, but their significance goes deeper. The dove is a call to renew, to cleanse and elevate, to break free from life's constraints. It's a beacon of gentle courage, encouraging calmness and harmony through love. With her pure white feathers and deep, caring nature, the dove is hope."

A loud round of applause erupted on all sides. Diana turned to face the cheering crowd. Molly beamed back at her, bringing her fingers to her mouth to whistle. Diana lifted her hand in thanks as the feeling surrounded her—lightness, excitement, a tingle that spread from the base of her neck to the tips of her toes.

When her attention fell on one woman in the crowd, the feeling surged, glowing and fluttering its wings.

***

After the last totem had been awarded, the staff moved the seating logs to one side, and the celebrations kicked up a notch. The band jumped into a lively acoustic set, encouraging everyone to dance and clap their hands. Ella and Riley led by example, twirling and spinning each other in circles, Ella's dress fanning around her as Riley guided her through the steps.

Despite the night's contagious energy, Diana kept to the edges, tapping her feet to the beat and watching the dancers, lit by the glow of the torches. Molly and Quin copied the accordion player's fast steps, tripping up in the process and laughing harder and harder. Diana's gaze landed on Faye. She was twirling with one of her dads, David, who'd flown out to celebrate. He moved with all the grace of a clumsy chicken in chinos.

Diana wanted to take it all in. The way the air buzzed with electricity and lingering smoke, the way laughter carried above the music, radiating pure joy. Above the canopies of flowers, stars sprinkled the indigo sky like fireflies. Beyond the cliffs, blanketed by darkness, she knew the sea continued to rock against the shoreline, forever changing, forever moving, but a constant all the same.

She thumbed the totem on her necklace. *The dove.* She'd never associate an animal so gentle with herself. It was a strange feeling. Like belonging—but also not. Something out of reach but eerily close. For a moment, she wondered if her familiar had any connection to her mum.

When a body bumped against hers, she turned.

"Don't look so disappointed," Ella teased, before she could mask her expression.

Diana leaned back against the wall. "Are you here to set me up again?"

Ella's gaze passed over the courtyard, where Faye was trying to teach her dad how to vogue. "It didn't work out too badly last time, did it?"

Diana shook her head. "Do I even want to ask how you know about that?"

"We have CCTV." Diana's mouth fell open, but

before she could reply, Ella nudged her again. "Kidding. I mean, we do have CCTV. But not like that."

Diana breathed a sigh of relief. "You're a menace. Has anyone ever told you that?"

"A few times." She gave her a small smile. "Do you want to know the truth?"

"Yes."

Ella eyed her, like she was assessing the validity behind her statement. "I can feel it. Some energies leave traces. Powerful ones. Like Hansel and Gretel but less lame and more epic." She waved her hand in Faye's direction. "You two are pumping out enough energy to make even Saint Valentine sick."

Diana bit the inside of her cheek, her eyes finding Faye across the room again.

"You feel it, though, don't you?" Ella pressed. "The way your bodies search for each other?"

Faye glanced their way, joy lighting her face, and something in Diana's chest squeezed. She didn't need to say anything. Judging by the knowing look in Ella's expression, she already knew.

Just like Diana did.

"You haven't got long," Ella said. Then she winked and skipped off towards the band. She whispered something in the singer's ear, they both grinned, and he brought the song to a close.

"Now for a group dance," he called, clapping his hands together. "Just follow me. Everybody!"

Ella shot her a glance from across the courtyard, and

Diana sighed. Whatever the woman was up to, she decided to play along. If she were to listen to the calling of her guide, she needed to push past life's restraints, and that included not waiting on the edge of the dance floor.

"Everybody, clap your hands." The man demonstrated over his head, stomping his big black boots. "Now spin the person on your left."

Diana had no choice in the matter; she was thrown into action by a short man, the courtyard circling around her. She stumbled, then righted herself, remembering her dance lessons.

"*Swap your partner!*"

Diana was catapulted to the left, landing in the strong arms of another man who smelled like cinnamon. Her eyes widened. She was dancing with Faye's dad, David. He grinned as they moved left and then right, the dance floor packed full of bodies. She caught sight of Faye as they circled around, her grin making her heart flutter again.

After another spin and clap, they swapped partners, and the two of them slotted together like magnets. Faye grinned, her hands warm and firm and sparking flames as they brushed against her skin.

"Are you having fun?" Diana asked, her own happiness tripling at the sight of Faye's.

"I am now." She held her tighter. "I want to talk to you properly, though."

"*Now spin your partner!*"

When Diana came back to meet those beautiful eyes,

Faye lowered her voice, though the music was loud enough to mask it. "Meet me at our bench?"

She nodded, then at the direction of the caller, they changed partners, the song kicking up tempo.

By the time Diana finally pulled herself from the dance floor, heart racing and heat creeping up her neck, Faye was already waiting. Away from the crowds, hidden by the darkness, the faint ocean breeze lifted the hair around her neck.

Faye let out a low whistle as she approached, her eyes roaming her body hungrily. "You look incredible. As always. Is there anything you can't make look a million dollars?"

Diana couldn't fight the feeling fanning in her stomach. She let her gaze drop over Faye's dress. "Green looks great on you."

"Thank you."

The two of them didn't say anything for a moment, the sounds of the party mixing with the hush of the waves below.

Faye scratched the back of her neck. "God. I don't know where to start. There's so much I want to say to you." Her attention fell on the totem hanging around Diana's neck, and she grinned again. "The dove… It suits you, you know."

"Do you think?"

"Definitely." Faye took a step closer, the moon hanging bright in the sky behind her. "Underneath those layers of perfectly tailored linen, you're a softie. I always sensed it."

Diana shook her head, but Faye reached out and took her hand.

"Really, though, getting to know you has been amazing. I've loved every second." She sighed. "Honestly, I've been struggling with it all coming to an end. The course, the island. Us." Her eyes flicked back to hers. Softer in the moonlight. "Diana, I…I know we had an agreement, but I don't want this to be goodbye when we step off this island tomorrow."

Diana swallowed, emotion thick in her throat. She didn't want that either, but the words were hard to say. They were her last layer of security; once they were out, she'd be disarmed and unguarded. Forever.

"Do you remember our conversation on the beach? About telling the truth?" Faye brushed her thumb over Diana's hand. The party cheered behind her, echoing in the quiet. "I don't know if being honest when it comes to my feelings will ever come without fear, but I know I don't want to leave here with any regrets. And if I leave without saying this to you, it'll be the biggest regret of my life." She blew out a big breath. "Here goes nothing. I know we should've spoken about this before now, but I was afraid of ruining a good thing. I suppose waiting until now, with only hours left, I've nothing to lose by laying my cards on the table." Her eyes crinkled, the passion swirling in her irises. "So here they are. I know there's distance to overcome. And a daughter," she added sheepishly. "But I want to try."

"You don't want me, Faye."

"What?"

Diana pressed her lips together. The words had come out harsher than she'd intended. But the ache in her chest called her back. The fear holding her there. She knew what people would say.

"When we get back to the real world, you won't want me. You're young, and you've got everything ahead of you. I don't want to stand in the way of that."

"Diana, that's bullshit." Her sharp tone forced their eyes to lock. "You don't get to tell me what I do or don't want. Did you not hear what I just said?" When Diana glanced away, unable to stomach the look in her eyes, Faye cupped her face, the action so soft and genuine, the backs of her eyes pricked. "I want to uncover more of your layers. I want to show you how beautiful you are, like you do to me. I want to love you in all the ways you deserve." She stroked her cheek, across the mole she'd declared her favourite. "I want you."

Those three little words pierced the veil Diana had shrouded herself with. She didn't have any of this under control. When it came to Faye, she wasn't sure if she ever had. And though the words still stuck in the base of her throat, her body always knew what to do.

She kissed her, threading her fingers through her hair and pulling her closer. The stars gleamed above, the music from the party playing like a soundtrack just for them. Her stomach flip-flopped, heat curling in all the familiar places Faye ignited as she deepened the kiss. Senhor had a point, didn't he? They needed to stop letting fear take the reins and live. They could do it. They could—

"What the fuck?"

A voice shot that hope straight in the head.

Diana jumped away, but it was too late.

Molly stood, the moonlight sharpening the shadows in her expression. "Tell me I'm not seeing this."

The air grew cold. *Oh shit, oh shit, oh shit.*

"This isn't what it looks like," Diana said, holding her palms up, but Molly cast daggers at her.

"Then what is it? Because it looks like my *mum* is kissing my ex-girlfriend." She shook her head, blonde curls trembling. "And that's so fucked up to even say, never mind look at."

"It's nothing. It's nothing like that. I…" But she had nothing to say. No words to explain. Panic eroded everything. She glanced at Faye, hoping to find something to help her, but the pain in her eyes was quick, unguarded, like she'd hit something raw.

"Is this to get back at me?" Molly asked. "For ignoring you for so long?"

Diana frowned. "What? No—"

"And that's why you didn't want to start things up again, is it?" Molly seethed, stomping towards Faye and giving her a push. "You'd traded me in for the older, saggier model!"

Well, Jesus Christ.

"Hey, that's not fair. You broke up with me, remember? We barely even dated. This is completely different."

"Oh, is it? Do tell me." Molly's eyes widened as she glanced between them, looking like a deranged tarsier. "Which one is it? Is it nothing or is it something *completely* different?"

"It's nothing. Faye just kissed me, and I...I just got carried away. It's nothing. It's..." As the words left her mouth, she felt the change in Faye's body, as though all the energy had drained out of it.

The world started spinning, shifting in a way she couldn't get back.

"I can't believe this." Molly's jaw tightened. "Not only have you gone behind my back, but you're lying straight to my face. Trying to blame it on her." She shook her head. "I should've listened to Dad. I never should've come on this stupid holiday with you. You are a selfish bitch, just like he said." She pointed a manicured finger at them both. "And this? It's sick. Hope you both rot in hell."

And she turned and ran, disappearing into the darkness.

A heavy sickness twisted Diana's gut, and she swallowed, trying to keep the contents down. *This is bad. This is really bad.*

"I guess it's good to know where I really stand with you," Faye said, the sadness in her expression clashing with the upbeat music. A tear spilt down her cheek. "I feel so stupid."

And then she was gone too.

Diana slowly lowered herself to the ground, trying to

steady her breathing, but her whole body trembled.

What had she said? What had she done?

In the blink of an eye, she'd ruined everything. Hooks clawed into her ribs again, her eyes stinging with tears, but she couldn't move. All she could do was feel it all as the drum from inside the courtyard continued to beat.

It no longer carried the message of a new beginning. It only marked the end.

TWENTY-FIVE

Faye - Three months later

Everything hurt. Her feet, her legs, her lungs. But the end was in sight. The benches by the canal signalled the biggest milestone yet—10k. So she kept moving, the distance shrinking, Self Esteem's "Focus is Power" pounding in her ears. *Just a bit more. Come on.*

When she reached the benches, her legs crying out with relief, she tilted her head back to the cloudy sky. A big grin stretched her face.

I did it.

A flock of ducks paddled towards her, puffing up their feathers and inspecting her hands for bread. The cold, crisp air nipped at her face, but her skin buzzed with adrenaline. Accomplishment. Another step closer to her goal.

I fucking did it.

Since her return from Sandy Springs, she'd started running three times a week, with the aim of raising money for the sanctuary. Though the poachers had been caught, the centre was still struggling, and Faye wanted to help. She wished she could say she was doing it for purely altruistic purposes, but she also desperately needed the distraction. Pushing her body and working towards the goal of a half-marathon helped to avoid thinking about a particular woman who had stamped on her heart.

She grimaced as the ache resurfaced. Everything had happened so fast. The elation, the betrayal, the goodbye. Faye wasn't a masochist. She wasn't going to let someone treat her like she didn't matter—no matter how hot they were. But it still hurt, like a hot scalpel scraping out her innards and slopping them on the pavement for the birds to feast on.

Leaving had seemed the best option in the moment. She'd completed the course, and there was nothing left for her other than memories of Diana laced in every corner of her cabin. So she'd stayed with Quin and left the island on the first boat in the morning, trying to avoid her dad's many questions. But getting away from it all without telling the woman how much she'd hurt her left the feeling festering. She didn't want their time on the island to be defined by that moment after the Fire Ceremony, for the title of *nothing* to be the lasting impression stamped on what the two of them had shared.

But did it even matter at this point? It had been three months of no contact. Three months of viewing the university website and lusting over Diana's profile. In a way, Faye was relieved she didn't have her number. At least then she wouldn't be tempted to call or send long texts to someone who didn't care about her.

She'd been doing well. She was back at work, looking for apartments with Quin, and she'd just run her first 10k, for god's sake. Something she'd never thought possible with Crohn's, never mind her ostomy bag. Training wasn't easy, especially in the beginning, when she'd had to watch herself for dehydration, a side issue with ostomies. But her support belt was a lifesaver, keeping everything snug and secure, and once her body had got used to the idea of running, Faye loved it.

The adrenaline. The pain. The accomplishment.

Running was infinitely more productive than curling up in the dark in her room and daydreaming about what might have been if Molly hadn't stumbled upon them. Because Diana hadn't replied to Faye's suggestion, but she had kissed her, and Faye thought that meant something.

She also denied it all and blamed it on you, her brain liked to remind her. *Yep. There was that too.*

She didn't need Diana to make her feel good about

herself. Yes, she loved the feeling when she was with her. The carefreeness, the confidence, the feeling she could do anything—but she could give that to herself. All this time she'd been searching for the enigma, and she understood now. She'd always had it.

A man rode past on his bike, pinging his bell in greeting. That was enough to snap her out of her pity party. She began her cool-down stretches, trying to refocus her thoughts on anything that wasn't the gorgeous blonde with impeccable posture.

"Stop thinking about her," she scolded herself as she sank into a hamstring stretch. "It's done now. If she wanted you, she'd have called."

"Damn straight," a woman quipped behind her. "You can't waste time trying to catch the wind, love."

Faye turned to the older woman sitting on the bench, a happy black schnauzer slumped across her lap. "Uh, thank you."

She put a cigarette to her puckered lips, lighting it with a match, and exhaled. "Keep putting one step in front of the other."

"I will. You too." Faye gave her a smile and then started walking, putting the advice into literal practice. She left the path and rejoined the road, the early morning air crisper now against her bare legs. The sun had already risen, but a grey mist hovered, threatening rain. Typical for her day off, but she could have been knee-deep in a bog observing frogs, so she'd not complain.

She blew out a breath, watching as the steam

contorted in front of her, and forced her tired legs up the hill. She was doing okay—she was—but she couldn't stop the niggle in the back of her brain, wishing that things were different.

She grasped the totem hanging around her neck, feeling its ridges. The elephant. *These gentle giants possess a phenomenal capacity to endure and overcome,* Senhor had stressed. *Their immense physical strength and intelligence make them a symbol of resilience and perseverance. The elephant teaches us to recognise our own strength and power. Harness that, and rule in the stability that our inner voice and instincts bestow.*

Faye wanted to believe that. In some ways, she did believe. Life with her ostomy had become her new normal, but when it came to her emotions, they flew all over the place. One moment, she was up on the runners' high, one step closer to her half-marathon goal. The next, she was standing in the courtyard, Diana crushing her heart in the palm of her hand.

What would an elephant do?

Other than stampeding across the Atlantic to drop a Titanic-sized poop on the woman's head, Faye wasn't sure.

She turned onto her street, rubbing the totem like it would suck out all the sadness sinking in her bones. She wanted to move on. But their last encounter played on a loop in her head. Had she been too rash? What might Diana have said if she'd waited?

But Diana hadn't contacted her. Diana didn't want

her. It was over.

So stop thinking about her.

The metal garden gate squeaked as she flung it open, the steps up to the mint-green door still damp from the morning condensation. In the hallway, she kicked off her shoes, placing them under the radiator to dry. The familiar sound of Tracy and Edna Turnblad was playing in the kitchen, and the knots in her chest loosened a little, knowing the scene before she even opened the door.

The music grew louder, the fresh scent of pancakes hitting her in a beautiful waft. As predicted, Lukas and Quin were mid-dance to "Welcome to the 60's" while David cooked batter in the pan, bopping his shoulders to the beat.

She'd barely had time to step foot into the kitchen before Quin tugged her towards them, encouraging her to twist her hips. Lukas held her other hand, the three of them bouncing in a circle—both more enthusiastic than her—until the song ended, to whoops and whistles from David.

"Alright, you lot." David turned down the speaker with one hand, sliding a fresh pancake onto the pile with the other. "Breakfast is served."

"Perfect timing, Faye," Quin said as they took a seat at the table. "You made a great Mr Pinky."

"Mr Pinky?" She scoffed, bending to stroke Mochi and Taco, who had come to see what the commotion was about. "I don't even need to ask who you were in the Broadway production."

"Well, duh." They grinned. "Of course, I'm Tracy Turnblad. I'm lead role material."

David took a seat next to Lukas. "I hope you've all worked up an appetite." His kind eyes flicked to Faye. "How was your run?"

"I did it." She forced her gaze to the stack of fresh pancakes, the smell making her salivate. David could see through her so easily, but she didn't want to talk about Diana again. She felt like a broken record.

"That's amazing!" Quin pulled her into a hug, knocking her elbow against the table. "You're a superstar."

"Well done," Lukas echoed.

"Thanks," she replied sheepishly, reaching for two pancakes and placing them on her plate. She scooped up a heap of fresh strawberries and blueberries and then drizzled syrup generously over it all. David's eyes tracked her, worry etched into his forehead. He'd need more to satisfy him. "And I've nearly raised 700 pounds for the sanctuary too."

"Wonderful." He beamed, and some of the tension in her shoulders loosened. "I'm sure Riley will be thrilled with that."

"Yeah," Quin added. "That'll be enough to give all the birds on the island a pedicure."

Lukas cracked up, squeezing Quin's shoulder before adding sugar to his stack of pancakes. Her dads had been amazing with Quin. Not that she'd had any doubt, but it hadn't taken long for Quin to become another part of the extended family.

She sliced through her pancake, putting the sugary goodness to her lips. Eating pancakes on a Sunday morning with people she loved, a job she adored, a life not confined to the four walls of her bedroom. It was enough. So why did she keep thinking about the spare seat at the table and how Diana might fit into this dynamic?

She chewed slowly, no longer hungry. She knew what her problem was. She was still holding onto hope. That last thread tethered to the balloon was wrapped so tightly around her finger, she couldn't let it go. Once the last strand was severed, banished to the atmosphere, that was it.

The end. Game over. Goodbye.

Senhor Arenoso had said that we need goodbyes to be able to transition. Faye needed closure, and no amount of running was going to give her that. She needed to speak with Diana. But how? When?

Diana confirming Faye's every fear about the time they'd spent together was only going to set her back…but maybe that's what she needed to sever the thread for good.

She finally swallowed her mouthful, the syrupy sugar too sweet for the churning in her belly. Truthfully, she didn't think she'd ever be ready. Good job they were thousands of miles apart, and the chances of bumping into Diana at Tesco and having that conversation were slim to none.

So she smiled through the rest of breakfast, accepting it was going to be one of those days where even certain shadows reminded her of the woman who'd crushed her heart. Normally, her run helped beat those stray thoughts into submission; today, tiredness consumed her.

Tomorrow will be better, she told herself. And it normally was. Throwing herself into work, taking care of the local ecosystems and doing something useful always helped to shake the funk. Plus, she and Quin had a couple of apartment viewings lined up.

She'd miss her dads, though. And the cats. Every transition really did come with a goodbye. She looked up from her plate. The three of them were discussing Chappel Roan. Her dads exchanged a glance as Quin ad-libbed a verse about pancakes to "Pink Pony Club".

The love was in the eyes. The way her parents watched each other without even realising it. Faye wanted that. She'd thought she had it.

Well, you didn't. So stop moping.

She stood and collected the plates, scraping her leftovers into the bin and then stacking the dishwasher. Mochi sauntered over, inspecting the contents. After confirming there was no food to be had, she pressed herself against Faye's legs, letting out a low chirp. Faye plucked her up, running her fingers through her thick grey fluff.

She'd miss this little rascal, too.

"Oh, sweetheart, there's some post for you on the side," David said as he stood, moving the frying pan to the sink. Mochi wriggled from her grip, darting to the stairs in anticipation of getting fed—though judging by the plumpness of her belly, she already had been.

Lukas caught David's elbow, guiding him away from the washing up and back to his seat. "Allow me." He planted a kiss on his cheek. "Although…isn't it still the newbie's job?" He shot a playful grin at Quin.

"I'm already on bin duty. These nails aren't made for manual labour." They aimed a dramatic sigh towards Faye. "The quicker we move out, the better, huh?"

"I don't know why you think that'll change things," she teased, plucking the stack of envelopes off the counter. "Bin duty suits you."

The room filled with laughter as she sifted through the mail. A check-up letter for her smear test, a right-wing leaflet that she immediately tore up, and then a manila envelope marked with a Portuguese stamp.

Her breath caught. A letter from Portugal? She quickly dismissed the suggestion that it was a warrant for her arrest. *It must be from the island.* But why?

Just open it.

As her parents and Quin fell into another debate about the worst household chores, Faye ripped the envelope and slid out the paper inside.

A dozen different emotions rolled over her as she read the words, excitement winning, fizzling through her veins. She read it again, just to be sure, then finally released a breath.

This invitation could be the closure she was looking for.

TWENTY-SIX

Diana – Three months later

Diana had never desired the attention that accompanied her numerous achievements and accolades. She'd strived hard for herself, not for the benefit of other people, whose false smiles and congratulations hid how they'd rather see you stumble than succeed, so they could use you for their own stepping stone. But still, formalities were formalities, she supposed.

At least on this occasion, it was a little different.

She zoned back in on the conversation around her.

Cilla Dorran was droning on to one of the young research assistants, whose excessive nodding showed desperation rather than agreement. Cilla was always in a bad mood. She survived not on oxygen but on complaints and moaning about anything and everything.

"It's just too clean, isn't it?" Cilla pressed, nose scrunching as she took in the room around her. "It's wonderful, of course, but it's just a bit too perfect for me."

And this coming from the woman who complained the coffee machine was also too clean.

Diana shared a glance with the young man. She sympathised; she'd been in his position before. Having to mingle and network and build connections with people who only wanted a subservient drinks lackey and often had a stick up their own arse.

"Evan, have you spoken with Dr Moore tonight?" Diana asked. "She's written a paper on the complexities of antibiotic-resistance evolution, which might interest you."

His thick eyebrows lifted, relief obvious. "I haven't yet, but that sounds fascinating."

"She's over there. Red dress. Big breasts and lipstick." She took a sip of her wine to hide her smirk.

"Ah...yes." He failed to hide the blush creeping up his neck but gave her a genuine smile. "Thank you, Dr Thompson."

He scurried away, then righted himself, remembering the assembly of significant professors dissecting every move.

The polite chatter resumed. Quiet. Respectful. Boring.

The sooner this was over with, the better.

Diana took in the low-lit familiar faces, the immaculate cream sofas and polished furniture. She took another swig from her glass, relishing the crisp taste. She would miss the wine, if nothing else.

"Have you tried the new hand soap in the faculty toilets?" Cilla asked, her voice droning like a faulty appliance. "The smell is reminiscent of…"

Oh god. Get me away from here.

A loud cackle came from the other side of the room. Selena Borgo threw her shoulder-length dark hair back, her hand on the shoulder of the dean like he'd said the funniest thing in the world.

Another thing I won't miss about this place.

Before Diana could shift her gaze, Selena locked eyes with her, her mouth curling in a delighted sneer. A year ago, Diana would've been up there, competing with her. Who could make the dean laugh the most? Who steered the conversation with the most esteemed group of colleagues?

Who cares? Diana didn't want it. She knew what she really wanted, but she wouldn't let herself think about it. About her. Or about the unanswered invitation sitting in her email inbox.

One thing at a time, she reminded herself.

The clink of a glass brought the room to silence. The dean, a man in his sixties, with thick, perfectly coiffed white hair, was standing by the unlit fireplace, flashing his pearly-white veneers. "Thank you for joining us tonight as we say goodbye to our brilliant colleague and friend, Dr Thompson."

Applause rippled through the room, and Diana lifted a stiff hand in thanks. She wouldn't consider any of them friends. The dean continued, listing off her achievements like a greedy child's Christmas list. And yes, they were important, and yes, they were impressive, but…who cares?

Really, it was about the money, the funding, the grades. It wasn't ever about Diana.

But she let him drone on, anything to distract from the hollow void in her chest that she didn't know how to fill. When he finally drew to a close, she smiled again through the applause, and the room settled back into chitchat. The food would be served soon, but she didn't want it. She wanted out of this room.

Unfortunately, everyone and their uncle chose this opportunity to commiserate and congratulate her on the new permanent position at Oxford. She kept her voice light, professional, delivering the rehearsed lines like a seasoned actress and not one in emotional distress. But she was over it; she was done. She just wanted to close her eyes and wake up back in England, without the insufferable seven-hour flight.

When the waiters brought out the food in silver-domed plates, and the crowd flocked to the serving table, Diana had room to breathe. This was her chance. She could slip away unnoticed and let the merriment continue without her.

She plucked up her black Prada handbag—and the leaving card inscribed with names she'd forget in a few months—and quietly slipped out the door. She'd said her piece with the dean earlier, genuinely thanking him for the opportunity to work there. For the most part, she had enjoyed it. It was just time to move on.

The hallway smelt of old polish and firewood, though the fires were scarcely lit. That old-money aura clung to every surface in the building. Something Diana used to admire but now found ostentatious.

She was heading towards the exit, heels sinking into the thick rug underfoot, when a voice called her back.

"Leaving without saying goodbye?"

Fantastic. She stopped, sucking in a breath, and turned around. Selena was standing in the hallway, one hand on her hip, her pencil skirt and red tailored blazer bridging the gap between intellectual and fashionable. She flicked her hair over her shoulder, then slowly swayed towards her, those misleading dewy eyes darting to the card tucked under her armpit.

"I didn't have you pegged for a runner," she said, smooth as silk.

"I have somewhere to be," Diana lied, keeping her expression neutral. If there was to be one final power play between them, there was no chance she was going to surrender.

"A woman in high demand." Selena clicked her

tongue, letting the silence stretch. Her gaze lingered, dripping down Diana's cleavage. "I've always admired that."

Diana kept her voice firm. "That's understandable."

Selena cracked a smile at her response, revealing perfect, straight teeth. She adjusted her thin gold-framed glasses. "I knew you'd make this difficult for me, but I suppose that's part of your charm." She took another step forward. "I was hoping we could leave things on better terms. It's no secret that I've enjoyed our rivalry over the years. It brings out the best in us, wouldn't you agree? Nothing quite like some healthy competition to keep bettering ourselves." She tilted her head when Diana didn't respond. "You're a powerful woman, Diana. I like that. If you find yourself with any time in your busy schedule before you leave tomorrow, you should pay me a visit." With the confidence of someone who'd just secured a million-pound grant, she placed a kiss on each of Diana's cheeks and turned, her hips swaying back down the hallway.

Diana could only watch her, wondering what on earth just happened.

***

When Diana finally made it into the comfort of a hotel room the next day, she let out a sigh, dumping her suitcases by the door. Not only had her flight been delayed, but she'd had to spend the journey next to a man who thought he had the right to both armrests and snored like a nasally grizzly bear. Normally, she enjoyed travelling. She blamed the lack of sleep for her discomfort, worrying if she was making the right decision—to return to England, that is, not whether or not to hate-fuck Selena.

The idea of releasing some of her frustration and sadness was tempting, but the reality of touching someone? Someone who wasn't *her?* She needed no time to think about that. The answer was obvious, even in her fragile state.

What she'd shared with Faye wasn't easily replaceable. It had started off as sex, yes, as a curiosity, to see if Diana could loosen up, but it had morphed into something much more than that long before she had the guts to admit it.

These terrible three months apart were telling enough in themselves. Plus, the giant ache in her chest whenever she allowed herself to think about her. Of course the ache multiplied with the absence of her daughter too. She'd exchanged a few words with Molly, called her dozens of times, but the message was clear, still sitting in their inbox as her last response.

Leave me alone.

So she had. For six long, agonising weeks. She'd given her space, hoping that would help, but she also dreaded whatever sewage Jason was no doubt filling her head with in the meantime. She'd handled the situation all wrong.

She'd talked at length about it with a therapist, Dr Andrews, who she'd started seeing after her return from Sandy Springs. Turns out it wasn't just the emotional baggage from her mother's death she was carrying, it was a whole bus full of unresolved issues. Her divorce, her relationship with her dad, and her avoidance tactics for most things that went wrong in her life. All that time she'd spent running away from her problems now felt like a waste. What was she so afraid of?

Maybe having everything and losing it in the blink of an eye. *Or with a kiss on the lips.*

She'd strengthened her relationship with Molly *and* had the possibility of starting something real with Faye. Then just like that, both were gone.

Needing to think about anything else, she pulled out her phone and checked her messages. She sent a text to Leanne, who replied in seconds.

Leanne: *Glad you're back on home soil. I'll be in London next month, so let's get dressed up and go for cocktails How's things?*

Diana: *Absolutely, thank you, you're a gem*
And no update, still radio silence

Leanne: *Give it time. Have a little faith. I'm sure Molly will come round*

Diana: *What if she doesn't?*

She watched the dots bounce.

Leanne: *She will. You need to stop beating yourself up. You're only human*

That hadn't exactly been her friend's response when she'd initially told her what happened—*what the hell were you thinking, Di?*—but she couldn't blame her. Diana could hardly believe it had happened herself.

She shot her ex-agent a reply, thanking her, then lay back on her bed, looking up at the clean white ceiling.

At least she and Faye had those wonderful three weeks on the island. She wished she could say that was enough, but the lie wouldn't stick.

Why hadn't she reached out sooner? Why hadn't she shared a bed with Faye? Regrets drip-fed into her brain until they pooled around her. She'd never hold Faye as night thinned into daylight, never feel the way sleep softened her in her arms. There were so many things she would never do and never say.

Faye had said once, "Don't let me be something you regret." But the regrets continued to rise, flooding the hotel room until she couldn't breathe.

She forced her body upright, remembering the grounding techniques Dr Andrews gave her to calm her racing heart. She searched for senses. *The twinkling city lights through the window. The hum of traffic below.*

Breathing in deep, she held it for a second before releasing. *The soft hotel bedsheets.*

Once she'd steadied her breathing, she flicked on the bedside light, casting a yellow glow about the room. When had it gotten so dark? The year, along with her brain, was running away with her. Always running. Always, always running. She was tired.

She scooped up her phone and opened the email she'd been avoiding.

Hello to all of you wonderful people!

I hope you're having a lovely day, week, and year. We have some news to share with you from Sandy Springs—two of our own are tying the knot! Riley and Ella want to invite all of you to share the joy and celebration of their wedding day, October 11th.

Cabins can be reserved for free on a first-come, first-served basis. Boats to and from the island will also operate more frequently if you choose to stay on the mainland.

We hope to see you there to celebrate love in its finest form. Please RSVP your attendance.

Diana bit her lip, torn between the possibility of seeing Faye and the implications of returning to the scene of the crime. The ache in her chest cried out for reconciliation, and the sensible part of her brain urged her to let it go. As much as she'd love to see Riley and Ella get married, she had to put her relationship with Molly first. She couldn't go back to the island. Seeing Faye again had the power to completely unravel her and annihilate any hope of fixing things with Molly for good.

She darkened the screen and tossed it away from her, tucking her knees to her chest.

She'd bounce back eventually. She always did. But for now, she'd stay curled up, marvelling at how she could simultaneously feel so close and yet so far away from those she truly cared about.

***

Diana lingered on the kerb opposite her family home. The red-brick semi-detached stood in front of her, unchanged by all the years that had passed. The empty hanging basket still hung there, flowerless since her mother's death. It creaked as it swung in the breeze, barely clinging to the rusted chain.

She pulled her coat tighter around herself, the chill creeping into her bones—or maybe it was the ghosts of her past gathering around her. What was she waiting for?

She'd been so sure this morning, but now the black door loomed before her, and she shrank under its shadow. Like she'd reverted back to that little girl crying alone in her room.

She'd made her mum a promise in her letter. To keep talking about her, not to shy away from her feelings. Diana had accepted the reality of her relationship with her dad. Some things couldn't be fixed. If she wanted an apology from the stubborn man, or a heartfelt epiphany, she wouldn't find one. But maybe she could find her mother's pictures.

She straightened her spine. He couldn't control her now. He hadn't for years. She could do this.

She forced her feet across the road and knocked loudly on the door. Her heart thumped hard, inching into her throat with every passing second.

There was movement on the other side. The thud of footsteps. Her breath caught as the door opened, and her heart plummeted into her heels.

"Molly?" she breathed.

Her daughter blinked back at her, confusion knitting her brows together until anger hijacked her features. "How did you know I was here?"

"I didn't. I…" She glanced at the house, even though she knew it was the right one. She'd been staring at it for the last god knows how long. "What're you doing here?"

"I could ask you the same question."

"I…came for the photos. Mum's photos."

Maybe it was a trick of the light, but she swore Molly's gaze softened, just for a second. Her fingers flexed on the handle, then the door inched open, inviting her in.

Not wanting to give her time to change her mind, she hurried inside. Not much had changed in all these years. The same worn green furniture crowded the coffee table, the same coals glowed orange in the fireplace. It was surprisingly tidy—no pots or glasses left out, no dust gathering on the bookshelf, just a stack of old shooting magazines stacked by the door. She removed her shoes, then hovered, feeling like a guest somewhere she used to call home.

Molly closed the door behind them, then took a seat on the sofa, crossing her legs.

Mum's old spot.

"Thank you for letting me in." Why was Molly here? She barely felt prepared to face her dad…this was something else entirely. She cleared her throat. "Is Grandad here?

"He's out," Molly grunted, shifting her gaze towards the TV, though there was nothing on.

"Molly…" Tears pricked Diana's eyelids as she sank into the chair beside her. Close enough but not too close. "I'm so sorry for how things ended in Portugal."

Her eyes cut towards her. "For fucking my ex under my nose, you mean?"

Hurt flared in her chest. "Yes. For all of it. But I want you to know, I didn't know about your history when it first happened."

"But then you did, and you still continued?"

It does sound bad when put like that. She sighed. "Yes."

"Jesus Christ, Mum. What the hell were you thinking?"

Her head dipped. She didn't know what to say. She had no excuse. "I'm sorry."

"So you keep saying. But that doesn't change anything, does it?" Molly shook her head. "I finally thought we were getting somewhere. Like you were treating me like an adult and not a stupid kid, and then you go and do something like this. I wanted to trust you, but you're always hiding things. Don't you get sick of keeping it all in? Of lying? Isn't it exhausting?"

Her words hung in the air. Thick like smoke.

Diana blinked, but it wouldn't clear. "It is exhausting," she admitted. "It's the only way I've learned to cope. But I'm working on things." She focused on the embers glowing red in the fireplace. "I'm continuing therapy. I've moved back to England and taken a job at Oxford. I'm trying, Molly. I really am."

Molly crossed her arms. "What do you want? A round of applause? How am I supposed to trust you after this?"

"You can. You can trust me. I promise."

She scoffed. "Yeah, right."

"No more lies. I swear."

Molly's stare sent heat rising up Diana's neck. "Did you sleep with her?"

She pressed her lips together, then answered, "Yes."

"More than once?"

"Yes."

"Fucking hell."

The silence stretched, Diana's neck pricking. When Molly finally spoke, her voice was softer, a stark contrast to the hard lines carved between her brows. "How do you really feel about her?"

Diana thought of Faye's grin, of her weird and wonderful brain, her gentle, caring nature, and how deeply she loved all animals. The way she touched her, looked at her, like she was something worth treasuring. How safe she felt around her, like she could lower her weapons and defences and still be someone desirable. "It's complicated."

"Complicated?" Molly huffed. "You'll have to do better than that."

"I…care about her a lot."

Molly was silent for a minute, suddenly interested in her hands resting on her thighs.

"I'm really sorry for belittling what happened, Mol. I panicked in the moment. I was terrified of losing you." Diana swallowed. "I said I'd be honest, and I am. It was just a holiday fling that got out of hand. I do care about her a lot. But that doesn't mean anything is going to happen. It's over now."

Molly nodded, seemingly satisfied. Diana let out a breath, hoping it would be enough. Hoping they could finally move past it.

"Why didn't you tell me Dad cheated on you?"

The change of topic was like a slap in the face. "I…well." She wet her lips, trying to gather her thoughts. "I guess I wanted to shelter you from it."

"Why?"

"I didn't want you to think differently of your dad or to be caught in the middle. Badmouthing each other doesn't do anyone any favours."

"He badmouths you."

She let out a humourless laugh. "Well, yes, that doesn't surprise me."

Molly snapped. "Do you know how frustrating it is to be kept in the dark about these things? Don't you think I deserve to know, so I can make my own mind up?"

"You do. But I was doing my best to protect you. I never want to see you hurt."

Molly sighed, putting her head in her hands. "It's quite a surprise to find out both my parents are set on lying to me about everything my entire life."

Diana looked at her daughter and started to piece things together. "Is that why you're at Grandad's? Are you staying here?"

"Just temporarily. I needed space to think."

She nodded. Pleased that, if nothing else, she'd raised a daughter who could think for herself. She'd been so worried about what direction her life was going to take, but she should've had more faith in her. Any person with half of Diana's DNA was bound to carve their own path. Molly was going to be fine.

She sighed. "I really am sorry, love. For everything."

Molly's blue eyes met hers, softening. "I know."

She breathed out a sigh of relief, and something shifted in the space between them. Like a fresh breeze through an open window, clearing all the heavy air.

"Did you receive the wedding invite?" Molly asked.

Her heart squeezed again. "Yes."

"Are you going to go?"

"No. Like I said, it's over. It's best to focus on my new start here."

To her surprise, Molly frowned. "You should go."

"What?" *Is this a test?*

Molly released a long, annoyed sigh. "Mum. You're one of the smartest people I know, but sometimes you're so dumb."

When Diana continued to look back at her, completely dumbfounded, Molly continued, "Look, I admit the idea of you shacking up with Faye wasn't on my list of top 100 moments, but, contrary to popular belief, I'm not stupid."

"Molly, I know you're not stupid, but—"

"But what?"

"But nothing can happen between Faye and me. I won't let anything jeopardise our relationship again."

Molly's brows pulled together. If this *were* a test, Diana was sure she'd get an F. "You said no more lies, Mum. But you're still lying to yourself."

Diana blinked, unsure if the words she was hearing were real or if she was still in a hypnotic state, standing outside on the street, imagining this whole conversation.

"This holiday ended in a shit show, alright," Molly said, "but you were different. You've always been so uptight, career-focused, but on the island, you were happy. Fun. I liked that side of you." She tilted her head. "Dad moved on, so why haven't you?"

Of all the lines of questioning, Diana hadn't expected

this one. "I have moved on. I haven't had any feelings for your dad in a long time."

"I mean, why haven't you found someone else?"

She sucked in a breath. "I…just haven't wanted to. I wasn't ready."

"And what about now?"

She looked at her daughter then, her face serious, eyes assessing. "Molly…"

"What?"

"Isn't it a little unusual to discuss this with you?"

"Honestly? Yeah. But didn't you learn anything from Sandy Springs? Life is short. Yeah, I was mad at you, but I think once the shock wore off, I was more angry about all the lies and the secrets. I'm not a kid anymore. I don't want you to keep things from me."

"No more."

"Promise?"

"I promise."

Molly nodded once, final. "So, what are you going to do then?"

Good question. Her brain had been through the blender in the last ten minutes.

"As much as it weirded me out, you deserve to be happy, Mum."

"Thanks, love." She blinked back tears. "I still don't know what to do, though."

Molly rolled her eyes. "You do. You've just got to listen."

Diana relaxed the tension in her shoulders, sinking

back into the armchair. So many conflicting emotions were wrestling inside her. Relief, apprehension, surprise, doubt, all bouncing around like ping-pong balls.

If Molly could have a change of heart, so could Faye. But maybe it was too late? Even if she did go to Sandy Springs, there was no guarantee that Faye would go at all.

But Molly was right. Deep down, she already knew the answer. So she closed her eyes and focused on her breathing, allowing herself to listen.

Breathe in...breathe out. And there it was. The flutter of wings beating together, starting small, then rising, louder, bigger.

Hope.

She opened her eyes, meeting her daughter's. "Thank you."

Molly nodded. "So..." Her mouth curved into a small smile. "Do you want to see Grandma's pictures?"

TWENTY-SEVEN

Faye

As she stepped off the wobbly boat onto the soft sand of the island, Faye was exhausted. Not from the journey itself, but from the constant yo-yoing in her mind from *what am I doing* to *I need this.*

Everything had ended so abruptly; she needed the closure. But now she was here, the sun and the sea greeting her like an old friend, reality hit her. Closing the book here would make it final.

You need this, she reminded herself, dragging her

small suitcase through the sand and onto the canvas walkway. She stepped under the arch of blue and yellow flowers welcoming her back to the island and breathed in the fresh, salty air. It was cooler than the last time she was here, but the October sunshine covered the island in a golden glow. The space hummed with activity. Dozens of people dressed to the nines, with fascinators dotted around like a lost flock of tropical birds, one gust away from disappearing into the North Atlantic. Guests gathered around the buggies, acting as a makeshift taxi rank to transport them further inland.

Faye scanned the colourful scene, looking for a phenomenal pantsuit, her pulse keeping a sturdy rhythm. She couldn't explain it, but she sensed that Diana was near.

She landed on a pair of kind dark eyes.

"You're here!" The force knocked the air out of her as Carla scooped her into a big hug. "Dog's Bollocks! I missed you."

"I missed you too," she mumbled into her shoulder, the world passing her in a spinning blur as Carla twirled her round.

Carla put her back on land and studied her appreciatively, letting out a low whistle. "Someone did not come to play, eh?"

Faye struck a little pose, fanning the blush pink dress so that the slit running up her thigh showed even more skin. Her dads and Quin had spent hours shopping with her until they'd found the perfect dress—one that screamed: "Diana, eat your heart out." The combination of the deep V-neckline and cinched ruched waist, and the smooth, soft fabric flowing over her skin, absolutely nailed the brief.

Carla nudged her. "Come on. You can ride VIP with me."

Riding VIP with Carla meant sitting at the front, wedged between a suitcase and a box of bottles, while other guests packed into the back. She chatted away as they navigated the island, a bombardment of memories flying at Faye: seeing Diana in the bar, throwing up in the flowers, running after Tiago, kissing Diana in the ruins.

That moment in the courtyard when everything shattered.

As they climbed the hill towards her cabin, a ghostly feeling passed over her. The presence of Faye who'd arrived here last time. How unsure she was. How afraid— how *hungover*. So much good had happened here that had changed her for the better. She was more confident and accepting of herself, and she knew what she wanted. She wouldn't let what happened with Diana taint or take away from that. Ultimately, finding her enigma was what she'd come here for in the first place.

She breathed in deep, letting the air touch every space in her lungs. When she exhaled, she picked her head up higher. *I'm a fucking elephant. Strong and resilient.* She touched the totem resting against her chest, letting the feeling sink further into her skin.

Faye left her suitcase at her new cabin, then Carla

dropped her off at the courtyard with the others, with the promise of seeing her later at the wedding. Flowers cascaded down the pergola in blues, pinks, and yellows, and she touched one as she passed, the silky petals soft between her fingers. A dozen round tables had been set up in the courtyard, their clean white tablecloths adorned with petals, with blue napkins folded into turkeys and dolphins—Riley and Ella's spirit familiars.

"Would you like a drink?"

The voice made her turn, and she burst into a big grin. "Romeo! How are you doing?"

He grinned back, wobbling his tray and almost spilling the flutes of sparkling liquid down his neat, beige vest. "I finally got the goats to master the hoop trick. Now I just need to add the fire."

The image of Sandy Springs doused with flames entered Faye's mind. "That's brilliant… Just be careful, Romeo."

He nodded, angling the tray towards her, his brown hair flopping over his eyes. "Would you like one? They're non-alcoholic."

She declined. Drinks with bubbles still didn't do her any favours—whether they were alcoholic or not. The last thing she wanted today was a bag-astrophe. Romeo made the rounds of the other guests, and Faye went for a wander. She chatted with some familiar faces from her time on the island. Louis and Charles were in the process of adopting a baby, and Faye couldn't be happier for them. Her eyes kept wandering, though, searching for that woman who could turn her legs to jelly and her heart to mush.

When Senhor Arenoso appeared, clapping his hands together and asking everyone to follow him down to the beach, Faye's heart sank.

Maybe Diana wasn't coming.

She'd known it was a possibility. One that she'd have to be content with. But she'd had a feeling…

She picked up her gaze, scanning the rush of colourful guests again. Maybe the connection they'd shared had been weakened by their time apart, distorted by the electromagnetic waves, and it was all wishful thinking.

She couldn't deny the disappointment. There was so much she wanted to say to Diana that would go unsaid, but she'd promised herself she'd be present for Ella and Riley's wedding. So she had to put a pin in that for now.

I'm a fucking elephant.

She joined the throng as they descended the walkway, dresses catching the wind like billowing ribbons, some holding their hats for dear life. The sea, as reliable as ever, beckoned them closer with rolling waves, the gentle crashing soothing Faye's internal storm.

On the sand, bamboo runners led the way to the aisle, which was prettily decorated on either side with shells and colourful stones. Blue chiffon drapes fluttered loosely in the breeze, matching the chairs paired with white gypsophila. At the head of the aisle, a beautiful wedding arch stood, wrapped in white and blue flowers.

Senhor Arenoso, wearing a magnificent blue kaftan lined with gold, exchanged hugs and kind words with everyone as he guided them to their seats. Faye removed her shoes by the wooden sign offering guests that option, letting her toes sink into the warm sand.

"Faye," Senhor greeted her, kind eyes assessing. "Lovely to see you. I trust the elephant is guiding you well?"

"As well as she can."

He let out a low chuckle before steering her towards a white wicker chair. "Have a little faith," he said with a wink, and turned to greet the next in line.

Faye smiled at her neighbours and let out a breath. *Just relax and enjoy yourself.* Her leg bounced, the material sliding off her thigh.

More guests filled the aisles, polite chatter humming around her as the waves broke gently on the shore and birds cawed overhead. She hoped Pinkie was doing well. Riley had told her the tracker showed her successfully reunited with her flock, so she took pride in that.

She let her gaze drift, admiring a raft of shearwaters bobbing along the frothy surface of the water. Then a figure emerged from behind the rocks.

Her heart squeezed. She forgot how to breathe.

Diana was approaching, black heels in hand, the breeze gently tousling that gorgeous blonde hair, like a shampoo advert. A sophisticated mid-length dress flowed around her calves, its long sheer sleeves and deep V-neckline revealing acres of perfect pale skin. As she drew closer, Faye's pulse firm and thick in her throat, the delicate, textured pattern on her dress grew visible; the deep burgundy colour was that of an exquisite red wine Faye wanted to drown herself in.

Diana carried herself just as Faye expected. Like that of a goddess, an angel, a queen. Her breath hitched as Diana scanned the seated guests. Was she looking for her?

She waited, heart fighting to beat out of her ribcage. The chatter of the guests around her faded into a pitchy ringing that only heightened her focus on the woman standing by the wedding arch.

Then Diana's gaze found Faye, and the world tilted on its axis. Everything she'd worked so hard to contain slipped away from her and towards the woman who held her heart. Like gravity itself were shifting.

She blinked, the pull behind her sternum deepening, the distance between them unbearable. But it was Diana's face… Her composed expression, her deep chocolate eyes tracing Faye's frame like they were committing it to memory. Then the twitch of her mouth. The corner curving into that smile that struck like an arrow through her heart, pinning her to her chair.

Then the scene snapped like a shutter. Senhor Arenoso hurried to greet Diana, blocking her from view as he ushered her into her seat. She'd made it just in time; the wedding was about to start.

Faye exhaled shakily as the band began. The light acoustic notes of the *cavaquinho* drew the guests into silence. Heads turned as the staff made their way down the aisle first, fronted by Carla and Romeo arm-in-arm. They joined Senhor Arenoso at the front, faces full of grins as Riley walked down next, dressed in a tailored beige-and-baby-blue suit. She greeted everyone as she passed, offering smiles and waves, until she reached the altar, where Senhor Arenoso pulled her into a big hug. The two bridesmaids were next. A forest green sculpted dress for one, blonde hair pinned up messily, while the other's was pink and loud and full of feathers, with an enormous fascinator resembling a satellite dish balanced on her head.

The acoustics swelled, the *viola braguesa* joining the *cavaquinho*, the paired strings weaving a flowing accompaniment as everyone got to their feet for the bride's arrival.

As she descended the last step, helped along by a man Faye assumed was her dad, Ella burst into joyful laughter. "Who thought it was a good idea to attempt all those steps in these heels?"

She stepped onto the bamboo, sunlight catching every movement of the delicate tulle and lace flowing around her curves. Her train trailed softly behind her with every step, catching sand under the silk like glitter, her grin growing with every second.

Riley held her hands to her chest, eyes threatening to spill as her bride drew closer. Faye couldn't help but steal a glance at Diana, who was watching the ceremony with glossy eyes. As though on instinct, her gaze flicked to Faye's. Faye's heart fluttered as she returned her attention to the brides.

Senhor Arenoso stood with Riley under the arch, his own features swelling with pride as Ella's dad kissed her cheek and gave her arm to Riley.

"Good luck!" he teased with a wink. "She's your problem now."

Ella swatted at him as he took his seat at the front, but Riley caught her hand, planting a kiss on her fingers. "Happily." Dimples popped in her cheeks. "You're so beautiful."

"So are you." Ella squeezed her hand. She pivoted to the guests, as though she'd just remembered they were there. "And so do all of you. All of this... It's so wonderful. Thank you so much for making the journey here. It means the world to both of us."

Senhor Arenoso brought his palms together. "Welcome, friends, family, to life's most precious and sacred event, the joining of two souls. There's something incredibly special about these connections. When a bond between partners recognises the light and shadow in their inner worlds, it transcends simple physicality and becomes a deep, powerful energy that feeds back into the world itself.

"True love is sacred. It's love that shifts our understanding of ourselves and the universe. When we recognise that, when we're brave enough to nurture and challenge it...it's the most potent and compelling force that exists." He glanced between the two of them with tears in his eyes, but his voice didn't waver. "It spills into the people around us. It feeds back into the earth. It restores balance and faith that true love, in its purest, most profound state, survives, blossoms, and endures." He placed a hand on each of their shoulders. "So let's unite them further, the turkey and the dolphin, brought together in life's imperfectly perfect harmony."

That brought a cheer from the guests and a loud wolf-whistle from the green-dress bridesmaid.

Faye blubbed through the vows and the exchanging of rings. Riley's words had most people dabbing their eyes, but tears streamed down Ella's face as she relived their journey of how they got here.

Ella's vows took a more comedic route, starting with how Riley had rescued her from a bramble bush in the middle of a rainstorm.

Then, at Senhor Arenoso's declaration of marriage, the two brides kissed, and everyone burst into a loud roar of applause. Riley dipped Ella, throwing her head back in laughter until she kissed her again. A flash from the photographer immortalised the moment forever.

Just then, a passing seagull dropped a load from the sky. Riley spun her wife out of the way just in time, the white monstrosity landing in the sand instead of on Ella's head. That drew an even bigger cheer.

Riley held up Ella's hand like a treasured prize. "My wife, everyone!"

The guests each took a handful of petals and cast them over the newlyweds as they walked back up the aisle hand in hand, back up to the courtyard, where music was already echoing.

Faye lingered at the back, caught in her emotions, her feet planted in the soft sand.

Then a presence settled beside her, one she could sense from a hundred miles away. Her stomach flip-flopped as she turned to Diana.

"Can I talk with you, please?" Diana asked.

TWENTY-EIGHT

The courtyard buzzed with energy. Drinks flowed as charming acoustic music drifted amid the hum of laughter and happy conversations. There was so much colour in the usual serene and calm place Diana had become fond of.

Ella and Riley had been whisked away to take wedding photos, their grins wide enough to split their faces, love spilling out of their pores. It was the complete opposite of Diana's wedding day. A simple gathering at their local church, Diana bursting out of her dress, and Jason complaining about his shoes being too tight. She should've listened to her gut then. No bride should experience a sinking feeling uttering the words "I do" when looking at their future spouse, or spend the evening trying not to cry in the bathroom because Jason had been very close to one of her bridesmaids. *Too* close, she later found out.

But she trusted her gut now. Her eyes followed Faye, and the subtle, soft vibrations thrummed across her skin, her senses searching, craving her. Like souls aching to reconnect. How had it been three months? Time had stretched unbearably since she'd last seen her. It was a sin, really. Just like that slit running up her thigh, revealing perfect pale legs.

They moved towards the bench without discussing it, the place a sentimental marker for so much of their time together.

Faye took a seat, looking out at the endless stretch of ocean. A faint layer of goosebumps rippled over her bare arms. Diana longed to touch them, to comfort her, the feeling so powerful it pained her keeping it restrained.

But she didn't want to overstep any boundaries, so she took a seat beside her. Ella and Riley were standing at the top of one of the cliffs, posing for photos. Riley twirled Ella in circles, the camera flashing, their laughter lost on the breeze. Ella's dress spun out around them both, sparkling in the sunlight, and Riley kissed her. Diana looked away, feeling like she was intruding on a private moment.

"I'm glad you came," she said, breaking the silence. "I wasn't sure whether you would."

"I wanted to be here for Riley." Faye's words were sharp, perhaps harsher than she'd intended, because she cleared her throat and smoothed out her dress, then added, more softly, "I wasn't sure whether you would, either."

"I wanted to see you."

Faye huffed. A dark lock of hair fell across her face. "You waited long enough, didn't you?"

"I know."

"It's been three months, Diana."

"I know."

Faye shot her a steely gaze. "Do you have any idea how much you hurt me?" The raw honesty sliced straight into Diana, and she fought the instinct to turn away. "Hearing you voice aloud the fear I had. That I meant nothing to you. Blaming me to try to save your own skin." She tucked her hair behind her ears. "I felt so stupid."

Diana's heart squeezed. "Faye, I—"

"I'm not finished." Faye held up her hand. "I need to get this out."

Diana nodded, surprised but impressed with the new fierceness.

"I know I'm not an innocent party in this," Faye went on. "When I found out you were Molly's mum, I still wanted to explore what we had. I wasn't thinking about Molly. I just wanted to know you. I do feel guilty about that, but I don't, and will not, regret it." Her eyes slowly found Diana's; the earlier feistiness melted away. "I will never regret you, Diana. Even after you stomped on my heart."

Diana blew out a breath.

"In a way, I should've known better," Faye continued. "But I was so enamoured by you. You made me feel special." She swallowed. "You made me feel wanted. I was naïve to think I wouldn't want more from you when our stay was over." Her gaze flicked to Diana again. "It took a lot for me to tell you that before we left. I spilt my heart to you and then… nothing…" She pressed her lips together in an attempt to fight off her emotion and exhaled a shaky breath. "I gave you my heart…and you just dropped it."

Goosebumps covered Diana's skin now, too, despite the Portuguese sun overhead. She swallowed the lump in her throat.

"Can I talk now?" she asked.

Faye nodded.

Diana reached for her necklace. The hard lines of the dove rough between her fingers. "I never really understood people's obsession with relationships," she admitted. "Very time-consuming, emotionally draining, a distraction mainly from getting you what you really wanted in life. I had a few arrangements, naturally, but the desire for more didn't interest me."

Faye muttered something Diana didn't catch and shook her head, assessing Diana as though she had a million thoughts racing through her mind—and not one of them good.

"I never understood it," Diana continued, "until I met you."

Faye's glare softened, and it took everything in Diana not to pull that perfect face to hers and kiss it. But just as much as Faye needed to get things off her chest, so did she.

"From that first moment I saw you, I was hooked. What twenty-something-year-old sits in a bar and does sudoku?" She let out a breath of laughter. "That shy confidence, the passionate speech about chickens… The way you rushed to save that idiotic man from choking." Her smile stretched. "I was completely swept up in you, Faye. I have been ever since. I told myself it was a researcher's curiosity. When something intrigues us, we encourage our brains, follow the trail, and try to uncover something new. But that 'something' isn't measured by data or by collecting samples. It just is." She looked out at the sea, the sunlight glinting off the rolling waves. "It's difficult to trust in a gut instinct that has always felt foreign to me. So imagine my surprise when I finally recognised the truth." She turned to Faye, catching those beautiful eyes. "I was forty-one when I finally understood love."

The words lightened the weight in her chest, and she breathed out. A breeze tickled the hair around her face.

"And not only that, I'd fallen in love with someone who was living in another country. With someone who, for many reasons, was off-limits. But in all my theories and dissecting, I've come to the same conclusion. Love just is. It doesn't discriminate by age or location. Nor complicated circumstances regarding previous partners. Love exists in the spaces between, without scientific reason or purpose. Love just…is."

Faye's eyes welled. That unexplainable feeling flowed through both of them. Pain mutual, joy shared.

Diana placed a hand on Faye's, her heart soaring when she didn't pull away. "I'm so sorry for the way we left things. For reacting the way I did. I panicked. Everything blew up in front of me, and I didn't know how to fix it. I should've reached out sooner—I wanted to. But I still didn't have any answers."

Faye looked at her through those long lashes. "And now?"

She swallowed, recalling the words Faye said to her on this very bench those few months ago. "I want to uncover all of your layers. I want to show you how beautiful you are. I want to love you in all the ways you deserve." She cupped Faye's face, hoping she knew she meant every word. "In a way I've never thought possible, with a hunger that made me completely reckless, with more certainty than I've ever known, I want you too, Faye."

"Diana…" Faye's voice broke on her name.

But Diana couldn't fight it any longer. She pulled Faye to her and kissed her, the kiss charged with three months' longing. As soon as their lips touched, something in her cracked wide open. Soft melted into hard, Faye's mouth welcoming hers in a way that made her whole soul fill with light. God, she'd missed her taste, the shape of her lips, the soft sounds she made when Diana kissed a little harder or nipped her with her teeth. Faye met her with the same desperation, their hands gripping each other like they were afraid to let go.

When they pulled away, breathless—Faye's fingers still tangled in her hair, Diana's lipstick staining her mouth—Diana's chest loosened. She was weightless, soaring up in the blue sky, looking into those gorgeous irises.

Faye brushed a strand of hair behind Diana's ear, her voice soft. "But what about Molly?"

She smiled. "She's the one who convinced me to come here today."

"*Molly?*"

"Yes."

Faye raised an eyebrow. "The woman who told us both to go rot in hell?"

"The one and the same. My daughter."

"Wow." Faye sat back, shaking her head. "I didn't see that one coming."

"Me neither."

"That's surprisingly cool of her."

Diana laughed. "Yeah, it undoubtedly is."

"So I can do this?" Faye's fingertips grazed Diana's thigh, and then she gripped it more forcefully, giving it a squeeze. "And Molly isn't going to come around the corner with a machete and murder me?"

Diana shook her head, heat curling in her centre under Faye's touch.

"And this?" Faye drew her thumb delicately across Diana's cheekbone, tracing the mole she favoured before leaning in close to capture her lips. She squeezed her thigh again, fingertips inching closer to where Diana missed them most, sending an ache pulsing between her legs.

A huge cheer erupted, jarring them both from their bubble. They turned to see a red-faced Riley carrying Ella up the last of the steps before placing her down unceremoniously on the stone flags. The guests whooped and hollered as Riley bent over, trying to catch her breath.

The singer called out, "Everybody, please welcome the newlyweds, Mrs and Mrs Murphy!"

Diana stood, offering her hand to Faye. "Come on, we can make up some more later."

Her eyes twinkled. "I'll hold you to that, Dr Thompson."

A hot shiver ran down Diana's spine. These months apart had stirred a new fieriness in Faye. One she really enjoyed.

With their fingers laced together, they walked back to the wedding party. They'd barely broken the outskirts before a loud scream came from Carla.

"Finally! Yes!" She ran up to them, wrapping her arms around them both, and turned to the man trailing behind her. "I told you. Pay up."

The man sighed, though his smile betrayed his amusement as he slid the euros into Carla's waiting hand.

Diana recognised him but couldn't think where from. She didn't know many people with a man bun.

Faye pointed an accusatory finger. "Hang on. Raul… What's going on here?"

Carla slipped her arm around his waist, and he tugged her closer, planting a kiss on her forehead.

"Finally!" Faye echoed back. "I'm so happy for you both."

Ah, yes. The man from the hotel.

Of course Faye knew them. Faye made friends wherever she went. She was a ray of sunshine. A ray of sunshine Diana didn't ever want to be without ever again.

After a few more minutes while Faye and Carla caught up on the details of their relationships—and Diana and Raul exchanged pleasant chitchat—they took their respective seats at the tables. Ella had seated Faye and Diana together—*of course she had, the little matchmaker*—with fellow graduates of the Sandy Springs course.

The speeches were short and sweet, but Faye shed a few tears when Riley thanked Ella for showing her how to live and love again with her whole heart. Ella dropped her head in her hands when one of the bridesmaids stood to retell some of her less flattering stories. Winnie, the blonde bridesmaid in the stunning green dress, had the guests in stitches reciting a particular date when Ella inadvertently went to the cinema with a woman and her boyfriend, having to sit through the entire film while they made out.

Light acoustic music played while the food was served—a combination of local delicacies: baked *bacalhau* with onion, garlic, and cream potatoes; seafood rice, a soupier version of risotto with fresh catches from the island; and a selection of freshly baked fruit tarts with mangoes and oranges.

Diana sipped her non-alcoholic fizz as she watched the guests mingling on the dancefloor. The Fire Ceremony had been remarkable, but the sheer number of flowers and the unmistakable joy in the air at this wedding stirred an ache in her chest. A good ache. A *"one day maybe I can have this"* ache. She smiled into her glass as she took another sip. She was becoming a stereotype. One hour after her declaration of love, and she was already hearing wedding bells.

Maybe there's some weight to this Princess Inês lore.

Her gaze wandered beyond the dancefloor to the table where Faye and Carla were engaged in excited conversation. Her heart fluttered at the sight of Faye. That beautiful pink dress complementing her pale skin and blue eyes perfectly. She couldn't wait to rip it off her later. Her body hummed with pleasure at the idea.

"Jeez. Get a room!" a playful voice teased. "You're gonna drown yourself in all that drool."

Diana laughed, turning to Ella with a shake of her head. "Guilty as charged." She kissed her on the cheek. "You look stunning."

"Hey, I'm a married woman now." Ella beamed, flashing her sparkling ring.

"Congratulations. You two are perfect for each other."

"Thanks." She blushed, her gaze finding Riley across the room. "I'm so glad you could make it."

Diana understood it now. The way the two souls searched for the other, the energy that Senhor Arenoso had spoken about. She felt it too, whenever she found herself looking at Faye, and those remarkable eyes found hers.

"Although," Ella continued, "if I knew you were gonna steal my thunder with your declaration of love, maybe I wouldn't have invited you." Diana glanced at her, and she cracked into a grin. "Kidding. I love it! It's about freaking time."

Diana laughed. "Funny. You're not the first person to say that."

"Sometimes love is the most obvious to everyone but those feeling it. One of those fucked-up, the universe-is-magical-and-weird things."

"Wow," Diana murmured. "Anyone ever told you that you should run a self-love course and share your wisdom with others?"

"No, but that is a fantastic idea." Ella winked.

One of the bridesmaids scurried over to them then, wild pink make-up smudged by sweat, and an enormous fascinator big enough to make contact with outer space. "Bestie! Sorry to interrupt." She shot Diana an apologetic glance. "But I've been teaching the band how to play the cha-cha slide. Are you ready for your first dance?"

Ella laughed. "Amazing, Pauline. Let's teach these locals a thing or two. Get everyone on the dancefloor. You too." She nudged Diana, then gathered Winnie and passed on the instructions.

The cha-cha slide? How has it come to this?

But with a happy sigh, Diana finished her drink and made her way over to Faye. The way Faye's attention fell over her cleavage and waist had her heart thumping. "Sorry, ladies. I've been instructed to get everyone on the dancefloor for the cha-cha slide."

Faye laughed. "Oh this I wanna see." She stood, pulling Carla with her, and they joined everyone in the courtyard. Riley and Ella stood at the front, chatting with the band, then turned around as the guitar began its opening notes.

In sync, they slid to the left, then the right.

This was ridiculous. This was brilliant. Diana couldn't get enough of it.

She turned to Faye, her happiness tripling in size, and kissed her right in the middle of the cha-cha slide.

The night continued with dancing, music, and laughter. In between timeless wedding classics reinvented with a Portuguese twist, the band played a mix of folk music and slower songs. As the sky darkened above them, torches and candles were lit, creating an intimate atmosphere that made Faye even more beautiful.

"I feel like I'm dreaming." Faye dipped her head, her warm breath tickling Diana's ear as they swayed to the romantic strings. "I can't believe I can dance with you like this."

Diana curved her hands around her waist, her dress soft and silky under her fingers. "I know."

"I don't know what's more unbelievable. This or seeing you do the cha-cha slide."

Diana tugged their bodies closer. "Who am I to deny the wishes of the bride?"

"What about mine?"

She pulled back, looking into her eyes. "Darling, I've never been able to deny you anything."

Faye smiled, and Diana kissed her, slow and deep, gripping her dress. Lost in the taste of her, heat burned through every place they pressed together, awakening an urge that wouldn't be satiated until she'd felt her come undone beneath her touch.

"So," Faye started, leaning to whisper in her ear. "When do we get to this making up you mentioned…" She threaded her fingers through Diana's hair. "Because I am *very* ready to make up."

"I hope so." Diana traced her nails up Faye's spine until she shivered. "Because I have a list of things I want to do to you."

"Another checklist? How sexy, Dr Thompson."

"I'm very thorough." Her lip quirked, her clit throbbing. "Now grab your clutch. I want you naked and needy by the end of this song."

Faye's eyes dipped. "I'm already halfway there."

TWENTY-NINE

Faye

Faye urged her hands to move faster. Emptying her bag was rarely a time-friendly activity, but when Diana was waiting on the other side of the door, voice laced with promises of wonderfully filthy things, she couldn't move quickly enough.

They'd already had the entire day building up until this moment—stealing kisses and touches throughout the wedding celebration—on top of their three months apart. Then Diana had insisted they walk the further few minutes to her cabin for reasons that *"will become clear soon"*. Faye couldn't move without the reminder sitting uncomfortably in her underwear. Whatever the suggestion implied, it had the desired effect. And the more she thought about Diana—her Diana—waiting for her in the bedroom, the more the feeling grew.

She triple-checked the seal around her stoma, making sure everything was secure, then quickly gussied up in the mirror and opened the bathroom door.

Diana was waiting for her on the bed, one leg crossed over the other, her burgundy dress riding up her thigh. Faye's mouth dried as she stood, closing the distance with the grace of a lioness.

Wordlessly, Diana gripped her hip, pulling her in for a kiss like it was the first time she'd seen her. Her mouth explored hers, soft, toe-curlingly slow, like she was rediscovering something special, not wanting to leave any place untouched. Faye couldn't stop the whimper leaving her throat. Her stomach bottomed out, the floor almost falling from under her.

Diana's hands slid lower, smoothing her dress and squeezing the curve of her arse. The force made Faye pull back with a gasp. Her heart thudded hard in her throat. Their chests pressed against each other, eyes looking deep into a place Faye had never reached before.

She pressed her lips to the soft spot on Diana's neck, trailing open-mouthed kisses to her ear. She took the lobe into her mouth, biting gently, causing a growl to erupt in Diana's throat.

Diana pulled her back by tugging her hair, her hungry mouth claiming her neck in return. She moaned as Diana's lips marked her, her teeth and tongue dragging over her delicate skin with such ownership, her knees buckled. She grasped Faye's dress, pushing the material up her thigh and bunching it around her waist, and slid her other hand through her soaked underwear.

Diana cursed as Faye pressed into her, the pressure from her fingers making her eyes dip. "Very needy. Good. Now for the naked part."

She lifted the dress over Faye's head, then let it pool at her feet.

"Yours too." Faye grasped Diana's dress between her fingertips, rooting her in place.

Her mouth curled. "If you want it, take it."

Faye crashed her lips to that perfect mouth, and Diana kissed her back, breaking the kiss to whisper, "You'll have to unzip me."

Faye turned her, placing a kiss that was all teeth at the nape of her neck before slowly lowering the zipper. She trailed kisses down the bare skin, letting the dress fall to the floor, leaving Diana in matching burgundy underwear.

"You're perfect," Faye murmured, tracing her nails up her spine.

Diana turned, pulling Faye's face to hers while slipping her other hand between her legs. Faye rocked into her, and Diana let out a low, satisfied hum. She removed Faye's bra with her free hand, releasing her breasts, naked bar her support belt.

"Is your checklist going well?" Faye breathed.

"Very well," Diana smirked, ripping the clasp on Faye's underwear and sliding two fingers straight inside her.

Faye gasped, digging her nails into the soft flesh of Diana's shoulders.

"Though you might have to watch that mouth of yours," Diana continued, her fingers deep, her thumb rolling slowly over her clit. "Or are you goading for a spanking?"

Fresh heat flooded her, coiling tight in her centre. Faye had never considered how incredibly hot it would be to have Diana's hand mark her.

Ignoring those fantasies of the cane, of course.

She squirmed under Diana's gaze as a new ache throbbed in her clit, caught between wanting to push her and wanting to give in.

"Maybe," she uttered, breathless.

Diana quirked an eyebrow. "Maybe?" She hooked her fingers upwards, a reminder of the control she had, and Faye inhaled. "That's not definitive enough." She guided Faye back to the bed until her thighs hit the mattress and leaned closer. Her tongue flicked out, wetting her lips, and Faye's pussy ached at the sight. She wanted that tongue in her mouth.

Faye closed the distance, but Diana pulled back with a playful grin, dipping close to bite her lip. When she released it, she removed her fingers, spinning Faye so her back was flush to Diana's chest. She bent her forward, tracing her fingertips up her spine, and pressed her pelvis into her. A jolt of pleasure spiralled in Faye's core.

"I need you to use your words, Faye." Diana caressed her arsecheek, gripping hard, before smoothing it. "Is this what you want? To be bent over like the naughty girl you are?"

Fuck.

Diana wrapped her arms around her, placing biting kisses along her shoulder and back, making her squirm. Her hands drifted lower again, leaving fire in their wake. She fisted Faye's cheek. "Is this what three months without me does to you? Do you need a reminder of who is in control here?"

Faye's entire body ached. "Yes."

She softened a little. "Are you sure?"

"Yes, Diana. I want you to do anything you want to me."

"Very well." She leaned Faye forward, pressing her into the bed so that Faye was supporting herself with her hands. Then she brought her hand to her cheek with a slap.

Faye gripped the sheets as heat spread through her.

"How was that?" Diana whispered, her warm hand smoothing the flesh.

"Good...I like it."

"Do you think you could take more?"

"Yes. Harder."

"You want me to leave a mark, don't you? Want everyone to know who you belong to?"

"Yes."

She spanked her again, hard enough to make her grit her teeth. Faye exhaled, tingling and buzzing with adrenaline. Her pussy ached, her clit begging for attention.

She wanted to be Diana's. In every sense of the word.

"Are you going to behave now?" Diana asked, caressing the area she'd just slapped.

"I will."

"One more. You're taking it so well. Think you can handle another?" When Faye said yes, Diana brought her hand to her cheek again, the force fanning the ache in her pelvis.

Diana gently caressed her sore behind, then her fingers crept closer to her pussy, spreading her open. Faye moaned, gripping the sheets, her head face down on the bed, her thighs dripping.

Diana sank her tongue into her, warm and wet, and Faye let out a cry. She lifted her hips, pushing into Diana as she pulled her closer. Her long, deep strokes were mixed with kisses and gentle sucks, every touch driving Faye further into the mattress.

When a finger teased through her folds, she whimpered, her legs violently trembling, three months of coiled-up tension already threatening to unravel her. Diana sank two fingers into her, and Faye arched on the bed.

"Fuck… Yes. Diana, *please*."

Diana thrust her fingers, hitting her so perfectly, she

couldn't contain it.

"Oh—god—yes!"

Seconds later, the pressure combusted, and she fell headfirst into an all-consuming orgasm. Her legs quivered, tightening around Diana's fingers, and the sound of Diana's pleasure catapulted her higher into the ceiling. She panted into the sheet, the grip tight in her fist, as hot white pleasure crested over her.

"God, I missed you," she said, somewhere in a daze.

"You like a little spanking," Diana murmured. "Noted."

Diana slowly removed her hand, replacing it with her mouth again. Faye whimpered as her tongue swept over her, her legs trembling with sensitivity. Diana's satisfied purr sent vibrations through every nerve-ending, making her pussy already ache for more.

"You taste so good," Diana said as she pulled back, leaving Faye a shaky mess on the bed, blinking away stars.

The sound of a zip opening caught Faye's attention. She let her tired body collapse, angling her head to see Diana foraging in her suitcase. Her eyes took in Diana's beautiful form as she stood.

Faye clocked the silky bag and swallowed. A bag like that only meant one thing.

"Have you used one of these before?" Diana asked, with a sly smile, pulling out a pink dildo and its harness from inside.

Faye shook her head, eyes widening at the length of

the toy. The thought of Diana using that on her stirred desire low in her navel.

"A little presumptuous, don't you think?" she teased, raising her eyebrow. "Bringing your bag of goodies?"

"I'd opt for…optimistic." Diana gave a sultry smirk.

"*Very* optimistic if you think you'll fit that whole thing inside of me."

"You'll be surprised." Diana laughed, and then her expression became serious. "Of course, we don't have to do anything you're not comfortable with."

"I want to. I want to try everything with you."

That made Diana grin. She crossed the room to capture her mouth with a fierce kiss. And just like that, the fire reignited, her body a helpless slave to Diana's every touch.

Diana pulled back. "Tell me if anything hurts or is too much. We can take it slow." Then, hearing the words leave her mouth and the look on Faye's face, her eyes sparkled with something only the two of them shared.

"I'm getting déjà vu."

"Shut up."

Faye kissed her again, just because she could, feeling Diana smile into her lips.

"I want you to put it on me," Diana said, breath hot against her mouth, sliding her hands to Faye's wrists.

"Me?" Faye hesitated. "But I don't know what I'm doing."

"I'll show you. Here." Diana laid the black harness on the floor and stepped inside the two leg hoops. "Pull it up."

Faye did as she asked, skimming the material up her freckled thighs and tightening the straps.

"Now place her inside there and make sure she's secure."

"Her?"

Diana's dark eyes held hers. "Do you see the need for any men here?"

Faye swallowed. "Absolutely not." Her fingers fumbled over the fastening, but once she'd snapped it closed, the large pink toy stood proud.

"Touch her. Have a feel."

Faye ran her hand along the smooth length, watching it spring back into place.

"She's yours. She's an extension of me. Remember that when she's inside you."

Sweet Jesus. That stirred the ache between her legs again, and she gulped, her heart beating faster.

Diana passed her a bottle of lube from her bag. "Get her ready for you."

Faye coated the toy with the liquid, smoothing it with her fingers until it was completely covered, shiny and slick.

"Now, lie back and use the excess on yourself."

Faye leaned back on the bed, supporting herself with the pillows, and let her legs fall open. She took her time, tracing her fingers through her pussy. Diana's eyes followed each movement hungrily, the look in those dark irises making her even wetter. She definitely didn't need the extra lube.

"Good," Diana murmured, voice thick with want. She bent down to kiss her, letting the strap graze against Faye's abdomen. The sensation was a little strange until she remembered Diana's words—*she's an extension of me*—which quickly alleviated the feeling.

Diana's lips started soft, kissing her jaw and neck before sucking hard below her ear. Faye dug her nails into her back, pulling them closer as her mouth continued laying its claim.

She groaned, pushing into Diana, rubbing herself against the strap. The thought of Diana putting it inside her made her restless. She couldn't think of anything she wanted more. She threaded her fingers in Diana's hair, tugging her up to meet her mouth in a rough kiss. Diana met her with just as much ferocity, her lips hard and bruising.

Faye's clit ached, her head dizzy with need. With another tug of Diana's hair, she guided her tongue into her mouth, her muscles loosening as Diana's warmth brushed against her. She probed deeper, and Diana sucked on her tongue.

Every atom melted, undoing her, leaving her a trembling mess in Diana's arms.

God. Faye was going to die.

"Please, Diana," she begged. "I want to feel you. Her. All of it."

Diana pulled back, her eyes pinned to Faye's as she gently teased the toy up her slit. Faye shuddered, her stomach rolling, anticipation eating at her. Then slowly, Diana pressed the strap to her entrance, easing inside.

Faye groaned as the toy filled her, inch by inch. Her eyelids fluttered closed, soaking in the feeling.

"That's it…good." Diana gripped her thighs. "Eyes on me."

She opened her eyes to the hottest sight she'd ever seen. Diana was towering over her, body wrapped in burgundy underwear like a gift, her hands parting her legs, her pelvis buried into hers.

"Fuck," Faye whispered.

"You like it?"

"Yes. Fuck, yes."

A smirk curled that perfect mouth. "I knew you would." She rocked her hips, slowly drawing the toy in and out, each thrust taking Faye deeper. She increased the pace, pushing a little harder each time, keeping those dark eyes on Faye's.

There was something so intense about the way Diana watched her. Assessing each movement, every reaction, as though her sole focus was making Faye feel good. The coils in her stomach tightened even more.

Faye gripped the sheets; she was unravelling in every sense of the word. To be so wanted and cared for, to be fucked so good…and by her. It was too good to be true.

What if it changed again? What if this was a taste of the life she could have before it was taken away?

She couldn't look at her.

"What are you thinking?" Diana asked, her voice low

and husky. The sound alone made Faye's toes curl.

She let out a soft breath, embarrassed by her train of thought. Diana stopped her thrusts, sliding her hands from Faye's thighs to her waist. *Oh god.* She'd really ruined the moment.

"What is it?" Diana asked. "Is something wrong? Did I hurt you?"

"No. Nothing's wrong." She shook her head, emotion bubbling up and pricking her eyelids. Oh no, she was crying now, too?

What are you doing, Faye?

Diana gently pulled out the shaft and lay down next to her, the heat from her body an immediate comfort. She cupped Faye's cheek. "Darling, talk to me."

"It's silly."

"Nothing is silly." Her voice softened. "Look at me."

Faye let her turn her face, her gaze blurring when she met those irises. She swallowed. "Nothing is wrong. Everything is right. And that's the problem."

Diana's mouth quirked. She brushed her cheek softly with her thumb. "Everything being right is bad?"

"All of this with you. I love the way you make me feel, Diana. But I lost you once. I don't want to lose you again."

"Darling…" She brushed the hair from Faye's face and cupped her jaw. "I don't want to lose you either." She let out a sigh. "I've waited forty-one years to meet you. Do you think I'm going to let you go so easily?"

"It happened once." A few stray tears slipped down

her cheek. "I don't know if I could do it again."

Diana caught the tears with her thumb. "I can't say that Molly was the only obstacle we'll face, Faye. But we'll face everything together. If you want me, if you want this…then have a little faith."

Heat bloomed in Faye's chest. "I like this new side to you."

Diana gave a small shrug. "We've got to have hope."

"Wow." She laughed dreamily. "Look at you speaking with all the wisdom of a dove."

"You have a way of bringing it out of me." She smiled that perfect Diana smile, and Faye brought her lips to hers.

It wasn't long before they were caught in a back and forth of want and consume, mouths territorial, imprinting. The vibrations from Diana's moan rumbled in Faye's throat, and her pussy tightened. She was suddenly very aware of the strap pressing against her leg. She palmed it in her hand, still wet from earlier, and guided it back inside, lifting her thigh over Diana's as they lay side by side.

"You have no idea what you do to me," Diana said, breathless in between kisses. "Do you?"

She adjusted herself, moving lower and hooking Faye's leg higher. The toy tilted, and Faye bent her torso, tweaking the angle so it didn't press on her bag. Diana pushed into her, and she groaned as the dildo hit a sweet spot.

"Oh my god. That feels so good."

"Open your legs wider for me."

Faye did as she was asked, allowing Diana to slide in and out of her easily. Diana held her thigh, gripping the soft flesh as she thrust her hips, meeting her with short, hard strokes.

Diana pressed her lips to her chest, licking a trail to her nipple. She swirled the tip with her tongue, sending pings of pleasure between her legs.

"Touch yourself," Diana instructed.

Faye immediately brought her hand to her clit, fingers slipping, already tensing under the touch.

Diana pulled and sucked at her nipples, the strap hitting Faye with a steady rhythm. Their heavy breathing filled the room, Faye's moans mixing with Diana's exertion as she drove into her. Diana tightened her arm around her, planting another kiss on her shoulder.

"Turn over." She rolled her so that Faye was on her front, her legs shaking, mind lost. "On those lovely knees of yours. That's it."

Faye could barely support herself on her arms. She sucked in a hiss as Diana scratched her nails down her back. Goosebumps rippled her skin, and she shivered, feeling empty without the strap filling her.

Diana teased the length against her entrance, and she moaned, needing it back inside her—needing *her* back inside her. Thankfully, Diana didn't wait, pushing the toy into her pussy. The heat of Diana's body followed. She pressed against Faye's back, teeth grazing her shoulder as she sank deeper, stretching her, until her pelvis rested flush.

"Wow," Faye breathed.

"You're taking her so well," Diana praised, placing a kiss on her neck. She pulled back, guiding Faye with her so she rested on all fours. She gripped Faye's waist, and then she started to move, sliding the shaft in and out, slow and deliberate so she could feel every inch. "Did I tell you to stop touching yourself?"

The sound of Diana's stern voice sent another roll of pleasure through her, and she brought her hand back to her clit.

Diana quickened her pace. "This is all for you, Faye. Tell me what you want."

"Harder."

The word had barely left her lips when Diana was fucking her with such delectable force, she whimpered.

"God—yes!" Her words were muffled in the sheet, her fingers pressing against her clit. She couldn't move; she could only take everything Diana gave to her, and she soaked up every second. Her orgasm pulsed inside her, threatening to burst.

"Let me hear you," Diana said, low in her throat. "Show me how it feels."

Faye moaned, not recognising the sound of her own voice, her fingers circling her slippery clit. Diana tightened her grip on her, continuing her pace while cursing like a woman on the edge. The thorough strokes combined with the filth leaving Diana's mouth tightened the pressure in Faye's core. She had never been so consumed by someone. So seen. She was so close to erupting, the brilliant white heat burning through her veins.

She pleaded, panting, pleasure coiling through her body until finally she came with such force she could hardly breathe. The intensity rippled through every sense, bursting through the surface with the weight of a tidal force, taking all the air with it.

Diana cried out as she tumbled into her own climax. Her hips shuddered against Faye's thighs, the sweet, raw sounds of her pleasure taking Faye's to another height. Her grip tightened around Faye's waist as the two of them spiralled, sinking into the feeling together.

Slowly, Diana pulled out, removing the harness and collapsing beside her. Their hot bodies lay curled together, sticky with perspiration, limbs entwining.

Faye traced Diana's cheekbones, while Diana drew slow patterns up her arm. Their heavy breathing began to slow, falling into one steady rhythm. Faye had never known anything so intimate. She never wanted the moment to end.

But then, she realised, it didn't have to. Their relationship didn't end at Sandy Springs.

Not this time.

"What's that smile?" Diana whispered, tracing the contours of Faye's lips.

Faye kissed her fingers. "I just…don't remember ever feeling this happy," she admitted.

"Me neither."

She let out a happy sigh, taking in all Diana's softness, shimmering under the sheen of sweat. "I don't know what the next chapter holds for us, but I'm excited to find out."

"Me too." Diana nuzzled into her neck, planting soft kisses down to her collarbone. "Although we still have a *lot* of making up to do yet."

"Is that so?"

"Mm-hmm."

Faye's toes curled as Diana hummed against her skin, her lips soft and warm.

Faye couldn't wait for their new start—but she also couldn't wait to find out what other surprises Diana had hidden in her suitcase.

It was going to be a long night.

EPILOGUE

Faye hopped from one foot to the other, nerves and excitement flitting through her veins. Around her, the crowd buzzed with the same mix of anticipation and eagerness, looking at the screen above their heads, waiting for the countdown over the speakers.

She'd warmed up, stretched, and used an extra hold seal on her bag. She was ready. It had been nine months of training in the making. Nine months of sore muscles, blisters, and bag malfunctions. Nine months of pushing herself and proving she could do anything if she kept going.

Nine months leading up to her first half-marathon—and six months of dating Diana.

Faye grinned. It'd been the best six months of her life—and not just because she'd been having the best sex of her existence, but because she'd never felt so confident in her own skin. Not just confident, but proud too. She'd spent a lot of her time after her operation locked away in her bedroom, wishing she could be more like those women she admired. The Emmaline Pankhursts, the Rosa Parks, the Ada Lovelaces, not realising she had those qualities, just in different Faye ways. In the beginning, it had been so easy to focus on the negative, especially when it was permanently strapped to her abdomen in a constant reminder, but accepting her circumstances—actually being thankful for the way her ostomy had changed her life, in all the bad, good, and in between—made a huge difference.

The countdown sounded, as the enthusiastic woman on the mic waved her arms in the air. "*Ten...nine...*"

The runners around her started jumping, shaking adrenaline out of their limbs and pinning their gazes forward. A man dressed in a Luigi costume gave out high-fives to his neighbours as the crowd's cheers grew louder.

Faye glanced down at her blue Sandy Springs Sanctuary T-shirt, checking the number was still attached. She'd raised almost £3,000 for the sanctuary so far, with her employers sharing her efforts on social media. Riley had told her it would be a huge help with their plans to expand and continue protecting the island's biodiversity.

She just had to run the damn thing now; she couldn't let them down.

"Six...five..."

She inhaled deeply, filling her lungs, letting the cool air calm her. She could do this. One step at a time.

I'm a fucking elephant.

"Three...two...one!"

Smoke fired from either side of the banner overhead, and the people gathered behind the barriers cheered and whistled as the runners started to move. A space opened, and Faye took her first steps forward, trying to settle into a steady pace.

She moved with the group as the slapping of feet hit the tarmac, high-fiving outstretched hands from the supporters, letting the energy fuel her. She'd need more of that for later.

The first few miles were easy. The crowd scattered along the route, clapping and holding up handmade signs, encouraging them to keep going. Faye passed the first water station, giving her best smile to the volunteers with outstretched bottles of water.

The roads wound through the city, the traffic lights still blinking their colourful sequences like their own form of encouragement. Someone on a microphone sang "Sweet Caroline" from the pavement, making her grin and mumble the words in a breathy attempt at singing.

Her mind jumped to Diana. It'd been a freezing December night when Faye had taken her to watch the

Lionesses at Wembley. Diana hadn't much interest in the sport, but when Faye explained how the women had triumphed and fought against a system that was always discouraging women from playing football, she warmed to the idea. Seeing her cheering along with the crowd, wrapped up warm in a black wool scarf, leaning in close to ask about the rules, singing "Sweet Caroline" at the top of her lungs, made Faye's heart swell. Doing ordinary things with Diana was always anything but ordinary.

The distance between them was challenging at times, but the three-hour train journey meant they could spend long weekends together, and even more time together during the half-term. Faye took on more fieldwork in the south, so they could relax in the evenings in Diana's apartment, and Diana dropped some working hours. It worked—but Faye always wanted more.

She wanted to wake up with Diana every morning, kiss her before sleep every night. To share breakfast and coffee, and cook with her guilty playlist of nineties boy bands playing loud. She wanted to make Diana's space *their* space. To get a cat or four. To build a whole life with her.

She loved living with Quin—don't get her wrong. The Drew Barrymore marathon was still underway, with different snacks of choice each week. Her current number one? *50 First Dates* and a sharing bag of Skittles. Quin had got a job at a local supermarket and had already charmed themselves into a promotion. It suited them well, chatting for a living. Ever since they'd cut contact with their dad, they'd been a lot happier. Her own parents had taken Quin under their wing, inviting them round for tea whenever Faye was away with work.

The onlookers cheered as a group of runners dressed like the Teletubbies passed her, their colourful antennae bouncing with every step. Faye's feet continued pounding the pavement, her breathing pulling the fresh air into her lungs. The road led under a bridge and curled back around as she overtook the giant seven-mile sign. She was over halfway.

Come on.

She passed another water station, accepted a bottle from a smiling volunteer and took a big swig. The cool liquid eased her dry and itchy throat. The runners flocked forward, the beating drum from a distant brass band marching them on. The thump grew louder, pushing her feet into the ground, taking her closer to the finish line.

As she approached the eleven-mile sign, Faye wanted to collapse. Her legs ached, her lungs burned, her feet had slowed to a pace where everyone was overtaking her. Two more miles? She couldn't do it. They'd have to come and peel her off the tarmac.

Everything hurt. Why on earth did she willingly sign up for this?

The weight of her familiar against her sternum suddenly pulled her into focus. The island needed this money; the animals did. She wasn't going to give up at the last hurdle. She was resilient. A fucking elephant. Strong and powerful.

She fixed her mind on the finish line. On Diana waiting for her. Her dads and Quin.

She forced her feet forward, keeping them moving. *Just don't stop.* She glanced at the people beside her, also red-faced and panting. They were all in this together, each person's determination encouraging the other. *Just don't stop.*

On the pavement, a choir wearing matching black robes bobbed side to side, singing "Dog Days Are Over" by Florence & The Machine.

You can do this.

She ran past the last water break. Past the last sign indicating the final stretch. The road unfolded in front of her, the passersby clapping and whooping as she drew closer and closer. The finish line in sight.

Music blared from the speakers ahead, growing louder with every step. *One, two. One, two.* The rhythm carried her forward, her feet and muscles aching, sweat stinging her eyes—until finally, she crossed the line and threw her arms up in the air.

"I did it!" She turned, breathless but still smiling, and high-fived the people closest to her. "We did it!"

Her legs burned, still feeling like they were running ahead of her body. She checked her bag—still attached, no leaks—and accepted her medal. It was heavier than she'd imagined. She immediately tossed it around her neck, beaming with pride.

Lungs heaving, she scanned the busy crowd of finishers hugging family and friends, and then her eyes landed on Diana, who was running towards her. They came together, wrapping around each other, happiness spilling out of them both.

"I'm so proud of you!" Diana kissed her cheek.

Her dads followed with Quin in tow, pulling her into a big group embrace.

"Oof." Quin chuckled, giving her arm a squeeze. "You stink."

"You run a half-marathon and see how wonderful you smell," she teased, unable to knock the grin from her face. Even when she spotted a familiar blonde walking up to her.

"Congrats, Faye," Molly said, offering her a gap-toothed smile and tapping her awkwardly on the shoulder. "You finally did it."

"Molly… What are you doing here?" Faye shot a glance at Diana.

"Don't be too pleased to see me." She flipped her curls over her shoulder. "Well, it's a momentous occasion, so it feels appropriate for a family affair, don't you agree?" At Faye's open mouth, Molly nudged her. "Come on, Faye. I'm pulling your leg."

Quin observed the exchange with far too much glee before clapping their hands together. "Right, everyone. Pint?"

***

The pub nearby was heaving with patrons, medal-wearers in Lycra, and family and friends clinking glasses. A man cracked open a sharing bag of cheese and onion crisps, offering them around, occasionally throwing a couple to the two greying spaniels lying by his feet. Chatter and laughter hummed around them, while the bartenders were rushed off their feet.

Faye and the others huddled around a sticky table, next to a Peppa Pig and Cinderella with a terribly tangled blonde wig.

Lukas raised his gin and tonic to the centre of the table, meeting Faye's gaze with his kind eyes. "As parents, one of the worst things in the world is to watch your child suffer and not be able to do anything about it. When you were rushed into hospital, David and I feared the worst. Waiting for you to come out of that emergency surgery was…" He shook his head, pressing his lips together.

David grasped his hand and gave it a squeeze. "It was pure hell."

Faye swallowed, her own emotions rising to the surface. She hated seeing her dads upset.

David adjusted his glasses. "When Lukas first suggested the Sandy Springs course, I was unsure. The idea of you being so far away from home and hard to reach seemed like a terrible idea."

"But we needed to get you out of that bedroom," Lukas insisted. "We were so worried about you."

Diana's hand covered hers, a simple comfort that

meant the world to her. Something she'd seen her dads do a thousand times with each other and always craved. Molly caught the movement. Faye's instinct was to hide the affection from her, but Molly smiled at the gesture before returning her attention to Lukas.

"You've come so far, Faye." He broke into a grin. "I don't think any of us would have believed a year ago that you'd be running a half-marathon. But I couldn't be more proud of you. Who knows what else you're going to achieve? The world is yours, *amore*. To Faye!"

Everyone clinked their glasses, chorusing her name around the table. The shared joy pulled at her heart. Having everyone here supporting her was incredible—even Molly. It made her want to run the damn thing all over again.

Then Diana raised her glass. "I would also like to make an announcement." All eyes fell on her, the chatter quieting, and she flashed one of those heart-stopping smiles at Faye. "First, congratulations, my love. You deserve all of this and more. I'm so proud of you." She kissed Faye's cheek, and all her insides warmed, slackening to jelly. "Second, I've just accepted a new job. Right here at the University of Manchester." Her eyes locked on Faye's, sparkling with joy. "I'm going to be moving up here permanently."

The table burst into congratulations, another round of glasses clinking.

"I can't believe it," Faye said, watching Diana's expression, the news not quite sinking in. They'd discussed the possibility before, but there had always been obstacles in the way. "But what about the pay cut? Your apartment?"

Diana simply smiled. "All inconsequential."

There was a crackle and a kerfuffle as someone switched on a microphone, drawing attention to the other side of the pub. A small TV screen flickered as a man waved his hands, greeting the crowd. Faye realised with a laugh that he was one of the Dingles from *Emmerdale*. He tipped his flat cap.

"Hello, winners!" He beamed. "I'd like to dedicate the first karaoke number to everyone who ran the half-marathon today. This is for you. You're incredible. Please sing along."

The opening notes sounded from the speakers as Tina Turner's "The Best" started to play. Red, blue, and green lights twirled over the ceiling as people made their way towards him, bobbing their heads, with their drinks in the air.

Diana leaned in, her voice a throaty whisper. "Is this the kind of normality I can expect living in the north?"

"Absolutely." Faye chuckled, squeezing her thigh as the man on karaoke unleashed a surprisingly in-tune opening verse on the applauding crowd.

"I was hoping…" Diana's breath tickled her neck. "That we could look at places together. Maybe even browse the animal shelter."

"You want me to move in with you?" Her heart squeezed, her voice turning squeaky. "And you want to get a cat?"

Diana chuckled, the sound filling her with light. "Yes and yes."

"I'd love to. Of course I do." She pulled back, meeting Diana's smile with one of her own. The smile slowly fell away. "I'll have to talk to Quin first, though."

"It's fine with me," Quin jumped in. They flashed a grin. "Sorry for listening in—but Diana already spoke with me about it, and I think it's a great idea."

She did?

She looked back at the woman who had completely captured her heart.

"I know Quin is important to you," Diana said, as if that explained everything.

The swirl of emotions in her chest was too much; she was going to burst. Completing the race, Molly showing her support, her dads being incredible, Diana moving up north, and the two of them moving in…it was all so perfect.

She glanced at Quin. "Are you sure you'd be alright with that? I can wait."

They shook their head. "I've never lived on my own. I think it will be good for me. Plus, I'm only round the corner from David and Lukas. Just promise me we will continue our Drew Barrymore marathon, and I'll be fine."

She pulled them into a hug. "Of course. I'll still see you all the time. You can't get rid of me."

"Then there's nothing to worry about." Quin squeezed her back.

As the song wound up to another chorus, the man at the microphone said, "Everybody, come on! On your feet."

Quin pulled Faye up, then Molly—who reluctantly agreed, rolling her eyes. Faye threaded her fingers through Diana's, tugging her with them towards the growing crowd. David and Lukas wrapped their arms around their mismatched, perfectly imperfect family, tilting their heads back to belt out the first line.

"You're simply the best!"

The room echoed the man at the mic, swaying as one, Peppa Pig and Cinderella waving their arms in the air.

Faye's face hurt from smiling. She tried to take it all in. The mixture of sweat, beer, and furniture polish that was oddly endearing; Molly and Quin huddled a little too close to be considered friendly; the heat from Diana's fingers in hers. Joy radiated from everyone in the room—especially those closest to her.

She'd never imagined a reality with her stoma where she could be so happy, so free, so…Faye. She'd gone to Sandy Springs in search of her enigma, that quality that had inspired her to be courageous and push outside her comfort zone. She'd done that with bells and whistles—taking down a poacher, snagging the most beautiful woman she'd ever met, and running a half-marathon. She could do anything.

Diana put Faye's fingers to her lips, planting a kiss that seared her whole body. She bathed in the happiness they shared, in their connection surging between them, the love in Diana's eyes. This was their beginning, their future, their present.

And Faye was going to enjoy every single second.

THE END

If you enjoyed this story, please do leave a review and let me know. Reviews and sharing/engaging on social media really make such a huge difference to indie authors like myself. The more support we get, the more novels we can write, and the more books there will be to read! If you got this far, I'm so humbled by your support, thank you.

ACKNOWLEDGEMENTS

Thank you so much for reading! I hope you enjoyed Faye and Diana's story. Sandy Springs is my first series as an author, and I've loved getting to revisit some of our favourite characters from the first book and introducing you to some new favourites too. The theme of self-love and accepting yourself for who you are carries over into this book. It's a huge part of what makes Sandy Springs the wonderful place that it is. This book was inspired by a friend of mine who recently had to have an ostomy, and that got me thinking about the representation in Sapphic books. I hadn't seen any characters like Faye—and so I wanted to change that. A huge thank you to all the lovely people that helped me represent that to the best of my ability. Jeanne Dagna, Katherine Laker, Kelly Woodhouse, Betsy Carswell, and Tara Beedle. Thank you for answering my questions, for your suggestions, and for being so open about your own individual journeys. You really helped shape Faye and her own acceptance, so thank you so much for that. Love to you all.

Why did I write the ex-girlfriend's mum trope? Honestly, why not? It's no secret I love older women, and older women deserve the spotlight too. I think I always saw Faye with someone older, but with two MCs attending the course, I needed some new conflict to keep it interesting. Molly played that role perfectly. I like to challenge myself as a writer and trying to figure out how to write a happily ever after for the three of them definitely came with its challenges! I think love shows up in many forms, and Faye and Diana's happens to be an elephant and a dove 🩶

Now for more thank yous. I wrote this story during a difficult period in my life. There were a lot of times where I thought I wouldn't ever be able to finish it. To all my readers who sent kind messages and support, you have no idea how much you helped me get back on track. Your kindness and encouragement is the reason why this story exists in its current form. Thank you.

Thank you to my wonderful beta readers, editor Helena, and proofreader Imogen—you're true superstars. Another big thank you to my ARC team! I love getting to know you all with each release, and your excitement and enthusiasm helps squash the anxiety around release day. I hope you know how much I appreciate you.

Another huge thank you to all the lovely people for

supporting me on Patreon. I love being able to share my WIPs with you. This year has been especially tough, and knowing you were there really encouraged me to keep writing. An extra special mention to Adrienne, Amanda G, Andrea Padilla, Andy, Britt of @jadedsunreads, Chance, Christiane, Danielle Raymond, Josh, Nancy Bardoni, Shannon C, Tammy, and Tun Ewald for being Sapphic champions of the world! Thank you for all your support and encouragement. It humbles me every day that you want to read my work (even it its uglier forms) and accompany me through this journey, book-to-book. There aren't enough words to express how much I value you. Thank you, thank you, thank you.

My next release is a rival pop/rock star romance, and I'm aiming to release it at the back end of summer. My WIPs are uploaded to Patreon weekly, along with some other fun benefits. If you're interested in checking it out and joining the club, my username is @emilywrightwriter.

Thank you to my girlfriend, LB, for supporting me throughout this tough year. For listening to all my panics and late-night stresses and continuing to believe in me even when I didn't. I'll never know what I did to deserve you. Thank you for being the person that inspires me to write about love every day by showing me what it means. I couldn't do this without you.

Last but not least, thank *you*, lovely reader, for taking the time to check out my story. Writing Sapphic romance books is all I've ever wanted to do. Thank you so much

for your support, you're making dreams come true (and
hey, that rhymed!)

Em x

ABOUT THE AUTHOR

Emily Wright is a dog-loving, book-sniffing, ukulele-playing author who lives in Barnsley in the UK. When she isn't attached to her computer writing, she loves the outdoors, especially the crash of the ocean and starry night skies that make her feel obsolete. She drinks far too much tea and eats an unthinkable amount of Bourbon biscuits but burns it off chasing her two naughty Spaniels around the house.

Connect with Emily here:

Website: www.emilywrightwriter.co.uk
Instagram: @emilywrightwriter
Patreon: @emilywrightwriter
Tiktok: @emilywrightwriter

Don't forget to subscribe to my newsletter to stay in touch and also receive a free sapphic novella, *All Bets Are Off*!

Abby Turner doesn't do relationships—she's very clear about that—yet, Sophia, her latest fling, obviously never got the memo. So, when a hot new woman moves into their business complex, both are eager to make a good first impression, and they strike up a bet: the first to win the new girl's heart. Abby's never said no to competition before, but there's something about new girl Gemma that leaves Abby with sweaty palms and the promise of trouble…

www.emilywrightwriter.co.uk/contact